THE
MYSTICS
OF
MILE
END

# THE

# MYSTICS

# OF

# MILE END

## SIGAL SAMUEL

Freehand Books gratefully acknowledges the support of the Canada Council for the Arts for its publishing program. ¶ Freehand Books, an imprint of Broadview Press Inc., acknowledges the financial support for its publishing program provided by the Government of Canada through the Canada Book Fund.

Canada Council for the Arts  Conseil des Arts du Canada  Alberta Government

Freehand Books
515 – 815 1st Street SW  Calgary, Alberta  T2P 1N3
www.freehand-books.com

Book orders: LitDistCo
100 Armstrong Avenue  Georgetown, Ontario  L7G 5S4
Telephone: 1-800-591-6250  Fax: 1-800-591-6251
orders@litdistco.ca
www.litdistco.ca

Library and Archives Canada Cataloguing in Publication

Samuel, Sigal, 1986–, author
The mystics of Mile End : a novel / Sigal Samuel.

Issued in print and electronic formats.
ISBN 978-1-55481-253-0 (pbk.). — ISBN 978-1-4604-0513-0 (epub). — ISBN 978-1-77048-553-2 (pdf)

    I. Title.

PS8637.A53875M97 2015      C813'.6      C2014-906987-1
                                         C2014-906988-X

Edited by Barbara Scott
Book design and illustration by Natalie Olsen, Kisscut Design
Author photo by Rebecca Lenetsky

Printed on FSC® recycled paper and bound in Canada by Friesens

FOR MY FAMILY

LEV

THE FIRST TIME I noticed my sister acting funny was also the first day of May. I remember it perfectly because it was the third funny thing that had happened that day. I don't mean funny like hilarious, jokey, a real shtick. I mean it as in *weird*.

The first thing happened at Normal School. Ms. Davidson said a new month meant a new beginning and that's why we'd be starting a new unit that day. The unit would be that every kid in grade five had to keep a journal from now until the end of the year, since it would improve our writing skills and also we would be happy we had this to look back on when we were fifty. She ran around the class giving out skinny blue notebooks with skinny blue lines on all the pages. Ms. Davidson was always running around giving things out, which made you wonder why she didn't just say *Take one and pass it on* like all the other teachers, but which made you also kind of like her.

Then Gabe Kramer raised his hand and said, "But a journal's only fun to look back on if you had cool things to write about," so she said, "And?" so he said, "And we don't," so she said, "You can just write in it like you're talking to a friend," so he said, "Whatever." He didn't really have a choice because at the end of the year Ms. Davidson was going to look in everyone's journal to make sure we wrote in them. She promised she wouldn't actually read them because a journal is a Very Private Thing, she would just sort of take a peek, which was good because it meant I could write about all of Dad's qualities and not just the ones that would make him seem like someone she might someday want to marry.

That was another thing Ms. Davidson was always doing, she was always talking about Very Private Things. She had a long list of them, which included but was not limited to: did she have a boyfriend, was red her real hair colour or did she dye it, was she older or younger than thirty-two, why did she ride her bicycle to school instead of drive, how much money did she make in a year, and who did she think should run the government, the English or the French.

We spent most of the period decorating the covers of our journals with photos that we cut out of magazines. Then Ms. Davidson said we had until the bell rang to write the first entry, but I had to go to the bathroom. On my way there I passed Gabe Kramer's desk, so I peeked over his shoulder and saw the words *this is dumb this is dumb this is dumb this is dumb* written out about five thousand times. I guess I stood there for a second too long because suddenly he twisted around in his seat and stared at me. He looked so mad his face was the same shiny orange as the plastic chair he was sitting on.

But the real funny thing happened when I came back from the bathroom. I passed Alex Caufin's desk, and he was leaning over his journal and smiling, so I peeked over his shoulder, too. I thought maybe he was doing the same thing as Gabe Kramer, cheating, but he was not. What he was writing was this:

```
0100100101100110001000000111100101101111
0111010100100000011001110110010101110100
0010000001110100011010000110100101110011
0010000001110010110111101110101001001011
0111001001100101001000000111000001110010
0110010101110100011101000111100100100000
0111001101101101011000010111001001110100
```

Line after line after line of numbers. There must've been at least eight thousand of them! I stood there staring, but Alex didn't even notice me. His tongue was sticking out from between his teeth, he was so concentrated. The secret theory that this put into my head was that maybe Alex was not cheating after all. Maybe he was writing a real journal, and maybe he was writing it in code.

The second funny thing happened on my way home from school. I was walking past Mr. Katz's house. Mr. Katz lived down the block and the reason why his name was Mr. Katz was not because he had lots of cats, it was because he was a Hasidic Jew. There were lots of Hasidic Jews in Mile End. You could usually see them walking around in long black coats and fur hats, even in summer. When it rained they wore funny-looking plastic bags over their hats that looked like shower caps, probably so the fur didn't get wet and start smelling. Mr. Katz was religious like them but he didn't really act or dress like them. Even though he had the same black pants, his were always wrinkled. Instead of a stiff white button-down shirt, he had a dirty white T-shirt. On top of that he wore the long white fringes that were supposed to be worn as an undershirt. Long dark curls dangled from the sides of his face, but instead of letting them bounce around, he tucked them away behind his ears like pencils.

When I turned the corner, I saw him sitting near the old oak tree on his front lawn surrounded by toilet paper rolls. He had a paintbrush in his hand and he was painting the rolls brown. I said, "Hello, Mr. Katz," and he said, "Hello, Lev," and I said, "What are you making?" and he said, "It's a secret," so I said, "Okay." I watched him paint for a while. His clothes were all covered in brown splotches, but he didn't care. His round face was smiling. It was really sunny and I didn't feel like going home right away, so after a few minutes I said, "Can I help?"

I felt bad for Mr. Katz because other people in the neighbourhood sometimes made fun of him. Even now, I could see out of the corners of my eyes that the Hasidic women pushing strollers were crossing to the other side of the street to avoid him. When their curious five- and six-year-olds tried to run toward him, the mothers pulled them back with a tug on their sleeves. Hipsters crinkled up their noses as they passed, like they couldn't stand the smell of someone so uncool, even though they were the ones leaving trails of cigarette smoke and loud music leaking out of their big headphones. Luckily, Mr. Katz didn't seem to notice the wide circles all of his neighbours were making around him when they passed.

Mr. Katz looked at me for a second and said, "Sure you can help, if you want to be a good boy and do a *mitzvah*, grab that roll and start painting." So I sat down on the grass next to him and started painting. It was not because I wanted to do a good deed, like they were always teaching us to do in Hebrew School. It was just because I liked Mr. Katz. I wondered what he was making.

The third funny thing happened at dinner. Sammy looked nervous and was acting weird. For one thing, she was wearing a long-sleeved shirt, even though it was a boiling hot day. Then when Dad asked her to pass the potatoes, her hand shook a little bit. She passed the bowl and he said, "Samara, is everything okay?" and she said, "Yes." But there was something else she wanted to say, a tiny word, I could see it in the corner of her mouth.

"So," Dad said between bites. "What did you learn in Hebrew School this week?"

All of a sudden, Sammy's face turned red. She opened her mouth like she was about to say something, and her eyes got really bright, which made me think it was going to be something important. But then she just poked her peas with her fork and said, "Nothing."

Dad raised his eyebrows, then asked what she was learning in Normal School. But she didn't answer right away, so even though I know it's rude to interrupt when someone else is speaking, I said as fast as I could, "We started a new unit in Language Arts today and the new unit is we all have to write in journals!" Then, because I knew this was a fact Dad would like, I added, "Ms. Davidson said she's going to check to make sure we wrote in them but she won't actually read them because a journal is a Very Private Thing!" Then, because no one else was speaking, I took the opportunity to say, "Ms. Davidson is highly intelligent and very funny and also she smells super nice," since one time I saw Dad sniffing an old perfume bottle of Mom's, which made me think that smelling nice was something he thought was an important quality.

"Well, good," Dad said into his water glass.

Sammy looked at me like I was crazy.

Then he asked her again what she was learning in Normal School.

"We just finished *1984*. I got an A on the essay. Now we're doing *King Lear*."

"*Lear!* That's great. So, maybe this weekend you and I can start going over the text together? Give you a little head start? Why settle for an A when you can get an A+, right?"

"Right," she said.

"Fantastic," he said. "You're sure everything's okay?"

"Yes," she said, and the corner of her mouth drooped under the weight. I took a closer look at my sister. The tiny word that she wanted to say but didn't say was *No*.


EVERY THURSDAY IN HEBREW SCHOOL we had to do a quiz. Mr. Glassman, our teacher who was also my next-door neighbour, asked us ten questions about the chapter of the Torah that would be chanted in synagogue on Saturday morning. Instead of grades, he gave us comments like *Tov* or *Tov Me'od* or, if you scored a perfect ten out of ten, *Metzuyan*.

One day in May, my quiz came back to me with the word *Metzuyan* scribbled across the top. After class, Mr. Glassman invited me over for tea and ruggelach. He always did that when I got a really good mark in his class. I had been to his house four times that year.

I liked Mr. Glassman a lot but I didn't really like going over because one, whenever I went Mrs. Glassman opened the door and pinched my cheeks and said, "Look at that *punim!*" and then spent about nine gazillion hours quizzing me on math while her husband waited on the welcome mat, and two, the air in that place had a weird feeling. I don't mean a weird smell, I mean a weird feeling. Like it was heavier than normal air. Like if you wanted to get from the front door to the kitchen, or from the bathroom to the living room, you practically had to go scuba diving. It made you wish you had a really small oxygen tank you could carry around in your pocket at all times, which is something I definitely would have bought if I had the money and if it existed but it didn't, I checked. The one good thing about going to the Glassmans' was that, when Mrs. Glassman was finally done talking in the doorway, she'd say, "Now if my husband would just move his *tuches* into the kitchen, I could bring you boys what to *nosh* on," and then she'd give you a big bowl of ruggelach, which was my favourite dessert.

While I was sitting in the kitchen, squishing the warm chocolate out of my fourth piece of ruggelach, Mr. Glassman looked up from his tea and said, "Lev, soon you will be thirteen. Bar mitzvah age."

"That's not for one and a half more years!" I said, licking my fingers.

"Still, for a smart boy like you, it is never too early to start pre-paring. Or too late. Take your sister for example."

"What do you mean?"

"She has been working very hard on her Torah portion."

"What Torah portion?"

"For the bat mitzvah."

I stopped licking my hand and put it down on the table. For a few seconds, I just stared at Mr. Glassman, his wrinkled face and straight grey hair and clear grey eyes. I knew that a bunch of girls from Hebrew School were having a group bat mitzvah in a month, but I didn't think Sammy was going to be in it because one, a bat mitzvah was something girls did when they turned twelve and Sammy was already thirteen, and two, when she was twelve Dad told her she wasn't going to do it since she was too young to tie herself to a religious tradition since she didn't really know how to think about religion yet. Did she understand how ahistorical it was? How anti-feminist? No? No, see, she was too young to understand. He wanted his kids to have a grasp on their culture, to know where they came from, that was why he was still sending us to Hebrew School, but that was it. Until we were old enough to think critically we were not in a position to be making any lifelong religious commitments. Even now, I wasn't really sure if that was true, because I was only eleven and a half but I was proud of being Jewish and I liked being in Mr. Glassman's Torah class. But I didn't want to tell Dad he was wrong because Mr. Glassman said the Talmud says a word is worth one coin but silence is worth two.

That night, after dinner, Sammy rinsed the dishes and I loaded them into the dishwasher while Dad put away food in the fridge. I started to tell Sammy how much I liked Mr. Glassman. Then I said, "And boy does he like you, he keeps telling me I should follow in your foot —" but all of a sudden she shot me a sharp look full of fear or maybe anger or possibly surprise or then again it could have been a warning and the sentence hung unfinished in the air.

THE NEXT MORNING was warm and sunny. At recess I saw Sammy laughing with her best friend Jenny in the lot outside Normal School. Then I looked into the nearby park and spotted Mr. Katz. He was wearing his usual wrinkled black pants and white T-shirt, and singing a happy tune to himself while he picked leaves off the trees and stuffed them into a big green garbage bag. I wanted to ask him what he was doing with all those leaves, but then I noticed that Gabe Kramer and Dean Toren were getting ready to corner Alex again.

Alex was one of those kids that got made fun of a lot, I guess because he was short and skinny and always reading a book about brown dwarfs and red giants and stuff like that. Probably his habit of keeping a book in front of his face at all times, even during recess, even when he was walking around outside, didn't help much. That was what he was doing right now, pacing back and forth with his nose buried deep in the pages, like all the kids playing basketball and dodge ball and hopscotch didn't even exist. Even though Alex's behaviour was maybe a little weird, I knew he didn't have any friends and none of the teachers were watching and I didn't want him to get beat up, so I went and stood next to him on the little patch of grass where he was reading.

When Gabe saw me, he nudged Dean and whispered into his ear and the two of them left Alex alone. Gabe probably thought I was going to tell on him for cheating with the journal, which I wasn't but he didn't need to know that yet. I stood next to Alex until recess was over, and it must've been a pretty good book because as far as I could tell he never even noticed I was there.

After school, I started walking down Saint-Viateur in the direction of Mr. Katz's house. Even though I never usually prayed outside of Hebrew School, because Dad said prayer was just an example of magical thinking, I decided to try it on my way over there. I prayed while the warm golden smell of bagels drifted through the air around me, making my stomach growl. I prayed while cool guys wearing skinny black ties with dark jeans climbed up twisting staircases, which were painted green and yellow and red, to get to their second-floor apartments, and girls with funky jewelry and short-shorts climbed down past them to unlock bicycles and pedal away. I prayed while teenagers listened to loud music at bus stops and old homeless men dug through the garbage searching for cans and small dogs barked outside Italian coffee shops and tourists snapped photos in front of bright graffitied walls.

The voices around me started to change: less French and English, more Yiddish. Now little boys were running past me with dark curls bouncing at the sides of their faces and white fringes trailing out from under their shirts. Their mothers, wearing long skirts and sleeves and wigs, rushed to keep up. I walked by the Judaica store, which was selling silver candlesticks and shiny Kiddush cups, and the Hasidic yeshiva, where men studied Torah for hours on end. All along the street, tiny front yards and iron balconies overflowed with kids' stuff, pink tricycles and blue toy cars. Most of the doors had *mezuzahs* on them. Two bearded men wearing black hats, coats, stockings, and shoes stood on a stoop, arguing in Yiddish and drawing circles in the air with their thumbs. I was still praying when I turned the corner onto Hutchison, asking God in my head to let me find Mr. Katz on his lawn so I could figure out what he was up to.

When I finally got there, the first half of my prayer got answered but not the second. Mr. Katz was sitting on the grass with all the leaves he'd picked lying on the plastic bag. The funny thing was, he was painting them all green, even though they were already green. When I asked him why, he said, "Not green enough."


IT WAS 8:15 on a Friday night and Sammy wasn't in the living room. Weird. On Friday nights we always watched the TGIF lineup, which started at exactly 8:00. I tried my best to be patient and wait, but when she still wasn't there at 8:30 I went to her room to get her, because it was boring watching TV alone and also she was the one who always made the popcorn.

Her door was open a crack so I peeked inside. The room was dark except for two white candles burning on the windowsill. Sammy put her hands over the flames and waved them three times, then covered her eyes and started whispering.

All of a sudden, I had a memory of Mom lighting the Shabbat candles when I was really little. I could see her pressing her fingers to her eyes and saying the Hebrew words. It made me feel weird because I almost never remembered anything about her, and remembering one thing made me wonder how many other things I'd forgotten. Hundreds? Thousands? Millions? Sammy knew more about Mom than I did because she was seven when Mom died and I was only five. But she didn't like to think about Mom, it made her cry, which was why I never asked questions anymore. Except now I could tell that she *was* thinking about Mom, because she was acting like her, so maybe that meant everything was different and I was allowed to ask again?

I tried to tiptoe into the room, but one of the floorboards creaked and Sammy turned around and saw me. She looked first shocked, then embarrassed, then extremely mad. She came toward me and yelled, "Haven't you ever heard of knocking?"

Then she slammed the door.

I went back to watch TV and tried to concentrate on the show but I couldn't because one, it was kind of boring and two, I kept wondering, why did Sammy look so embarrassed? And also how long had she been lighting Shabbat candles?

After a while, I fell asleep on the couch.

When I woke up again, it was because the noise of the TV had suddenly disappeared. The silence confused me, so I opened my eyes and there was Dad, standing over me and smiling. I could tell he'd just come back from the university because he had that tired look in his face and his briefcase in one hand. He held the remote in his other hand. He fell with a big plop into the armchair and said, "Hello. Sorry I woke you. How come you're not in bed?"

I yawned. "Fell asleep watching TV."

"Nothing good on, huh?"

"Not really." I twisted my neck to look at Dad and saw that he was flipping channels. "What are you doing?"

"Mmm? Oh, just seeing what's on."

"But I mean, why are you watching it on mute? You could turn the volume back on, since I'm up anyways?"

A funny smile came over his face then. "It's something I picked up from your mom, I guess," he said. "You know, she used to like to find the stupidest shows on TV, I mean the most truly awful soap operas in the world, and then turn the volume all the way down so that she could make up what the characters were saying. God, she loved to do that. I would find her sitting here sometimes, making up dialogue and laughing her head off."

I froze. Dad was like Sammy, he almost never talked about Mom. Once in a while something would remind him of her and he would tell me some random fact, like the name of her favourite chocolate bar (Milky Way) or her favourite Beatle (George). But that was it.

For a second I forgot to breathe. Then I had a genius idea. Maybe if I did the voices for the characters on TV, it would make Dad laugh and he would be so happy that he would want to tell me stuff about Mom all the time!

I concentrated hard on the screen and figured out what was playing. It was an episode of *Star Trek*. A Klingon guy was talking to a pretty woman while their ship crashed through space, lights flashing like crazy all around them. I took a deep breath and put on a woman's voice: "Excuse me, sir, but your skin is really breaking out. Your forehead looks like it's got a mountain growing out of it! You know, you should really try that new face wash I got you for your birthday. It worked wonders for my mother." Then I switched to the man's voice. "Um, can we talk about this later? Our ship's about to crash!" Then I did the woman's voice again: "Stop trying to change the subject. You're always so sensitive!" Then the ship tilted over and the characters fell down, so I said, "Your turn, Dad!" But when the man's mouth started moving again, Dad didn't say anything. I looked over my shoulder and he was just sitting there, staring at me.

His eyes flashed with anger. The muscles in his face were all twisted up for a second, then they went flat again. He turned off the TV and got up. "It's late," he said. "Time for me to turn in. Good night."

As his back disappeared down the dark hall, I caught a whiff of perfume coming off him. That's when I understood why he'd gotten so mad. If he was still sniffing Mom's old perfume bottle, sometimes even spritzing it on himself, that meant he still really missed her. It probably hurt him to be reminded of her, just like it hurt Sammy.

"Good night," I whispered, but I don't think he heard me. The door to his room was already closed.

**THE NEXT DAY** was hot and quiet. Most Saturdays, me and Sammy played games like Snakes and Ladders or Monopoly or Scrabble, but today she had her best friend over. Actually, Jenny was her only friend. Even though Sammy was one grade above her, they'd known each other forever because our dad and her dad both taught at the same university and our families were friends. When Mom died, Jenny's parents said they could watch me and Sammy for a few hours after school every day so that Dad could work late at the university and wouldn't have to hire a housekeeper. He told them sure, thanks, why not.

Now Sammy was playing with Jenny in her room, and the door was closed, and I didn't want to knock in case she was still mad at me.

So instead I turned around to face the door to Dad's study. It was closed, too. But I couldn't stop thinking about what had happened the night before: how he'd told me something really cool about Mom completely out of the blue, and how maybe, if I was lucky and patient, if I didn't push, he might do the same thing again today. A second later, I went ahead and did something I hadn't done in ages. I knocked.

"What?" He didn't like being interrupted when he was working.

I opened the door a few inches and said, "Hi."

Without taking his eyes off the book in front of him, he said, "Do you need something?"

"No."

"Are you hungry?"

"No."

"Sick?"

"No."

"Well then? What is it?"

I didn't know what to say. Finally, I said, "I'm bored."

He sighed. Then he put a finger on the page to mark his place and looked up from his book. I couldn't tell what it was but the letters on the cover were in Hebrew. There were a dozen other books stacked up all over the desk, and a million more on the messy shelves behind him. One of them, I knew, even had his name on it: *The Unorthodox Kabbalah*, by David Meyer. Near his elbow were a slice of toast and a half-finished cup of coffee, but I could tell he'd forgotten all about them. "Where's your sister?" he asked.

"In her room."

"What's she up to?"

"Hanging out with Jenny. Painting or drawing or something."

"Well, why don't you ask them to play a game with you?"

"They won't want to play with me."

"You don't know until you ask."

"Okay," I said. "I'll ask."

"Great." He shot me a quick smile and then looked down at his book again. "Would you close the door, please?"

I closed the door.

In the hall, my eyes landed on a couple of picture frames that had been sitting on the same table for as long as I could remember. One showed Dad the year before Mom died, back when he was still religious and had a beard. He was sitting in his study with a book in his hand and a look in his face like he was itching to get back to it.

The other picture showed Mom around the same time. I picked it up and ran a fingertip over the glass. I traced her smiling eyes and her big, laughing mouth. I wished I could see more of her, but her long-sleeved dress hid every inch of skin, all the way up to her neck. Her hair was tucked away under a plain blue scarf. Still, she glowed.

The last time I saw Dad with a beard was ages ago, when I was five. Dad had bought a new book and he and Mom were having a big fight about it. I was in bed, so they thought I was asleep, but I could hear every word coming through their bedroom door. Then Dad stormed out of the bedroom and into the bathroom. I tiptoed into the hall and saw him shaving his beard, but he didn't see me. A few days later Mom came home with her head shaved and a wig to wear over it instead of her usual scarf. I felt sad because one, I used to like playing with her long shiny hair, and two, after she did that Dad didn't say a word all day and then the next day it was too late to say anything because Mom got hit by a car and died.

For the millionth time, I wished she were still alive so she could play with me right now, and also so she could get Dad to come out of his study more often. Ever since she died, he stayed mostly cooped up in there. Somehow I thought if she was around, he would be a lot happier, and probably he would want to spend a lot more time hanging out with me and Sammy. But she was gone, and his door was closed, and there wasn't anything I could do to fix that — at least not right then.

I put down the photo, opened a closet and took out the Snakes and Ladders board. But instead of knocking on Sammy's door, I went into the backyard and set up the game on the grass. I rolled the dice and moved my token six spaces forward. I rolled again and landed on a ladder and shot up two rows. I rolled three more times and landed on a snake and dropped all the way down to the bottom again. When I got tired of playing against myself, I lay back and stared up at the sky until my eyes started to close. The next thing I knew my ears were full of ringing and somebody was calling my name.

Inside, I followed Sammy's voice to the front of the house. She was standing with her hand on the doorknob and making small talk with Alex, who was glancing back and forth between her face and his shoes with a half-excited, half-terrified expression.

"So, what do you like to do when you're not at school?" she asked.

He mumbled something that sounded like "look at the stars."

"Cool," she said. "I love looking at the stars."

"Really?" He beamed. "But actually, I said 'listen,' not 'look.'"

"You listen to the stars? How can you *listen* to stars?"

"They send us messages all the time," he said seriously. "And I mean, if there's intelligent life up there, don't you think it would be trying to communicate with us?"

Sammy stared at him. His cheeks and the tips of his ears glowed bright pink.

"Hello," I said.

"Oh!" Alex said, glancing at me. "Hi, Lev. Do you want to go play? Um, basketball?"

I blinked at the basketball in his hands. I couldn't believe he was here, at my house, and I couldn't believe he wanted to play sports. Because I couldn't think of anything else to say, I said, "Where?"

"At my place, I have a hoop in my driveway, remember?" Then I guess he realized that I'd never actually been to his place before and he added, "Well, I mean, you don't have to, I just thought you might want to." He was sweating a lot and his glasses kept slipping down his nose and he kept pushing them back up with one finger. If I had to describe the expression on his face using only one word, the word I would use would be *please*.

I asked Sammy if it was okay. She shrugged and said she didn't see why not. Then she turned back to Alex. "What did you mean, the stars are sending us messages all the time?"

"I can show you, if you want. I've got all the equipment set up in my room. You can come with us, if you're not busy?"

"Yeah, I'd like to see —"

"Samara?"

We all turned around. Jenny was standing in the doorway of Sammy's room. None of us had noticed her, but I wasn't too surprised by that, because Jenny was the kind of person you could not notice for a long time. She pushed a strand of blonde hair away from her freckled face and said, "My mom's not coming to pick me up for another half an hour."

"Oh, that's okay," Sammy told her. "I don't have to go right now! I'll stay till your mom gets here, definitely."

"And then you'll come over to my house, right?" Alex asked.

"Sure," Sammy said. "What's your address?"

He gave it to her. Then we waved goodbye and the two of us headed off down the block.

On the corner, we bumped into a couple of old Hasidic men, who stopped all of a sudden when the streetlight turned red. They were wearing fur hats and short black pants and white stockings, and talking really fast in Yiddish. The fringes that poked out from under their coats were dangling almost to the ground. Then the light turned green and they rushed ahead. We kept on walking.

"What's with those white stockings?" Alex whispered. "They look like girls' clothes."

"I asked my dad about them once, actually. Because some of the Hasids around here wear white stockings and some wear black and I didn't understand why."

"And?"

"And he said it might have to do with which sect they belong to. There are lots of different Hasidic sects in Mile End: Belz, Satmar, Bobov, Munkacs, Skver, Vishnitz, you name it. But when I asked how you could tell the different sects apart, he just said, 'Who cares?'"

Alex shrugged like maybe that was a logical response. After a minute he said, "Lev."

"Yeah?"

"That's a weird name."

"Oh. I guess."

"What does it mean? Does it mean something?"

"It's Hebrew for *heart*."

"Where'd you get a name like that?"

"Um. My parents gave it to me?"

"Obviously. But like, what made them decide to call you *heart*? I mean were you named after somebody famous or something?"

"I don't think so."

"They just thought that would be a cool name?"

"I guess."

"Oh. Well."

I was going to tell him not to sound so disappointed when he came to a stop in front of a red brick driveway, the only one on the street with a basketball hoop. I didn't know what to say. All these years we'd been living just two blocks apart and I'd never even noticed.

I wanted to start playing right away but Alex said I should really let him give me some lessons first because he'd seen my layups in gym class and they weren't very scientific. He kept shooting and missing and saying, "Oops, okay, I miscalculated there, but this game is all about physics, trust me, just watch," and then he'd shoot and miss again. After about twenty minutes, I stole the ball from him and dribbled it up to the net and shot and scored.

"Nice one!" called a voice.

I turned around and saw Sammy. "Thanks!" I called back, then added, "Alex was just giving me some pointers."

"Oh really? That's nice of you," Sammy said to Alex. The tips of his ears went bright pink again.

Then he led us inside to get popsicles out of the freezer. There were only three left, a cherry, an orange, and a grape. I claimed the cherry. Alex let Sammy have the orange one even though I could tell that he didn't like grape, because, really, who does?

Except for us, the kitchen was empty. As far as I could tell, there was no one else home.

"Where is everybody?" I asked.

"My mom's at work. She's a nurse at the hospital."

"What about your dad?"

"He lives in Toronto."

I didn't want to say the wrong thing, so I didn't say anything. Six seconds passed.

Then Alex announced, "I was named after somebody famous."

"Really?" Sammy asked. "Who?"

"My grandfather. My mom's dad."

"He was famous?"

"Sure."

"What was his name?"

"Aleksandr Leonidovich Zaitsev."

"What did he do?"

"Aleksandr Leonidovich Zaitsev? He was only one of the most important astronomers of all time! Who do you think came up with the idea for SETI?"

"What's SETI?" we asked at the same time.

"*What's SETI?* The Search for Extraterrestrial Intelligence!" Alex cried. Then he pointed upstairs. "Come on, I'll show you."

Alex's room was small and messy and full of light. In one corner was a big white computer set up on a big white desk. In another corner was a huge white bookcase packed with books. The bed took up the third corner, and the sheets were decorated with spaceships and comets and shooting stars. In front of the window stood a white telescope, skinny and long. The floor was almost impossible to walk on. It was covered in heaps and heaps of ancient stuff: telephones, batteries, keyboards, computer mice, wires in red and blue and green and yellow, and, on top of the nearest pile, a TV remote control that someone, probably Alex, had taken apart. I picked up the remote and studied the blue wires crisscrossing the grey plastic. They reminded me of what rivers look like when you see them from above, for example in an airplane, and also of the bluish veins on Mr. Glassman's arm.

"What's this?" Sammy asked, trailing her finger along a shiny antenna.

"That's my ham radio," Alex said proudly. "It lets me communicate with amateur radio operators all around the world. My mom got it for me for Christmas last year."

"And is that how you hear the other messages, too? The ones from the stars?"

He smiled, then shook his head. "For that, you need a way bigger radio."

Alex explained that there was a group of astronomers who, instead of using normal telescopes to look at the universe, used radio telescopes to listen to it. Instead of picking up light, a radio telescope picked up noise.

"Here, check it out," Alex said, waving us over to his computer. "This is SETI."

We went and looked at the screen. It was full of weird symbols I didn't understand. Squiggly waves, charts, and numbers. In the top left-hand corner, it said, *The Search for Extraterrestrial Intelligence at Home*, and then there was a picture of a satellite.

"Okay, so pretend you're a radio astronomer. What you're listening for with your radio telescope is a pattern hidden in the noise coming from outer space. That type of signal doesn't happen naturally, so if you detect it, that could mean evidence of alien technology. Okay?"

"Okay," we said.

"So, once you pick up a pattern, what do you do? Well, so maybe you analyze the data digitally on your big ginormous supercomputer. But the more computer power you have, right, the more frequency ranges you can cover — and the more sensitivity you've got, too. So the more computers you have working for you, the better. Okay?"

"Okay."

"So, in 1995, this guy named David Gedye said, hey, why don't we use the internet to hook up, say, a million computers, like the ones in people's houses, to do some of this work for us? And that's exactly what he did. And that's what my computer is doing right now."

"Why?" I asked.

"Why what?"

"Why would you want a bunch of people you don't even know using your computer?"

Alex looked at me like he couldn't believe his ears. "Because it's *cool*," he said. "Because it's *science*." Then, just to make sure I understood how cool it was, he did a search for "Arecibo Message." He explained that SETI astronomers broadcasted this radio message into outer space back in 1974. It was the first message human beings ever sent out on purpose. They aimed it at something called globular star cluster M13, which was approximately 25,000 light years away. It was their way of saying hello. They were still waiting for a response.

Sammy pointed to an image on the screen. It showed a telescope, a stick figure, and something that looked like a strip of human DNA. "What's that?"

"That's the message."

"It's a picture."

"So?"

"So I thought you said the message was noise."

"So?"

"So how can the message be a picture if it's also noise?"

"Well, because the message is written in binary."

She looked confused, so Alex smiled and typed in "Binary" and what came up on the screen then was numbers.

Line after line after line of numbers.

Not just any old numbers, but zeros and ones specifically.

I was so excited, I had to bite the insides of my cheeks to keep from showing it.

Alex explained that in the binary system you could use zeros and ones to say anything you wanted. How exactly it worked was kind of complicated, which was why only Sammy understood it and not me, even though Alex kept tapping his fingers on the desk and telling me to think of each tap as one and each rest as zero. But he said this was how the astronomers had sent the Arecibo Message. The whole entire picture was made up of zeros and ones.

"Think of it like code," he said. "Morse code also has two symbols: dots and dashes. It's always either one or the other. Zero or one. Dot or dash. And that's all you need, really — you can say anything you want in the whole universe using just those symbols, and anyone else in the universe, as long as they know the code, can understand you and send a message back."

"*Cool*," Sammy said, and Alex grinned.

Then she looked at her watch and said we should probably go home, since Dad would be wondering where we were. Alex said okay, but before letting us leave he made us each pick out books to borrow.

Sammy chose *Cracking Binary Code* and *Patterns in the Chaos: Listening for Intelligent Life in the Cosmos*. I didn't know what to choose, so Alex picked one out for me: *Important Names in Astronomy Today*. The book was gigantic, and even though I was positive I would never actually read it, I took it anyway because I could tell from the way his eyes started to shine that it would make Alex happy.

By the time we left his house and started making our way home, the sky was already dark. The streets were empty. It was Saturday night and all the Hasids were probably still in synagogue. I looked up at the clouds. I tried to imagine all the different voices that must've been travelling on the wind at that moment — radio signals, TV signals, messages sent into outer space — but the air around us was still and silent. We turned onto our block and it was hard to believe anyone on the planet had ever spoken a single word. To reassure myself, I squeezed my eyes shut and pictured a series of zeros and ones streaming through the universe. Sammy turned her key in the lock and we said hello into the darkness of the hallway. Nobody answered. For some reason, my stomach began to ache.

WE ALWAYS HAD Language Arts last on Mondays. I knew that Ms. Davidson liked to lock up her bike in the second-to-last rack behind the school, so on Monday morning instead of walking to Normal School I decided to take my bike. I locked it up next to the big blue bicycle with the shiny bell and the basket on the handlebars that I knew was hers. Then I went to class.

When the bell rang at the end of last period, I hunched over my journal and kept right on writing. Ms. Davidson always took a few minutes to gather up her stuff, so I leaned over the page and pretended I was very concentrated on my thoughts. After a while, I saw her dress out of the corner of my eye, so I pressed my nose close to the page for extra believability. Then she said, "Lev? The bell rang a few minutes ago. Shouldn't you be getting home?"

I looked up fast and checked the clock, then made my eyes wide to show how surprised I was. I followed her out of the class and down the stairs and into the empty lot behind the school.

"I left my bike over here," I explained. "I love biking, don't you?"

She smiled. "Love it!"

We reached the second-to-last rack and she started unlocking her bike. I leaned over to unlock mine, which was so close to hers it was actually touching. For a second I was nervous that she might get suspicious, but when she saw what I was doing she just laughed.

"Well!" she said. "Look at that."

She was already pulling her bike out of the rack, so I knew there wasn't any time to lose. Using my most casual voice, I asked, "When's your favourite time of day to go biking?"

She thought about this for a second, and while she thought, I prayed. Then, because God sometimes listens to you if you pray really hard, she gave the exact answer I was hoping for.

"Night," she laughed. "I like a good middle-of-the-night bicycle ride! Why do you ask?"

"That's so funny! My dad loves to go biking at night. He does it all the time!"

"Is that so?"

"Sure!" I said. Then I started to tell her about the time Dad took me and Sammy out for a bike ride in the middle of the night. "It was *four in the morning*," I said, to make sure she knew how much he liked the thing she also liked. "We went all the way from our house, which by the way if you want to know is 5479 Hutchison, all the way to the mountain and then all the way back! And we didn't get home until *sunrise.*"

"What a fun adventure!" she said, climbing onto her bike. "Well, Lev, I'll see you —"

"Wait!" I wanted to tell her some more interesting things about Dad, like that he was a professor and highly intelligent and understood completely about Very Private Things and could make macaroni and cheese better than anyone else's dad in the neighbourhood, which I knew for a fact was true even though he hadn't actually made it for us in ages, but all of a sudden I looked down and something very small and very white caught my eye.

There was a flower in her pedal. From the way it was sticking out, I could tell she hadn't put it there on purpose. It'd just gotten caught as she rode her way through a forest or meadow or something like that. It made me feel sad, but I didn't understand why.

"Lev? Was there something else you wanted to tell me?"

I shook my head.

"Okay," she smiled. "I'll see you tomorrow!" And she pedalled away.

I walked my bike slowly down the street, trying to find the reason why I'd suddenly felt so sad, but I couldn't think of it. This was a thing that happened to me sometimes, I got sad for no reason. Once, when I was eight years old, I'd asked Sammy what she thought was causing it. I thought maybe it was some kind of sickness, and if it was a sickness it probably had a name, and I wanted to know the name of it. But she just told me not to worry, it happened to her, too, it happened all the time.

When I turned the corner, I saw that Mr. Katz was out on his lawn again. He was sitting on the grass surrounded by the cans of green paint. He had the paintbrush in his hand, and even though he'd already gone over all the leaves once, he was going over them all again.

Because I had nothing better to do, I asked if I could help with the second coat. He said okay, so I sat down and picked up a leaf. The sun was shining and the birds were singing and I felt like I could sit there for hours, warm paint squishing between my hands. I knew I was doing a good job because after I painted a leaf it looked even realer than the leaves of the old oak tree on the lawn. Mr. Katz was really happy, too, and when I left he said I could come back and help out some other time if I wanted.

There was almost no light left in the sky by the time I got home. Dad and Sammy were in the kitchen. He was making dinner and she was setting the table.

"Why are your hands all covered in paint?" he asked me.

I stared down at my green hands and froze.

"You haven't been talking to that old quack down the street, have you? Because when I passed by his house this morning, I saw him sitting there with green paint."

"I, um —"

"The man's delusional. One too many religious ideas gone to his head." He frowned down at me. "Well? Were you with him, yes or no?"

Out of the corner of my eye, I saw Sammy shake her head, very slowly, from side to side.

"No."

"Then why are your hands all covered in paint?"

"I'm working on a project? With Alex? From Normal School?"

"For what class?"

"Science?

"What's the project on?"

I froze again. But in the next second, Sammy was standing right beside me.

"Chlorophyll," she said.

He looked at her. "Oh?"

"Yes," she said. Then she stared down at her feet and added, "And just because Mr. Katz is religious, that doesn't make him delusional. He looks lonely. I feel sorry for him."

"Is that right?" Dad said. But she didn't answer him, so he just told me to wash my hands and then turned back to face the stove.

As I walked to the sink, I snuck a look at Sammy. I rolled my eyes in Dad's direction and her face cracked into a smile. I grinned. Me and my sister didn't just share the same nameless sickness. We also shared a secret language that only we could speak.

IN HEBREW SCHOOL, we spent most of the time listening to Mr. Glassman read the Torah out loud. He'd read a section, then try to get one of us to translate it into English. Because nobody ever wanted to do it, nobody ever volunteered, which meant lots of seconds passed without anybody saying anything, which made you kind of wonder why Mr. Glassman didn't just call on someone and make them translate it like any normal teacher would. After a while, you realized Mr. Glassman didn't need to call on anyone because he sort of had his own trick, which was to just stare at us in perfect silence until finally, eventually, somebody cracked.

But that week the temperature shot up like crazy. Mr. Glassman, who wore his usual neat shirt and vest and tie even though it was a million degrees, had big circles of sweat under his arms. I counted off seconds in my head. Ten, twenty, thirty, forty, fifty, sixty. After sixty-three seconds passed without anyone saying anything, Mr. Glassman did something he'd never done before. He closed his book and asked if we wanted, just this once, to hear a story instead.

Right away everyone yelled, "Yes!" and slammed their books shut. Mr. Glassman ran his fingers through his damp grey hair and smiled.

Rabbi Akiva, he said, lived two thousand years ago, but he wasn't always called Rabbi. For the first forty years of his life he was just plain Akiva, a poor shepherd who didn't know how to read or what the alphabet was or even how to pray. He said he was so jealous of the Torah scholars in his village that if he had the chance he would have bitten them like a wild donkey. But then one day, when he was out with his sheep, he saw a big rock lying in a riverbed and a tiny stream of water dripping onto it from up above. It was a very slow drip, but Akiva saw that over many years that drip had worn down the rock. Now there was a hollow space in it big enough for a pool of water to collect. He thought: If a drop of water can make its way into a stone, the Torah can make its way into my heart! The next day, he went to school with his youngest child to learn how to read the alphabet.

By the end of his life, he had the most knowledge and the most students of any Torah scholar in the world.

That night, at dinner, Dad asked again what me and Sammy were learning in school. He wanted to know how Sammy was liking *King Lear* so far, but she just stared down at her skirt, so instead I told him all about Ms. Davidson and how she went for bike rides in the middle of the night and wore happy colours and really made you think. After a few minutes, he yawned. I could tell he was extremely bored but I kept on talking because that was the only way, because if I kept on talking, word after word, drop after drop, sooner or later a space would open up.


ON MY WAY HOME from school in the last week of May, I saw Mr. Katz sitting on his lawn in between the old oak tree and a second tree trunk that seemed to have sprouted up overnight. But when I got closer, I saw that it wasn't a real trunk at all, it was the hundreds of toilet paper rolls that we painted brown tied together with dental floss. I went over and said, "Hello, Mr. Katz."

"Hello, Lev."

"Are you making a tree, by any chance?"

After a very long time, he said, "Yes." Then he grabbed my wrist and pulled down hard so I kind of fell onto my knees on the grass. When I was sitting next to him, he whispered, "Can you keep a secret?"

I rubbed my wrist and said, "Yes."

"You promise?"

"I promise."

"This is not an ordinary tree I am making."

I dropped my wrist and said, "What kind of tree is it?"

"This," he said, "this is the Tree of Knowledge."

THE NEXT DAY, I decided to ask Mr. Glassman about the Tree of Knowledge, because all I knew was that it was in the Garden of Eden and that eating from it was what got Adam and Eve kicked out. I waited all afternoon for Torah class to be over, and then I went up to him and said, "Mr. Glassman, I've been thinking about how you said it's never too early to start preparing for your bar mitzvah, and I was wondering if I could study with you some days after school?" He looked really happy when I said that, and he even pinched my cheek and said, "*Geshmack!*" He told me we could start right away, so I followed him home.

When Mrs. Glassman opened the door and saw me, she said, "Two times I get to see Lev in the same month, tu-tu-tu *kenaynohora*, but if I knew my Chaim was going to be *schlepping* you here practically every day I would prepare for you more things to eat!" She told me to sit at the kitchen table and brought us some hot tea even though it was about a zillion degrees outside. She said, "Drink!" so I drank.

Mr. Glassman asked when my Hebrew birthday was so he could calculate when my bar mitzvah would fall during the year. That way he'd know what Torah portion I'd have to read. I said, "I don't actually know when it is because my dad says that calendar's based on a backwards idea of when the world was created, which scientists are still iffy about but which was definitely more than 6000 years ago." Mr. Glassman raised his eyebrows, then shook his head and sighed.

Since what I really wanted to learn about was the Tree of Knowledge, I asked Mr. Glassman if we could study Genesis instead. He gave me a funny look but then his face lit up. He said, "Begin at the beginning, excellent idea, I see you're just as thorough as your sister!"

We started reading the first chapter of Genesis, but after an hour we had only gotten up to the part about the grass being created. Even though I wanted to ask about the Tree right away, Mr. Glassman could see the toilet paper roll version of it right from his window and I didn't want to make him suspicious that maybe I was trying to help Mr. Katz.

The reason why was that Mr. Glassman was not the Hasidic kind of Jew that believes in personal miracles and prayers full of dancing and curls that bounce at the sides of your face. He was the Misnaged kind of Jew that believes in logic and straight lines, like the lines of his shirt and vest and tie, like his combed grey hair. Once when I came over after Hebrew School, Mr. Glassman said that Mr. Katz was a nice person, but he was all faith and no knowledge. What good was one without the other? An animal also had faith! Mrs. Glassman poked him in the ribs when he said that, but I could tell from her face she thought he was right.

That's how I knew I had to be patient and come back as many times as it took. I didn't mind that much because Mrs. Glassman's ruggelach was the best in the neighbourhood. And even though she talked to me for about nine gazillion hours before letting me leave, asking questions like "You are liking your math class?" and "You have learned about the Fibonacci numbers?" and "A syllogism, you know what it is, yes? No? How can you not know?" she only pinched my cheeks three times.

Luckily it only took me a few seconds to get home because the Glassmans' house and our house were so close they were practically touching. Actually there was so little space between them that when we were little Dad used to always tell me and Sammy to keep it down, noise travelled easily through the windows and he was sure the Glassmans could hear us. I pointed out that *we* never heard any voices coming from *their* house, and noise travels both ways, but Dad just said that must be because the Glassmans talk very quietly. I didn't want to tell him he was wrong, but I knew for a fact that wasn't true, because sometimes when Mr. and Mrs. Glassman talked to me their voices were so loud I could feel it in my teeth.

As soon as I opened our front door, I knew right away Sammy was already home. I could hear her voice coming from her room. She was chanting in Hebrew, so I knew it was the Torah portion she was preparing to read at the bat mitzvah next month.

I crept into my room very quietly so that she wouldn't hear me and get embarrassed or mad. I clicked the door shut and held my breath for nineteen seconds straight, and she kept right on chanting. But five minutes later, Dad came home, and the second she heard his voice in the hallway she stopped.

He called, "Samara?" and she said, "Yeah?" and he said, "Would you help me get dinner started?" and she said, "Okay." I heard Dad ask, "How about cheeseburgers?" so I ran into the hallway to say, "Yes!" but when I saw Sammy's face I said, "Ye — No, could we have grilled cheese instead?" When Dad went into the kitchen, Sammy gave me a funny look, like maybe she could tell that I could tell that she was trying to keep kosher in secret.

THE SECOND THE BELL RANG for lunch, I knew something was up. All the kids jumped up from their desks, got their lunches from their lockers, and raced out to the empty lot behind the school. Gabe was in the lead and I could tell he had something hidden in his jacket, because the corner of it was peeking out, a lighter blue against the dark blue of his ripped-up jeans.

Alex was taking his time getting his lunch out of his locker. I told him to hurry up and he asked why and I said to just do it and he asked why so I pulled him by the sleeve and rushed with him outside. I had a very tight feeling in my stomach, and once we reached the empty lot it took me about three milliseconds to understand why.

Gabe was standing at the far end, near where the grade sixes usually played dodge ball. Swarming around him were twenty kids from our class, and they were all pushing and shoving at each other to get a better look. The thing they were trying to get a better look at was in Gabe's right hand, and the thing Gabe's right hand was holding was —

"The Secret Diary of Alex Caufin," announced Gabe, and the entire class cheered their heads off. "Who wants to hear what this loser *really* thinks of us?" Again the kids roared. Very slowly, with a huge grin on his face, Gabe opened the journal to the first page.

He frowned. The kids waited. He turned the page. The kids waited. He flipped to the middle of the notebook. One kid shouted, "Come on already!" and even Dean shouted, "Yeah!" but Gabe just scowled. I turned around to look at Alex but he was walking up to Gabe and Dean. Half the kids spilled onto one side of him and half the kids spilled onto the other in a way that reminded me of something in the Torah but I couldn't remember what. I couldn't figure out why Alex looked so calm, but then I saw the journal in Gabe's hand and remembered what I'd seen on the first page, which was line after line after line of numbers. The whole entire thing was written in code, and that's why Gabe couldn't read it, and that's why his face was turning so red!

Alex stretched out his hand and said, "I believe you have something that belongs to me."

Behind Gabe's shoulder, Dean grinned and raised his fist like maybe he was planning to give Alex something else instead. But just then Ms. Davidson came outside and we heard her voice call out, "What's going on here?"

Dean lowered his fist. Alex snatched his journal back. The two of us went inside.

I could tell Alex was feeling really proud of himself, but all day long my stomach stayed tight because I could see Gabe shooting us laser looks of hate out of the corners of his shiny, black, too-small eyes.

Which was why, hours later, after I'd gone to bed and crawled under the covers, I turned on my flashlight and took out my journal and read through all the pages I'd filled so far. I wanted to make sure there was nothing too private in them, nothing that would be too embarrassing if Gabe and Dean ever decided to read it out loud in front of the entire class.

Luckily I didn't have much to worry about because mostly what I'd written in my journal was lists. For example, one list was called Very

Important Qualities According to My Father, which was an excellent list even though the title was maybe not one hundred percent true since some of the qualities were thought up by me and not by Dad. I flipped to the page and checked it for embarrassing details just in case.

VERY IMPORTANT QUALITIES ACCORDING
TO MY FATHER:

1. Highly intelligent
2. Good cook
3. Easy on the eyes
4. Likes watching TV on Friday nights
5. Likes playing board games on Saturday mornings
6. Very funny
7. Interested in Judaism but not too interested
8. Smells nice

That list looked okay to me. I still wished I'd had the idea to write everything in code, but so far there was nothing too bad and I figured I was probably safe for now.

I closed my journal and stuffed it under my pillow, but I didn't turn off the flashlight. Instead I pointed it at my door so that Sammy could see the light from her room across the hall. Then she would come to my room and say, using her most grown-up voice, "Lights out!" or "It's past your bedtime," which was this thing she did for me sometimes. Sure enough, a few seconds later my door creaked open and she said, "It's past your bedtime," and I said, "Just five more minutes?" and she said, "No," and I said, "You're not the boss of me," and she said, "Yes I am," and I said, "Whatever," and then I pretended to be all upset even though I was not. I turned off my flashlight and she closed my door and I smiled up at the ceiling, and when I fell asleep the smile was still on my face, because what I really was right then was happy.

THAT FRIDAY, I got home from painting at Mr. Katz's house and went straight to the kitchen to get a fudgesicle from the freezer. A minute later, Sammy came in and got a cherry popsicle and started eating it while balancing on one foot. The red light on the answering machine was flashing, so I pressed play and listened.

The first message was from Dad. He said he was going to be at the university late because he was giving a special lecture about evolution and fundamentalism and that we could make whatever we wanted for dinner. I made a mental note to look up "fundamentalism" in the dictionary, then hit delete.

The second message was from Ira, Jenny's dad, who taught at the same university. He was calling to make sure Dad knew about the faculty meeting on Tuesday, so I made a mental note to remind him. Then, just when I was about to hit delete, Ira's voice started up again.

"I almost forgot! You'll be getting an invitation in the mail, too, but I wanted to let you know that Jenny's bat mitzvah is in just a few weeks! We're all so excited, and of course we'd be honoured if you'd come and celebrate with us. So! June 23, save the date!"

He hung up, and two things happened: the answering machine beeped, and Sammy lost her balance. The foot that had been dangling in the air fell to the floor. I looked at her face and saw that it was red. She looked at my hands and saw that they were green. We looked at the floor and said nothing.

Then I had a genius idea. I asked if we had any M&M's and she said that she had just bought some, so I went to look for her backpack, which was near the front door. I unzipped the biggest pocket and the M&M's were right on top. When my hand grabbed the package, I felt something soft and velvety underneath. I pulled it out and saw that it was a long blue dress.

Just then, Sammy appeared in the hallway. When she spotted me holding the fancy dress, she jumped. I thought she was going to yell at me for snooping in her stuff, but she just told me to hurry up so that we could make dinner. I put the dress back and followed her into the kitchen.

I took a box of Kraft Dinner out of the pantry. While boiling water, I thought maybe the blue dress was what Sammy was planning to wear to the bat mitzvah. I poured the macaroni into the pot and stirred. Sammy looked at my green hand and said, "Another project on chlorophyll?" I opened my mouth to laugh at her joke but then I had a better idea, so I said, "Actually, it's for the special thing I'm making with Mr. Katz, which by the way if you want to know is a tree." She asked, "What kind of tree?" and I put on my best I-have-a-juicy-secret voice and whispered, "Can you keep a secret?" She said, "Yes," so I said, "You promise?" so she said, "I promise," and then I told her exactly what Mr. Katz was making.

My idea was that maybe if I told her one of my secrets she would feel like telling me one of hers. It worked! She said, "Can you keep a secret?" and then she told me all about how she was going to be in the bat mitzvah in a few weeks. I told her it sounded cool. She said that it was very cool, the only problem was that if Dad found out he'd never let her go through with it. The only people who knew were one, Jenny, who would never tell anyone because she was Sammy's best friend, and two, Mr. Glassman, who was also a safe bet because he practically never talked to anybody unless they were his student and it was class time. She'd been taking private after-school lessons with him at Hebrew School because she had to learn how to chant from the Torah because she had never learned how to do it when she was twelve years old.

I told Sammy not to worry and that I would help keep her secret safe. Then I asked her if she was keeping kosher and she said that she was trying to and also that she was trying to keep Shabbat but it was hard to do without making Dad suspicious. I said that if she wanted I could do it with her. She gave me a funny look then, but what she didn't say was *No*.

Then we divided the M&M's into six bowls — blues, oranges, reds, greens, yellows, and browns — and mixed some of the Kraft Dinner in with each, so that the macaroni in each bowl turned a different colour. Blues and yellows were okay, but reds tasted best.

IT WASN'T UNTIL my third lesson with Mr. Glassman that we finally got to the part about the Tree of Knowledge. We spent half an hour going over it at the kitchen table while Mrs. Glassman stood at the counter baking ruggelach and talking to herself. It always confused me when she did that because usually when people talk to themselves it means they're missing a few marbles, and Mrs. Glassman was a smart woman with marbles to spare. She was muttering under her breath, "If not $p$ or $q$ entails not $p$ and not $q$, and $p$ is true if and only if $r$, then we prove that for every $r$..." Mr. Glassman kept right on studying like he didn't hear anything, so I did the same.

But by the time the lesson was over I didn't have any more answers than when I started, only more questions. There were lots of things about the story I didn't really get. For example, it said that eating from the Tree was supposed to make you wise and know the difference between good and evil. But when Adam and Eve ate from the Tree, all the story said was that their eyes popped open and suddenly they realized they had no clothes on.

Another thing I didn't get was at the end of the story when it said: *Man has become like us to know good and evil, and now lest he put forth his hand and take also of the Tree of Life and eat and live forever, therefore the Lord sent him forth from the Garden of Eden.*

I'd never known before that there were two special trees in the garden. I thought there was just the Tree of Knowledge. I asked Mr. Glassman what this business about the Tree of Life was all about, but he shook his head and smiled. He said that, according to the kabbalah, the Tree of Life was what God had used to create the universe out of nothing. But it was a very dangerous idea, so dangerous that you weren't allowed to study it until you were forty years old and married.

"Why's it so dangerous?" I wanted to know.

"Because, when you are studying it, it is easy to become obsessed," he said. "Suddenly everything you see looks like a sign from above. Many of our sages, blessed be their memories, lost their heads chasing after such signs."

"What do you mean, they lost their heads?"

"Well, it is not so clear, really. But there is a story, a famous legend, of four great rabbis who entered the holy garden. You remember Rabbi Akiva, from the story I told you in school? Akiva was one of the four. The only one who entered in peace and departed in peace."

"What happened to the other three?"

"The second sage, Ben Azzai, looked around and died. The third, Ben Zoma, looked around and went mad."

"And the fourth?"

"The fourth... well, the text only tells us that he 'cut down the plantings.' What that means, I do not know. There are many symbolic interpretations."

"What was his name, the fourth one?"

"His name? The text does not call him by his name. It calls him only 'Acher.'"

"What's that mean?"

"It means 'Other.'"

I frowned. Other? What kind of name was that? But then I thought of another question. "If the Tree of Life is really so dangerous, like you said, then why would being forty years old and married make it okay?"

"Because, according to the sages, at that point you are already wise."

"Oh. Well, you're older than forty."

"Yes."

"And you're married."

"Yes."

"Are you studying the Tree of Life, then?"

"No."

"Why not?"

"Because I am not wise," he said, with a funny smile on his face.

He looked down at the numbers tattooed on his arm. I looked up. And that's when I noticed that Mrs. Glassman had stopped talking to herself and her hands were frozen in the air, hovering over the balls of dough she was supposed to be rolling into ruggelach. She stayed like that for a long time. Mr. Glassman didn't move a muscle either. He stared at his arm for so long that I thought maybe he had fallen asleep. My head was exploding with all the questions I wanted to ask, but it didn't seem right to ask anything else after that, so I just went home.

I RAN UP THE SIDEWALK, confused and hungry, and opened the front door.

"I'm home!" I shouted. "What's for din —"

But I never finished my question.

Just then, I looked down the shadowy hall and saw something — someone — moving fast.

Jenny burst out of Sammy's bedroom. Her freckled face was all scrunched up and her eyes were open wide. She looked scared or maybe shocked or then again she could have been angry. In the doorway, Sammy tried to grab her wrist, but Jenny was too fast for her. She rushed past Sammy and past me and out the front door.

Then she was gone and my big sister was standing with her hands dangling empty at her sides. Her face crumpled up and her eyes filled with tears. I opened my mouth to say something. I tried to take a step toward her. My body wouldn't move.

I couldn't remember ever seeing her look so small.

MR. KATZ HAD almost finished making the Tree of Knowledge but now he had a problem. When I passed by on my way to school one morning in the first week of June, I found him sitting on the lawn with his hands full of dental floss. He was busy tying knots in it. When I asked him what for, he said he was making cradles for the fruit to hang in, and the cradles were coming along beautifully, the only problem was that the Torah never said what fruit.

When I got to Normal School that day, Ms. Davidson announced that our grade was going to be competing in a science fair. She would divide the class into pairs and each pair would present one project at the fair in the last week of the school year. All the kids from all the other grades would come and watch. Then the kids would vote on which project they thought was best and the group that got the most votes would win a secret prize.

Alex was really happy because the two of us got paired together, which I knew Ms. Davidson had done on purpose and which proved that I was right about her being a highly intelligent person. Dean and Gabe also got paired together. When Ms. Davidson turned to face the blackboard, they whispered that they were going to wipe the floor with us, but I knew we had nothing to worry about because Alex had more brains than the two of them combined.

After last period, Alex said we needed to go to the library right away. All I could think about was the line of popsicles waiting for me in the freezer at home. I asked, "Why?" For the second time that spring, Alex looked at me like he couldn't believe his ears. "Because we need to do research to come up with a winning project," he said. "I want to *win*. Don't you want to *win*?"

We went to the library.

At a table near the window, Ms. Davidson was grading homework. Ignoring her, Alex marched through the stacks and started pulling down every book with the word "radio" or "astronomy" or "physics" in the title. When he had about thirty books, he dumped them all on an empty table and started reading, his eyes zipping from side to side so fast it made him look like a cartoon.

After wandering through the library, I sat down across from him and picked up *101 Physics Projects for Tomorrow's Rocket Scientists*. I propped it up on the table in between me and Alex. Then, because I had my own research to do, I slid another book in front of it so that only I could see. It was called *Fruit of North America and Beyond: Exotic and Common Species*, and I hoped it would contain the clues I needed.

Seeing Ms. Davidson in the library had given me an idea. So that I wouldn't forget any of the clues I found, I dug my journal out of my backpack and opened it to a fresh page. Alex looked up for a second and gave me an encouraging nod. From the way he smiled, I could tell he thought I was taking notes on physics, but really I was not. Really what I was writing was this:

FRUIT THAT MAY OR MAY NOT HAVE
BEEN ON THE TREE OF KNOWLEDGE:

1. Apples
2. Oranges
3. Peaches
4. Plums
5. Tangerines
6. Nectarines
7. Bananas
8. Pears
9. Grapes
10. Strawberries
11. Cantaloupes
12. Coconuts
13. Pomegranates
14. Watermelons

Just as I finished adding number fourteen to the list, Alex said, "Psst!"

I looked up to see him waving his book in my face. "What?"

"Listen to this!" he said, and then read aloud: "Astronauts aboard the International Space Station have the equipment available to make unscheduled ham radio contacts with radio amateurs all around the world on a one-to-one basis during their personal time. With a very limited investment in amateur radio equipment, licensed hams, *including students*, can make individual contact with astronauts by learning to follow the published orbital schedule."

"So?"

"So! This right here is a winning project!"

"What is?"

Alex pretended like he was talking to an idiot. "We bring in my *ham radio* on the day of the *science fair* and call the International *Space* Station and talk to an *astronaut!*"

"Yeah, right. They're never going to waste their time talking to us. Why would they?"

"Didn't you hear what I just read to you? They talk to students all the time!"

"Okay, but —"

I was about to tell Alex that even if the astronauts were willing to talk, there's no way we would figure out how to contact them in time, when a movement near the window caught my eye. A tall man with messy brown hair and a nice smile was walking up to Ms. Davidson. She was so concentrated on what she was reading that he had to tap her on the shoulder to get her attention. But, as soon as he did, her face filled with light and opened up like a giant flower.

All of a sudden I felt happy and sad and lonely, happy because my mysterious sadness had a reason after all, sad because there was nothing I could do to make the reason go away, lonely because I now knew that I didn't really have a nameless sickness, and losing that sickness meant losing one more thing that had tied me and Sammy together.

The reason why the white flower on Ms. Davidson's bike had made me sad was because what it probably meant was that she already had a boyfriend. Long bike rides through meadows was something people did when they were in love with other people. I was only eleven and a half, and so far I had never been in love with any other person, but it didn't take a genius.

Trying to get my attention, Alex waved his hands around in my face, but I pushed them aside and shushed him. From behind *Fruit of North America and Beyond: Exotic and Common Species*, which was behind

*101 Physics Projects for Tomorrow's Rocket Scientists*, which was behind Alex and his fort of books, I spied on Ms. Davidson and the man with the nice smile. Whispering in his ear, she piled all the homework assignments into her bag. He took it from her and she grinned at him. They walked to the door of the library. She opened it and held it for him and he laughed. Then, just before he walked through the door, he leaned down and kissed her.

That's when I realized that, even though Ms. Davidson might be a highly intelligent person, she was not the person who would fill the empty spaces in my father's heart.

**THAT FRIDAY**, Dad left us a message on the answering machine. He wouldn't be coming home until very late because of another university thing. We decided that this time we would make pizza for dinner, so Sammy started slicing the cheese and I started opening the packages of Nibs and Gummy Bears. The kitchen was quiet except for the sound of rain hitting the windows. After a while, the phone rang. We let the machine pick up and a familiar voice filled the room.

"Hello, David? It's Ira! Listen, I just wanted to wish you and the family a big *mazel tov* on the upcoming bat mitzvah! I can't believe I didn't know Samara was participating, Jenny just told me now, that's wonderful news! Sammy, if you're listening, we're all so proud of you, we wish you the very best of luck, and we can't wait to see you on the big day!"

The machine beeped. I looked at Sammy and she looked back at me and I saw that her eyes were filled with sadness. I hit delete.

Then I went back to dividing the candy and Sammy went back to slicing the cheese. But after a few seconds, she put the cheese slicer down. She said she'd be right back and that I should go right ahead with the toppings, so I covered one side of the pizza with Nibs and the other side with Gummy Bears.

Just as I finished, I heard a sound like someone trying to light a match. I went to Sammy's room and saw her standing over the candles she'd put in front of her window just like the other night. She'd finally got the match lit and was holding it out over one of the wicks. Then the floorboard creaked and she turned around, but this time she didn't get mad or tell me to go away. Her cheeks were wet. I went and stood next to her. She lit one of the candles and gave me the match and I lit the other one. She waved her hands over the flames — one, two, three — so I did it, too — one, two, three — then we covered our eyes and she whispered the blessing. I didn't know the words but I said Amen when she was done because that's what you say after a blessing. That's what Dad used to say, back when he would hurry home to watch Mom light the candles, which was something he stopped doing a few months before she died. She cried the first time he didn't show up and I worried that her tears would put out the flames and she'd have to light them all over again.

Sammy wiped her cheeks and we went back to the kitchen to finish making the pizza. While it was baking, I had an idea. I went to the pantry, found a bottle of grape juice, poured some in a cup, and brought it back to her. Before we ate the pizza, we said the Kiddush over the grape juice. Normally people said the blessing over wine but I knew Dad would probably be mad if we drank wine, even though he mostly never made rules about what we should eat or drink or do because he said parents should trust kids to learn for themselves instead of imposing their own authority. Afterwards, Sammy washed the cup so that Dad wouldn't suspect anything, and I put the grape juice bottle in the back of the fridge.

Then we watched the last two shows on the TGIF line-up. We'd missed the first couple of shows but I didn't really care because one, I liked doing Shabbat with Sammy and two, they were almost always repeats anyway.

That night, before falling asleep, I made another list in my journal.

THINGS THAT MAKE MY SISTER SAD:

1. Memories of our mother
2. Answering machines
3. Her old bicycle
4. Swing sets
5. How her hair gets frizzy when it's hot out
6. Watercolour paintings
7. Musical instruments
8. The smell of perfume
9. Jenny (?)

ON MONDAY AFTERNOON, me and Alex spent our recess on the patch of grass behind Normal School. All the other kids were running around, throwing balls and chasing each other. Sammy, who used to always spend recess with Jenny, was wandering alone on the far edges of the lot. A couple of teachers paced around us, looking up at the sky or chatting.

Alex ignored them all and started teaching me about astronomy, which he said was something you should really know about unless you wanted to be a total ignoramus. "Do you want to be a total ignoramus?" he asked. I figured this was one of those cases where silence is worth two coins, so I just stood there while he told me about all the different kinds of stars and showed me pictures in the new astronomy book his mom got him for his birthday.

"Proxima Centauri is the closest red dwarf to our solar system but it's still 4.2 light years away."

Somewhere behind and above us, we heard a voice like a low growl. "Nope," it said. "The closest red dwarf is way closer than that."

We whipped around and twisted our necks up. Gabe and Dean were looming over us with crazy smiles on their sweaty faces.

For a second, Alex looked too surprised to say anything. Then he pointed at a chart in his book and started to say no, Proxima Centauri was definitely the closest, it said so right *here*, but he didn't get to finish because all of a sudden Dean was grabbing the book out of his hands and ripping out pages.

Alex froze. Pages fluttered away from his body like birds. I could tell he was fighting hard not to cry because his whole face was turning bright red.

Gabe said, "Well look at that, now there's a red dwarf right here on Earth."

Dean dumped the shredded book at Alex's feet. Then he and Gabe laughed and started to walk away.

But Sammy was walking toward us. Alex looked from her to them and something in his face changed. "Hey!" he shouted at their big wide backs. "You think you're so great? Just wait until the science fair, you losers, we'll show you!"

Gabe and Dean slowly turned around. There was something scary about that slowness. Then Gabe sneered and leaned in close to Alex again. "Oh yeah? What're you going to do, turn from red to purple? Go from four-eyes to eight-eyes? Grow even shorter than you already are?"

"We're going to talk to an astronaut on board the International Space Station!" Alex blurted out in a crazy half-scream.

I blushed with embarrassment then, knowing this would only make things worse.

Gabe and Dean were already laughing, doubled over and slapping their knees. They pretended to need a second to catch their breath. Finally they said, "Yeah, great, can't wait for the big day, this won't be humiliating for you *at all*," and left.

Sammy was quiet, biting her lip. She gave us a little nod, then wandered off in the opposite direction, toward no one, toward nothing.

I felt so mad, all I wanted to do was kick something. I tried to remind myself that Mr. Glassman said the Talmud said you were supposed to be slow to anger and quick to forgive, but I couldn't help it. I decided then and there that we were going to win first prize in the science fair, even if it meant I had to go over to Alex's house every single day for the rest of the year.

UP IN ALEX'S ROOM after school, we tiptoed through the maze of silvery radio guts on the floor. He went straight to his computer and sat down. I asked him what he was up to and he said he was researching the space station's orbital schedule, what else would he be doing? He had to find out what time the astronauts would be flying over Montreal so that we could establish contact!

I said, "Great, but what am I supposed to do?" so Alex pointed at a poster board and some markers and said, "Why don't you make the backdrop for our presentation?" I sat on the ground and started to draw a replica of Alex's ham radio, making sure to get the shading just right, which was something Jenny had taught me the year before because she was really good at art. She hadn't been over in a while and I missed her. Another new thing me and Sammy had in common.

After a while, I got bored, so I wandered over to the telescope. I brought my eye close to it but I couldn't see anything. I thought maybe it was because you had to have one eye closed and one open so I tried to wink but it was hard. Then Alex pointed to the far end of the telescope and there was a black cap there I hadn't noticed before. I took it off and pressed my eye to the lens, and then I saw. The sky. A bird. A roof.

"Hey! Do you ever use this thing to spy on people?"

"I'm a scientist."

"Okay."

"From a long line of scientists."

"Okay."

"Scientists don't spy."

"Okay."

"They observe."

"I think it'd be cool to be a spy!"

Alex sighed. "You're not supposed to touch the lens like that," he said, taking the telescope and showing me how to hold it.

I brought my eye close again but not too close this time. The neighbours' windows sparkled in the afternoon light. "Hey, look!

It's Mr. Glassman's house! And look there — that's Mr. Katz, sitting under the tree on his lawn!"

I moved aside to give Alex a turn and saw his blank face and right away realized that never in his whole life had he thought to look down at other people instead of up at the sky. He shifted the telescope to the right, then brought his eye up to the lens and gasped.

"What? What? What do you see?"

Alex kept still and said nothing. His face and the tips of his ears went bright pink. I tried to be patient but inside I was going crazy so I pushed him out of the way to see for myself. But just as I got up to the lens, something hard hit me right above my eye.

"Ouch!" I said, clapping a hand to my forehead. I could feel the skin pushed aside from a small dent where the telescope had hit me.

Alex danced around, flapping his hands like a bird. "Sorry, sorry, sorry! Are you okay?"

I took a deep breath and told him yes. "Is there a mark?"

Alex bit his lip and nodded. But he said the cut wasn't deep, and there was only a little blood on my hand, and I could tell he felt really bad, so I just asked if I could have a Band-Aid. He got me one and while I was putting it on we heard Alex's mom calling from downstairs.

When we got to the kitchen, Alex gave her a hug and then introduced us. She said to call her Lesley. She was still wearing her hospital clothes, and three thoughts flew into my head: one, she was a nurse, which meant that two, she must be a highly intelligent person, and three, she was very pretty and young-looking. Her red hair and bright green eyes shone in the light.

Even though her eyes had dark circles under them, she asked if we'd like her to fix us dinner. Alex said, "No, it's —" but before he could finish his sentence I said as fast as I could, "Yes please that would be great I'm starving!" even though I was not. She smiled and said that in that case she would throw something together right away, and how did I feel about spaghetti, meatballs, and roasted butternut squash and apple soup? Excellent, I said. I felt excellent.

While she cooked, me and Alex set the kitchen table and he tried to get me to understand the difference between a pulsar and quasar. Even though it sounded interesting, I stopped listening, because I was busy watching Lesley and I needed to pray to God. My prayer was *please please please please please* and I prayed it so many times that it started to feel like my heart was saying it, one *please* with every beat.

An hour later, Lesley put a steaming bowl of orange soup in front of me. It looked creamy and bright, and it smelled delicious, but there was only one way to be sure. I picked up my spoon and brought it to my mouth.

That's when I knew for sure that God was real.

THE NEXT DAY, during lunch, me and Alex went back to the library. We had to do more research since we'd need to carefully calculate the space station's trajectory since it travels 386 kilometers above the Earth's surface at a speed of 27,358 kilometers per hour. As soon as Alex sat behind his fort of books, I picked one of the books out of his pile and flipped to a random page. Behind it, I opened *Fruit of North America and Beyond*. I needed to narrow my list down a bit.

FRUIT THAT MAY OR MAY NOT HAVE
BEEN ON THE TREE OF KNOWLEDGE:

1. Apples
2. Oranges
3. ~~Peaches~~ (they came from China, and the Garden of Eden was probably in Israel)
4. Plums
5. Tangerines
6. ~~Nectarines~~ (belong to same species as #3)
7. Bananas
8. Pears

9. ~~Grapes~~ (probably not, since grapes make wine, which makes people drunk, not wise)
10. ~~Strawberries~~ (do not grow on trees)
11. Cantaloupes
12. ~~Coconuts~~ (how would Adam and Eve break the shell, since tools were not invented yet?)
13. Pomegranates
14. ~~Watermelons~~ (same as #10)

I was thinking about adding a new possibility to the list (*15. Dates*) when I heard a gasp behind me. I whipped around and saw Alex glaring at the page.

"You're supposed to be researching the space station!" he said. "And instead you're — you're — what are you doing?"

"Nothing," I said, closing the journal fast. But he'd already seen the title of my list.

"The Tree of Knowledge? What's that supposed to be?"

"It's — it's the holy tree in the Garden of Eden. You know, the one Adam and Eve ate from? So they could get knowledge? I'm trying to figure out which fruit could've grown on —"

Alex snorted. "That's not how you get knowledge, all at once, by eating some fruit off a tree! You get it through the scientific method!"

"No, you don't understand, see..." I sighed. Alex was not Jewish, so I had to do a lot of explaining to get him to understand about the Tree. I told him about Adam and Eve and the fruit and the snake. But when I was done, Alex said that he was an atheist, which meant that he didn't believe in God because he believed in science instead. I tried to convince him that God was real, but Alex said, "I don't see any evidence, if God is real then where is He?"

"My neighbour Mr. Katz says He's everywhere."

"No, but, where *exactly* is He?"

Waving my arms in all directions, I said, "Up, down, here, there — everywhere!"

But Alex still did not look convinced. So then I told him about how the Jews were slaves in Egypt and God took them to the Promised Land and they built the Temple in Jerusalem and then it got destroyed so they built it again and then it got destroyed again but they still write their prayers on tiny scraps of paper and stick them into the Wailing Wall and then God answers them.

"You really believe all that?" Alex asked.

"Sure I do. Why wouldn't I?"

Alex shrugged. He was watching Gabe Kramer, who had come running into the library, dribbling a basketball and laughing loudly. Then Alex leaned over and whispered, "If God exists, then why would He always let Gabe beat us at basketball when we play in gym class?"

I opened my mouth to answer, but just then the bell rang and lunch period was over.

As we left the library, Alex said we should come back right after last period, but I told him I couldn't because I had to go to Hebrew School. He looked disappointed, so to make him feel better I reminded him about our secret plan that we had come up with after spaghetti and meatballs, which was to set up his mom with my dad so that we could be related and live in the same house forever. I told him to come over to my place in a couple of hours so we could drop some hints about Lesley at the dinner table. His eyes shone a bit but he still looked very impatient, and once I got to Hebrew School I understood exactly how he felt.

All through class, I waited for the right moment to ask Mr. Glassman what fruit was on the Tree, but it never came. Then, when we were finally sitting at his kitchen table about to pick up where we left off in the Genesis story, all of a sudden Mrs. Glassman took a break from the dishes she was rinsing and the proof she was working out under her breath ("If $t$ then $r$ and if $r$ then $t$ entails $t$ if and only if $r$...") and brought us a plate of apple slices. Mrs. Glassman never brought us fruit and I had the idea that maybe God made her bring it so I'd have an excuse to ask my question. Here was my chance. "Take!" she said, so I took.

I said, "Is it true that the fruit on the Tree of Knowledge was apples?"

Mr. Glassman looked surprised, but he smiled and said, "No, absolutely not, there were no apples in that part of the world at that time."

So then I asked, "Maybe it was oranges?" I thought this sounded like a good guess because I'd heard of Jaffa oranges and I knew that Jaffa was in Israel. But he shook his head no. So then I asked, "Maybe bananas? Pears? Cantaloupes?" He kept shaking his head and smiling until finally I said, "Pomegranates?" Jews eat pomegranates on Rosh Hashanah, which made me think there was a pretty good chance that pomegranates were a biblical fruit.

Mr. Glassman stopped shaking his head and said, "Possibly."

"What do you mean possibly, don't you know for sure?"

"No, not even our ancient sages, blessed be their memories, knew for sure."

He went to his library and came back holding a tall book with a brown cover that I knew was called the Talmud. He opened it up and started reading out loud. I didn't understand, but I knew when he got to the end he'd translate into English for me, so I just waited.

Finally he said, "You see? There is disagreement amongst the sages. According to Rabbi Meir, it was a grape which Eve made into wine. Rabbi Nehemia says that the fruit was a fig. Rabbi Yehuda says, what are you, *meshugganeh*? It was wheat! Some other rabbis say don't be ridiculous, it was a pomegranate, everyone knows the Land of Israel was overflowing with pomegranate trees at that time!"

When I heard that, I was really disappointed, because I knew I had failed Mr. Katz. If the rabbis didn't even know what fruit was on the Tree, how was I supposed to figure it out? And how was Mr. Katz ever supposed to get Knowledge?

I looked down at the Genesis text, feeling sad and frustrated. "None of this Adam and Eve story even makes any sense," I said. "Like this, here: *And they heard the voice of the Lord walking in the garden.* How can you hear a voice walking?"

Mr. Glassman's clear grey eyes got very serious. "Do you really want to know, Lev?"

"Sure I do."

"It will take me some time to explain."

"I've got time."

"I will have to tell you a story."

"I like stories."

He paused. "The answer to your question lies in the story of my wife's brother."

Out of the corners of my eyes, I saw Mrs. Glassman's hands lose control over a soapy bowl. It slipped out of her fingers and clattered into the sink. She snatched it up again and kept on rinsing. But she didn't take up her mumbling proof again.

Mr. Glassman glanced at her back for a second and then started to talk in a quiet singsong voice. "Once upon a time, you see, my Chayaleh had a brother. A big beautiful brother with big beautiful eyes. Yankel, his name was, but she called him Yankeleh. He was everything to her then, sun and moon and stars. But he was a strange boy. When he was young, he didn't laugh. He was... grave. A very grave and silent little person."

Mr. Glassman was rocking back and forth while he talked. "At first, they thought maybe he was a simple soul — sometimes the Kadosh Baruch Hu makes them like that — simpler souls, no better, no worse, only different from the rest. But he was not so simple, was he? No, no. It took them some time but after a few years her parents realized what he really was: deaf. He was deaf! And he had never learned to speak.

"Already thirteen years old, he was, when they moved to the village, and still he had not spoken one single word all his life. But

Chayaleh, she didn't care, little things like that did not matter to her, she loved him. His big dark eyes and long dark lashes. Like a prince, he was, wasn't he? And a writer — Kadosh Baruch Hu, save us from writers! A writer of strange little stories that he would scribble down by the river, birds singing in the sky, sunlight in the trees . . . this was before all the *tzures* started.

"She followed him there once. She was ten years old. A little *nudnik*, she was. Couldn't leave him alone even for two seconds. She found him standing in the water, his feet bare, his ankles blue with cold. And a smile on his face — ah, what a smile! But what did it mean? What did it mean, she asked herself, dancing from foot to foot, hidden behind the trees.

"First he was still. Then his lips were moving, but no sound was coming out. Then he was still. He was listening, she thought, only he could not be listening because he could not hear. And then his lips were moving again, smiling almost, inviting almost, encouraging almost, and then! Then, all of a sudden, a fish was leaping out of the water! She saw it, the flash of colour against his ankle, big and bright and blue before it disappeared. He had called out "Hello!" into the river and the fish had answered, the fish had kissed his ankle, the fish was saying, "Hello! I heard you." Her brother, he was *talking* to the fish. He was talking to them and listening to them and she could see this, with her ten-year-old mind, already she understood this. And it stole her heart.

"She ran out of her hiding place and splashed into the water — I can see it perfectly, her skinny feet — and bent down in the river. And what did she do? She grabbed his ankle — and kissed it! And then got very shy. Shy and scared, too scared to look up. What if he was angry? What if he hated her for spying? She closed her eyes and waited for judgment to fall. But, what? Did he punish her? Did he hit her? No. He bent down in the river, grabbed her ankle, and kissed it. And ah, that was it, it was all over for her. She stood. He gave her a kiss, a small kiss, right in the corner of her mouth. She gave him a kiss, a small kiss, right in the corner of his mouth. He pressed his finger to her lips. She pressed her finger to his. *Sha*, he told her without words. Quiet, be quiet, listen.

"Was it then that it happened, Lev? So fast, just like that? Or did it take her many more lessons, days maybe or weeks, to hear what the fish were saying? And the birds and the flowers and the trees and the sunlight and the wind? His secret language, his silent laugh?"

I opened my mouth to answer, then closed it again.

"There must have been many lessons. A whole language like that — it can't be easy. A grammar and a vocabulary and a — but what do I know from languages?

"Ah, how she loved him. Him and his strange little stories. He did not have anymore to write them for her — he could speak them to her now, in his own way, and she would hear him. How happy they were in their two-person world! How much taller they were than the rest of the village! All the poor people going about their little businesses, using words, pathetic spoken words — how sad and silly they all were! Didn't they see that the language of silence was the most beautiful, most precise language of all? The only language that did not need to be invented by humans — the language that was actually spoken by God? *And the voice of the Lord was walking in the garden* ... They did not see. And ah, how she pitied them. Because the tiny footfalls of silence, its tiny levers and pedals, you could feel them pressing on your skin if you learned how to open yourself to their music..."

I sat up a bit straighter. So that was it! The "voice of the Lord" was the silence all around you, and if you listened carefully enough, you could feel it "walking" all over you...

Mr. Glassman cleared his throat. "That was the happiest summer of her life. That summer of pity and music." He sighed. "But her brother, his stories were sad. And she did not like this. She loved him, he delighted her, she wanted he should be happy! She wanted he should make pretty things! 'Make the world pretty,' she begged him. So, for her, he tried. For a few weeks he told happy stories. Stories about talking animals — giraffes, lions, birds — that sort of thing. But these stories were all failures. They did not tell the truth, and she, already, at ten years old, she already could feel that these stories were lies. The giraffes and the lions were lies. The sweet little birds were lies. They did not tell the truth about how the world was and so they did not delight her. 'Make true things,' she told him after a while. She gave him her permission and in return he gave her his most beautiful, most serious smile. And then, at the end of that summer, he told her another story. Ah, but what a story! The Kadosh Baruch Hu should guard us from such stories as that…"

The kitchen was now weirdly quiet. The only sound was the water rushing into the sink. But Mrs. Glassman wasn't rinsing dishes anymore, she wasn't moving at all. I didn't know how long she'd just been standing there, with her mouth hanging open like she'd had the breath knocked out of her. I watched her stay still a few seconds longer. Then, all of a sudden, even though there were still dirty dishes left and even though the water was still running over them and even though her hands were still dripping wet, she turned away and walked out of the kitchen and slowly, maybe painfully, climbed the stairs.

Mr. Glassman let out a deep sigh. Seconds slipped by. Outside the window, a bird flew across the sky and cawed. Finally he said, "I have kept you too long, you will come back another time and I will tell you Yankel's story, yes?" I said, "Yes, sure," and then I added, "Thanks for the lesson, Mr. Glassman!" before racing out the door into the fresh night air, which I gulped down into my lungs like a person who's just been rescued from a shipwreck, and then I ran down the sidewalk and up the path to my house and turned my key in the lock.

HALFWAY THROUGH the dark hallway, I heard voices in the kitchen. Sammy was talking to someone and I was sure it must be Dad, but then I saw Alex and remembered that I'd invited him over for dinner. They'd obviously already eaten without me because Sammy was rinsing the dishes and Alex was loading them into the dishwasher, which was supposed to be my job. I was about to walk in but stopped when I heard what they were talking about. Me.

"Well, I just don't get how Lev can think that," Alex was saying. "Those people he was talking about, the ones who stick messages in the Wailing Wall, they're praying to something that doesn't exist! To some magical, all-knowing, unobservable life form that —"

"I don't see how that's any different from the messages SETI sends out," Sammy laughed. "The Arecibo Message was also sent out to 'unobservable life forms' —"

"Yeah, but life forms that, if they do communicate with us one day, will be *one hundred percent* observable and verifiable! Whereas God's messages are *never* —"

"Which, by the way, that's another thing I don't get about SETI," Sammy said. "If there is intelligent life out there, and if it does send us a signal with a pattern, won't it be drowned out by all the other noise in the universe? It'd be like us listening for one radio station that's broadcasting news when a million other stations are broadcasting rock music."

"Don't worry," Alex said, stacking the last dirty dish with a smile. "SETI scientists are experts at listening. They've had loads of practice."

Sammy turned off the tap, dried her hands, and turned on the dishwasher. "What kind of practice?"

He sat down on the floor in front of the machine. "Come here, I'll show you!"

She gave him a funny look, then shrugged and sat down cross-legged next to him.

"One time," he said, "I read about these SETI scientists who would spend hours and hours listening to dishwashers and washing machines, searching for patterns in the chaos."

"Does that really work? I mean, can *you* hear the patterns?"

"I'm not very good at it. At least not yet. But —"

She shushed him and pressed her ear up against the machine.

He did the same. She closed her eyes, probably to help her hear the noise better. But he kept his eyes on her.

After seven gazillion minutes, Sammy started to smile.

"What?" Alex whispered. "Can you hear something?"

"Even better," she whispered back. "I can feel it." Without opening her eyes, she reached for his hand and placed two of his fingers on her wrist, her pulse. "See?"

A few seconds passed. Alex's eyes grew huge. He stared up at her, then squinted, like what he was seeing was so bright it was almost blinding. Sun and moon and stars.

I walked backward on tiptoes until I reached the front door. I stepped outside and softly closed the door behind me. Then I opened it, stepped inside, and slammed it shut.

"I'm home!"



LATER THAT NIGHT, after Alex had left, I walked down the hall and stood in front of Sammy's closed door. She was chanting again, but there was something weird about her voice now.

It buzzed for half a second, then went quiet for eighteen seconds. It hummed for another half a second, then went quiet for thirty more. Goosebumps rose on my arms and I pressed my ear to the door and then I realized what the weird thing was.

Most people, when they read, read one word at a time. But my sister was not most people. She was reading one *letter* at a time. She was letting each vowel or consonant roll around in her mouth for almost a whole minute before releasing it onto the air. In between when she pronounced one letter and when she pronounced the next, I could hear huge stretches of silence. And the silence was strange and layered, and it made me feel happy and sad and lonely all at the same time.

I walked across the hall and lay on my bed and stared up at the ceiling. I didn't really feel like doing anything just then, except maybe praying, but I didn't know what for.

ON MY WAY to school the next morning, I stopped at Mr. Katz's house. He was standing in the middle of the lawn, staring up at the Tree. The clouds kept moving back and forth over the sun, and if you squeezed your eyes shut and tilted your head to the left, the toilet paper rolls really did look like branches. I stood next to Mr. Katz and we both squeezed our eyes shut and then I could see the cradles that he'd hung up in the branches, around twenty or thirty of them swinging in the breeze. They looked a bit like empty spider webs, shining in the sunlight, waiting for a fly to land. I said, "I'm sorry," and he said, "What for?" and I said, "For not knowing what fruit was on the Tree," and he said, "Don't worry, we just need to have a little *emunah*, and the Kadosh Baruch Hu will teach us what fruit it was, He'll make a miracle, just wait and see." We tilted our heads to the left and waited.


THE NEXT TUESDAY, I woke up and realized there were only a few days left before the science fair. I was feeling nervous that the whole thing was going to be a huge disaster since Alex had been practicing radio calls to the space station every day and so far he hadn't gotten through even once. Alex said that was just because he'd been miscalculating the orbital trajectory, but he would get the timing right in the end, not to worry. I worried.

So after school, we walked to his house and went straight to his room to practice calling some more. I was supposed to be putting the finishing touches on the poster, adding stars and planets to the sky I'd drawn up above the ham radio, but really I was watching Alex test the actual radio out.

"This is VA2KFO, this is VA2KFO, come back?" Alex said. VA2KFO was his call sign, which is like your code name if you're a radio operator. "Hello, N1ISS, do you read me, come back?" N1ISS was the call sign for the International Space Station. "This is VA2KFO, this is VA2KFO, calling N1ISS, is anyone out there? Hello?"

Half an hour passed. Nobody answered. My stomach began to ache.

Finally, Alex turned around and caught me watching him. "I'm sure they're just busy right now," he shrugged. "Astronauts have a busy schedule. Did you know they have to do four hours of exercise every single day, because of the microgravity? That's probably what they're doing right now, exercising. Anyway, their next orbit is in 90 minutes, so I'll call again then." He was trying to sound confident but I could tell he was just as worried as me.

When he went to the kitchen to get a snack, I decided to take a break from the poster board. I walked around his room. I looked into his telescope but I couldn't see anything because it was daylight. I sat on his bed, which had dinosaur sheets on it now, which made me feel a bit embarrassed for Alex. Then I looked at his bookshelves and noticed how, even though Alex's floor was a huge mess, his books were arranged in an unbelievably logical way.

All the books about astronomy were together. One shelf was full of books about the human brain. Another shelf had books about animals, the bottom shelf was completely packed with science fiction, and the top shelf was bending under the weight of three gazillion comics. Inside each perfect category there were smaller, hidden categories, because all the books were also arranged alphabetically by author — last name, then first name — and also by height, and also by colour, and also by whether they were hardcover or softcover.

Then I saw a small hole in the wall beside the bookshelf. I got down on my knees to look at it and there was a tiny scrap of paper stuffed inside. I pulled the paper out of the wall and opened it.

The first thing I noticed was that it had a very tiny map of all the streets in our neighbourhood, and a red X where Alex's house was. The second thing I noticed was that it had a few words scribbled at the bottom. It said: DEAR GOD. I AM HERE *EXACTLY*. WHERE ARE YOU *EXACTLY*?

THE NEXT DAY, I went to Mr. Glassman's house to see if he was around to teach me more about the Tree of Knowledge.

When he opened the door, at first he looked right through me, then he looked at me like he didn't recognize me. Then he said to come in, so I came in. I asked, "Where's Mrs. Glassman?" and he said, "Chayaleh is not feeling well." His hair was sticking up like crazy around his ears and the buttons on his shirt were done up all wrong. He kept staring down at the number tattoo on his arm. I said that maybe I should come back another time, but he said no, we should learn some Torah, it might help her get better, so I said okay.

We went into the kitchen, but practically the second we sat down we heard a loud crash from upstairs, like maybe Mrs. Glassman had knocked over a lamp or something. Mr. Glassman looked scared and ran up the stairs.

I waited around in the kitchen but after a while I got jittery so I climbed the stairs, too. I'd never been up there before so I was nervous that Mr. Glassman might get mad, but when I poked my head into the doorway of the bedroom he just whispered at me to come in.

Mrs. Glassman was lying in bed but I could tell she wasn't exactly sleeping, just resting, because her eyelashes were fluttering. Mr. Glassman gave her a sip of water from a glass and then put it down on the floor, near where a lamp had fallen onto its side. Next to the bed there was a desk with a chair. He waved me into it.

"Chayaleh is ill," Mr. Glassman told me. "She will recover with the help of the Kadosh Baruch Hu but it is very serious. The doctor gave her a new medication. He says now we must wait and see how she reacts. Wait and see, wait and see, all he ever says is wait and see! You would think a doctor could tell you something one hundred per-cent, but no, they like to toy with us. Well, and why should it be so surprising? After all, He toys with us, too."

Mr. Glassman pointed up at the ceiling. I didn't know what to say, so I didn't say anything. He seemed to be in a weird mood.

"Did Chayaleh ever tell you the story of how she and I met? No? Well, you know, when I was a boy — fourteen, fifteen — I wanted to be a mathematician. I was the best student in mathematics, and the teacher, Mr. Krakowski, told me that if I worked hard he would give my name to the university in Göttingen, to recommend that I study there. Then one day Chayaleh enters the class. I soon learn that she is smart — very smart — annoyingly smart. I do not admit it to anyone, not even myself, but I know she has a better *kop* for mathematics than even me. She is so curious, for every fact Mr. Krakowski teaches she has seven questions. He says that the shortest distance between two points is a straight line, she wants to know *why*. He says that even nature is made according to the rules of mathematics, she wants to know *how*.

"For many months we are rivals and I hate her bitterly, more bitterly than Haman and his evil sons, may their names be erased. Then one summer afternoon I walk into the forest and see her tall shape walking through the trees. Every so often she bends to pick something up, studies it for a minute, then wraps it up in the scarf she is carrying and keeps walking. I follow her, hiding behind trees so that she should not see me. But eventually I am so curious to know what she is doing, I forget to hide, and she whips around and catches me. 'What are you doing?' we shout at the same time. 'Were you following me?' she says. She is very mad. 'What are you collecting?' She does not answer me, so I grab the scarf and open it. Inside I find a bunch of pine cones. 'What do you need with all of these?' She looks at me, still very angry, and lifts her chin up in the air and says, 'I am checking to see if what Mr. Krakowski said is true. About the Fibonacci numbers appearing in nature.'

"And that's it. That's all. Something inside me releases, like a thousand elastic bands letting go all at once. I am so happy that a little laughter bubbles out of my throat, I can't help it — but this is a big mistake, because Chayaleh thinks I am laughing at her, and she does not talk to me for an entire month after that. She is a very stubborn girl, but eventually she forgives me. I lay a pine cone on her doorstep every day for a month, and eventually she forgives me.

"We spend the last few weeks of the summer lying in the forest together, in the sunshine, we talk, we kiss, we examine the pine cones, we fall in love. One day, toward the end of the summer, she suddenly gets very serious. She turns onto her stomach and tells me she does not want to love me anymore. 'Why not?' I want to know. 'Because you cannot depend on people. They are always changing. They are not like math, like numbers, that always stay the same. People, they come and go. You cannot trust them.' I am shocked, I don't know what to say. We lie there in the sunlight, not saying anything, listening to my silence. It makes a very loud noise. She gets up and leaves me.

"For weeks I am miserable. Then one day at the end of September, our teacher Rabbi Loew is telling us about how the great commentators, blessed be their memories, used *gematriya* to interpret words in the Torah. Have you learned it yet in school, the system of *gematriya*? No?"

I shook my head, so Mr. Glassman took a paper and a pen off the desk. He put the paper on his knee and started scribbling.

"You see, in the system of *gematriya*, every letter of the Hebrew alphabet has a number. Aleph is one. Bet is two. Gimmel is three. When I hear this, I am so excited I can barely contain myself. I rip a page from my notebook and spell her name, then my name."

I looked at the paper on Mr. Glassman's knee and saw:

| | |
|---|---|
| 8 = ח | 8 = ח |
| 10 = י | 10 = י |
| 10 = י | 5 = ה |
| 40 = ם | 30 = ל |
| | 5 = ה |
| Chaim = 8101040 | Chayaleh = 8105305 |

"At the bottom of the note, I scribble: *You see? People and numbers are not so different.* She sits three seats to the right and two rows back. I watch impatiently as the note travels to her, uncurls in her hand, sits beneath her gaze. Suddenly she smiles. She looks at me and I am so happy, a little laughter bubbles up in my throat, I can't help it.

"The next year is when the *tzures* start. They, may their names be erased, begin with their deportations. I am deported one day, with no warning, no chance to say goodbye. In the cattle-car all I can think is, what if Chayaleh forgets about me, who knows how long we will be separated, what if we don't see each other for years and years and by the end of it she does not recognize me? They take me to the camp and make me stand in a line. Left, right, left, right, my eyes flick from side to side, I should be praying to end up in the good side but who knows what is the good side, if there is a good side, what do they know from good sides? I lose track. Suddenly it is my turn. I am told to turn right. I turn right.

"I am standing in front of an officer. His mouth is moving but I can't hear what he is saying. He frowns and rolls my sleeve up for me. The needle presses down on my arm. I don't scream, I don't say anything, I can't make a noise. I see the first number it makes: 8. Then the next number: 1. Then 0. I cannot believe it. Then 1. A miracle. Then 0. This way, she will always recognize me. Then 4. He is about to write the last number — I almost have a heart attack — I can see he is about to make it a 1. Suddenly all the noise in the world rushes out of me, I plead with him like an idiot, like a *shmendrick*, like a *shlemiel*, 'Please, please, a zero, I need a zero, surely it won't make any difference, such a small difference between one and zero, what can it hurt' — I start to babble, I cry, I spit, and do you know what? This officer gives me a strange look. The needle presses down — and I see — zero! I am so happy, the officer sends me to have my head shaved, a little laughter bubbles up, the hair is falling all around my ankles and I am laughing and laughing like a *meshugganeh*, I can't help it.

"My Chayaleh, she is deported just a few days later. When her arm is under the needle — it was a miracle performed by the Kadosh Baruch Hu — she sees the same thing start to happen, only it is *her* name that starts to appear: 8, then 1, then 0, then 5, then 3, then 0 — and before the needle presses down one last time, she pleads with the officer to make it a 5. He gives her a strange look. A very strange look. He makes it a 5.

"After the camp is liberated, I end up in New York City. For months I live like a ghost. My mind is a slate that's been wiped clean, empty of memories. Then one day I remember Chayaleh. The next day I remember about the numbers. The day after that I call the telephone company and have them give me a new number. I print business cards with just that number on it, seven digits, no name, no nothing, just the number. Scatter them about the city like pigeons.

"My Chayaleh, she has the idea very early on. She is living with her cousin just a few miles away, and she doesn't see my cards, yet she thinks to call a number. But she calls the number that is on *my* arm. She calls my name, not her own. Doesn't she realize that her name is sweeter in my mouth than my own, that I remembered her existence before I remembered my own? She doesn't realize.

"Years pass.

"One day a seed of faith sprouts in my mind. I don't know who planted it there. The faith to believe that maybe — who knows? — maybe the idea that occurred to me occurred to her also.

"I call my name. She picks up. I say nothing. She hangs up.

"I call my name. She picks up. I say nothing. She hangs up.

"I call a third time. She picks up. I open my mouth, I try to make a noise, but nothing comes out. She doesn't hang up.

"She recognizes me by my silence."

Mr. Glassman grew quiet. A few seconds passed. Then, without opening her eyes, Mrs. Glassman raised one of her hands. It rose slowly, slowly, slowly, until it reached the side of Mr. Glassman's face. She ran her fingers along his cheek, just once, gently, and then her hand sank back down onto the bedspread.

OVER DINNER THE NEXT DAY, I was listing off all of Lesley's great qualities, which would have been a lot easier if Alex had been there to help, but Dad just kept on yawning.

I took a deep breath, trying to think up more qualities Dad might like, but then I caught a whiff of perfume in the air. He must have been missing Mom even more than I'd thought if he was spritzing himself with her old perfume every day now! The secret theory that this put into my head was that maybe he would never love another woman again because he was still too in love with Mom. I tried to figure out if I should be happy or sad about that but it was hard.

Suddenly Dad said, "I almost forgot. Ira stopped me in the hall to remind me that Jenny's bat mitzvah is in two days. I really wish we didn't have to go to that, but he and Judy were so good to you after... Well, I guess we'll just have to go. You must be excited to see your friend perform?"

Sammy blushed and shot me a warning glance. "Yeah, I guess."

Dad obviously hadn't noticed anything weird because he just started asking her how *King Lear* was treating her, and would she like to continue going over the text later on, since they'd finished the part about Lear's regret for banishing his daughter and they were ready to move on to the second act. But what she said next was that her class had finished *King Lear* weeks ago and besides she had lost her copy of the play. Dad looked at her like she was crazy and said, "But you never lose anything," and she said, "I know," and he said, "And yet," and she said, "And yet," and then we ate watermelon and nobody said anything. So that I wouldn't crack and spill the beans about Sammy's bat mitzvah, I repeated the word *watermelon* in my head, I was ready to *watermelon watermelon watermelon* all night if I had to, but everyone ate extremely fast and then Sammy cleared the plates.

Dad was just leaving the kitchen when the phone rang. Me and Sammy already had our hands wet with soap and water, so we didn't pick up, and Dad kept walking down the hall in the direction of his study. The answering machine kicked in and a very loud and very happy voice filled the kitchen.

"David, hi, it's Ira! I was so excited about Jenny earlier that I forgot to say good luck to you all. I'm sure you're just as excited as we are! So, we'll see you at the synagogue, and Sammy, if you're listening, good luck with your —"

Dad was walking back toward the kitchen. On the counter near the sink was the glass bowl that had held the watermelon a few minutes ago. It still had some sticky seeds in it. I hit it with my elbow and watched it fly in slow motion through the air, down, down, down and —

*Crash!*

" — soon! Bye for now."

The machine beeped. I looked at Sammy and saw that she was frozen. I looked at Dad and tried to figure out from his face if he had heard the message or not but it was hard.

Then he asked, "Who was that, Ira?"

Sammy breathed a sigh of relief. He hadn't heard. I nodded.

"What did he want?"

"Just to remind us about Jenny's bat mitzvah coming up, that's all," I said.

"Again? He already did that in person." Dad frowned, looking puzzled. "Do you two need help cleaning up this glass?"

"No, it's okay, we can do it."

He nodded and walked back in the direction of his study.

I started picking the sticky seeds off the floor. Sammy got a broom out of the pantry, swept up the pieces of glass and dropped them into the trash.

We stood together at the sink. She rinsed dishes and I stacked them in the dishwasher. She was very quiet, so to distract her, I told her I'd asked Mr. Glassman what fruit was on the original Tree of Knowledge so I could help Mr. Katz with his, but nobody knew. She still didn't say anything, so I said, "What fruit do you think it was?"

She turned off the tap and stared straight ahead with a funny expression on her mouth, like a smile, only sad. Her lips opened and then closed. They reminded me of a bird that opens its wings to fly but then decides not to.

THE NEXT DAY was the science fair. At 3:15, all the kids from the other grades started pouring into our class to see the projects. Each group had their own table. Me and Alex stood in front of ours, which held his radio equipment and my poster board, until he told me to hold down the fort because he was going to scope out the competition. He walked up and down the rows and the more he saw, the more he smiled. Then he came back to give me the rundown, counting off projects on his fingers.

"There's four model solar systems, which, please, are we in kindergarten? Two paper plate speakers. One x-ray demonstration. Three baking soda volcanoes — truly pathetic. Two potato clocks — been making those since I was five. One solar-powered microwave — not bad, but clearly made by the parental units hovering right over there. Oh, and Gabe and Dean — *plus six other teams* — made tin can telephones!"

"Tin can telephones? Those are cool! Me and Sammy made one once."

"When?"

"A few years ago."

"Exactly. That's kids' stuff. I'm telling you, we've got this thing in the bag."

"Yeah, *if* we can get this radio call to work…"

Alex checked his watch. "Speaking of which, it's almost showtime. The space station is going to pass overhead in 3.5 minutes. We've got to start gathering everyone around!"

I saw Sammy walk in alone just in time to hear Ms. Davidson clap her hands and announce that me and Alex were going to be calling astronauts on board the International Space Station. Right away all the younger kids started swarming toward us. Gabe and Dean pushed them aside and came right up close to our table. Even the teachers seemed interested, or maybe they were just nervous about all the commotion, because they pressed in too until practically the whole crowd was standing around us in a big circle, looking from Alex to his radio to Alex, who was busy looking down at his watch. The room got quiet.

Alex raised three fingers, then two, then one. Then he started speaking into his radio.

"This is VA2KFO, this is VA2KFO."

A moment passed.

"This is VA2KFO, this is VA2KFO, come back?"

Just static.

"This is VA2KFO, this is VA2KFO, calling N1ISS, do you read me, come back?"

Still nothing.

Alex turned his back to the crowd to fiddle with one of the dials and the antenna. I prayed as hard as I could, my stomach tight. The little kids in the audience were getting antsy. A couple of them wandered away toward the potato clock. Dean let out a loud, mean laugh. Alex turned back toward the crowd, ready to try again, but just then his eyes landed on Sammy, who looked worried. His face went bright pink. The next time he spoke, his voice sounded thin and high.

"This is VA2KFO, this is VA2KFO."

Thin and high and desperate.

"N1ISS, do you read me, come back?"

Thin and high and desperate and lonely.

"This is VA2KFO, calling N1ISS, is anybody out there? Hello?"

The radio static crackled, and then a loud and friendly male voice filled the room. "Hello VA2KFO, this is N1ISS, we're reading you loud and clear up here on the International Space Station, over!"

The audience gasped. A couple of teachers clapped their hands to their mouths. Even Alex looked shocked. The voice boomed out from the radio again.

"Where are you calling from, VA2KFO?"

"We're — we're calling from — Mile End, Montreal, Canada!" Alex spluttered. "We're at school, um, at a science fair!"

"Science fair, huh? Well then, hello to everyone listening, and welcome aboard! Do any of you students have a question you'd like to ask about space exploration?"

A flood of kids pushed forward. Alex let one little girl talk into the radio.

"Hi, I'm Carly. My question is, how do you take a bath in space?"

"Excellent question! Luckily it's not too dirty up here, but sometimes we do get sweaty because we run or bicycle or lift weights. To take a bath, you just put warm soapy water on a washcloth, rub it around your body, and rinse it off."

A boy spoke up next. "What do you miss most about Earth?"

"I really miss my dog, actually. A small Jack Russell Terrier. Today's his birthday, and he's turning 11 years old."

A few kids laughed. Then another boy came up to ask a question, but Gabe shoved him aside. "This is so fake!" he shouted. "Do you idiots think you're really talking to space? You're asking stupid obvious questions and they're playing you stupid pre-recorded answers! Give me the radio, I'll prove it!" He snatched the radio away from Alex and said, "Hey astronaut, my name is Gabe Kramer and if you're talking to us for real then tell us something only you could know!"

There was a pause, heavy with static. Then the voice said, "Well, Gabe Kramer, it sure is nice to meet you. For one thing, I know that you are a true skeptic, which is a very good quality in a scientist. Crucial to scientific inquiry, in fact! Just make sure you don't become *so* skeptical that you refuse to believe the truth even when it's right there in front of you!"

The audience roared. Alex grinned and snatched the radio back. "Thank you so much for your time, N1ISS! But monitoring your trajectory here, I can see that we're about to lose your signal, over."

"You're absolutely right, VA2KFO, we're heading out of range now, so I'll say goodbye. Thanks for taking an interest in the International Space Station, you all have a great day, over!"

The room buzzed with static, then the sound of everyone talking at once.

Ms. Davidson said, "Well everyone, I don't know about you, but I think we have a winner here! Am I right? If you think Alex and Lev deserve to win first prize, raise your hand!"

Sammy's eyes were shining. She raised her hand high above her head. As if she'd pulled them all up with her, a bunch of other hands shot into the air.

A few minutes later, school was over and Alex was calling his mom and she was picking us up and driving us to Baskin-Robbins, since the secret prize for winning the science fair was two free ice cream cones plus sprinkles plus any toppings we wanted in the whole entire store.

We placed our orders and sat down at a tiny round table to eat. While I attacked my one scoop of Cookies and Cream and one scoop of Mint Chocolate Chip with marshmallows and Reese's Pieces and rainbow sprinkles and maraschino cherries, Alex started talking about how our project had beat all the other projects out of the water. Then he did an impression of Gabe's face when he realized that his tin can telephone had lost, and me and Lesley laughed. But Alex got so excited that he accidentally smeared hot fudge all over his face, which made me and Lesley laugh even harder, until finally Alex asked what was so funny and Lesley told him and then he went to the bathroom to wash his face.

"I'm so glad you and Alex are friends," Lesley told me, smiling. "He talks about you all the time, you know. Says you're the best friend he's ever had."

I didn't want to say the wrong thing, so I didn't say anything.

"I don't know if you've noticed, but he doesn't make friends very easily. Big reader, that one. Are you a big reader, too?"

"Sort of. Not like Alex, though."

She laughed. "No, nobody reads quite like Alex, do they? He's the brains of the family, I've always told him that. The budding scientist."

"He must get that from your dad, right? Liking science and astronomy and all that?"

She laughed again. "What in the world gave you that idea?"

"Well, he was a scientist, wasn't he?"

"My father? He was a plumber."

"A plumber?"

"Yep. Fixed toilets for a living."

"You mean he wasn't the one who came up with the whole idea for SETI?"

"SETI? What's that?"

"Um. The Search for Extraterrestrial Intelligence?"

"Sorry," she smiled, turning her palms up to the ceiling. "You'll have to talk to Alex about that kind of thing. He's the astronomer. I buy him books on the subject, you know, when I can, but I really don't know anything about it."

I opened my mouth to say something, but just then Alex came back from the bathroom. His face was clean and a little pink from where he'd rubbed it too hard with paper towels. I finished my ice cream and Alex finished his and a few minutes later Lesley drove me home.

That night I went to bed early but I couldn't sleep. I went to my bookshelf and picked up the book that Alex had given me weeks ago and that so far I hadn't opened even once. It was *Important Names in Astronomy Today*. I took it under the covers with me and turned on my flashlight. I flipped to the back of the book and brought my finger down the list of names in the index and there, hiding near the very end, I found it.

Zaitsev, Aleksandr Leonidovich. 1945–.

A dash and a dot. Like a coded message. I was only eleven and a half, but it didn't take a genius. What the symbols meant was one,

Zaitsev was still alive and two, he was only in his fifties which meant that three, he was not Lesley's father which meant that four, Alex had been lying to me when he said that he was named after somebody famous.

I squeezed my eyes shut and tried to think of why Alex would lie to me but I couldn't. Then I thought of how, for months and months, I'd seen him walking around at recess with his eyes glued to the pages of a book. All that time, I'd thought he did it because he was really into whatever he was reading. But now I thought, what if he did it because he liked the way it made the world go blurry at the edges of his vision? I knew it was possible, if you got the angle just right, to peek out of the corners of your eyes in a way that made everything around you go bright. You squinted. You had patience. You tilted your head to the left and waited.

I closed the book and put it on my desk, but I didn't turn off the flashlight. Instead I pointed it at my door so that Sammy could see the light from her room and come and say, using her most grown-up voice, "Lights out!" or "It's past your bedtime!" But even though I counted off two hundred seconds inside my head, she didn't come. I was about to give up and turn off the flashlight when all of a sudden I had an idea.

I took my journal out from under my pillow and flipped back a few pages, until I came to Things That Make My Sister Sad. Under number nine, which was *Jenny (?)*, I added a tenth reason for my sister's sadness. It was the kind of thing that, once you saw it, seemed so obvious you couldn't believe you hadn't seen it there before. *She doesn't have a bedtime*, I wrote. Then I fell asleep.


THE NIGHT OF the bat mitzvah was hot and humid. When we got to the synagogue, one hundred guests were squishing their one hundred bums into the one hundred seats of the congregation. The bat mitzvah girls were already sitting up on stage. They had red velvet chairs arranged in a half-moon shape, and all of them were full except for one. The chair at the left end of the red half-moon was empty.

The synagogue was so packed that Dad started to worry out loud that maybe it would be hard to find three seats together, but then he saw that there were a bunch of empty spots in the second row, right behind where Mr. Glassman was sitting. While we walked toward them, I looked at Sammy and saw that her face was white. Dad squeezed into the row and sat down, so I squeezed in after him and sat down, too. Then Dad told Sammy to sit next to me, but she just stood there, looking down at her fancy blue dress.

Mr. Glassman turned around in his seat and beamed at her. Dad frowned and told her again to sit down, but she didn't move. He stared at her. She stared at Mr. Glassman. Then, very suddenly, she turned around and climbed onto the stage and walked to the chair at the left end of the half-moon and sat and stared at her knees.

Mr. Glassman twisted around and gave Dad a slow, careful smile, like a test. "She is quite something, your daughter, yes, Mr. Meyer?" he said. "She is the best student in her class. Best student I have ever had! Very smart. Very curious. You must be… you should be… very proud of your daughter… yes?"

Dad said nothing.

I was afraid to turn right and look at him, so instead I turned left just in time to see a very fat lady squeezing herself into the seat beside me. She was out of breath, and I wondered if it was because she was very fat or because she had rushed to get to synagogue on time. I thought about what might have happened to make her need to rush so much, and then I thought about what might have happened to make her need to eat so much, and then the bat mitzvah started.

First Mr. Glassman got up and made a speech. Then the first of the girls, the one at the right end of the half-moon, stood up in front of the microphone. She also made a speech, a very long one, and then she read from the Torah. Then the next girl in the half-moon stood up and the whole thing happened all over again, except this time the speech felt about five times longer. I started to pick my nose, but then I realized what I was doing and stopped. I took a deep breath and looked out at the crowd and felt how the air was heavy with all the people and all the words they wished they could say but couldn't say because girl after girl was crossing the *bima* and saying a speech and chanting from a very ancient scroll.

I couldn't really see, because Mr. Glassman's grey hair was standing up right in front of me, but one thing I noticed was that all the girls either read too fast or too quiet. Sometimes they stumbled over their words and lost their place and had to go back and everyone in the audience sunk a little lower in their seats. Another thing I noticed was that the fat lady sitting to my left kept fanning herself with the program and yawning. She had on a purple silk suit and a gigantic pearl necklace, and she looked unbelievably bored. I thought, who could blame her?

After about four billion years and three gazillion songs, the last of the girls got up on the *bima* and I made my neck long to see over the hair in front of me and it was my sister. My sister who was not most people. Her hands were shaking when she grabbed onto the scroll, but then she started chanting.

And there it was, the weird something in her voice. It was not too fast or too quiet but slow and steady, as if she had all the time in the world, as if it was just for her, just for this moment, that the whole world had been created. I closed my eyes. Inside her voice I could hear each letter, and each silence between each letter, and I felt happy and sad and lonely, because in each perfect silence was a smaller, hidden silence, like dolls inside dolls that go on and on forever, and inside the smallest doll I could suddenly see the list curled up, the list of all the reasons, the reasons for my sister's sadness.

The answering machine on the kitchen counter. The sticky seeds on the floor. The red bicycle in the garage. The closed door. Two small palms smeared with strawberry jam. A store full of musical instruments. A woman's fingers braiding ropes of dough. Voices singing.

Feet dancing. Two boys, laughing, pointing. Hundreds and hundreds of old books. A dead bird. A familiar freckled face with a streak of paint across it, the mouth twisting down. A group of girls standing on a playground, seen from up above, their thin backs turning. And underneath all these pictures, down below the deepest one, a single question burning. It was coming closer, growing bigger and bigger like a shadow on the wall, and I turned away because the question was too big and too cold and too much and because it wasn't meant for me, it was not my question to answer, and then the voice fell away and it was all over — I opened my eyes.

I blinked once and the synagogue reappeared. It reappeared so suddenly, it almost hurt. It was like the feeling you get coming out of a dark movie theater into a bright sunny day. For a second, I felt almost dizzy. Then I blinked again and everything was normal.

Everything was so normal that now I wondered, maybe it was just me? Maybe it all just happened in my head? What if I'd fallen asleep from boredom and missed the whole entire thing? I was still afraid to turn right and look at Dad, so instead I turned to my left.

The fat lady's hands were trembling. Her eyes were squeezed shut and a single tear was rolling down her cheek. It slid down her skin and fell with a plop onto her purple silk skirt.

It wasn't just me.

There was a pause, and then Mr. Glassman crossed the *bima* to make the final speech. He had cue cards in his hands, but his fingers were shaking, and he could barely get the words out of his mouth. He seemed confused and a little blind, like his eyes hadn't adjusted to the sunlight either. He kept turning around to look at Sammy. Finally he said good night, and then there was the sound of one hundred bums lifting out of one hundred seats, and Sammy came down from the *bima* and stood very still beside me.

She looked at Dad and for a second he didn't say anything. Then he opened his mouth, but before any words could come out, Ira came rushing up the aisle toward us. His eyes were watery and his face was red like maybe he'd been crying. He stared at Sammy as if there was so much he wanted to say but he didn't know where to start. His mouth flapped like a flag in the wind, opening and closing and opening. Then he took Dad's hands in his hands and looked right into his eyes. "Miriam would have been proud," he whispered. "So proud."

Dad ripped his hands out of Ira's and balled them into fists. A vein in his forehead was jumping up and down, and if I had to describe the expression on his face using only one word, the word I would use to describe it is *fury*.

Then Ira's wife Judy came up to join us, dragging Jenny by the hand. "That was wonderful, oh, just wonderful!" the woman cried. She kissed Sammy on both cheeks, making her blush and look down at her shoes.

Jenny was staring at my sister. Her eyes were so wide I thought they were going to pop out of her head. They were filled with a feeling that looked like awe and regret and sadness all mixed together at the same time. I tried to come up with one word to describe her expression but it was hard. Five minutes later we got into the car and drove away.

Almost immediately, it started raining. The windshield wipers swished back and forth, filling our ears with a loud clicking noise. Raindrops slid across the windows like comets. I traced their tails with the tip of my finger.

Dad's knuckles were white on the steering wheel, and he didn't say a word the whole way home. Except once at a red light I heard him mutter something about "sharper than a serpent's tooth." I didn't understand what he thought was sharper than a serpent's tooth, unless maybe he meant the rain, but it wasn't even coming down that hard. In the backseat, I was sitting up close to Sammy, and when he said that I could feel her whole body shiver.

When we got home, Dad went straight to his room and Sammy went to hers. I heard their two doors close like echoes of each other. I got a cherry popsicle from the freezer and stood in the hallway licking at it with the tip of my tongue. The framed photos of Mom and Dad stared up at me. I looked at the one of Dad and noticed that he didn't look very happy in it. He was bent over the books on his desk, and he was frowning. But Mom, she was smiling. I picked up her photo and looked at her laughing mouth, her shining eyes. Her face had a light in it that Dad's face didn't have, and I wondered if maybe that was *emunah*. I thought, was Mom a happier person than Dad because she had faith and he didn't? Then I bit straight down on the popsicle, pushing my front teeth deep into it until I shivered.

I knocked on Sammy's door and then opened it. She'd changed into shorts and a т-shirt, and she was stuffing a bunch of things into her trash can. The blue dress. Her candlesticks. A box of matches. The triangle she used to play in band class. The Kiddush cup. Her prayer book. I asked, "What are you doing with all this stuff?" and she just shrugged, so I asked, "Can I have it?" and she just shrugged again. Then she pulled her backpack over her shoulder, so I said, "Where are you going?" and she said, "To the supermarket, go to bed," and then she left.

I poked around in her trash can, took out all the things except the blue dress and the triangle, and stuffed them under the bed in my room. Then I tried to fall asleep but I couldn't. After a while, I heard the phone ring and ran to the kitchen to answer it. Even though I said hello three times, nobody answered. I hung up, but a second later the phone rang again. This time I let the machine get it. Instead of a voice, I heard a long stretch of silence, with a few taps thrown in here and there. Then the machine beeped and went quiet.

I went back to bed and crawled under the covers. I turned on my flashlight, made another list, and turned off my flashlight again. I squeezed my eyes shut but I still couldn't fall asleep, so instead I calculated how much my name equals in *gematriya*, which by the way is 32. I calculated Sammy's name and then I calculated Dad's name, too, trying to see if all our names added up together equalled something I could still recognize, something maybe not that different from family.

ALL THE SILENCES I KNOW AND WHERE
THEY CAN BE FOUND:

1. In libraries
2. In synagogues
3. Between sleep and waking
4. Right before something terrible happens
5. Right after something terrible happens
6. Inside the bodies of musical instruments
7. Anytime you want to say something nice to somebody but are too shy to say it
8. Anytime you want to ask somebody a question but are too shy to ask it
9. Between knocking over a glass bowl and seeing it hit the ground
10. Late at night, after everyone has gone to sleep
11. Early in the morning, before anyone has woken up
12. Between the letters on a page
13. On the other side of the telephone wire
14. 25,000 light years away
15. After the rain

**THE NEXT DAY** a miracle happened.

When I woke up in the morning, it was still early. The house was asleep but the sun was already shining. I walked outside in my pajamas. The rain had cleared everything away and the neighbourhood smelled clean and fresh and blue like the inside of clouds. I started walking in the direction of Mr. Katz's house.

When I got there, he was standing in the middle of the lawn staring up at the Tree. He was also in pajamas, and his mouth was hanging open. I stood next to him and looked up.

In each one of the cradles sat a perfect yellow lemon.

The longer I squinted up at them, the more my eyes started to hurt, but I didn't want to look away. It was as if the lemons were giving off a light of their own, a bittersweet light. Mr. Katz pulled at my sleeve and said, "You see? When you have *emunah*, the Kadosh Baruch Hu answers your prayers." His eyes were glowing like maybe he'd been staring into the light for too long. He went over to the Tree and picked the lemon from the lowest cradle. "Taste and see that the Lord is good!" He bit into it and his eyes popped open.

I got really excited to tell Mr. Glassman that I knew what fruit was on the Tree of Knowledge, so I ran over to his house. On the way I saw somebody disappearing around the corner and it looked a bit like Sammy but I couldn't tell for sure because the sun was in my eyes. I skidded to a stop in front of Mr. Glassman's door and knocked, my heart thumping like crazy.

When I saw his face, I remembered that Mrs. Glassman was sick a few days ago, and maybe she still was and I shouldn't be here, banging on their door so early in the morning. But then I heard her voice calling, "Lev, *boychick*, is that you?" Mr. Glassman smiled and brought me into the kitchen, which was full of the smell of fresh ruggelach baking. Mrs. Glassman pinched my cheeks and said, "Skin and bones, sit and let me bring you what to eat!"

While I sat and waited, Mr. Glassman started talking about Sammy's bat mitzvah reading. He couldn't stop saying how amazing it was and how much she had touched him. His voice was relaxed and happy and I decided not to tell him about the things I'd seen her throwing into the trash can last night.

Instead, I put my hands in my pockets. In my right pocket I could feel Mr. Glassman's scrap of paper, the one with his name and his wife's name calculated out in *gematriya*, which he'd let me keep the other day. I started to think about the story he'd told me and what it said about the tattoos they got in the camp. The more I thought about it, the more made-up and *meshugganeh* it all sounded. What kind of Nazi officer would let you choose the number of your tattoo? It didn't work that way! Mrs. Glassman was wearing a shirt with rolled-up sleeves, and while she moved around the kitchen getting the tea and ruggelach ready I tried to sneak a good look at the number on her arm, to calcu-late and see if it really did add up to her name, but she kept moving too fast and the sunlight was making everything fuzzy and all of the numbers blurred together and I couldn't tell anymore what was what.

DAVID

N O SOONER HAD I bolted awake than I spluttered the words, "Where is she?"

Above me, an unfamiliar face swam into view. A dark-skinned, dewy-eyed, thirtyish man was saying, "Mr. Meyer, please, try to calm down —"

"Where is she?"

"Who?"

"Samara. My daughter. Is it over?"

"Is what over?"

"Did she leave already? I have to tell her — to apologize — the bat mitzvah —"

"The what?"

"Bat mitzvah! I have to —"

"Dad," said a small voice. "That was ten years ago."

I looked to my left as someone moved into my circle of vision. It was Lev, my Lev, but it took me a second to recognize him. The little boy I'd just seen fidgeting in my mind's eye was gone; in his place, the grown-up version of my son. Here, in real life, he looked even more scared than he had in the dream — because it was a dream, I understood suddenly, the synagogue and speeches and Samara's downcast eyes, that was a memory — past, not present.

"Where am I? What happened?"

"You've suffered a myocardial infarction — a heart attack," the man explained. "Don't worry, you're in good hands now. You're at the hospital. I'm Dr. Singh."

I squinted up at him. Something metallic swung in front of my eyes, catching the late afternoon light and temporarily blinding me. The doctor applied a gentle pressure to my shoulders, making me lie back. Then he grabbed his stethoscope, pressed it to my chest, and asked, "Mind if I have a listen?"

Instead of replying, I stared out at eye level. My gaze fixed on Lev's hand. His index finger marked his place in a small leather-bound book, its spine stamped with Hebrew letters. I frowned. He'd been praying for me — reciting psalms, as if that would save me. Then I remembered that he was a yeshiva boy now and only doing what the rabbis there taught him to do in situations like this one. Still, it pinched: I'd gotten one kid off of religion — at great personal cost — only to have the other one turn.

"Your sister," I whispered to my son's hand, "is she coming?"

"Of course!" Lev said. "I called her a few minutes ago, and she said she was getting on the metro from McGill right away, so she should be here soon."

I nodded weakly, unsure whether to believe him — Samara almost never came home of her own volition — and disoriented by the recollection that she was now college-age, a university student more than halfway through her undergraduate degree. Moments ago, in my dream, she'd stared down at me from a synagogue *bima* with a young girl's hopeful, vulnerable eyes.

"Are you okay, Dad?" Lev asked. "Do you need anything?"

Dr. Singh stood up and smiled. "Oh, he'll be all right. What your dad needs now is lots of rest. Lev, why don't we go out into the hall and let your dad sleep for a bit? You and I can talk later, Mr. Meyer."

Exhausted, I dozed off.

When I next awoke — it could have been minutes or maybe hours later — the shadows in the room had lengthened. Someone was hovering in the same spot Lev had occupied when I'd first regained consciousness. Samara. As soon as she saw me recognize her, she flinched. I looked into her face and she looked into mine and we held a silent moment between us. I opened my mouth and she ran from the room, too scared to talk to me, too scared to see me in this weakened state. And then I knew that the news of my collapse had terrified her, and I cried. Not because I was sad that she wouldn't come closer. But because I was happy that, despite everything I'd done wrong, she still loved me enough for my mortality to fill her with a fear so strong she couldn't quite look it in the eyes.

FOUR DAYS AFTER the heart attack, I was ready to be released. Stooped over my hospital bed, Singh pressed his stethoscope to my chest one last time. He listened intently, as if a Verdi opera were playing beneath the metal, then straightened up and handed me the instrument. "Have a listen."

"Why?"

"I think you'll want to hear this."

I placed the buds in my ears, the disc to my chest. It was not Verdi, or Scarlatti, or Mozart, but something like music was happening inside me. "What is that?"

"A heart murmur."

"Is that — dangerous?"

He raised his palms apologetically. "Not usually. Yours is a bit unusual."

"Unusual?"

"Well, as you can see — hear — it's audible. The murmur occurs during systole — that's the phase of the cardiac cycle in which the tissue experiences contraction —"

At that word, I sat up a little straighter.

"And the volume is, you might say, irregular. Once you're stronger I may ask you to come back for a few tests. But for now, try not to think about it. No work, plenty of rest, and minimum physical exertion over the next few weeks. Do you have any questions?"

"I assume it's all right for me to go running?"

"Well, a little bit of exercise is fine, yes, but don't overdo it. Remember that running is what landed you here in the first place, so steer clear of anything strenuous or prolonged. Jogging might be better. Or walking. Okay?"

I nodded, though it was not. "And what about, you know, sexual activity?"

Singh smiled. "It's not nearly as risky as many patients seem to think. You can safely resume sexual activity in a couple of weeks. Okay?"

I hadn't seen Valérie since I'd been in here, though she'd repeatedly called to check up on me. I'd asked the nurses to assure her there was no need to visit. The kids had been here pretty much non-stop — especially Samara, who, though she didn't say much, stalked the hospital with a haunted look and insisted on sleeping in a chair in the hallway — and I didn't want them running into Val. But I knew I'd want to see her before long.

"Okay," I said.

"Your daughter and son are here to take you home, then. Ready to go?"

"Yes."

"I'll ask the nurse to wheel you out. Take care, Mr. Meyer."

I nodded again, and Singh left. A nurse materialized at my side and transferred me, despite my protestations, to a wheelchair. She smiled at me with bright green eyes — oblivious to my rage at that traitor, my body — then offered to wheel me into the hall. When I told her I could take it from here, she smiled again and withdrew.

The first person I saw upon wheeling myself into the hall was Samara, her arms crossed against anxiety or the artificial cool of the hospital wing. Behind her Lev was frowning nervously, but even that could not detract from the luminous quality of his boyish face, a face just saved from too-beautifulness by a tiny but conspicuous scar above the brow. It was a sight that never failed to make me smile, and so, approaching him, I smiled — but only for an instant. In the next instant I realized that, just a few feet away, still and silent in an old-fashioned black dress — the one I jokingly called her Saint Teresa dress — was Valérie.

The kids came toward me and said their hellos. I hugged them both, all the while signalling at Valérie behind their backs, trying to convey through subtle dilations of my pupils that she should keep her distance. She must have understood my code well enough, because she just stood there, eyeing me darkly with a gorgeous torment in her face and hands.

Lev wheeled me down the hall toward the elevator, chattering happily. Samara followed at a distance. Craning my neck backward, I saw her flash a glance at Val, but couldn't catch the meaning of her expression. Did she know? The elevator arrived, its doors opened, we were swallowed up. Probably not.

The second we got outside, we were struck by a wave of humidity so powerful as to wipe out any higher functions of the brain. I was tempted to turn back and stay in the hospital forever. The pills I had taken were making me tired and woozy, and because the June air had a stickiness that made any movement whatsoever, speech included, seem gratuitous, I was silent as I watched the dark clouds rolling in overhead.

While Samara went to bring the car around, Lev's overbright voice filled the space between us, babbling about how glad our neighbours — Glassman, Katz — would be to see me back at home. I didn't bother to remind him that these were his friends, not mine. When the car appeared, Lev asked, "Do you need help getting in?" and I grunted, "Yes," feeling like a pathetic child as he eased me into the back seat.

Samara turned on the air conditioning, and her long dark hair billowed around her shoulders, just as her mother's used to do before we married and she started covering up. Look how adult she seems behind the wheel, I marvelled, as though years, not weeks, typically passed between sightings of her. I wished she would say something. Banalities like Lev's, questions like Singh's — something, anything. She said nothing.

On the seat beside me were a couple of hastily packed oversize purses, a sleeve and a hairbrush peeking out of one of them. "Are you going somewhere?" I asked her.

She glanced in the rear-view mirror, then turned her attention back to the road. "Oh, that. No, I'm going to move back home for a couple of weeks."

"Oh?" I whispered.

"It's no big deal. Classes are over now anyways, so."

"Right," I said, more casually now. "Summer break." But the idea that she was concerned enough to come back, even if only temporarily, even if she insisted on minimizing the gesture, touched and surprised me.

As we turned onto Côte-Sainte-Catherine, the humidity finally, mercifully, broke. The downpour was slow at first. Then, before you knew it, it was a flood. That was how it always happened in this beautiful, lunatic, impossible city. A cold rain fell down like manna into the gaping mouths of potholes, and, overflowing these, cascaded down into the sewers. Samara turned on the windshield wipers. They swished back and forth, back and forth, with that small clicking sound that most people found comforting but that I, for reasons that were now opaque to me, had come to detest.

I took a deep breath and placed a hand on my chest. Beneath the sounds of the rain and the cars, beneath the clicking of the windshield wipers, I thought I could now detect another sort of noise entirely. The sound of my own heart beating. The sound of a murmur. I closed my eyes and listened. Opened them and smiled. Closed them again and prayed for traffic.

THE MORNING AFTER I got home from the hospital, everything looked different. Not better or worse, just different. The framed photographs, the mounted diplomas on the walls — they all bore a certain *unheimlichkeit*, an uncanniness that set me on edge.

In my bedroom, opening a small trunk that had not been cracked in several years, I thought I could detect the smell of Miriam's perfume lingering in the clothes. This was doubly ridiculous; not only had she been gone for over fifteen years, but the scent I imagined myself to be picking up was that of a very ancient perfume, one she'd worn when we were both newly religious yeshiva students — she at the women's seminary and I at the men's. It was a pale vanilla scent that clashed absurdly with the perfumes I'd encountered since her death: the bold musk and spicy cardamom notes favoured by my grad students were so strong they'd soaked into my shirts, making me worry that my kids would one day ask why I kept coming home smelling like the fragrance aisle of a department store. Luckily, they never seemed to notice.

As the sounds of Lev's prayers drifted toward me from his bedroom — a joyful, nasal voice singing out one psalm after another — I glanced around the room. Sunlight filled the space, glossing the pages of open books. I picked up the autobiography of Teresa of Avila — required reading for Introduction to Catholicism, which I had taught the previous semester — and opened to a random page, smiling at the thought of Valérie's dress.

> I saw in his hand a long spear of gold, and at the iron's point there seemed to be a little fire. He appeared to be thrusting it at times into my heart, and to pierce my very entrails; when he drew it out, he seemed to draw them out also, and to leave me all on fire with a great love of God. The pain was so great, that it made me moan; and yet so surpassing was the sweetness of this excessive pain, that I could not wish to be rid of it.

I'd read this passage just hours before the heart attack and thought nothing of it then, having little use for Saint T and all that self-indulgent mortification of the flesh. But today her description seemed all too familiar. After all, wasn't that what I had felt during the attack? A point of fire that pierced the heart, an excessive pain, a desire to scream *no no no no no* — and yet, coiled within the no, an intricate sweetness, an ineffable yes.

Closing my eyes, I placed a hand over my heart and listened. Once again, I thought I could hear the murmur. A rush of blood moving back and forth, back and forth, and behind it all a subtle whistling or whispering, like wind through a flute or breath through a harmonica. It had an unmistakable musical quality — crescendo followed by decrescendo — a quality that could be called, almost, linguistic. What had Singh called it? Systolic. *The phase of the cardiac cycle in which the tissue experiences contraction...*

My eyes flew open. The academic manuscript I'd been working on lay on my desk, but I didn't make my way toward it. I didn't need to; I remembered it word for word, and the particular words I had in mind were to be found in the very first paragraph. *The great kabbalists taught that God began the process of creation by contracting His infinite light and pouring it into the ten vessels that formed the Tree of Life. As the light trickled down through these vessels, it condensed into physical matter and gave rise to the world as we know it...*

My lips moved soundlessly for a long time, forming the words I was most intimately familiar with. A haze descended on me; I fell asleep.

I WOKE TO A persistent ringing that filled the house. After a moment, I realized it was the telephone. Shuffling into the kitchen in bathrobe and slippers, I picked up the receiver. "Hello?"

Silence.

"Hello?"

Silence.

"Hello?"

Silence.

I hung up, but my hand remained on the receiver for a long time, as if contact with the plastic would allow me to divine, through osmosis perhaps, the identity of the mystery caller with the blocked ID. For the thousandth time in the past ten years, I found myself wondering who it could possibly be. It was not a wrong number, prank call, or simple coincidence; a decade of repeated calls had ruled those three options out. But who, then, did that leave?

The air in the kitchen was thick and clammy and I was sweating profusely. I needed some air.

When I opened the front door, I found Samara and Jenny sitting on the stoop, their shoulders touching. "Hello, Jenny," I said.

They sprang apart like startled animals.

"Hi, hey, hi, Mr. Meyer."

"Nice day, isn't it?"

"Yes, um, very. How are you feeling?"

"Much better, thanks. Do you two have anything fun planned for this afternoon?"

Samara stared at me but said nothing. Jenny said, "Not really."

"Good day for a bike ride," I suggested, keeping my voice as casual as possible and nodding toward the garage where Sam's old bike was stowed.

"I haven't used that bike in about—" Sam muttered, but stopped herself. "The tires are probably flat."

"Yes. Well. Just a thought. See you girls later," I said and retreated into the house.

Closing the door, I made a mental note to add bicycles to the litany of things Sam and I did not talk about. I wondered whether she remembered that time, just weeks after her mother died, when I had taken her and her brother cycling in the middle of the night. She had complained, earlier that day, that we never did anything fun together. And so, besieged with parental guilt, unable to sleep, I had woken them up in the small hours and insisted that they come outside — I would not tell them why. They balked when they saw their bicycles in front of the house, Sam's red ten-speed and Lev's green one-speed all newly polished and poised for flight. And fly we did: up suburban streets and down back alleys, through empty play-grounds and past deserted schoolyards. By the time we got to the mountain they were laughing and singing and swinging their bikes, back and forth beneath the streaming stars. It was 6:30 by the time I finally got them to bed. Years later, I still remembered the sibilance of Samara's breath as she slipped into sleep; the cupid's bow of her mouth, not quite closed, suffused in the orange glow of dawn. But she was too young, then, to remember such a thing now. As far as she was concerned, I had probably never taken them for a single ride. I had probably never taken them anywhere.

Back in the kitchen, I poured a glass of lemonade and took the pills Singh had prescribed out of the cupboard. Honestly, for such a smart girl, Samara could be surprisingly naïve sometimes. As if any-one could fail to notice how happy she'd been since she and Jenny bumped into each other at a college art show, rekindling their friend-ship ("friendship") after a years-long rift and later moving in together. How her features softened whenever the girl called or appeared at her side. Who could fail to understand exactly what this softness meant?

I knew, I knew, of course I knew — but she didn't know I knew. Why wouldn't she just come out and say it already? Did she think I would judge, disapprove? Didn't she understand that I didn't believe in any of that traditional twaddle, that Leviticus 18 junk?

I drank the pills down with the lemonade, then put the glass in the sink. Through the window I could see right into the Glassmans' kitchen, and there was Mrs. Glassman, whose recent stroke had forced her to walk with a cane yet who was now pulling fresh challah out of the oven while Mr. Glassman sat at the table, sipping tea and not saying a word. I endeavoured to remember a time when Samara and I used to speak freely. As a child she'd been talkative, even bubbly: at six or seven, she would sit on the floor of my study, running her fingers through the carpet, listening to me explain about Zeno and Pythagoras and Plotinus, asking me questions and spouting her theories... Six or seven. Right before her mother died. Was that when she became so secretive, so silent?

The smell of freshly baked dough wafted over from the Glassmans'. I closed my eyes and saw myself coming home from work, briefcase in hand, to find Miriam in the kitchen teaching the kids how to bake challah. Sam giggled, trying and failing and trying again to copy her mother's motions as she braided the ropes of dough. Lev's pudgy fingers kneaded purposelessly, hitting the dough just for fun, and then he reached for the brush and dipped it in orange juice and sneaked up on Miriam and painted her cheek. She snatched him up and rubbed flour on *his* cheek — and then Sam was into it, too, squealing with delight, smearing both of them with flour and juice and dough. I stood there, marvelling at the three of them together, their robust physicality. It hit me that although these were my children as much as hers, I had no idea how to interact with them. Certainly not with that simple solid faith of Miriam's, a faith that was perfect for kids but that I knew even then I would never be able to access. She died that summer and a yeasty silence filled the house and rose, inch by inch, until it filled the space between us.

FULLY A WEEK had passed since my release from the hospital before I finally screwed up the courage to call Val. When I did, she answered on the fifth, not the first, ring: a great relief.

"*Allo?*"

"It's me."

"Oh." Guarded. Concerned but distant. "How are you?"

"Much better now. Listen, I saw you at the hospital, I'm sorry I didn't get a chance to —"

"It's okay. I saw your kids, by the way. *Ils ont l'air très sympa.*"

"Thanks."

"Especially your son."

"Yeah, that's what everyone says."

"Your daughter, she was giving me a bit of a funny —"

"Listen, how are you? Eckhart treating you okay these days?"

"Yes, he's being very nice. In fact, I just finished a chapter this morning, so. Maybe we could take a coffee?"

"What, now, you mean?"

"Yes. I can pick you up in, we'll say, half an hour?"

I hesitated.

"The kids are at home?"

"No, actually, they're gone." Samara was out, presumably with Jenny. Lev was at Alex's, probably building some telescope or model rocket.

"So I can come get you."

"I — okay. But I'm not very — I mean, I may be a bit tired still."

"Of course. What's your address?"

With a certain amount of constriction in the vocal cords, I gave it to her. Then, hanging up, I walked to the bathroom and assessed my reflection in the mirror. For a man who had long prided himself on his physical appearance, his health, his ability to get by just upon a smile, baby, this was a sorry sight; hardly the stuff of student fantasy. My hair seemed greyer. My skin looked sallow and strained. I saw, or imagined that I saw, a faint yellowish tinge around the eyes. So much for the sexy professor trope, I thought, nevertheless doing my best to clean up. I shaved, put on a fresh shirt and pants and, for the first time in a week, substituted loafers for terrycloth slippers.

By the time I heard her car pull up in the driveway, I was hemorrhaging confidence fast. I opened the door; she was walking up the stone path, her green dress swirling about her knees, her step buoyant yet measured, as if she came to this house every day. Her smile, too, had the ease that comes with daily routine — but this was not that, could never be that, and I gripped her firmly by the elbow and steered her back toward the car. Only once we were shut up inside it did I kiss her; curiously, as soon as I did so, my anxiety melted away. I kissed her again, harder, and beneath my mouth I felt her smile with all the winsome coyness, all the premature cunning of her twenty-six years.

"I see you're getting your strength back," she said.

"Well. You have that effect. And you — I'm happy to see you chose green, not black today. When I saw you in the hospital wearing that funereal dress…"

She smiled, but the smile was only in the mouth. She turned the key in the ignition and we pulled away from the house. For a moment there was silence.

"So where are you taking me?" I asked, strenuously jocular.

She named the place. "Have you heard of it?"

I hadn't.

"You'll love it," she said, and grinned at the road.

Our destination turned out to be a coffee shop in Val's neck of the woods, the Plateau Mont-Royal. Outfitted with mismatched chairs, "radical" zines, Scrabble boards, and a strictly vegan menu, it projected the look-how-quirky-and-idiosyncratic-we-can-be air that I'd come to associate with undergrad students.

No sooner had we sat down with our coffees than a scruffy, plaid-wearing guy came toward us bearing a pamphlet. He was angry about pesticides, or the overuse of plastic spoons, or coffee shops' failure to replace wooden stir sticks with fettuccine — and he wanted us to help him fight whatever corporate interests were perpetrating this travesty. Val smiled and nodded and accepted his pamphlet and he ambled away. By the window two girls wearing dark-framed oversize glasses and baggy thrift-store dresses were talking in righteous, high-pitched tones about "development porn" and "post-structural semiotics." At the table beside ours another girl, sporting yellow stockings and a maroon dress and what appeared to be the exact same oversize glasses, was attacking Žižek's *Sublime Object of Ideology* with a highlighter.

I raised an eyebrow at Val. "It's all so — vaguely cultish, isn't it?"
She smiled into her mug.

"Why did you bring me here, of all places?"

She looked up, eyes sparkling, and shrugged. "Isn't it obvious? They make really good coffee!"

I laughed and took a sip. She was right: it was hot and clear and bright. I studied her over the rim, my appreciation for her deepening. The other students I'd slept with would never have brought me here; they'd have known I would hate it, and they'd only permitted themselves to love what I loved. But Val had no interest in ticking boxes, no patience for costuming. She loved what she loved — and that was what made her my Valérie, *ma valkyrie*.

With an upward puff of air, she blew the bangs out of her eyes — one of her lovely, unconscious gestures — and then, glancing at her watch, said she needed to make a quick call. Take your time, I told her. I was happy to watch as she stepped into the slanting rays, to marvel at her litheness, her tallness, to contemplate how lucky I'd been to land her in my graduate seminar last spring.

The only Québécoise student to enter the department in years, from a staunch Catholic background to boot; intelligent and engaged, but without the slightest trace of earnestness; lacking both the grades-crazed fervour of her academically-minded classmates and the ersatz zealousness of her more mystically-minded peers. As I had discovered over the years, graduate students in Religious Studies came in two flavours: aspiring professors and aspiring saints. Personally, I preferred the former — or, rather, found them slightly less detestable than the latter.

Myra Goldfarb, for example, in last year's Eastern Philosophical Texts — there was something grotesquely unsettling about the way she stared at you, unblinking as a cat, with the enormous, blue, near-sighted eyes of the bodhisattva-in-training. You could tell from her seminar papers that she secretly believed she would achieve *satori* if she just plowed through enough books, ladled up enough pea soup at the soup kitchen, and managed to squash that pesky little illusion we called the self. Minus a catechism and a wimple or two, she was like Mother Teresa on speed: she padded her spiritual resumé with the furious zeal of a high school senior intent on getting into Harvard or Yale. Val, praise be, had none of that.

She re-entered the coffee shop, tossed her phone into her handbag, and sat down across from me, radiant. Her stylish bob had grown out a bit in recent weeks, so that the tips of the hair now skimmed the tops of her shoulders. The effect was extremely becoming. We drank the rest of our coffee, chatting about the courses I'd be offering next year (Development of Jewish Mystical Thought, The Gnostic Worldview) and about her dissertation (Meister Eckhart and Zen Buddhism: The Unthought Debt). Words tumbled across the table — Neoplatonism, *Gottheit*, *merkava*, demiurge — and sat there, and that was what I loved: neither of us felt the need to beat our words into swords, or to roll them toward some overwhelming question. Free from the burden of persuasion, the words became simple carriers of pleasure. So that by the time the sky had been recast in a series of pinks and purples and oranges, I began to feel as though someone had opened up all the taps in my nervous system and flooded the veins with red wine. Taking her elbow for the second time that day — but with a different kind of pressure in the grip — I steered her down the street toward her apartment, looking forward to an evening of *luxe, calme et volupté*.


**BACK HOME IN** my study the next morning, with the red wine glow gone from my system, I stared at the heaps of research on my desk.

Before the heart attack, I'd begun a book on kabbalah, focusing on the Tree of Life and based on notes for my lectures in Development of Jewish Mystical Thought. Leafing through the pile, I realized that for all their physical thickness, the notes I'd put together were shockingly thin. Cursory. Lazy. Scanning page after page, I was struck by the shallowness of my textual exploration. I'd written: *The goal of the* kabbalist is to climb the Tree of Life by spiritually binding himself to each of its ten vessels in turn, until he is united with the divine source of all being. Okay, I thought now, but "bind" how? Why hadn't I gone into more detail? Wasn't the "how" the most interesting part?

In my discussion of two vessels — Ani, the lowest, and Ayin, the highest — I'd noted: *Scholarly commentaries warn that undirected meditation on Ayin is one of the most perilous methods in classical meditation, and that it should not be attempted even under the guidance of a master. Prior to the Hasidic writings, there is virtually no mention of this method, and even in the Hasidic writings it is mentioned only obliquely.* Yet I hadn't given a single example of these "oblique" references.

A scrap of paper fell out of the pile and landed on my knee. Here, right here was one of the phrases I could have mentioned: "Ayin is the crown of Ani." Why hadn't I cited that quotation? It seemed to indicate that the highest of the divine vessels was intrinsically linked to the lowest — but how, exactly? I repeated the phrase over in my head, pausing on each word. Then I got a pen and a sheet of loose-leaf paper and wrote out first "Ayin," then, below it, "Ani."

נ י א

י נ א

In Hebrew, these names were anagrams, made up of the same three letters scrambled. This had to have some significance beyond mere wordplay: while Ayin meant "nothingness" and was associated with ego-annihilation, Ani meant "I" and was associated with the ego or unified self.

But what did that mean, practically speaking, for the kabbalist trying to get from point A to point B? I had no idea.

It was painfully clear now that my notes were hopelessly banal. If I let them form the basis for my course lectures, they would put all the students to sleep. Well, almost all the students. Even now, I could picture the frisson of agonized delight on Myra Goldfarb's face upon seeing her new brick of a course pack. The fact that I'd created a lesson plan that would thrill just such a person came as an unpleasant, almost sickening jolt.

Something on my desk began to ring. I dug the source out from underneath heaps of paper. "Hello?"

"David? Is that you? It is *so good* to hear your voice."

"Who's this?"

"It's Ira! Ira Rosenthal!"

"Oh, yes, Ira... of course." I could picture him perfectly, seated behind his oak desk, his fingers forming a tent above his rather significant belly. The famously congenial smile that had landed him the title of Dean of Religious Studies nearly a decade earlier, the rosiness in his cheeks, the dimples in his clownish face, the glint of sincerity in his eyes — all the qualities he had deployed to smooth out the wrinkles in the political fabric of the department and to make the eggheads play nice. The remarkable thing was that his own niceness was not at all put-on; he really was a likeable guy, and in the years before Miriam's death our two families had enjoyed something that might even have been called closeness. After Miriam died, he and his wife Judy offered to take Samara and Lev to their house for a few hours every day after school — they were picking up Jenny anyway, so it was no trouble, really, no trouble at all — and because I needed time to finish my dissertation, I gratefully accepted. But when Samara and Jenny's friendship mysteriously dissipated years later, I allowed that gratitude to lapse. Shabbat dinner invitations piled up on an answering machine that I conveniently pretended never to check — until, one week, the invitations simply stopped coming.

"How are you, Ira?"

"I should be asking you. Are you doing all right?"

"Yes, I'm doing —" I paused, looking at the notes in my hand. When I spoke again, it was with a faint tremolo in the voice. "Well, I'm doing as well as can be expected."

"Aha, yes, mm-hmm. Well. You gave us quite a scare, you know that? Yes. And how are the kids?"

"They're fine. Summer break, you know."

"Great. That's great. Listen, David, I was wondering — and, now, I know you must be needing to take it easy, I mean obviously after the, ah — but what I'm wondering is, have you had a chance to look over those term papers? From spring semester?"

With a tremendous effort of will, I wrenched my mind out of my notes. "Term papers?" My gaze canvassed the room and lit upon a stack of papers half-obscured beneath a heavy green desk lamp. I held the phone against my shoulder and pried the eighty-odd papers out. "No, I'm afraid I haven't felt quite up to the task."

"Yes, well, that's, ah, to be expected. No rush — it's just that we need the grades for the undergrad courses by, well, three weeks ago actually — but, again, no rush."

"I see."

"Yes. Again —"

"I'll get back to you with the grades as soon as I can."

"Well!" he laughed. "That sounds fine then, David, just fine."

"Give my best to Judy."

"What? Oh, yes, yes, thanks, thank you, I will. So. Take it easy now!"

"I will. Goodbye."

As soon as I'd hung up, I suddenly needed — not wanted, not the banality of wanted — to go for a run. I knew this would be anathema to Singh, and to Val, and to my kids, and to whatever spectre-shadow of their dearly departed mom they liked to imagine might still be watching over me from above, but. Ever since Miriam's death, I had been exercising twice a week, every week, without fail. Eager to finally shed the physical wimpiness associated with yeshiva culture, I'd become acquainted with the perverse pleasures — the masochism, really — of long-distance running. Now, because I wasn't about to let one little heart attack undo over a decade's worth of training, I dug out my T-shirt, jogging pants, and running shoes and snuck out of the house on tiptoes.

Freedom! The morning sun was high up in a cloudless sky, glinting off the brick row houses' wrought iron gates and balconies, sparkling in the dewy grass of their tiny front yards. The air had that just-mowed scent that always put me in mind of childhood and summer camp and Ralph Waldo Emerson and his "transparent eyeball." I took in gulp after gulp of it and felt it polishing my lungs from the inside.

For once, the neighbourhood was quiet. The young professionals had already left for work; the twisting staircases they'd painted in lively purples and greens and oranges were free of the bicycles that usually lay propped against the rails. In their various yeshivas, the Hasids were gathered for morning prayers — beating their breasts during the Silent Devotion, or bouncing on the balls of their feet as they sang Holy Holy Holy et cetera during the cantor's repetition.

Rounding the block at a quickening pace, I noticed a lone figure squatting on a lawn under a majestic old oak tree: Katz. The knees and shins of his pants were damp with dew, and yet he seemed oddly separate from the unkempt grass and the ground beneath it. A religious nut, the man might have been pitiable had he not made a habit through the years of buttonholing me in the street to debate the merits of various rabbinic commentaries on this or that biblical verse. Suffering from some mental affliction that everyone in the "community" was too anti-gossip to name, he'd spent his adult life as the ignored manqué of a yeshiva world that should have been his birthright.

But ignored only to a point. Ten years ago, for reasons unknown to the good citizens of Mile End and, for that matter, to the non-tin-foil-hat-wearing segment of the population, he had hung dozens of lemons — in dental floss cradles, no less — not from the old oak he currently sat under but from the branches of a makeshift construction, the cardboard imitation of a real tree. At first, the neighbours had viewed this as an innocuous if odd display of the poor sap's quirks and quiddities. Then summer arrived: the lemons ripened and rotted, grew mottled and moldy, and people began to want them gone. Katz explained that this was miracle fruit, dropped down from above, and human beings had no right to destroy it. Unfortunately, this miracle turned out to have a putrid stench, which, as the weeks wore on, became unbearable. Katz, too, imbibed the smell, and the flies that had begun to swarm around the tree took a shining to him as well.

One night an angry mob of caftaned men rushed his front lawn. They ripped apart the toilet paper roll branches and painted leaves, and set them aflame in a garbage bin in the middle of the street — a bonfire into which these Savonarolas' children tossed lemon after lemon. Katz looked on and wailed, high keening notes escaping him like the sounds Jews emit when mourning the destruction of the Temple. Driving by with the kids in tow, I couldn't help laughing. But, to my surprise, Lev looked miserable, even tortured, and Samara's eyes flashed with anger.

That experience appeared to have cured Katz of the creative impulse; for years after, his hands lay dormant in his lap. Yet what he was doing now was so eerily reminiscent of that long-ago summer that I slackened my pace to observe him. Surrounded by a three-foot-high fort of unlabelled tin cans, he was using a screwdriver to poke holes into the bottom of each one. A spool of twine waited on the grass beside him. Katz looked up and waved merrily. I nodded and, not wanting to become entangled in the sticky web of conversation, quickened my pace.

I raced along the tree-lined street in a tunnel of green light, then turned onto Bernard. Pulse pounding, I sped past the boutiques and bakeries, and was just beginning to get an enjoyable endorphin rush going when all of a sudden I heard it again — the odd music — the oddly *linguistic* music. The murmur was audible now, yes, definitely audible. I could hear it thrumming, I could hear it — almost — *saying*. Saying what?

At that instant I had the kind of intuition generally enjoyed only from that rear-view mirror known as hindsight. Now — *right* now, before it was too late! — was the time to flick this idea away from me. Nip it in the bud. It was absurd, the thought of an internal organ speaking in human language — and dangerous, too, because there is nothing more seductive to an intellectual of a certain generation and class than an absurdly romantic notion about his relationship to his own body. I remembered Emerson: *The eye reads omens where it goes, and speaks all languages the rose.* A heart, I reminded myself with each footfall, does not speak in words — that is not what is meant by body language!

Yet instead of slowing down to silence it, I sped up. My heart rate accelerated accordingly. The blood was pounding in my ears, a whooshing, whistling sound. My knees ached, my shins cried out for respite, I pressed on, I needed to be sure. Monosyllabic? No. Definitely disyllabic. A vowel, followed by a consonant, followed by... another vowel? It was unclear, I gathered speed, my lungs shrivelled, my brain whined, but now, at last, I could make out the first syllable: aaaahhhh.

And the second? The second syllable was more elusive, but this only made me want to hear it more; nothing had ever seemed more vital. Was it an *n* — or, perhaps, an *m?* It might have been a *y* — but, then again, could just as easily have been an *l*. Picking up still more speed, dripping with still more sweat, I cranked up the volume of my heart.

But I took an unfortunate turn: instead of darting along one of the neighbourhood's deserted back alleys, I made the mistake of bolting down Durocher, which, at 8:35, was already teeming. Morning prayers over, Hasids flooded the street, and I was drowning in a sea of fur-trimmed hats and black satin coats. Dark beards and scrawny shoulders pushed past, while the gazes of their owners slid right through me; I felt, for a moment, the loneliness of the invisible. And they were loud, so loud, calling to each other in a tumult of Yiddish and Hebrew, in the vulgar vox populi of the European *shtetl*.

Beginning on the steps of the synagogue and slowly but surely filling the entire street, a thousand separate cries of *gut shabbes!* rang out, and joined forces to become an inescapable wall of sound. I couldn't hear what my heart had been trying so hard to tell me. Not for the first time, I experienced a bitter surge of hatred for this particular type of Jew, whose shrill holiness dominated the bandwidth of religious sensibility, silencing stiller smaller voices until the only signals that were audible were those spoken in the first person plural, in the cultish key of we.


**I LURCHED INTO** the kitchen to find Lev and Alex making cheese and jam sandwiches. Samara sat at the table, reading a book. They had their backs to me and didn't notice my entrance. Alex, who had just finished his first year at McGill, was gushing on with his usual intensity.

"But it's not just intentional messages we've got to think of, really we've been sending signals into space for years and years, because our radio signals flow way out across the galaxy, and conceivably, I mean, with a big enough telescope, someone could pick up on all that —"

"Hello, Alex," I said. "Still waiting for E.T. to call?"

The boys spun around. Alex, blushing, was rendered momentarily speechless. Samara shot me a sharp glance that held the tinge of a warning: she was ready to leap to Alex's defence. Then Lev saw the patina of sweat glazing my face and throat.

"Did you go running?" he asked quietly. Opprobrium was so foreign to Lev's voice that it invariably gave it a hushed quality.

"Yep."

"Is that, you know, healthy? I mean, shouldn't you be resting?"

"Probably," I laughed. "But I feel fine. In fact, I've never felt better."

Alex, who seemed to have regained his voice, muttered, "You should be careful. The heart is a delicate organ."

"Excuse me? Delicate? Did you say *delicate?*"

"Sure. Yeah. I mean the slightest frequencies — like, even radio frequencies — can impact the tissue, so."

I opened my mouth, then closed it. "You're saying my heart is a radio?"

Alex smiled the grateful smile of a person who is, for once, in his element. "Well, not exactly a radio, maybe, but definitely able to pick up signals. More like an antenna," he said, his body turning ever so slightly toward Samara. Even after all these years, he never missed an opportunity to show off in front of her.

"Did the doctor say it was okay for you to be running?" Lev said.

"What kind of signals?" I asked Alex.

"Oh, well, you know. Like, doctors use radio frequencies to repair damaged passages in the heart sometimes? Like, radiofrequency ablation of an accessory pathway, let's say?"

"Maybe I should call Dr. Singh," Lev said.

"Oh, I already called," I lied. "He said it's fine as long as I take it easy. Which I am." Lev looked dubious, so I picked up the pill bottle on the counter, popped it open, and poured some of the white capsules into my palm to show him. "Besides, Dr. Singh gave me this. Digitalis, it's called."

"What does it do?"

"These little white helpers? Lub-dub, lub-dub, lub-dub."

"What?"

"They help the ticker tick faster."

"What?"

"The heart. They make it contract. Make it pump harder."

"Harder? But is that, you know, safe?"

"Doctor's orders," I shrugged, tilting the pills back into the bottle. "Don't worry. I've got an appointment with him on Thursday, so I can double-check then."

Lev nodded, placated at last, and bit into his sandwich. But now Samara was looking me over as if I might collapse onto the kitchen tiles at any moment.

I weighed the advantages and disadvantages of asking Alex to elaborate on the radio heart concept. Showing interest in this kid's field of study was dangerous, a fact I knew from watching Sam get trapped listening to his hour-long lectures. There was a bloodhound devotion to the way he pursued his science, and a certain hazardous sadness in the relentlessness of it; you had the impression that he looked skyward not just for pulsars and quasars but for emotional companionship and spiritual solace. I decided to research radio waves on the internet instead. Taking a glass of lemonade from the fridge, I went back to my study, where the manuscript was waiting.

TWO WEEKS AFTER the heart attack, I found myself back in the hospital. Singh had called to say he wanted to run additional tests. What kind of tests? I asked. And was told: the usual. A chest x-ray. An ECG. A cardiac MRI.

Because I didn't want to give Singh the satisfaction of seeing that his spooky medical acronyms unsettled me, and because I didn't want to worry my kids any more than was strictly necessary, and because my sexy professor image had been diminished enough in Val's eyes as it was, I'd come alone. And remained convinced of the rightness of this decision throughout the first two tests. An x-ray was nothing, really; I'd done it a dozen times at the dentist's office over the years. An ECG? Piece of cake. Singh placed probes on my chest and monitored the signals in and around my heart. His eyebrows shimmied higher on his forehead, and even when his face struggled and failed to hide his growing consternation, I did not pester him with questions. I was, in short, a model patient.

It was only once we got to the MRI that I felt something like fear. Lying flat on my back in the tubular machine, I imagined I could feel the magnetic field buzzing around me. It was a strange feeling made all the more unsettling by its filmic quality. How many movies had I seen in which, at the crest of the protagonist's travails, he was reduced to lying in one of these dreary tubes? And how many of those protagonists had escaped death? The statistics on this point were not encouraging and so, to keep my mind from spiralling into panic, I took refuge in naming. Adam had tamed the animals by christening them *lion* and *bear* and *snake*; the first step toward mastering one's world is to bend it to language. Quickly, I dredged up that most comforting of languages — science — and tried to describe in its vocabulary what was happening to my body.

The MRI machine was emitting a magnetic field. The magnetic field was aligning atomic particles in my cells. Radio waves would then be broadcasted toward these particles, producing signals that varied according to the type of tissue they were. Images of the heart would be created from these signals, and Singh would study these images to determine the cause and nature of the murmur...

I found myself wishing, for the first time in decades, that my parents could be at my side. Wishing for the iron-fisted but stolid presence of my engineer father, the meek and comforting presence of my mother. Their scientific-mindedness. Their zero tolerance for mystical mumbo-jumbo. The total and utter *secularness* of them. All the qualities that had driven me away from them at age seventeen, and straight into the arms of the yeshiva world where I'd met Miriam — and then, years later, straight out of that world and into the world of academia.

Theirs had been a life of dinner parties and office parties, carved turkeys and apple pies: two personalities happily constrained by the trappings of the nuclear family and the traditional values that went along with it. There was no room in that tight-lipped world of theirs for doubt. It was an environment built for certainties, not for faith. Because there could be no faith, there could also be no miracles, and as a lonely geeky teenager I had wanted miracles, had needed the exhilarating upward swing into intimacy with something greater and wiser than myself, had been prepared to sacrifice anything — intellectual integrity included — on the altar of that great need.

But extreme swings of the pendulum lead, almost inexorably, to extreme swings in the opposite direction. And so, just a few years after Miriam gave birth to Lev, naming him "heart" in the full burst of our shared devoutness, I began to realize that my wife — like my whole religious life — embodied nothing more nor less than another iteration of certainty. Her belief was exactly like my parents', only reversed. Repulsed by the bright glow of faith in her cheeks, I scurried into the cool and comforting shadows of forbidden bookstores. There, I read the sorts of secular treatises that would have made my yeshiva teachers spit in disgust. I was drawn to philosophy at first — Nietzsche, Kafka — and then to biblical criticism. As I surrendered the idea that every word in the Bible came directly from the mouth of God, another idea — that life was utterly meaningless and that was perfectly okay — leapt up to take its place. I dropped out of yeshiva and enrolled in university. Because I gave the impression that I wasn't abandoning the faith, just the school I had attended for the past several years, Miriam accepted it. She wasn't happy, but she accepted it.

And then I discovered Gershom Scholem. The founder of the academic study of kabbalah was doubly forbidden to me: for an Orthodox Jew under the age of forty to study mysticism was already taboo; to study it using this secular apparatus was unimaginable. I didn't care. I couldn't stop. In Scholem, I found a thinker who thrilled not to the long et cetera of petty details typical of organized religion, but to the transcendent aspects of Judaism — and who applied critical tools to those aspects without transforming them into desiccated dogma. To read Scholem was to run along a razor blade, its sweet edge cutting into me again and again. With every page I became more bloodied and more brazen.

For Miriam, that was the last straw. When I'd brought Nietzsche's *Beyond Good and Evil* into the house, she'd frowned. When I'd brought books on biblical criticism, the frown had deepened to a scowl. But the day I came home carrying Scholem's *Major Trends in Jewish Mysticism* was the day we had our first yelling match. She lost it then — maybe because she could see the light in my eyes, the light of a new love, a love that didn't include her. She ripped the book apart in front of me. I did the only thing I could think to do, the thing I knew would hurt her most: I marched into the bathroom and shaved my beard.

For a day, two days, three days, she could barely bring herself to look at me. On the third day she came home wearing her usual scarf and, summoning me to the bedroom, swept it off to reveal a shockingly bald head. I stared at the egglike surface and something inside me cracked. Her long, sensuous black hair — which she'd kept covered ever since our wedding, but which had always been a source of behind-closed-doors pleasure for me — gone. This wasn't just a competition anymore; we were locked in a war. I went to bed shaking with rage.

And that was why, when Miriam left the house the next day and went to the grocery store to buy saltines, fucking *saltines*, and got hit by a car and *died*, a part of me was horrified but a part of me was vindicated, was triumphant, and that was the part of me that felt like screaming from the rooftops: Yes! Yes! Exactly! Yes! *That* is how meaningless life can be!

I heard a beep. In the dark confines of the tubular machine, I opened my eyes. The MRI was done. My atomic particles, like kids at the end of a long school day, breathed a collective sigh of relief as the machine released them to their natural alignments. When I emerged, Singh told me to return in a couple of weeks; he would have the results then, and we would know more. He handed me a prescription refill. I took it shakily and passed him without a word.


YOU HAD TO GIVE Saint Teresa credit. She must have been pretty spry for a nun; not just any old woman could have reformed those naughty Spanish Carmelites the way she did. With an outstretched arm and a mighty hand. To think that before she turned up, they

were only engaging in ceremonial flagellation once every few weeks —
the laxity!

But really, the remarkable thing about her was her mystical philosophy, her description of the stages of the soul's ascent toward God.
Particularly the stage she referred to as the "prayer of quiet," in which
the human will is lost and subsumed in the will of the divine. The
mind, Saint T reasoned, had to abandon all superficial activity if it
was to engage in the deeper activity of opening itself to God. It must
be self-emptied and still. Don't think anything, was the basic idea.
*No pensar nada.*

I wondered, as I plowed through texts in my study, if this quietist
philosophy might have influenced the European Jewish mystics — the
Hasids. Though you'd be hard-pressed to show a direct line of influ-
ence, I thought I could sketch the outlines of a plausible story. The
Hasids of Eastern Europe would have been in contact, not always
ungentle, with their gentile neighbours. Among these neighbours
would have been the Russian spiritualists, who would have inherited
the ideas of certain fathers in the Eastern Orthodox Church — quite
possibly their doctrine of *hesychasm*, of "quietude." Silence the mind;
abandon the ego; detach, detach, detach — when the Hasids spoke of
rising to the vessel of Ayin, of ego-annihilation, they could almost be
describing quietude. Had the Jews adopted this gentile notion, garb-
ing it in the vocabulary of their own tradition to make it seem more
kosher, less intellectually *treif*?

Struck by a sudden memory, I stood up, left my study, and walked
across the hall.

Lev's bedroom, with its pale blue walls and neatly made bed,
felt peaceful even in his absence. It was as if, simply by living here,
he had rarefied the air around him. I scanned the titles on his bookshelf until I found the volume I was looking for: one of Lev's early
primers on Hasidism, a sort of religious digest that cobbled together
the ideas of various disciples of the Baal Shem Tov, the father of the
Hasidic movement, recasting them in language simple enough to

entice new followers. I picked it up sheepishly — years ago, I had tried to warn Lev off this proselytizing genre — then flipped to the passage I remembered:

> You must make your heart like an empty instrument
> so that the spirit of God can blow through you. Any
> blockage at all will prevent the making of this divine
> music. Even something that is traditionally considered
> good and worthy can constitute a blockage: knowledge,
> for instance. What is required is a certain emptiness,
> or quietness, of mind.

Here was a dead ringer for old Saint T! And as much as I had always found the anti-intellectual *no pensar nada* approach distasteful, wasn't this kind of right? Knowledge *was* a blockage, or at least it sometimes could be. After all, birds didn't fly by studying the laws of aerodynamics; any brain capable of carrying that type of knowledge would be too heavy to stay up in the air. A certain lightness, a certain weightlessness, was what was required for flights up into the Godhead — that seemed to me now the main, if not the only, mystical prerequisite.

It was the reason Myra Goldfarb would never make it anywhere near Ayin, or Nirvana, or any such thing. It was the reason, if I was honest, why I would never make it there either. I had wanted to believe that she and I were polar opposites, but now I saw that we had this in common: we were both too weighed down by the cumbersome luggage of a graduate-level education.

Taking Lev's book with me, I returned to my room and laid myself carefully on the bed. Outside, a light rain began to fall. Tiny raindrops pattered on the roof. For a moment, I imagined that they were penetrating the ceiling and landing directly on my heart. *Gutta cavat lapidem*, I thought to myself. Then I closed my eyes and waited for sleep to claim me.

BY THE TIME the doorbell woke me, twilight filled my bedroom with a soft blue glow. I heard footsteps shuffling down the hall to the front door, then voices from the stoop filtering in through my window. Samara and Alex chatting while they waited for Lev to get back from evening prayers. As always, the talk turned to Alex's favourite topic.

"And yet it's so weird, you know, because Einstein was totally right!" Alex was saying now. "Except he didn't have the courage to stick to his results! He was all like, no, yeah, the universe can't be expanding, I must've forgotten to carry a one, I must've miscalculated there. And then — can you imagine? — *years later*, the Hubble Telescope suddenly starts sending back all these crazy photos, and the scientists are like: um, hello, you were right! The universe *is* expanding!"

Samara laughed.

I groaned inwardly. She thought she was being kind, but this was not kind. She was stringing him along. Case in point: When, for her sixteenth birthday, he'd given her a vintage five-volume box set of *Scientific American* books, she'd accepted it. Not only that, but she'd arranged these five books in an alternating pattern with the five books of the Torah, so that, trailing your finger along her bedroom bookshelf, you hit: Genesis, *The New Astronomy*, Exodus, *The Physics and Chemistry of Life*, Leviticus, *Twentieth-Century Bestiary*, Numbers, *Atomic Power*, Deuteronomy, *Automatic Control*. What exactly she was trying to convey about the relationship between science and religion, I had no idea — but whatever it was, Alex loved it. And his love was painful to see.

"Later, Einstein said it was the greatest blunder of his life. Sad, isn't it?"

"Yeah," Samara said. "Definitely."

"Yeah. And now all scientists pretty much agree that the universe is just getting bigger and bigger and bigger, which, you know, is kind of weird to think about." Alex paused, presumably to let the full weirdness of this sink in. In an oddly serious voice, he continued: "The funny thing is, Newton had sort of predicted, way back in the

17th century when he discovered the law of gravity, that the universe can't be finite. Because every object in the universe attracts every other object, right? So if the universe were really finite, then the attractive forces of all the objects should've forced the entire universe to collapse on itself. But that obviously hasn't happened, right? Even though gravity is always attractive."

Before Samara could respond to this observation, Lev's voice announced that he was back.

I got out of bed, made my way down the hall, and opened the front door.

"Hi, Dad," Lev said. "Alex's mom invited me over for dinner. Is it okay if I go?"

"Of course."

He scrutinized me, as if trying to gauge the effect of his absence from the dinner table in terms of the minutes, hours, or years it might take off my life. "Are you sure? I could stay if you want. I mean if you wanted to have —"

"No, go. Really, it's fine. Samara and I can eat together, right?" She nodded — almost imperceptibly. As if the thought caused her physical pain. "See? It's fine. Give my best to your mom," I added to Alex, even though I had never actually met her. Even though I had actually studiously avoided meeting her. Not because I suspected there was anything wrong with her — if the praise Lev persisted in heaping on her over years' worth of family dinners was any indication, she was a thoroughly lovely person — but because the boys' blatant attempts to set us up had always made me feel uncomfortable.

Alex acknowledged my words with a polite nod, shot Samara a quick backward glance, and led the way down the path. Lev said, "Bye, Dad," and followed.

With the boys gone, the house seemed colder and darker. In the kitchen, the natural light had all but drained from the windows. I flipped the switches, laughing, "Let there be light!" but the vague upward tilt of Samara's lips was only the caricature of a smile.

Working side by side in a kind of meditative muteness, we threw together some leftover roast beef and stir-fried vegetables, and sat down to eat. At Lev's request, Samara had been coming home for Friday night dinners since she moved out of the house three years ago. But she often made excuses not to, so her presence at the table still felt strange, unexpected.

"So," I said. "How's summer so far?"

"Good," she said.

"Yeah?" When this met with no response, I tried another tack. "How's Jenny?"

"She's fine."

"What's she up to this summer? She working?"

"Well, no, she just graduated. She's taking a bit of a break."

"Oh, that's nice. That's good! Does she want to pursue music professionally, I mean, now that she's graduated?"

"You mean painting. She studied painting."

"What? No, I thought she was in music?"

"Nope."

"Oh."

"Can you pass the stir-fry?"

"You're sure it wasn't music?"

"Pretty sure." Reaching across the table, she took the dish.

I tried to laugh. "Guess my memory's not what it used to be." She said nothing to this, so I said, "You used to be kind of into music, though, remember? Remember, when you were nine and I took you to Steve's to pick out an instrument? Remember what you picked?"

She muttered something inaudible.

"Sorry?"

"Eight. I was eight."

"Right," I said impatiently. "But do you remember what instrument you picked out?"

"The triangle."

"Yes! The triangle!" I laughed again, but she didn't seem to see the humour in this. Didn't seem to understand what was funny about a kid being taken to a top-of-the-line music store, cram-jammed with violins and flutes, Fenders and Strats, and, upon being told she could select any instrument in the store, choosing to leave with a dinky triangle!

I'd tried, gently, to interest her first in the Steinway piano, then in a couple of nice wooden recorders, even in an electric guitar. She wanted nothing to do with any of them. She wanted the triangle and only the triangle. Trying to be supportive, I'd bought it for her, assuring the salesperson that we'd probably be back for another, more serious instrument, you know, once she tired of this one.

But she hadn't tired of it. She would sit there, on the floor of her bedroom, dinging that triangle for hours on end, as if all the secrets of the universe were audible in the rest between one note and the next. As she grew older she got less obsessive about the triangle, but not about listening in that strange way. When she was thirteen, I would find her sitting with the telephone pressed to her ear, saying nothing, hearing nothing, except, presumably, the dial tone. The next day, she'd be crouching in front of the dishwasher, attending to its chaotic rumblings as if she were in possession of a primer that allowed her and only her to hear its hidden harmonies. I told myself this was creepy. I told her to stop it. Didn't she have homework to do, tests to study for?

But now, placing a hand on my heart to still its murmuring, I began to doubt my motives. What if I'd tried to stop her not because I found her behaviour weird, but because, watching her, I had felt a twinge of something like envy? It was as if, by listening to the static embedded in musical notes, dial tones, dishwasher noise, she believed she could attain enlightenment. An enlightenment I already knew would never be mine. There was no secret chord I could play to please the Lord.

"That triangle," I said, "do you still have it?"

"No," she said.

We ate our dessert in silence, cleared the dishes, and went to our separate rooms.

**THREE HOURS LATER**, I was lying in bed with Valérie, spent and exhilarated by the fuckfest that had ended minutes earlier. I felt relieved that she still wanted me in that violent reckless way — and that I could still get it up — but also strangely sad. Her old landlord was moving around upstairs, and the lonely sounds of plodding footsteps, clinking beer bottles, droning television reruns — all of these struck me as singularly depressing.

It was a clear night. A star was winking at me through the window. The wink seemed congratulatory, like a dorm-room high-five bestowed on a geeky freshman who has bedded a girl everyone knows is out of his league. Then I remembered that the light had actually been emitted eons earlier. For all I knew, that star was probably dead.

Turning away from the light, I gazed instead at Val's left leg, where a large and slightly raised birthmark sat an inch above the kneecap. This had always been my favourite part of her body. The bluish spot looked like a map of an imaginary continent. If you peered closely, it was possible to see tiny streets and houses, rivers and forests, men and women and birds and fish all going about their business. I pressed my ear to the birthmark, hoping to hear... what? The hallowed harmonies of the grand design, the music of the spheres? Stroking the back of her knee, I listened with one ear for the sounds of her sighing and with the other for the spinning of this lost and secret world. But the sound of a lighter snapped me out of my trance.

Lying back, I saw that Val had a lit joint pinched between thumb and forefinger. In the glow of the Zippo she took a toke, then handed it to me. This was one of the rituals into which she'd inducted me months ago: the post-coital joint. Infinitely preferable, she believed, to the post-coital cigarette. Most nights I was happy to oblige; there had even been one or two occasions when we had gotten so stoned that I still felt the effects the following morning. Tonight, however, I held up a straight-edge palm to say: no thank you.

"*Ça va?*"

"*C'est rien.* Just not in the mood."

A pause, wherein she regarded me intently. Then, with her joint-holding fingers, she brushed the hair out of her eyes and straddled me. "So serious," she said in a put-on baritone, imitating my furrowed brow. "And what are you thinking about so seriously?"

I studied her face suspended above mine, its soft vatic lines. The mouth was smiling. The cheeks were smiling. And the eyes? They were also smiling. But in them there was something else as well: an uncivilized, howling aloneness that never failed to make me feel grateful to know her, because it was the very facsimile of my own.

And yet: how could I tell her what I was really thinking? If I started babbling about Ayin, about how it was supposed to be the "crown of Ani," about how this idea nevertheless made me feel vaguely sad and lonely, wouldn't she look at me like I was crazy? Our relationship was based on irony, studied distance, intellectual detachment — not this earnestness, not all of these goddamn *feelings*.

I took her face in my hands and said, "I was thinking about Hubble."

She laughed. "Of course."

"I was thinking about how really fundamentally odd it is that the universe is expanding. Odd and, I don't know, disturbing I guess."

"Why?"

"Why what?"

"Why do you find it disturbing?"

"Don't you?"

She exhaled smoke. "No."

I stared at her. After a minute, I shook my head. "No, I didn't use to either. I don't know why it seems strange to me now. All that empty space."

"You don't know that it's empty. There might be other people — creatures — out there."

"No, you're right, that's true. But I meant..."

"The abyss, *c'est ça?* The void."

"Yes," I said. "I keep picturing us, our little planet, zooming off into this never-ending space that only gets bigger and bigger, with nothing to zoom toward." She was looking at me quietly, with the halved patience of a young mind that has spent its best years behind ivy-covered walls. The strands of ivy were already in her hair; soon they would be tangled in her eyes. "It's stupid, I know."

"No. It's not." She touched my brow, then leaned down and kissed me.

It was a gentle kiss, and I knew that she meant it as a token of affection or support, but the gesture only made me feel old. I was reminded, suddenly, of the increasing greyness of my hair. Of the parched skin of my hands, my face, my lips. In the apartment above us, the old landlord pushed back a chair, stood up, walked across the room. The sound of a door opening and closing followed. I shut my eyes for an instant and, opening them on the doorway of the bedroom, thought I saw the shadowy profile of an ancient man. The Angel of Death, proffering my coat and hat, beckoning me out into the night. With a violent motion like that of a dog shaking water out of its fur, I shook the image from my mind.

Val looked at me oddly, but somehow, in the next second, she seemed to know just what to do. She ashed the joint, turned off the lamp, and lay down beside me. Our warm bodies just barely touching. Not the supernova of two people newly in love, not the sticky melding together of disparate identities, but a constellation of adjacent alonenesses, a parallel glide through space.


THE FEELING I HAD after running for forty-five minutes was midway between nausea and vertigo. I stood hunched over with my hands on my thighs, a grimace on my face, sweat pooling in the salty cradle of my neck. Three Hasidic boys, all dressed in identical striped shirts, whizzed past me on their scooters. A pair of little girls raced in the opposite direction, yellow silk bows flashing in their hair. Plastic dolls ogled me from the neighbours' peeling porch steps.

As I waited to regain my breath, my eyes fell on Katz, who was sitting cross-legged on his front lawn in the blistering summer sun. He had dabbed sunscreen on his face, but had done a careless job of it; a big glob of white was visible on the bridge of his nose, while the entire right side of his face was pink and sunburnt. He looked happy as a lark.

He was still surrounded by an inestimable number of tin cans, but now he was running the twine through the holes he'd created in each of them, humming as he did so. The tune was the sort of wordless, joyful melody often heard in synagogues on Friday nights — a Polish *niggun* — yet Katz's face registered none of the simple pleasure usually worn on the faces of *niggun*-singers. Instead, his eyes had a laser-beam focus that reminded me, strangely, of Alex preparing a science experiment.

The stitch in my side had finally relaxed. I gave Katz a perfunctory wave; then, seeing that he had been completely unaware of my presence, I began to jog down the block, ducking into a backstreet when I saw the indefatigable Mrs. Glassman tottering toward me, muttering under her breath. The green of the trees and the red of the fire hydrants zinged on the undersides of my eyelids. The countless baby strollers, scooters, tricycles, and toy cars that overflowed the porches and littered the curbs — I hurtled over all of them. Houses whipped past. My hands, flat as silverware, sliced the wind on either side of me. First my feet, then my legs began to ache, each strike against pavement sending a shock through the arches and around the ankles and up into the calves, which seized up, relaxed, then seized up again. Bouquets of pain blossomed in each muscle and I welcomed them. In the past few weeks, pain had become, paradoxically, my greatest source of pleasure. Had become my pathway to the still small voice — which was not so still now, not so small — which was growing louder with every heartbeat...

Aaaahhhh...

The first syllable was audible — I tilted murderously forward — the second syllable was welling up, I could hear it wanting, waiting to burst forth…

Aaaahhhh… aaaahhhh…

Ani.

I froze in mid-lunge, crumpled to the ground. A stinking heap of screaming tissues and beaten, battered bones. Ani. I let my body stretch itself out. The pavement felt cool and welcoming against the base of my skull. Ani. Not the indeterminacy of Ayin but Ani, Ani, the nexus of great absolutes — Authority, God, Meaning. I closed my eyes.

Somewhere a voice was calling. Another voice was answering. I opened my eyes. A flock of blackbirds was darting across the whiteness of the clouds. I stared, for a long minute, at the piano key sky. Then I got up and slowly, painfully, began to walk.

Judging from the position of the sun, it must have been at least noon; I marvelled at the fact that I had lain undisturbed on a suburban sidewalk for upwards of an hour. Then, bending my steps in the direction of home, I found myself marvelling at everything around me. The parked car at the corner of Lajoie and Querbes was leaking gasoline onto the pavement, and the iridescence of the resultant rainbow seemed magical and poignant and also terribly human and wasteful and also, for that very reason, achingly beautiful. Tears sprang to my eyes. How vastly things could change in a matter of minutes! In the space of a single heartbeat! Light streamed down, imbuing everything it touched with purpose. On the neighbours' lawns, each blade of grass was swaying with a deliberateness, a grace, that could only have been preordained. I thought of the Hasids in Chagall's hometown, who claimed that behind every blade of grass stands an angel urging it on: Grow! Grow! I thought of Epictetus: I move not without Thy knowledge!

I reached home, drew a deep breath, and smiled at my own obtuseness. Everything my mind had been pitting itself against all these years, I thought as I turned my key in the lock, was everything my heart had been labouring so hard to teach me.

ON THE FIRST MORNING in July, I was reading in my study when the ringing of the phone laid siege to my ears. I sprang up to get the portable. "Hello?"

Silence.

"Hello?"

Silence.

"Hello?"

The sound of the phone being replaced in its catch followed.

Cursing the mystery caller under my breath, I returned to my book only to be disturbed a minute later by renewed ringing. With an edge of irritation that I didn't bother to keep out of my voice, I snapped, "Hello."

"Hello! Um, David, it's Ira."

"Oh. Ira. Hello."

"Hello," he repeated, somewhat stupidly.

"Yes. Now that we've established that, was there any specific reason you called?"

"I thought I'd see how you're feeling these days. How are you feeling these days?"

"Not very well," I answered, with increasing tremolo. "Unfortunately."

"Ah, mm-hmm, yes? Well. That is unfortunate, yes." A pause. "Nevertheless, I —"

"I've been working on grading those papers, though." I glanced at the corner of my desk, where the eighty exam booklets were gathering dust beneath a jumbo-size box of tissue. The rest of the desk was strewn with my notes on the Tree of Life.

"Ah! The term papers? Really?" he said with manufactured surprise, as if that had not been the very — the only — reason for his call.

"Really," I said, adding, "slow but steady wins the race."

"Yes, absolutely! Slow but steady, as the saying goes. That's great. So, ah, when can we expect, I mean, when do you think you might have the papers ready by, approximately?"

"Oh, well…"

"Yes?" he encouraged.

"It's hard to say…"

"Yes?"

"But possibly…"

"Yes, yes?"

"Next week. Assuming —"

"Great! That's great. Well, I'm glad to hear you're feeling so much better, and I'll look forward to seeing those grades next week. How are the kids?"

The shrewd bastard. "Excellent. Really excellent."

"Glad to hear it! Well, David, I'll let you get back to your work. Bye for now!" he said and hung up.

I stood in place for a long moment, listening to the dial tone as if it were speaking to me in a foreign dialect, which, with some little skill, I might be able to parse successfully. After several seconds of concerted effort failed to yield any tangible results, I gave up and dialled.

"*Allo?*" answered the voice at the other end.

TWO HOURS LATER, Val and I were sitting across from each other at her kitchen table, late afternoon light haloing her warm brown hair. She was reading *Meister Eckhart: The Man from Whom God Hid Nothing*. I was reading term papers on Saint Teresa's quietist philosophy.

But I wasn't getting very far. Whereas most of the papers had simply been pathetically misguided — the work of bad writers and even worse thinkers — the one I now had propped up on my knee was the work of an intelligent mind. The prose was impeccable, the diction high, the argument complex. And yet the whole thing was so strictly English Department, so clearly the product of a Lit Crit course, that it made me want to hurl it across the room.

Saint T, the writer argued, was not the saintly figure her orthodox admirers made her out to be. A close reading of her autobiography revealed a subtle yet striking anomian strain. To show just how deep this strain ran, the writer quoted Saint T extensively. Her analysis of every quotation was seductively logical — but how it turned my stomach! Because underlying the whole project was a way of reading that took for granted the indeterminacy of the text, that saw it as little more than a free play of signifiers, which was the reader's to do with as she wished. The Author was dead, and dead, too, was the idea of absolute meaning or ultimate reality. Meaning was free-flowing, cried *la nouvelle critique*, meaning was up to the reader to produce! You wanted to read Saint T as a closet heretic? Why not! You wanted to make her into a radical feminist, anarchist, punk, goth, modernist, neoliberal, vegetarian? Go for it!

The Author must die so that the reader may live: it was an idea that was very familiar to me. I, too, had been taught to read enthusiastically and badly, to cherrypick, to indulge poetic license at the expense of textual particulars. And I, too, had enjoyed being given such freedoms. Yet now this refusal to fix meaning repulsed me. It was idiotic, it was absurd.

I laid down the paper and looked at Val. Her gaze was trained on the page, but something in her expression caught my eye. "Are you studying?"

"Yes."

"Really?"

"Yes."

"Because you've got a thoroughly extracurricular look on your face."

She laughed — a warm, roundish laugh — and slipped into my lap. The perfume of her collarbone filled my head with a kind of rosé haze, a schoolboy tipsiness I hadn't felt in decades. She leaned into me and I kissed her until, glancing at her watch, she excused herself for just a minute, leaving me to grin at the kitchen tiles.

I wandered into her bedroom and sat on the bed. On the nightstand, three photographs showed Val and a friend on their recent trip to Europe. I sighed, remembering how much I had always wanted to travel the world — to see it all — to see everything. The birth of my kids and the death of their mother had made that impossible; still, I had found other ways...

Beside the photographs, an issue of the *New Yorker* was opened to a page tightly crammed with text. The heading read *Vladimir Nabokov: Letters from a Touring Writer.* In a letter addressed to Nabokov's wife, someone had flagged the middle paragraph:

> ...tiresome conversation, which lasted right to Hartsville.
> At six on the dot I was driven into a magnificent estate,
> to the magnificent multi-pillared mansion of Mrs. Coker,
> and here I remain as a guest until Tuesday. As soon as
> I barged in she told me that in ten minutes the guests
> invited in my honor would arrive, and at breakneck speed
> I began to bathe and tug at my dinner-jacket armor. I love
> you. The shirt came out so starched that the cufflinks
> would not go through the cuffs and it ended with one of
> them rolling under the bed (to be discovered only today).

I stopped there. Exactly three words of the passage were underlined — *I love you* — and I thought I could see why. Between a sentence about his dinner jacket and one about his missing cufflinks, the writer had snuck a hint of something genuine, the way Jews tuck their notes of prayer into the Wailing Wall. Nestled amid ego and petty details, a glimpse of truth, a flash of revelation.

I replaced the magazine on the table and looked over at the photographs of my lover. I could not offer her any such three-word phrases; she'd get no revelatory flashes from me. And my inability to utter that simple sentence would one day be the shibboleth that would turn her against me. What did I stand to give her, anyway? A radiant mind, a decaying body, a sick heart. That was it, that was all. The longer I stood there, warming myself by the lamplight of her youth, the more

I could feel death gliding toward me with the slow, inevitable grace of a mathematical proof. It would come upon me one of these days, ripping my hands from the branches of a half-grasped Tree — and then what use would I have made of my life?

I heard the click of a door opening, then closing. Val came into the bedroom, slipping her cell phone into her jeans. She put her arms around my neck and kissed me.

"It's getting late," I said.

"Hmm?"

"It's past five, I should go."

"*Tu veux pas rester ici?*"

"No, I should get home. Have dinner with my kids, for once."

"Okay. I can drive you, *si tu veux*."

"*Non, ça va, je vais prendre un taxi*."

"Ah, okay," she repeated, and looked at me quietly. "How are they taking it, by the way? Your kids — they must have been scared by the heart attack — by what could have happened, no?"

I blinked. With all their anxious inquiries about me, had I even asked them?

I took Val's face in my hands and pressed my mouth first to her lips, then to the crown of her head, where it lingered for a longish moment. "*Tu es tellement belle*," I whispered into her hair, and left.

When I got home, Samara was nowhere to be seen, and Lev was getting ready to head out somewhere, too.

"Where's your sister?" I asked from the doorway of his bedroom. And suddenly realized, with a surprising surge of irritation, how often I was found skulking in doorways. As if this weren't my house. As if these weren't my children. I took a step forward into the room.

"With Jenny, I think. They said they were going to a concert?"

"Oh. Right." Earlier, Samara had mentioned that she would be out late. Or, to be more precise, had called it carelessly over her shoulder as she disappeared out the front door in the afternoon, a laughing Jenny orbiting around her like a waxing gibbous moon.

Lev was zipping up his ratty blue backpack.

"And where are you heading?" I asked.

"I'm going over to Mr. Katz's house for a bit."

"What for?"

"Um, he asked me to help him out with a project?"

"What sort of project?"

"I don't know, exactly."

"This wouldn't have anything to do with those tin cans he's got piled up on his lawn?"

"I don't know, Dad." He braced his shoulders. "But, you know. He doesn't have that many friends, so."

"So. How's he doing these days, anyway? Mentally, I mean?"

Lev's eyes widened with surprise. He stared at me for a moment, as if he were entertaining some novel possibility — the possibility, perhaps, of confiding in me. The features of his face seemed to open up, to broaden out — I had the impression of blinds being lifted, windows being raised — and through his unshuttered eyes I could see straight through to his most inward self, and it was a perfect sky, as clean and fresh and blue as the inside of clouds. But in the next instant the shutters came down.

"He's okay, I think. I have to go, Dad — sorry, I'm late. Bye!" He swung his backpack onto his shoulder and disappeared.

A moment later there was a knock at the door. I opened it to find Mr. Glassman on the stoop.

"Oh — hello," I said, taking in the man's white hair, his cobwebbed skin.

"Hello, Mr. Meyer," he said. "It is so good to see you are back home, safe and healthy. You are recovering nicely, yes?"

"Yes. Thanks. Uh, are you looking for Lev?" My son didn't take lessons from our old neighbour anymore, but as the two of them were still friendly, that seemed like the safest guess.

Softly, almost apologetically, Glassman shook his head. "I am looking for Samara, actually. Is she here? She has moved back home, no?"

"No — I mean yes, she did move back home for the summer, but no, she's not here."

"Ah." Glassman sighed. "I was hoping... she might explain... some things to me..." His hand, the victim of a faint tremor, lifted a book into view. *King Lear*. Not just any *King Lear*: Samara's old school-issued copy.

"What are you doing with that?" I asked, my voice harsher than I'd intended.

Glassman bowed his head, looking very sorry, even ashamed. "I found it... in my things... your daughter, she forgot it..."

In my mind, I completed the sentence for him: *she forgot it when she was studying with me in secret. When she chose to read books with me, not you.*

"Well, she's not here."

"Perhaps I could leave this here for her then? That way, if she wants, she could come and talk with me about it?"

"Just keep it."

"But it is her book — she should have —"

"Keep it," I repeated, and shut the door.

I crossed the hall and entered my study, breathing heavily. From the window, I could just make out Katz's house, where Lev was getting up to who-knew-what. A moment later, I saw old Glassman re-enter his home, his slight frame silhouetted in the second-floor bedroom. I stood there for a long time, thinking about how these two men had, over the course of a single summer, stolen my son's heart away from me. Their piety had drawn him in a way my skepticism never could. Ironically, just as Samara's interest in religion was dropping off — after her bat mitzvah, she never showed any interest in it again — her brother surprised us all by taking up the discarded mantle of observance and announcing his intention to wear it to the end of his days. At the time, I had blamed these two men for driving a wedge between my son and me. Yet, even then, I realized I could not say the same for my daughter. No, I had done *that* all on my own.

**IF VAL KNEW** I was avoiding her, she was doing a good job of hiding it. And this was typical Val: calm, composed, utterly non-clingy. In the past, I'd have counted myself lucky to have found someone of this description; now, two weeks after our last encounter, it gave me an unsettled feeling to be rubbing up against the surface of all that cool.

I knew that I had to break things off with her, and I was dragging my feet about it, and knowing this only made me drag my feet more. Worse, there was a clairvoyant quality to the silence she was broadcasting: I was sure she knew what was coming, though she didn't say a word. The fact that she didn't say a word was how I knew she knew. But I still couldn't bring myself to do it. To deliver the speech, make the call, get tangled up in an emotional upheaval — it's not you, it's me, mea culpa, mea culpa — that would distract from the thing I really wanted to be devoting all my mental and physical energies to: the Tree.

I was throwing myself into work like never before, burying myself in arcane manuscripts, checking and re-checking the variant texts and making assiduous notes. Intent on getting my hands on everything to do with the ten vessels — but especially Ani and Ayin — I hauled myself over to the university libraries late at night, when I was sure the stacks would be reasonably empty. I Xeroxed any manuscripts I wasn't allowed to take home, and the photocopied pages rose on my desk, forming a precarious structure that threatened to collapse at any moment but managed miraculously to endure. Surrounded by these religious texts, I laughed, thinking that like my namesake I'd found a hell of a way to ward off death: according to an old rabbinic tale, King David studied the Bible nonstop because he knew that the Angel of Death could not lay claim to his soul so long as it was immersed in Torah study.

I interrupted my research only to go running — which I had begun to do with increasing frequency and, also, with increasing confusion. Racing down the same streets, expecting to hear the same message,

I suddenly was not so sure of what I had originally heard. About the first syllable, yes, I was certain. That aaaahhhh was unmistakable. But now the second syllable seemed to slip and quaver like an arrow which, buffeted around by the breeze, has trouble meeting its mark. Was it really an *n* sound? Didn't it sound, after all, much more like a *y*? The more ground I covered, the more convinced I became that my first impression had been mistaken, and that what I was actually hearing was not Ani, Ani, Ani but Ayin, Ayin, Ayin.

My mistake seemed clear in retrospect, as well as pathetically psychoanalyzable: it was fear of death, of the void, that had closed my ears to the true message of my heart, making me prefer the pretty lie of somethingness to the terrifying truth of nothingness. I would steel myself, now, against the comforting lie. I would not make the same blunder twice.

I had thought I was too weighed down to reach the lofty regions of Ayin — but maybe I'd been wrong. Because, for all the psychopathic undertones to be heard in a man's insistence that his heart was speaking, yes, actually speaking to him in human language, the murmur was beginning to sound like something distinctly greater than a murmur. It was beginning to sound like a promise: stick with me and you'll go far. Stick with me and you'll fly straight to the top.

There was, unfortunately, one problem. My body was habituating to my new fitness regime, with the result that I had to run at higher and higher speeds to get my heart rate to the point where the words became audible. To keep achieving the necessary clarity of pitch, I would need to run impossibly fast. Yet, impossible or not, I had no choice: I was driven by a dreadful fatalism, a kind of two-plus-two logical implacability that is the way with all *idées fixes*. It spurred me on in the same way and for the same reasons that desire spurred lovers to enter into disastrous affairs: because the human brain seemed hardwired for this sort of obsession; because it was the root of all figures of beauty; because, as Marcus Aurelius said, it loved to happen.

SINGH STOOPED OVER ME, stethoscope pressed to my chest, while I tried to breathe normally. I could barely contain my excitement. Finally, I was going to get some answers. But why was he still using the stethoscope? Why didn't he just stand very still and, well, listen?

At last, he straightened up and gave me a stern doctorly look. "Have you been working?"

"No."

"Doing any kind of physical exercise?"

"No."

"Sexual intercourse?"

"N-no."

He looked satisfied. "Good. Well, Mr. Meyer, you seem to be recovering nicely."

"Excuse me?"

"Very nicely, all things considered."

"What do you mean?"

"Well, naturally it's not an overnight process, but I see no reason for con —"

"You've got to be kidding. Can't you ... I mean surely you can ... don't you hear it?"

"Hear what?"

"The — murmur."

He smiled patiently. "Well, yes, the murmur is there, but as I said, it appears to be benign, if a bit — unusual."

"Unusual! Yes. That's what I meant. Its — its unusualness. Its, ah, volume."

Singh shot me a quizzical look, then grabbed the ends of his stethoscope and raised them to his ears. But before they were even midway to their hairy destinations, I stopped him.

"But — what are you doing?" I said.

"I thought I would have another listen, since you seem so concerned."

"Yes but, but, why do you need that?" I said, pointing at the instrument. "I mean, you said yourself, right before you released me — it's *audible*."

His face now bore an expression that was akin, plus or minus an iota of condescension, to that of a kindergarten teacher whose young charge has just made a terribly charming, terribly *cute* mistake. "I think you must have misunderstood," he said. "When I said audible, I meant, audible *with the stethoscope*."

I chose my next words with great care. "So you don't... hear... anything, now."

"No."

"Right."

"Do you?"

"No."

"Right." He paused. "Let me ask you something. Have you been exposed to any abnormally loud noise in the past few weeks? Rock concerts? Construction work?"

"Yes, I regularly blast Metallica while performing crane demolition in my backyard."

"I'm just trying to rule some things out."

"Such as?"

"Just conditions that are apt to produce ringing in the ear. Tinnitus, Ménière's —"

"Isn't that what van Gogh had?"

"Possibly."

"So, what? You think I've got some kind of hearing damage, on top of everything else?"

"Well, no, nothing's certain, we're just examining all the possibilities. Tinnitus, for example, has been known to produce certain musical hallucinations —"

"So now I'm a madman."

"Please, Mr. Meyer, I'm just trying to —" He paused again. "I'd be happy to run some more tests, if you'd like."

"No more tests," I said, hopping off the examination table with what I hoped was a sprightly step. "Thank you!"

I drove home and contemplated the fact that the medical profession in this province — *vive la patrie!* — was clearly, undeniably, and most depressingly going to shit. I ate dinner alone and railed inwardly against the rabid medicalization of everyday life, the therapeutic society seeking pseudoliberations from pseudodiseases. And yet as soon as I retired to my room, I found myself — like so many bored midwestern housewives with nothing better to do than to self-diagnose into round after round of clinical depression — trawling the internet for answers.

"Tinnitus" yielded over 16,500,000 results. After scrolling through paragraphs marked Objective Tinnitus, Subjective Tinnitus, Pathophysiology, Prevention and Prognosis, I clicked on Notable Individuals. Van Gogh was there, sure enough, along with Goya and Michelangelo. Bono, Eric Clapton, Phil Collins, Moby, Paul Simon, Barbra Streisand, Neil Young, Schumann, and old Ludwig van himself. For a moment, I felt better about the possibility of being included in such a lineup. Then, smack dab in the middle of the list, I spotted another name: Adolf Hitler.

I closed the browser.

The phone rang.

When I went into the kitchen to answer it, the green numbers on the microwave gleamed at me in the darkness. The three digits — a 9, followed by a 1, followed by another 1 — seemed eerie and full of import. Squashing that childish thought, I picked up the phone. "Hello?"

Silence.

"Hello?"

Silence.

"Hell —"

Suddenly it occurred to me. The perception of sound within the human ear in the absence of corresponding external sound. A persistent ringing in the ears. Wasn't this the very definition of tinnitus? I broke out in a sweat. Was it possible that, all these years, I had merely been imagining the ringing of the telephone? It was not a wrong number, it was not a prank call — like the murmur, it was just your garden variety, run-of-the-mill, materially reducible musical hallucination. Wouldn't that explain why no one ever answered when I said hello? A conversation I'd overheard years ago, between thirteen-year-old Alex and Lev, suddenly loomed up — a frightening shadow puppet — against the black canvas of my mind:

*You're not seriously going to go through with this whole bar mitzvah thing, are you?*

*Sure I am. Why not?*

*You believe in all that stuff? The burning bush? The big booming voice from the sky?*

*Why wouldn't I?*

*Because it's so — so — so unscientific! How can that not bother you?*

*I don't know. It just doesn't.*

*Have you ever heard of Occam's Razor?*

*No.*

*It means that, all things being equal, the simplest explanation tends to be the right one.*

*Okay. So?*

*So which is more simple? Which is more likely? That God sent your people into slavery to kill themselves over Pharaoh's pyramids, spoke to Moses from a* burning bush *in the* middle of the desert — *convenient, eh? — and plucked them out of Egypt, only to make them wander for forty years and then get* slaughtered *about six million times by, oh, more or less every nation on the planet? Or that the whole thing was just one big delusion?*

I was delusional: was *that* the simplest explanation? The blackness of the kitchen felt doubly dark, as vast and lonely as interstellar space. The room accordioned in and out, green numbers on the microwave throwing their feeble glow into the expanding void. *No,* I said to myself, and then I repeated it aloud: *no no no no no.*

The doorbell rang.

I froze. What if this was another hallucination? The latest instance of my sickness, my delusion? I dreaded the thought of opening the door to see only night, night, night, and to hear the stars in their thick velvet beds mocking me with tinkling laughs. But the doorbell kept ringing, and finally I marched myself to the front door and opened it.

"Hello!"

I couldn't help it: I breathed a sigh of relief. "*Ira.* What are you doing here?"

"I came to check up on you! And — to bring you this," he said, producing a casserole dish with a flourish.

I groaned inwardly. Not again. When Miriam died, Ira and Judy had been relentless in their delivery of home-cooked meals like this one — a casserole every other day for a month — so that even now, my sharpest memory from that period was of a pile of Tupperware containers that overflowed the fridge and mounted on the kitchen counter — a kindness that took up too much space, intruded on our grief.

"I'm sorry it's taken me so long to come by for a visit," Ira said, misinterpreting my silence. "Judy and I meant to drop this off *ages* ago, but, you know —"

"Oh, no, no — thank you for this. It's very kind of you — really, very kind." I gestured inside. "Would you like to...?"

"Ah, sure, okay, thanks!" He stepped over the threshold and looked around. "It's, ah, been a while since I've been here, hasn't it?"

"Yes, it has."

"Yes, mm-hmm, well. Oh! Here you go." He handed me the casserole, then turned his attention to the various knick-knacks and photographs on the credenza in the hall. He picked up a picture of Miriam, then put it down again.

"Thank Judy for me," I said. "I'm sure this is delicious."

"Mmm? Yes, I will," he murmured, apparently lost in thought. Then, with alarming abruptness, he turned around and swooped in for the kill. "David," he said.

"Ira," I said.

"Is everything all right? I mean, with you?"

"Sure it is. Of course it is. Why wouldn't it be?"

"Well, there's the, ah, medical condition..."

"Minor setback."

"Is it?" he asked, again with alarming abruptness. "I mean, can we expect you to be, ah, ready to teach again in September? Will you feel, ah, rested enough?"

My eyes narrowed. "Of course."

"That's good to hear," he said, and looked as though he genuinely meant it. "I was starting to get a bit — concerned. It's not like you to be late submitting grades, even given the, you know, the present circumstances. So I just thought I'd come here to make sure everything's okay... as a friend," he added.

"Everything's fine, Ira. Really."

But he seemed not to be listening anymore. He was wandering instead down the hallway, where a faint stripe of light was visible beneath the door of my study.

I followed him. "Really, really fine, in fact I'm very excited about this upcoming semester, I've got some fascinating new texts that I think the 505 kids are really going to *plotz* over..." I trailed off, allowing myself to be momentarily distracted and amused by the image of Myra Goldfarb *plotzing* — but this was a mistake. Ira was already several steps ahead of me, opening the door to my study.

"Mm-hmm, yes — oh!" he gasped.

I stood beside him and saw the room as if for the first time. The surface of the huge glass-topped desk was entirely covered with books.

A zoo of loose-leaf papers, manila folders, gilded folios, cracked-spine quartos, and assorted paraphernalia was overflowing the bookshelves, stacked upon the windowsills, propped beneath the potted plants. You could barely see the furniture or the floor. To the untrained eye, the collection would have looked haphazard, but I knew there was a secret order hidden in the chaos.

Ira appeared to have been struck dumb. He meandered over to the desk, to where the exam booklets that had no doubt occasioned his impromptu house call still peeked out from beneath the giant tissue box, but said nothing. Instead, he turned to the various sheaves of papers that all dealt, in one way or another, with the Tree of Life. He picked up a Xeroxed page from *Shaar Hakavanot*. His eyes flitted from right to left, reading the Hebrew passage for what seemed a long time. He swivelled around and stared at me strangely.

"Ira?"

"You haven't been…"

"What?"

"You're not toying with the idea of…"

"What?"

"Making the climb yourself?"

"Don't be ridiculous. You know I haven't been interested in religious practice for years."

And as easily as that — because, no doubt, his desire for normalcy to be restored was great — he smiled. The cool breeze of relief entered and filled the room. It fluttered between us for a roundish minute, making speech superfluous.

Escorting him to the front door, I said, "We'll be in touch."

"Yes. Yes, we'll be in touch. Thanks for your understanding, David."

"Of course."

"Take it easy now."

"I will. Goodbye."

The door closed behind him with a soft thump. I wandered back into the hall and stared at the photo of Miriam he had picked up earlier. *Miriam would have been proud*, he'd said on the night of the bat mitzvah. *So proud.* He was actually trembling, as if Samara's reading had plucked at some innermost chord. But I had heard nothing, felt nothing. Or so I told myself in the days following the bat mitzvah, when a question dangled in the air of the house, in Samara's downcast eyes, that I didn't know how — didn't *want* to know how — to answer.

But I *had* heard it, *had* felt it — that desire to scream *no no no no no*, and yet, coiled within the no, an intricate sweetness, an ineffable yes. It had plucked at a part of me I had rejected, and that made me angry, and anger kept me silent. Yet now my heartstrings were murmuring against the silence, they were vibrating with the resonance of her question. And for the first time in a decade, I was listening. It was so loud I could barely hear anything else.

THOUGH I HAD COME with the express purpose of breaking up with Val, we had somehow managed to end up fucking instead. A major setback, yes, but surmountable — perhaps even understandable in light of recent events. This had been the last hurrah, and now, well, now I'd exhausted my excuses and exhausted myself and there was nothing left to do but cut the cord.

I propped myself up on an elbow to contemplate Val, her ocean eyes and skyscraper eyelashes, her dark hair spread out on the pillow, her perfect breasts rising and falling with the rhythm of her breathing. I marvelled again at the sheer lankiness of her, and felt a surge of preemptive sadness at the sight of the birthmark on her left leg — how I would miss that pale blue dot! And all the tiny streets and houses, rivers and forests, men and women and creatures on that imaginary continent — would they miss me when I was gone?

"I —" I said. But then she was looking at me, and her eyes were gorgeously, irresistibly serious. Gravity *was* attractive — Alex had been right about that, at least. "Should probably get home," I finished lamely.

She turned her gaze back to the ceiling. "Why?"

"Well, it's almost ten-thirty."

"*Et alors?*"

"My kids will be wondering where I am."

"But your son is staying with his friend tonight? The astronomer?"

"Yes, that's true, but my daughter — she'll be home. And I don't really want her to see me sneaking back in the middle of the night, or doing the walk of shame at six in the morning."

"Why?"

"Because, well, I'd prefer it if — I mean, I don't exactly want her knowing. About us."

"She knows."

"There's no real ev —"

"She knows."

"But maybe she just —"

"She knows."

"Okay," I said. "What makes you so sure?"

Her mouth contorted in a strange smile. For a while she was quiet. Then, in an apparent non sequitur, she said, "You know those old telephones they used to sell? The ones where you had to spin that plastic thing if you wanted to dial a number?"

"Rotary phones?"

"Yeah, exactly. When I was a kid, we used to have one of those phones. My mother kept it on a table in the hallway. And my father, he used to call her every day in the afternoon to tell her he loved her and he was coming home from work. Every day at five o'clock the phone in the hallway would ring. I remember my mother used to twist the cord around her fingers whenever she talked to him. I always thought she did that for fun, but later I realized — it was a nervous habit, you know? And she had a good reason to be nervous, I guess, because one day — I was eight years old — the phone didn't ring. It was five o'clock and the hallway was so silent I thought maybe I had gone deaf. You've never had such a silent sixty seconds in your life."

She glanced at me, then fixed her eyes on the ceiling again. "My mother, I think she thought he was dead. She disconnected the phone from the hallway and dragged it into bed. She stayed there for four days. Four days she didn't move and didn't say a thing. Like if she didn't make a sound, she could freeze time and he wouldn't be gone and the phone would ring and he would come home again.

"But the phone didn't ring. It was locked in this battle with her, like it wanted to see, who would break down first and make a noise? And so for four days I prayed, please, *Jésus,* please, *Vierge Marie,* he doesn't even have to come home, just let him call so at least we can get on with our lives. Finally, on the fifth day, the phone rang. At exactly five o'clock it rang. Nobody spoke — there was no voice at the other end, no 'I love you' — but it was enough. My mother got out of bed. And every day after that, at exactly five o'clock, the same thing happened all over again. The phone rang and nobody spoke but for the next twenty-four hours the look in my mother's eye said: enough. She could go on."

I said nothing. A moment passed. Then she said, in a voice that sounded, suddenly, terribly depleted, "*Tout ça pour dire* — I knew. Right away, from the first day he didn't call, I knew it at 5:01. He was with another woman." Abruptly, she sat up, gathering her knees in her arms. Then, thinking better of it, she lay back down again. "A daughter has a way of knowing such things. And once she knows them, she stops needing in the way she did before. Of course, she still needs, you and other people, future people, but. She will no longer say, 'I love you,' 'I don't love you' — even if she is very young, she will already be too old for words like that. She will not… *subject* you to that vocabulary anymore. So, you might as well stay, if you want to. I mean here, if you want to. You can," she said. And I did.

THE NEXT MORNING, I got home at nine o'clock. Val's assurances notwithstanding, I had timed it so that Lev would be at the synagogue saying his morning prayers, and Samara would in all likelihood be asleep. But when I tiptoed down the hall, I heard a steady stream of music leaking from Samara's bedroom. Because it was unusual for her to be awake at this hour, never mind listening to dance club electronica, I wondered if she had put on the music to muffle the sounds of my embarrassing arrival. Maybe she knew, but didn't want me to know she knew? I crept into my study and closed the door.

I sat down at my desk. It should have been a peaceful moment — usually, when I did this, it was with the feeling of a sailor setting foot on *terra firma* after a dangerous and grueling time at sea — and it would have been, had the eighty ungraded term papers not been staring back at me. I picked one up at random, then put it down again. Yes, I decided, it was time for a run.

I had barely left the house when I started to sweat in the mounting humidity. On Bernard, a few cars whizzed past, but on the whole the streets seemed quiet and deserted. Grateful for the silence, I began to pick up pace, racing until beads of moisture soaked through my T-shirt, sticking it to my chest and shoulders. The old rush was coming back. And along with the rush, that torrent of whispers, the throbbing of voices on membranes, the knocking of breath on all my most internal doors.

Aaaahhhh... It was Ani, and I opened my arms wide, embracing absolutes, embracing all the deities, and with them authority, meaning, quest, self, eros. And then, in the next instant — no, I was wrong — it was Ayin, it was really Ayin after all. The self was fluid and fragmented, there was no authority, no unified I, everything was thick with threat and thanatos. And then, in the next instant —

I stopped, trembling and furious. What good was a message from above if it couldn't even be decoded? What good was a signal if it was always getting drowned out by interference? Couldn't the powers that be afford better equipment — was heaven so murky as that? My hand curled into a fist and began to beat my breast. Out, damned *dybbuk!* Out, out! But it would not out, and all of a sudden doors were opening and voices were pouring all around me, cries of *gut shabbes!* were filling the air, and I found myself surrounded by the thick mid-morning traffic of Congregation Toldos Yakov Yosef.

A young Hasid paused on the steps of the synagogue to study me, his expression neither malevolent nor benign but, perhaps, simply curious. I realized that my fist was midway to my chest — I must have looked like a worshipper begging forgiveness for his sins — and dropped it, embarrassed. Then I recognized the person staring at me.

It was Lev. My Lev.

My jaw dropped. Of all people! Look at him: already he was wondering what the hell I was up to; any second now he'd be walking toward me, ready to turn the interrogation lamps of his eyes on my squirming, sweating face. For one wild second, I considered confessing — the murmurs, the vessels, the Tree of Life — but no. I'd already confused one kid's religious development; did I really want to make that same mistake twice?

I fled.

Racing down the busy avenue, I didn't ease up until I'd rounded the bend onto a familiar tree-lined street. The sounds of church bells and crying children filled the air. I strode with eyes down, searching the pavement for tectonic instabilities, praying that one of its cracks would open up and swallow me, Korah-style. And so it was a while before I registered the fresh cacophony of voices now assaulting my ears and looked up.

A large knot of people had gathered around the base of a tree. Katz's old oak tree. Many of the bystanders were muttering in barbed tones; some of them were pointing.

Hanging from the branches were the innumerable tin cans that had been piling up in Katz's yard for months. Long pieces of twine linked each can to several others, giving the impression of a gigantic spider web suspended in midair. It made you think of the tin can telephones that every child seemed fated to make between the ages of eight and twelve, as if to signal their entrance into the burgeoning mastery of technological adolescence.

As kids, Lev and Samara had suffered many frustrated attempts before realizing that the twine connecting the two cans had to be pulled extremely taut in order for the device to work. Now, squinting up at the tin cans in the branches, I noticed that these strings *were* pulled taut. Katz had done his research. Or someone had done it for him.

To a certain kind of eye the device might have possessed a crazy, quirky beauty — you could imagine it striking the fancy of the twenty-something hipsters living in the Plateau — but no such eyes were in attendance here. To the Hasidic citizens of Mile End, the device was simply a property-value-lowering eyesore, and an example of the individualist spirit that plagued the non-God-fearing world with socially useless and sinful frivolities.

Katz was sitting on his front porch, taking in the crowd from a safe distance, rocking back and forth and muttering to himself. What was he saying? Trying to read his lips was like playing charades with a partner who didn't realize there was a game going on. Two words. First word: one syllable. *Please*. Second word: one syllable. *Call*. I stared at his face. *Please call?* What was that supposed to mean? Was he actually expecting someone to call him on that crazy contraption? I turned my back on the scene and trudged homeward through the dizzying heat.

Dinner that night was a somber affair. Samara and Lev chopped vegetables for a salad, handed each other ingredients for the pasta they were cooking, and later, when dinner was served, passed each other dishes without recourse to words. I saw for the first time that their bodies spoke the secret language of ballet dancers and synchronized swimmers and Trappist monks: they moved together in a practiced state of unfocused attention that allowed each person to anticipate the needs of the other. Even before he knew he wanted the mashed potatoes, she was passing them. Before she could point at the jug of lemonade, it was halfway to her hand. How long had they been speaking this esoteric family language? I tried, and failed, to parse the syntax of their silence. And so they ate and I ate and they spoke their comfortable creole while my paternal pidgin, with its reduced vocabulary and limited grammatical structure, flopped and flapped its way across the table, a series of unfunny jokes and halfhearted anecdotes and lame questions which they, perhaps as a courtesy to me, interpreted as rhetorical.

I could tell from Samara's flushed cheeks that she had heard me come in that morning. I could tell from Lev's downcast eyes that he had seen me flee the scene. But none of us mentioned either of these things. Instead we sat, and strands of silence floated up between us, linking me to her to him, a silver web suspended over the dinner table, capturing everything, communicating nothing.

Then dinner was over and the kids were clearing up, she washing and he drying, their custom from childhood. And because they did it as a matter of course, did it without needing to be asked, I permitted myself a moment of relief over the fact that my parenting-by-proxy — leaving them in Ira and Judy's unneurotic care — had worked out well enough after all. But the moment evaporated quickly and left something darker and colder in its place. If I were to suffer another heart attack, lethal this time, they would probably make out just fine without me. Taking small sips from my glass of water, I watched the scene as if from above, an awkward stranger beholding a family portrait months after it is taken. And wondered: was this what was meant by out of body experience? Was this what it was like to die?

**ON THE THIRD SUNDAY** afternoon in August, Val invited me to a picnic on what was known to tourists as Mount Royal and to everyone else simply as "the mountain." She was looking especially pretty that day — like one of Sappho's maidens — in a pink sleeveless dress, delicate golden sandals, and a thin embroidered headband that might well have come from Sardis. It was impossible to turn her down.

The punishing heat would have been intolerable were it not for the shade offered by a clump of trees near the gazebo. To cool off, Val opened a bottle of chilled Maudite and poured it into two glasses she'd brought along in her handbag. We clinked glasses. "L'Chaim," she said, with a wink.

And then we ate — strawberries and zaatar bread — the light, insubstantial diet of lovers. She leaned over to kiss me with her ruby mouth and I made a game of plucking berries from between her lips. Her iridescent throat had never seemed so lovely or so worth biting.

When we were done picnicking, Val lay down in the grass with an arm over her face, her strawberry smile still visible. I was happy to let her lie there for as long as she liked; merely to sit beside her had become, suddenly, reason enough to live. Visoring my eyes with one hand, I peered out past the gazebo to where a large group of people was drumming on tam-tams and dancing. Men, women and children, in various states of undress, losing themselves to the music. A dizzying spindle of sound, a sort of counterfeit rapture. This kind of bacchic frenzy put me in mind of Euripides — the Ancient Greeks called it *ekstasis*, literally to be outside one's self. And though I had no desire to join in the frenzy myself, I was able to appreciate, at least abstractly, the appeal of such an altered state. There was relief there, I thought. There was release.

But my appreciation ceased, suddenly, to be abstract, and became instead alarmingly concrete. Against the sea of rapturous faces all blurred together in anonymity, one familiar face stood out in sharp relief. Samara was dancing with her eyes closed, her mouth parted in a strange smile. Otherwordly. Detached. Terrifying. I battled the impulse to run up, grab her by the shoulders, shake her until she fell out of it. It was a smile I had never seen before, a smile she would never want me to have seen. For this type of situation, we had a strict protocol. That protocol was: don't talk.

And so I added the smile to the litany of things we did not talk about, which by this point included but was not limited to: Jenny, music, bicycles, my health, intellectual elitism, Kraft Dinner, Zionism, her mother, bat mitzvahs, Shakespeare, my sexual activity, her sexual activity, Alex, *Winnie the Pooh*, saltines, capitalism, loneliness, the relationship of Virginia Woolf to Vita Sackville-West, wrong numbers, the colour blue, *The Birth of Tragedy*, her friends (or lack thereof), her marketable skills (or lack thereof), popsicles, Volkswagens, swing sets, lepidopterology, the correlation between intelligence and melancholy, Vincent van Gogh, drugs, "The Love Song of J. Alfred Prufrock," collapsible telescopes, the name Miranda, chess, Djuna Barnes, flying, and the theory of evolution.

These were the sticking points in our conversations, the unsayable, unvisitable black points on the map, which had at first required sharp detours and violent twists of the steering wheel and which we had later learned, by means of a stunning array of conversational acrobatics, to avoid entirely. And yet, precisely because these points were unvisitable, they had, over the years, begun to exercise a strange power over my imagination. They were blacker than black. Their shadows shone, bright with excessive dark. They stood out sharply on the map and formed a collection of points that the human brain, geared for gestalt, longed to link together. It was the same impulse that had made our forebears connect the dots in the sky into the imaginary pictures we now called constellations. The same impulse that had driven us to search for codes in the Bible, and that would one day drive us to see poetry in nucleotides, reading rubaiyats in sequences of G and A and T and C, as if meaning could be genetically encoded in verse. It was an irresistible temptation and a fatal idea.

After some time, Val opened her eyes and smiled at me. Then, like a person slowly waking from a pleasant dream, she brought herself to a sitting position. She took out her cell phone and said, "Can you excuse me for a second? I have to make a call." Her face, which had been so radiant a moment ago, was suddenly overcast, little bits of cumulus clinging to the corners of her eyes.

"Sure," I said. "But why not make the call here?"

"No reception. I'll be right back."

She gave an apologetic little wave and I watched her golden shoulders recede into the sunlight as she walked down the grassy slope. She came to a stop a dozen feet away, far enough that I would not be able to overhear. But, strangely, she didn't appear to be saying anything. Her back was only half-turned to me, and in the bright light I could clearly make out the outline of her lips, which weren't moving.

On impulse, I took out my own cell phone and, doing so, noticed two things.

The first was that the phone had perfect reception.

The second was the time.

It was exactly five o'clock.

I was overwhelmed with compassion for the eight-year-old girl she had been, admiration for the choice she had made. To think that all these years she'd kept up her daily devotion — it was all I could do to leave her secret unsung. When she came back up to me, I took her phone-holding hand and kissed it with something like reverence. She looked at me quizzically, but said nothing. Soon she was buried in her Eckhart again and I was fanning the ungraded term papers out on the grass. In the space of five minutes, I had graded all eighty of them. Though the gesture reeked of the stickiest kind of poetic self-indulgence, though my better judgment warned against it, though it was probably professional suicide, everyone got an A.

**THAT NIGHT**, alone in my bed, I woke suddenly. The clock read 4:58 a.m. I lay still for a moment, trying to figure out what had woken me, but there was nothing. No loud music. No slamming doors. The house was silent.

But it was like the silence that follows on the heels of a power failure, when the hum of refrigerators, the buzzing of streetlights, the whole concerto of urban living goes missing, the volume of the world dipping down to a level you never thought possible. That was it, I thought: something, some noise, had just gone missing.

After a long moment, I realized what it was.

My heart had ceased its murmuring. For the first time in weeks, I couldn't hear it at all.

I frowned. Rationally, I knew that the disappearance of the murmur should have come as a welcome surprise. Instead, it came as a tremendous letdown. That whispered message had been my golden ticket! Without it, what did I have? Nothing.

No, not nothing. I had a middle-aged, middle-class, suburban life. A family. A girlfriend. Everything I had ever been taught to aspire to. But I had been promised the holy of holies, highest of heights, and the idea of being shunted back to the *via media* now was unacceptable.


**AN HOUR LATER**, I was running. It was barely six o'clock and already the heat was oppressive. The sky was grey and low. My heart rate was ramping up. I forced my body through wall after wall of humidity, revelling in the sensation of speed, motion chasing blood out of tired muscles, adrenaline ripping through arms and legs. My shirt pasting itself to back and stomach. Even my eyelashes dripping sweat.

Now the sky was darkening with an influx of clouds, and I was racing fast beneath them.

The thrashing of ventricles and aortas was gratifyingly audible again. Audible but still unclear, because one moment the muscle was saying Ani, and in the next moment — Ayin. This time I would press myself up against the cool viscous membrane that divided something from nothing, being from non-being, existence from void. I would outrun my body's limits, I would —

My heart spasmed. I clutched at it and gasped for breath. This pain was not pleasure. A point of fire pierced my chest. I fell to my knees and shuddered. Something inside me was turning, twisting, burning. I gasped again and wished for water. I thought: this is it, this is it, but where is the Angel of Death? And, in search of his face, I looked up.

A shadowy, ancient man was turning the corner. Black coat. White hair. Just as I'd always imagined. He whipped past, a single hand extended into the air — he was beckoning me up into the sky — or was he shaking his fist? — and then he was gone.

Katz's tree loomed over me.

The web of tin cans still hung there, taut and tense and waiting, as if expecting a call at any moment. Something — it might have been a moth or a butterfly, or even a small bird — whizzed past my ear and landed with a ping in one of the cans. The soft wing-flap was a ripple in the air — delicate at first, localized — then thrumming from can to can, from branch to branch, until the whole tree sang and groaned.

A door banged open and Katz burst out of his house, looking to the tree with deranged rapture. A gust of wind ruffled his clothes and swept the yarmulke from his head, but he didn't bother to run after it. He was moving his lips in response to a conversation only he could hear.

The wind grew rougher, encircling him in a private whirlwind as he — what was he doing? He was bouncing on the balls of his feet, like a synagogue worshipper hearing Holy Holy Holy. The bounces got bigger; he was leaping, lifting, impossibly light on his feet. It looked as if he might be taken up, Elijah-style, and I craned my neck skyward, scanning the clouds for a chariot of fire or an unidentified flying object that might whisk him off into the lofty regions he so clearly wished to inhabit.

Then it rained.

As the humidity broke and the heavens opened their windows wide, emptying themselves of water, I squinted hard at Katz. If I tilted my head to the left, I could just make out his shape through the downpour. He was rising and falling, running and returning, up and down and up and down and up. And suddenly it all came clear — I had my answer — not Ayin or Ani, not either/or, but both/and. Ayin-Ani-Ayin-Ani-Ayin-Ani-Ayin-Ani and my soul a boomerang back and forth between these two poles forever.

But it was not forever.

My heart was exploding, my heart was on fire, my heart was cloven in two.

The pavement felt cool and welcoming against the base of my skull.

I had wanted an answer. But how I suddenly loved the question, black coffee and the smell of books, and a fine wine on a white table-cloth, and middle-of-the-night bicycle rides, and middle-of-the-way forays into old age, and the pale blue dot on Val's left leg, whizzing away into infinity, and the new manuscript waiting to be written, and the old silences waiting to be spoken, and the girl attacking her copy of Žižek with a highlighter, and all of the trunk drawers full of jewelry and sadness, and the telephone ringing all day, and my children. My children. And Valérie saying, "You might as well stay, if you want to. I mean here, if you want to. You can."

SAMARA

**A** TOWER OF CASSEROLES teetered on the edge of the kitchen sink, their aluminum foil pans glinting in the sunlight. I reached out a hand to steady them, then grabbed the counter and steadied myself.

The doorbell rang. I walked past the kitchen island piled high with deli meats and specialty salads, fruits and chocolates, through the sea of people who had brought these trays and platters and baskets, and who were now clutching me by the wrists, murmuring traditional blessings. *May God comfort you among the mourners of Zion and Jerusalem.*

Opening the door, I just had time to see a miserable-looking Jenny sandwiched between her parents before Judy fell upon me with a hug that choked the air from my lungs.

"Samara!" she cried, very close to my ear. "I'm so, so sorry. Your dad was *such* a good man. *Such* a good man. I just couldn't believe it when I heard. If there's *anything* you need —"

"She needs air, Mom!" Jenny said, pulling Judy off me. I shot her a grateful look.

A solemn Ira held out an offering and said, "This here is for you and Lev."

A casserole. "Thank you," I said. "That's very kind."

"The least we could do," he said sadly. "How are you two holding up?"

At that moment, Lev appeared at my elbow. Judy now fell upon him, exclaiming about what a beautiful eulogy he'd given his father, just beautiful, and her exuberant praise saved me from having to answer Ira's question.

Behind Lev, Alex stood looking inconsolable, as if the man we'd buried an hour ago had been his father, not mine. As I raised my hand to give him a small waist-level wave, Jenny grabbed it, thinking I'd reached out for her. She led me into a corner of the living room and leaned in to kiss my mouth, then remembered where we were and pecked me on the cheek instead.

"Sorry about my mom and dad," Jenny said, taking the casserole from my hands. "I'll put this in the kitchen for you. Have you eaten anything? Can I warm a bit of this up for you?"

I nodded, because it was easier than forming the words "I'm not hungry." She gave my hand a little squeeze, then wove her way through the crowd.

Someone touched me on the shoulder.

"Sama —" Mr. Glassman said. Before his mouth could fully form my name, his wife shuffled up behind him, leaning heavily on her cane and murmuring, "If it is not true that $p$ if and only if $q$ then either we derive $p$ and not $q$ or we derive not $p$ and $q$, and therefore…" When she reached me, she took my arm — whether to stabilize herself or comfort me was unclear — and gazed at me with such profound sympathy that I worried I, and not she, might fall over.

"Mrs. Glassman, hi, you really didn't have to come, I know you haven't been feeling —"

The ancient woman made pshawing motions with her free hand.

Mr. Glassman said, with a tight smile, "My wife is doing very well, thank God. Very, very well. Already she is mostly recovered from the stroke, you see? The only thing is, she forgets sometimes to take her pill in the afternoon…"

Mrs. Glassman reached a trembling hand into her purse, retrieved a pill bottle, and shook a pill into her palm. "Samara, *neshomeleh*, you have for me some water maybe?"

"Of course, I'll bring you a glass —" I said. Mr. Glassman reached out an arm to stop me, to keep me there — to tell me something — but I cut him off with "I'll be right back," and hurried off.

In the kitchen, Jenny was placing a gigantic serving of casserole in the microwave. I filled a glass with water and was just about to dredge up the energy to tell her that I'd lost my appetite when Lev came up behind me and said, "There's someone in front of the house."

"Who?"

"I don't know. She looks kind of familiar, but I don't know. Can you come see?"

I asked Jenny if she would take the glass of water to Mrs. Glassman. She took it with a smile and headed off in search of the tiny woman while I followed Lev to the living room windows.

"See?" he pointed. "That woman in the silver car?"

I nodded.

"Who is she?"

I shrugged.

"She was at the funeral, too. Why is she just sitting there? Why doesn't she come in?"

I said nothing. I'd recognized her instantly: my father's lover. An hour ago, she had shown up at the graveyard, pacing the periphery of the crowd. Throughout the burial, her shadowy presence hovered at the edge of my vision, a wretched someone in a black dress who didn't say a word to anyone, but whose silence screamed sadness, whose body radiated loss.

I didn't have the heart to explain who she was to Lev.

Luckily, I didn't have to. As if she sensed we were watching her, she turned her key in the ignition and drove off.

My chest felt tight.

"Are you okay?" Lev asked. "Did you know her, or what?"

"I —"

Someone tapped me on the shoulder. I whipped around.

"Samara," Mr. Glassman said, "I was hoping to talk to you, if you have a minute? Just a minute? I wanted to —"

"But if $p$ and $q$, then not $q$ or $r$, so we can assume either not $p$ and $q$ or not $q$ or $r$..."

"To return something to you and also ask if you may be able to help with —"

"I —" I said, looking around wildly.

My eyes landed on Alex. He must have seen the panic in my face, because he came toward me and said, "Sorry to interrupt, but can I borrow you for a second, Samara?" and, before anyone had a chance to object, he was leading me down the hall.

"You looked kind of trapped back there," he whispered as we came to a stop in front of my dad's study. "Lev and I can handle the food and everything, if you want to escape for a minute?"

I nodded at him — full of gratitude, but too breathless to say thanks — and ducked inside. The door clicked shut behind me.

I leaned against it and surveyed the room. There was the majestic desk I'd marvelled at as a child, the thick shag of the carpet I'd played on while Dad studied, the endless rows of books along whose spines I'd trailed a reverent fingertip. Dust motes spun lazily through the air. Tears surged up my throat. This was the first time I'd been in here since —

On his desk, books were scattered haphazardly across the blotter. The books he was reading right before he died. When he collapsed in the middle of the street, his last thoughts had probably been of them.

A wild and terrifying anger ripped through me — after so many years of leaving us alone, he'd gone and left us alone again, really alone this time, and forever — and all because he insisted on running! Even after the heart attack, even after the doctor's warnings. Had he stopped for one second to consider what it would do to us if he died? No. He cared about running, so he ran. It was suicide — literally that's what this was — so why wasn't anyone calling it that? And why had

I kept on clinging to a childhood grudge instead of trying to warn him, stop him, talk to him —

My hands began to shake. Eyes stinging, I paced the room. No, I thought. No. No. Don't cry. Not now. Not with everyone still out there. If you let yourself go now, how will you ever pull yourself together?

I reached for a tissue from the giant box on the desk, and there it was.

A manuscript lying on a pile of term papers.

*Something Out of Nothing,* the title page said, *by David Meyer.* I flipped to the next page and found a drawing of the Tree of Life.

I flipped the page again and read the dedication.

*For my daughter.*

I froze, then read it again. And again. And again. *For my daughter.*

Then somebody knocked and Jenny's voice called, "Samara?"

I hid the papers behind my back just as she opened the door.

"What?" My voice, louder and harsher than I'd intended, boomeranged around the room, ramming me right between the eyes.

"Alex told me you were in here," she said. "Are you okay?"

"Yeah, fine," I said. "Thanks."

"Are you coming? I warmed up that casserole for you."

"Casserole?"

"Yeah — the one my parents brought?"

"Oh. Right. Sorry. I'll be right there."

She smiled softly and turned away, leaving the door ajar. I waited a few moments, then hurried to the front closet, stuffed the sheaf of papers into my backpack, and zipped it up tight.

I heard quick, shuffling footsteps out on the stoop and took a few deep breaths to brace myself against a fresh onslaught of casseroles, or deli meats, or other unwanted offerings. But by the time I opened the door, whoever it was had already gone.

I stared down at the welcome mat and tears sprang to my eyes.

There, unaccompanied by a note or card, sat a perfect yellow lemon.

OVER THE NEXT WEEK, I paged through the manuscript whenever I had a moment to myself. Which wasn't often: the day after the funeral, I had packed my bags, taken the bus from the house in Mile End, and moved back into the Plateau apartment I shared with Jenny. I couldn't stand to be in the house a second longer, couldn't stand Lev's sad gaze following me up and down the halls, waiting for me to say something comforting and big-sisterly. But now I had Jenny's gaze trailing me around our much smaller apartment.

Worse, school had started up again. It was the first week of September and the last year of my undergraduate career. I was enrolled in five courses: Literary Theory, Postcolonial Literature, Materiality and Sociology of the Text, a Milton seminar, and (at Jenny's urging) a 300-level Art History course called "The Female Body in Postmodern Visual Culture." I couldn't bring myself to care about any of them.

The theory class was the worst. Professor Zimmerman spent exactly two minutes going over the syllabus — it ranged ambitiously from Plato to Foucault — then spent the next twenty-five minutes reading aloud from Roland Barthes' *The Death of the Author*. "In precisely this way," he declaimed in his reedy voice, "literature (it would be better from now on to say *writing*), by refusing to assign a 'secret,' an ultimate meaning, to the text (and to the world as text), liberates what may be called an anti-theological activity, an activity that is truly revolutionary since to refuse to fix meaning is, in the end, to refuse God and his hypostases — reason, science, law."

I glanced around the class in search of the mutual eye-rolling this bullshit deserved. Instead I found thirty heads nodding solemnly and in unison.

Finally, with five minutes to spare, Zimmerman looked up from his Norton anthology and asked what we thought. A preppy student I recognized from my philosophy elective last semester raised his hand and said in a loud, confident voice, "It makes total sense. Everyone knows that a book is just a tissue of signs and there isn't actually any objective meaning to it. Like, the whole modern notion of the Author as this thing that decides the meaning of a text — it's just such obvious bogus."

"Yeah," added a ponytailed girl to his left, "I mean it's just an outdated concept, right? Like the whole idea of God? Because, like, fixed meaning, that's basically what religion is all about."

"Very good," Zimmerman said. "As Barthes explains, reading a text is not about uncovering a single, objective, 'theological' meaning — the message of the Author-God — lying beneath the surface. On the contrary, it's about carrying out a systematic *exemption* of meaning, which —"

But class time was over, and the rest of Zimmerman's sermon was drowned out by the sounds of thirty chairs scraping backward on worn linoleum. Students shuffled, robot-like, to their next classes.

Outside Moyse Hall, I pressed my forehead against a cold stone pillar and squeezed my eyes shut. The harsh fluorescents had imprinted themselves on my retinas and I could see dashes of white light, like the dividing lines on a road. The voices in the lecture hall had crammed my skull with noise; the beginnings of a headache ate at my brain. An angry ache gnawed at my gut. All those nodding heads, those eager faces. How could they get so excited about such stupid ideas? What was so wrong with meaning? Why should we view a refusal to fix it as "an activity that is truly revolutionary"? If Barthes really thought a text gave him nothing, the revolutionary thing would be to make something out of it. I opened my eyes and walked as quickly as I could, bending my steps eastward, away from campus and toward the Plateau.


HANNAH LOOKED UP as I came into the café, a huge smile spreading across her face. "Hey!" she cried from behind the counter, putting down her dishtowel to pour me a cup of coffee. "How was your first week of class?"

"Terrible," I said, taking the drink with a grateful, tired grin.

Hannah had been slipping me free coffee since she first started working at Two Moons Café back in our first semester at McGill. We'd been assigned to the same room in one of the on-campus dorms, and we'd quickly become friends, despite — or maybe because of — our opposite personalities. Born and raised in Vancouver, Hannah had never even left the West Coast until a week before school started. Her hippie parents believed in the gospel of urban farming and organic food, and the apple hadn't fallen far from the tree. Hannah had spent her teenage years helping them tend their plot in the local community garden, tagging along to ashtanga yoga classes and developing an interest in reiki. With tattoos on her arms and feathers in her blonde hair, she was the most balanced human being I knew — and also the most talkative. After the funeral, she was the person I most wanted to hang out with. Her laughing eyes and simple chatter put me at ease; they made it possible for me to say nothing without being rude, and nothing was exactly what I wanted to say.

Surrounded by the free spirits and flower children who typically populated this café, we spent a few minutes talking about my new English classes and her Political Science ones. Then I excused myself, saying I already had a bunch of reading to do. This was technically true, even if it wasn't exactly the type of reading I knew she was imagining. She waved me toward my favourite table by the window.

I pulled my backpack onto my lap and took out my dad's crumpled manuscript. I never took it out at home, knowing that if Jenny saw it, she'd dish out a look so compassionate, so concerned, it would only make me feel worse. Here, I was free from the burden of other people's sympathy. I flipped to the first chapter and read:

> ANI, the first vessel on the Tree of Life, is considered feminine. This is because, within the kabbalistic framework, the masculine is that which bestows and the feminine is that which receives. Given her position

at the bottom of the Tree, Ani receives divine light from
the vessels above her, but is not capable of emitting her
own. For this reason, she is associated with the moon,
the orb that reflects the light of others.

I frowned. "The feminine is that which receives"? The less-than-enlightened perspective on gender relations annoyed me, but I kept
going.

The most evocative image associated with Ani is that of
"the beautiful maiden without eyes." In the medieval
period, it was believed that the eyes emitted rays of
light; these rays landed upon objects, and in this way
the phenomenon of vision was produced. To be without
eyes, then, was to be without the ability to emit one's
own light. This applied wonderfully to Ani, always the
receptacle for divine light but never the progenitor of it.

"Evocative"? "Wonderfully"? Since when had my dad ever been able
to appreciate the beauty of a religious idea? This from the man who
had told me a bat mitzvah was just a worn-out tradition, who had
called Mr. Katz "delusional" when a mystical tree rose up on his front
lawn? *Now* my father decided to get it? Half angry, half suspicious,
I flipped to the next page. There, crouching at the foot of a margin,
was a hand-scribbled note:

*Ani as shortcut to Ayin? (Cf. "crown.") Dangerous if
I jump from first to last? Skipping steps: check Lurianic,
Hasidic sources for precedent.*

My gaze zeroed in on one word at the note's centre, that fulcrum from
which all other words slid off into invisibility: "I." The most abhorred
word in academia. The forbidden personal pronoun. What if this
hadn't just been academic for him, what if it had been personal, and he

was actually engaged in the famously dangerous business of *climbing* the Tree of Life? And not only that, but looking for shortcuts to boot!

I jammed the manuscript into my backpack, said goodbye to Hannah, and left the café. But instead of going straight home, I stopped in at the public library. At the back of the special collections area, I walked through the stacks, letting my index finger trail along the spines, which was this thing I did sometimes. The air was thick and musty, and on the shelves were rows and rows of crumbling books. I didn't pick them up, I didn't open them, but I let their scents wash over me. Then I left the library and went home.

WHILE I WAS OUT, Jenny had found a new job. And a new friend. The new friend had found her the new job.

"Her name's Kyle," Jenny said as I hung up my jacket.

"Kyle?"

"Yeah. She lives right across from The Word, and she's in her last year of undergrad, she's studying design? And she said that a bunch of her friends are in this art collective, they meet on weekends and stuff, and they're looking for a model. You know, like to sit for them?"

"I know what a model is."

"Yeah. So, what do you think? They're students, so they don't have a lot of cash, but Kyle said she could pay me like —"

"Wait, she's going to be there?"

"Well, yeah."

"I thought she was studying design."

"Well, yeah, but she likes to paint on the side."

My phone beeped. I took it out of my pocket and found a text from Lev. *I know we weren't that close, but I still miss him, you know?*

"So what do you think?" Jenny said.

I switched off my phone. "About what?"

"The job."

"Well, it beats bagging groceries."

"That's what Kyle said!"

"What?"

"That it beats bagging groceries! That's what she does — that's where I met her — at the grocery store." Jenny looked triumphant, delighted, as she added, "And maybe with the extra money we can fix the place up a bit."

I flopped onto the couch. It was true that our small but beautiful apartment was still barely furnished, even though we'd moved in together two years ago. Because she'd just graduated from her arts certificate program and I was still a student, we didn't own much of anything; what we had was a kitchen table, a lamp, a bed, a radio clock, mismatched dishes, two chairs, books, an easel, and about seven thousand tubes of paint. The entire floor of the apartment was made up of black and white square tiles. As a result, I sometimes felt like we were living inside a chess game, one in which very few pieces remain.

"Anyway," Jenny said. "How are you?"

"Fine," I said and met her eyes, just for a second, but this was a mistake. They bludgeoned me with a look of such infinite kindness that I flinched and turned away.

"Samara," she said. "Do you want to talk?"

"I have to pee."

"What?"

"Just a sec," I said and locked myself in the bathroom.

Once I was in there, I figured I might as well go. No luck. But I sat there anyway, savouring my moment of freedom from Jenny's pity — a pity that was all the more painful because it was so well-meaning. When I couldn't put it off any longer, I flushed, turned on the water, and pretended to wash my hands. The face in the mirror had bleary eyes and chapped lips. "You look like shit," I whispered to my reflection and started putting on eyeliner.

When I came out ten minutes later, Jenny was folding tiny paper cranes.

"Hey," she said, "I'm going to make dinner, do you feel like spaghetti or — are you wearing makeup?"

"Yeah. Have you seen my black halter top?"

"On the lamp," she said, pointing with the crane's crisp beak. "Where are you going?"

"There's a dance thing tonight."

"Where?"

"Downtown."

"I didn't realize you were the clubbing type."

"I'm not. But, well, Hannah invited me, so."

She nodded at this lie, then dragged her fingernail across the crane's back to form the tail. I pulled off my ratty T-shirt and put on the halter. I could tell she was trying not to press me for details, not to push too hard. To give me some space.

"What time will you be home?"

"I don't know," I said, dropping a kiss on her lips before grabbing my jacket and jamming my feet in my boots. "I'll call you," I said, even though we both knew I wouldn't.

I RUSHED OUT into a tangled nightwood of rank bars and dirty dance clubs, not stopping at any one place but flitting from room to room, bottle to bottle. I folded my frame into foreign bodies, and this was where I felt relief, free from *how are you* and *I love you*.

I was never the type of girl who goes to clubs, the type of girl who parties. I was not that sort of character, that was not my story — and wasn't that reason enough to go? I wanted to empty my mind, to free myself from the familiar. To be anyone but this unbearable person I could feel myself becoming: a heart full of anger, a head full of abstractions. So I worked my way into the centre of the dance floor, letting the music crash on my ears, the bodies beat on my body. I swayed under the strobe lights and thought, this is me, on the dance floor, emptying myself. This is me stepping into an alternate storyline.

WHEN I GOT HOME, Jenny was asleep. I wanted to shower but knew the noise would wake her, so I stripped down to my underwear and slipped into bed beside her curled form. The radio clock read 3:48 a.m. She was drenched in moonlight.

Jenny, my sepia girl. As a child she'd gone unnoticed by both her parents: Judy, a bossy and busy lawyer, and Ira, a kind but weak and no less busy dean. Their unseeing eyes had rubbed the colour right off her, so that by the time she was old enough to go to school, there was nothing left for her teachers and classmates to see. Her name sat quietly in the middle of roll call, plain and forgettable. She had a tendency to blend into backgrounds, with pale hair and skin the colour of dishwasher detergent. In class photographs, her face invariably showed up as a smudge.

Maybe that was why, when I saw her sitting across from me on my bedroom floor at age thirteen, her translucent face focused on the watercolour she was painting, I lifted my paintbrush and, on impulse, spread a faint blue streak across her cheekbone. Her eyes widened with surprise — and then she laughed. She raised her own paintbrush and staged her counterattack, the bristles reaching for my nose and forehead and eyelids, but I was too fast for her. I grabbed her skinny wrists and wrestled her to the ground. She lay under me, squirming and giggling. I stared at her mouth and suddenly it was not colourless, in fact it was bursting with colour, I had never seen anything so red. I leaned down and kissed her. For a second her eyes were wide and still. Then her face twisted as she wiped her mouth with the back of her hand, pushed me away, and ran out of the room — a room she wouldn't enter again for almost ten years.

For a long time afterward, Jenny steered clear of all painting. But then one day, at the age of sixteen, she told her mother she wanted to redecorate her room and her mother bought taupe paint and Jenny revolted. She began to fill canvases with bouquets of wild colour, to fill white with explosions of light and profusions of impossible brightness. She showed up at the dinner table with hands splattered in oils and acrylics, flicking their exotic names off her tongue one by one: amaranth, cadmium, chartreuse, burnt sienna, vermillion, xanadu, cerulean, heliotrope, atomic tangerine. She might as well have said *fuck you*.

When high school ended, she chose Concordia over McGill, fine arts over liberal. She left the wealth of Westmount and deliberately moved into the dirtiest, shittiest apartment to be found in the student ghetto. She had money but wanted to live as if she had none. She had parents but wanted to live as if she had none. She painted in her dank apartment and waited for something she could neither name nor remember. She told herself she was learning the opposite of grey, the opposite of disappearing, but for all her efforts over the coming months she remained invisible.

Until the day I showed up at her student art show, not knowing it was hers, and she let me walk her home afterwards to her tiny one-and-a-half. I touched her face and, one by one, her features sprang away from the cracked wall behind her. I held her by the hip and the grey drained away. I pushed her against the wall and she laughed a vermillion laugh, feral and throaty, her mouth stained red. I kissed her there and the colour spread — she was amaranth, cadmium, cerulean, heliotrope, atomic tangerine — and I pulled her into bed and inside the walls were raining, paint was pouring down, and outside the sky was darkening to a deep pitch black. In the morning, when I held the mirror up to her face, she wept the impossible tears of one who has never known what it is to see her own body.

I never would have thought that one day those colours would sting my eyes, forcing me to look away.


**BY THE SECOND WEEK** of the semester, the voices of my professors and classmates were needles entering through my ears and piercing my brain. When I looked down at my Norton anthology, the words on the page quietly picked up and rearranged themselves. *How long are* *you going to sit here listening to this crap?* the letters read. *Don't you have more important things to do?* I skipped one class, then two, then three. It didn't faze me. The letters were right; Barthes and his cronies would get along just fine without me.

As to the "more important" things — well. My dad's manuscript lay crumpled at the bottom of my backpack, but I couldn't bring myself to look at it.

So instead I spent every other night at the clubs, drinking and dancing until dawn. I slept in until two in the afternoon, and when I woke up, Jenny followed me around with big, worried eyes. "Don't you have school today?" she asked. "Do you want to talk?" she asked. I pretended not to hear the panic in her voice.

Then Saturday rolled around and Jenny started her job as a nude model. By the time I woke up, she was already gone. She left me a note on one of the paper cranes: *Gone to sit for Kyle & co. It's 486 Milton, in case you get lonely. Might not be back for dinner. Leftovers in fridge.*

This note filled me with an immense sense of relief — and excitement. She would be out all day, I had the place to myself, I could do anything I wanted! This excitement lasted approximately three seconds, which is how long it took me to realize that there was nothing at all I wanted to do. I picked up a novel but couldn't focus. Poetry wasn't any better. I tried to fold a paper crane but couldn't remember what to do after the first few steps.

I got dressed and went to a downtown café. When I ordered a bowl of soup, the cashier asked for my name and I told her it was Miranda, which was this thing I did sometimes. I liked to have strangers call me by other names, names that were not my own. It made me feel like I was getting away with something, hoodwinking the universe in some small cosmic way. Five minutes later, the cashier called out "Miranda!" and a bubble of happiness floated up inside me.

When I was done eating, I walked outside and tried to think of something else to do. What would Miranda be doing right now? She would be shopping for new shoes. They would come in unusual colours like turquoise and purple. They would be stylish but not painful. If she didn't feel like shoe-shopping, say if she'd just done that the day before, then she would almost certainly be acting in an independent film. Miranda was quirky and eccentric like that.

Because I didn't know how to act and couldn't bring myself to wear turquoise, I did neither of these things. What I ended up doing was thinking, but this was a mistake. I thought about Jenny, naked, surrounded by a ring of beautiful girls with boyish haircuts and over-sized glasses and androgynous names. Kyle, I was sure, would have red hair and freckles, but not in an *Anne of Green Gables* kind of way. In a sexy, look how cute I am as I eat an apple/hold a paintbrush/hand you your clothes kind of way. Would she trail her fingertips along Jenny's neck, the back of her knee, the curve of her spine to guide her out of one pose and into another? I felt sure that she would.

When I finally got home, I could hear Jenny's voice through the front door. She was speaking in a flat, grey voice, so I knew she was talking to her mother. I stood still with my key in the lock, listening to her side of the phone conversation.

"Yeah, I just ate. I don't know, salad and pasta and stuff. She's out, I think. How should I know? Out. No, I'm fine, I'm just tired. She's fine. It's okay, I got a job, I don't need more — No, really, what you sent last week is enough. Besides, I've got money saved up, I never even cashed my graduation checks. What do you mean? That's totally what savings are for. Yes, it is. *Yes*, it — Samara? She's got her scholarship, that'll tide her over for a while. What? Yes, a *long* while. Mom, it's one of the biggest scholarships in the university! It's —"

I shuffled my feet and jiggled my key in the lock. Jenny's voice stopped abruptly. Then: "Listen, I've got to go. Yeah, she just walked in. I'll talk to you soon. No, we're fine, I swear! Okay. Say hi to Dad. Bye." She looked up from her phone. "Sam?"

"Hey. How was work?"

"Boring."

"Really?"

"Yeah. I had to hold my arm in the air for like three hours."

"Did it go numb?"

"Yeah."

"Are you going to do it again?"

"Yeah."

"Can you do me a favour?"

"Anything."

"Can you pass me that magazine?"

For a second, Jenny looked dumbfounded. Then she handed me the magazine, and I sank into the couch and pretended to read. She sat at the kitchen table.

"Your brother called," she said after a while.

"He called you?"

"No, you. You forgot your phone at home, so. I saw his name come up on the screen."

I turned the page.

"I mean, I didn't answer or anything. But I think he left you a voicemail?"

I picked up my phone from where it lay on the far edge of the couch and checked my messages. Lev's voice filled my head: *Hi, um, it's me. I just wanted to tell you, I started looking through Dad's stuff, his clothes and books and stuff, to figure out what we should give away and what we should keep. Is there anything you want? Let me know soon because my yeshiva's organizing a charity drive and I —*

I deleted the message.

"Is everything okay?" Jenny said.

"Yeah."

"What did he want?"

"Just saying hi."

"Are you going to call him back?"

"Yeah."

"I could go out if you want some privacy?"

"It's okay, I'll call him later."

She didn't say anything. Instead, she took out a piece of paper and started folding another paper crane. This one was even tinier than its predecessor. I stared at my knees. She picked up a paintbrush and painted an eye onto the bird. I could feel it peeking out from under her palm, watching me.

"Or, hey," Jenny said, "maybe you want to write him a letter?"

"Lev's not really the letter-writing type."

"Still. Everyone loves getting mail, right?"

I considered this, but I knew I couldn't do it. He would want me to move back home. He wouldn't say that, of course — he was way too good to say it — but it would be obvious. And he would be right: I *should* be there to help him through this, of course I should. But. I couldn't.

And yet, to do away with the look of kindness in Jenny's eyes, I nodded. She handed me a piece of paper and a pen. Because she was still watching me, I scribbled *Dear* at the top of the page; satisfied, she turned back to her flock of tiny birds. I continued to move my hand in case she looked up again, but really I was just doodling absent-mindedly.

Then I saw what my hand had drawn and I jumped.

I'd sketched the Tree of Life.

The pen fell from my palm.

Jenny turned around and smiled at me. Even without looking directly at it, I could tell it was her brightest, most encouraging smile. It was coming. I could feel it. Three, two, one —

"So," she said. "How are you?"

We went to bed early that night. Jenny gave that nudge of her hip bone that she always gives me when she wants to have sex, but I pretended not to notice and finally she gave up and fell asleep. It was cold of me, and selfish and inconsiderate and mean, but I just couldn't help it. And I couldn't fall asleep either. So I stared up at the ceiling and felt guilty and thought about the Tree I'd drawn and then about my mother and how, when I was little, she used to tell me stories before bed. It was one of the few things I remembered about her. They were complicated Jewish folktales, and most kids probably conked out before the story was half-over. But I always refused to close my eyes until she got to the end and answered the question my schoolteachers had drilled into me: what is the moral of this story?

So, for example, when my mother told me the legend of the four rabbis who entered a holy garden, counting off their fates on her fingers — "One died, one went crazy, one 'cut down the plantings' (not sure what that means exactly, but it's not good!), and only one came out okay" — I asked her what the story was supposed to teach me about how to handle that kind of situation. She laughed and laughed, and I asked her what, what, until finally she told me that I had nothing to worry about, girls didn't go wandering into strange gardens, girls didn't climb the Tree of Life! What did girls do then, I wanted to know. Well, they grew up to be good women who married good learned men, she said, stroking my hair. And once they got married they covered their hair and raised their God-fearing children and that was that! Wasn't I looking forward to that? Didn't that sound like fun?

Beside me, tangled in the moonlit sheets, Jenny shifted in her sleep.

THE NEXT FRIDAY, Jenny and I took the bus to Mile End and Lev greeted us at the door. His face was a pale blur above the whiteness of his button-down shirt, contrasting sharply with his black dress pants. He motioned us inside with a smile. But it was a smile hitched up by elastic bands. His eyes, big and blue and blinking fast, were untouched by it.

As we stepped over the threshold, Jenny gave my hand a little squeeze. She knew that her presence at these Friday night dinners was the only thing getting me through them, that if she didn't keep pushing me — gently but insistently — to come, reminding me I was all Lev had left in this world (as if I could forget!), I would probably beg off. It wasn't that I didn't want to see him. It was just becoming too hard.

Lev recited the blessings over the wine and the bread, and we sat down to eat. Jenny launched into a series of cheerful questions about Lev's school life. Was he liking his yeshiva classes this year? Were the rabbis really super-strict? Why did they all wear the same black coats, black hats, black shoes, and black beards? Lev fielded her questions calmly, politely, but with a strange new distance in his eyes.

Then Jenny asked, "So, did Samara tell you I got a new job?"

I shifted uneasily in my chair. I had let Jenny assume that I was speaking, or at least writing, to Lev on a regular basis. His eyes flickered toward mine, then away.

"No, she didn't," he murmured. "What's the job?"

"Oh, it's with these art students. They're learning to draw the human form, and they need a model to sit for them." Jenny paused. "Sam didn't mention it?"

Lev was blushing now. I could tell Jenny thought my pious brother was embarrassed at the thought of a woman's naked form, because she swiftly changed the topic by asking if we were ready to move on to dessert. Relief eased the tension in Lev's face; he nodded. But instead of offering to clear up, I excused myself and went down the hall.

I had to be quick. I only had five minutes until Jenny, increasingly concerned about my mental state, came looking for me. And I didn't want her to find me in my dad's study again. I snuck into my old bedroom and dug my flashlight out from the space between the mattress and the wall. Then I ducked into the study and closed the door behind me, turning on the flashlight and pointing it at the desk. A beam of light illuminated the volumes scattered across the blotter.

I grabbed the first book that came to hand and flipped through its pages, searching for something — an underlined passage or a dog-eared page — anything that would help me understand my father's fascination with the Tree of Life. Nothing. I grabbed the second book.

Nothing. I was running out of time. I abandoned the books on the desk to scan the titles on the bookshelves behind his chair. Nothing leapt out at me. Growing frustrated, I went from shelf to shelf, plucking a book out at random, testing its weight in my hands, jamming it back into place only to run back a moment later and pluck it out again — but still nothing.

I slumped down at the desk in despair. Through the window, I saw the silhouetted form of a stooped man who could only have been Mr. Glassman. He was standing at his window, watching me. He raised his hand as if to wave — but, before he could complete the gesture, I killed the flashlight and ducked under the desk.

Calm down, I told myself. Calm. Down. It's just Mr. Glassman! But the sight of my old teacher had always instilled in me a confusing mixture of nostalgia and guilt. Before the bat mitzvah, he'd spent countless hours teaching me, then countless more in after-school attention. Day after day, he graced me with his gentle smile, his ear patiently inclined as I rehearsed and re-rehearsed my Torah portion. After the bat mitzvah he naturally assumed that I would continue my studies. Instead I shunned him. I couldn't bear to explain to him why, and so he was forced to come asking me what was wrong, didn't I want to study anymore, it was such a shame, really such a shame, I had such a *kop* for Talmud! Every time I ignored him, it became that much harder to do anything else but ignore him the next time he came around. Even after his wife got sick, I hadn't gone to visit him. Even then I'd kept on punishing him for a failure that was not, never had been, his fault: my failure to make my father hear me.

All of which struck me now as profoundly ironic. Because if anyone could help me understand my father's journey up the Tree, it was Mr. Glassman. But I felt too guilty to ask.

How long had I been here? Realizing I had better get back, I flicked the flashlight on again — and that's when I saw it.

The book jumped out at me, not because it was lying on the floor under the desk, not because of its bright blue dust jacket, but because it was the one thing in this room that didn't belong. The one thing here that was not like the others. This book was not part of my dad's collection. It was part of Lev's. I picked it up and it folded open like a flower in my hands.

> You must make your heart like an empty instrument
> so that the spirit of God can blow through you. Any
> blockage at all will prevent the making of this divine
> music. Even something that is traditionally considered
> good and worthy can constitute a blockage: knowledge,
> for instance. What is required is a certain emptiness,
> or quietness, of mind.

Written in pencil beside this paragraph was a single, telling "!"

One exclamation point. A clue. A sign. Not one that I'd been searching for — but then, wasn't that mostly how people came upon signs — when they weren't searching for them?

Quietly, the words on the page picked up and rearranged themselves. *If you really want to understand the Tree, you've got to empty yourself completely. You've got to be willing to go all the way. The only question now is: do you want to understand?*

I closed the book, turned off my flashlight, and walked out of the study. I rejoined Lev and Jenny at the kitchen table for dessert and was halfway through it before I realized that they were looking at me strangely. That I was nodding in response to a question neither of them had asked me: *yes, yes, I do, yes, yes.*

IN MY DREAM I was climbing toward something. I didn't know what but I knew I was getting close. A deep voice sang over my head, calling me higher, urging me into the light. The sound and sight were mixing with a bitter smell. Turpentine or paint. Heat was on the rise. I kicked off the sheets and opened my eyes.

Sunlight poured through the open window. Jenny stood with her back to me, a purple silhouette, her pale hair swept up in a messy bun. She liked to have her hair away from her face when she painted, and she was painting now, her brush skipping lightly across the canvas.

"Morning," I mumbled and wiped the sleep from my eyes.

She didn't answer. Squinting, I saw that she was wearing earphones. Her hips swayed back and forth, dancing to a music I couldn't hear. The sight made me smile. I crawled across the sheets to kneel on the foot of the bed and grabbed her round the waist. She spun around, startled.

"You scared me!" she said, but she didn't look angry. As I pulled her toward me, one of the earphones fell from her ear, dangling over her warm shoulder. I brushed it away and kissed her. Her mouth pressed against mine, her hands moving toward my face — hands covered in green paint. I pulled back, the image stirring something in me I couldn't quite remember.

"Sam, what is it?"

"Nothing."

She leaned down to kiss me again but I was already rising; her lips brushed my collarbone instead. I pecked her on the cheek and dressed quickly, then shuffled into the bathroom, turned on the tap, and splashed water on my face. After a minute, she came up behind me. I continued throwing handfuls of water at myself.

"So, do you want to see a movie today?" she asked. "There's a Truffaut retrospective at Cinema du Parc. Unless you have reading to do for school?"

"I don't."

"Great!" she said. Then, in a slightly suspicious tone, she added, "But, wait, how do you not have reading to do? You always have reading to do. Plus, I thought you said that Zimmerman guy was trying to get through the entire Western canon in one semester, so —"

I met her gaze in the mirror. I might as well tell her now. It would come out sooner or later anyway. "I'm dropping out," I said.

She stared at me, then laughed. "You're joking."

"Nope."

"But — why?"

"It's just not the right time."

"Not the right *time?* For what, getting an education?"

"I just — it's just not something I can handle right now."

"Do you hate your classes? Is that what this is? Because you can withdraw, it's not too late to withdraw, you know. Is it the Zimmerman class? If you hate him, you can totally —"

"I do hate him, but it's not that. I'm just dropping out, okay?"

"No, it's not okay. You're — Samara, you're so smart, you have practically the biggest scholarship in the university, and you're just going to — throw it away?"

"Yes."

She squeezed her eyes shut and took a deep breath, trying to steady herself. I turned on the hot water and let it warm the back of my hands, which was this thing I did sometimes. Slowly, she said, "Okay. If this is about your dad, okay. I get it. If you need to take a leave of absence, that's fine. You can go back next semester, and graduate in the winter instead of the summer, that's fine, that's not a big deal." She took another deep breath. "But if that's what's going to happen, I think we should get jobs."

"You already have a job."

"I think —"

"You think I should get a job."

"Well, would it be such a bad idea? It might take your mind off —"

"That's not even what this is about. This is just about my scholarship money, isn't it?"

"You know it isn't," she said quietly.

I glanced down at my hands in the sink. They were turning red.

"Listen," she said over the sound of the water, and I could tell she was trying to be patient. "I just think we both have to try and pull our own weight. The first of the month is coming up and money doesn't grow on —"

"Yeah well, you're not exactly paying rent either."

She stared at me, mouth agape. Then: "Fuck you."

I didn't even bother to turn off the tap. I walked out of the apartment, my hands dripping soap and water, and slammed the door.


**I FOUND HANNAH** working the cash at Two Moons Café. When I asked her if there were any job openings she looked surprised, but said yes. If I waited twenty minutes the manager would be coming in and might even be able to interview me on the spot. Could I wait? I guessed I probably could.

Leaning against the counter, I saw a little girl sitting alone at a table for four. She had a huge sketchpad and a watercolour kit in front of her. She was alternately painting, scowling, and picking her nose. I looked for the parent or adult who must have accompanied her here, but there was none.

Hannah followed my gaze. "That's Lily."

"Lily?"

"My niece. She's five."

I glanced at Hannah, then back at Lily. I could see the resemblance now: wispy blonde hair, blue eyes. The kid's scowl — so different from Hannah's yogic smile — had thrown me off. "What's she doing here?"

"My sister brings her by sometimes, when she doesn't have time to watch her. Just dumps her there and comes back to pick her up at the end of my shift. Her boyfriend — Lily's dad — it looks like he's taken off for good now, so." Hannah shrugged. "Free baby-sitting."

I nodded. I'd met Lily's deadbeat dad and ex-hippie mom exactly once, at a birthday party of Hannah's. They'd shown up high and spent the entire night fighting in the bathroom. It wasn't hard to understand why their little girl was now painting with such reckless abandon, such fury in her eyes. I had never seen anyone look so unhappy while colouring.

Just then the manager came in and Hannah introduced us. Tyler was tall and muscular, with reddish blonde hair, a loud laugh, and a frat-boy expression that contradicted his thirty-odd years. He looked me up and down, placed a hand on the small of my back, and guided me toward a table. I glanced over my shoulder at Hannah, who rolled her eyes.

I expected Tyler to ask me about my skill set and previous work experience, and I was getting ready to break it to him that I had none. But he seemed more interested in my personal life. So, I was a friend of Hannah's? How come he hadn't seen me in here before? He definitely would have remembered a face like mine. How old did I say I was again?

A few minutes later, I was hired.

By the time I got home, it was that violet hour right before dusk. Jenny sat at the kitchen table, but she wasn't eating. The entire surface of the table was covered in miniature paper cranes.

I told her about my new job. She put down her paintbrush but said nothing.

I spoke again. "Happy?"

"Ecstatic."

But a moment later she stepped into the bathroom and closed the door. The apartment felt very quiet, like a library or a cathedral. I looked down at the birds, stiff and flightless in the bruised, washed-out light. A thousand beady eyes stared up at me. When I looked closer, I noticed that all the eyes were crying.

ON THURSDAY, I started my new job at the café. Right away, I liked it. Standing behind the counter, twisting a dishcloth over the same mug ten, then twenty, then thirty times — it was a motion that calmed me, beautifully boring and repetitive, like counting beads on a rosary. I measured out minutes with coffee spoons and they trickled down easily — one, two, three, four — carrying me through the morning with something not unlike peace.

Whenever there was a lull, my gaze would flit from customer to customer. I recognized a lot of the regulars, the anarchists who sat at the long tables in back and the little old lady who whispered to the empty seat beside her. Their reliability gave me a cozy feeling, but my eyes kept returning to a boy by the window, his head bent over a note-book, scribbling furiously. "What's with the kid?" I asked.

"What kid?" Hannah replied, her hands fluttering over the teacups. She was stacking them into a pyramid that always looked precarious but managed miraculously to endure.

I pointed.

"Oh, him. I don't know, he comes in here almost every morning for breakfast. Afternoons, too, sometimes. Orders a drink and sits for ages."

The kid was probably around thirteen or fourteen years old. His yellow hair gleamed in the sunlight and I resisted the urge to go up and touch it. But the intense focus in his face and the curve of his shoulders hunched over the page reminded me of Alex. I looked away, twisting the dishcloth over the mug in my hand — five, six, seven, eight.

And I wondered: is this what Jenny feels when she sits in the cen-tre of the circle, posing? Does she measure out minutes in the flick of brushes, in the flash of light? Does the numbness that gathers in her hand gradually spread to her arm, moving from arm to neck and from neck to mind, wiping out sadness, wiping out sound, leaving only a faint white noise? I wondered: is her work as boring as mine? Does it allow her to alchemize time?

**I RETURNED TO** an empty apartment. Relieved not to have to answer any questions, I undressed and ran a bath. But just when I was standing with one foot in the tub and the other in midair, two things happened: Jenny came home, and her phone rang. She called my name and I didn't answer. She picked up the call, but I didn't put the other foot in the water. I stayed standing, half in and half out, while she mumbled into the phone.

"Hello? Yeah. I'm fine. It's — Well, if you want to worry about someone, worry about Sam. No, I didn't mean — she doesn't need — she just needs time. I don't know, these things don't run on a clock, I can't tell you exactly — What? She's working. A café somewhere. No, I don't know the name, who cares? Are you crazy, she wouldn't do that. Because I know her. *We* know her. She wouldn't lie. No, we don't need money. Because, we've got jobs, I just told you that! Oh my god, what do you want me to do, follow her to work to make sure it exists?"

She slammed down the phone. As if my ankle had been tied to it with a piece of invisible string, I lost my balance. The foot that had been dangling in midair plunked into the water. From the next room, I heard a sharp intake of breath.

My heart was beating like crazy. It was so loud, I could almost hear it. Suddenly, I had an overwhelming desire to take a shower, not a bath. I turned the nozzle, the showerhead spurted on, the rush of water was a beautiful music drowning out everything.

When I emerged from the bathroom a half hour later, I found Jenny stringing up paper cranes from the ceiling. I dressed and told her I was going out. She flinched, but said nothing.

My hair was still soaking wet. As I walked along the street, drops of water clung to the strands. They held on for as long as possible, as if intent on defying gravity, and then they let go, darkening the pavement behind me like a secret stain, like a trail of breadcrumbs.

"**YOU CAN'T GET IN** like that," said the bouncer outside the club on Saint-Catherine Street.

"What?"

"You can't come in here dressed like that."

"Why not?"

"It's the first Thursday of the month."

"So?"

"So you don't know what happens here on the first Thursday of the month?"

"I guess not."

He considered. "Take off the dress and I'll let you in."

I gaped, then did as he said. I felt self-conscious in just my bra and leggings, but this feeling disappeared the instant I crept into the club. There was skin everywhere, standing out bright against the darkness. What little of it wasn't exposed was covered in leather or latex or lace. I must have looked like a nun by comparison.

The music was loud, with a heavy bass line, but for once I had no desire to dance. A man leaning against the wall tested the strength of a whip in his hand. A few feet away, a woman watched imperiously as a crouched figure licked at the toe of her leather boot. I lacked the will to turn away or even register shock. Empty, I stood on the side-lines and surveyed the scene.

The place was full of yellow smoke. It licked bodies, snaked around ankles, tongued the farthest corners of the club. I followed it away from the dance floor and into one of the chambers off the main room.

A dark-eyed girl wearing only a collar, a bra, and a short schoolgirl skirt cowered at the feet of a large woman. The woman, dressed in a black silk corset and rubber pencil skirt, had one arm raised above her head; she was holding a riding crop. She whispered a question to the girl, who nodded once and murmured something under her breath. The woman lifted the skirt. The riding crop came whistling down.

The girl groaned and her eyes flew open, her face an ecstasy of surrender. I gasped and the large woman gave me an encouraging smile: "Your turn?"

Suddenly I was nine years old and all the other girls in the playground were jumping off their swings. This was a game they had invented the year before. Each girl pumped her legs furiously. When her swing reached its highest possible point, she stood up on it and jumped. I was the only one left, and I could see them waiting down below. "Fall! Fall!" they shouted, but I was dizzy just thinking about it. One girl called, "Falling is like flying!" and all the other girls started yelling, "Fly! Fly!" but still I couldn't do it. And now the girls were getting bored. I could see their thin backs turning. It was this sight, more than anything else, that spurred me into action. "Falling is like flying!" I repeated, and was just about to let go of the chains when I looked up and realized that everyone was gone.

I shook my head to erase the memory, and saw that the woman's eyes were now strangely focused. Not on me. On a point slightly below and to the right of my head.

I swung around — and it was her.

She turned away before I could see her face, but I recognized her anyway.

My sepia girl.

She pushed her way onto the dance floor. Oh no. You followed me, now I will follow you. She tried to lose herself in the crowd but I kept my eyes fixed to her back. She wriggled on the pin of my vision, but I could see her white fingertips, now spindling above her head, now touching a boy's cheekbone, now meeting empty air. I shoved through the dancers — uppercuts, right and left hooks — until at last I reached her.

Jenny.

I grabbed her by the hips, twisted her round and stared into her eyes — only she had no eyes.

Everything went silent. The volume of the world dipped then plummeted then crashed to zero. I stared and suddenly knew. Ani, the beautiful maiden without eyes, the key to the first vessel on the Tree. A girl who reflects the light of others but is incapable of emitting any light of her own. A girl who remains invisible until the beam of your attention is turned on her body. How had I not seen it before?

As the key fell into my palm, all my anger vaporized. I put my hands on her hips. Inside my skull, nothing was left but an inchoate clicking and swarming, a prelingual consciousness, a guttural awe. I kissed her.


AFTER THAT NIGHT, we became lovers again. We shut the blinds and stayed in bed. We tore at each other with hands, teeth, all the accumulated misery of the past few weeks. She sank her nails into my back; they formed a hundred half-moons, perfect crescents that waxed and did not wane. She dragged her nails downward and comets streaked between my shoulders. When I bit her, bruises rose like tulips on her skin. Her thighs were bouquets of blue and yellow and purple, her throat a riot of colour. We grew fierce and then gentle and then fierce again.

This state of bliss lasted exactly three days. On the morning of the fourth day, my phone lit up with a text from Lev.

*Mr. Glassman asked about you again today. Wants to know how you are. What should I say? Also, charity drive is tomorrow so I'm giving away all of Dad's clothes. Unless you want to keep something?*

I hurled the phone across the room.

Jenny glanced up, startled. "What's wrong?"

"Nothing."

She studied my face. Then, in a quiet voice, she said, "I think we need to talk."

"Oh?"

"I'm worried about you."

"Yet you hide it so well."

"Sam, don't get all sarcastic with me. I know it's only been a few weeks since — you know — since the funeral, and everyone grieves in their own way, but you need to stop taking it out on me. Okay?"

I glared at her.

"And you need to start... well, don't you think it's time to rejoin the land of the living?"

Blood was pounding in my ears.

"What I'm saying — what I'm trying to say — is that you used to be so — ambitious. I mean — motivated. You had all these projects and like, goals, but now —"

"I've got goals."

"Name one."

"I'm climbing —" I screamed, but stopped myself. I'd been about to say: I'm climbing the Tree of Life! Which I hadn't meant to say. Which I hadn't even really realized I was doing. Yet now that it popped into my head, I thought: *of course* that's what I'm doing! That's what I've been doing all along! I didn't choose this path, but it's chosen me — and I'm going to go all the way.

"You're climbing...?" Jenny repeated uncertainly.

"I have to go," I said. And I left.

I HAD THE MORNING SHIFT at Two Moons. For three uninterrupted hours, I served decaf lattes and cappuccinos as if nothing at all extraordinary were going on. I withstood Tyler's flirtatious grins and did my best impression of a normal person, and this was very convincing, because it was a trick I had perfected over the years.

With the morning rush over and a deep lull setting in, Tyler left me to watch over the café alone. Behind the counter, I pulled the sheaf of papers out of my backpack and read, not my dad's words, but a dream I had recorded in the margins of his manuscript.

*Everything was made of light. Above my head roots reached toward me like tiny outstretched hands. I gripped them and they pulled me up. When I climbed into the branches, I saw that they bore a luminous kind of fruit. Except that it wasn't fruit, exactly. It was books, and the books too were made of light. There was no breeze, but the pages were rustling, and they looked delicious. Irresistible. I slithered across a branch and plucked a book off its stem. I took a bite — and my eyes popped open.*

This was something I had started doing recently. Writing comments in the margins. At first it was just thoughts that sprang to mind as I read, but after a while I started scrawling down everything, especially my dreams. Getting them out onto the page helped to clear my head. But it was more than that. All my life my dad had locked himself away in his study, spending hour after hour writing manuscripts like this one, while I waited outside the door. Now he was the one outside the door. I was the one scribbling furiously all over his book. Covering his words with my words, glossing his dreams with mine.

The yellow-haired boy who reminded me of Alex came up to order a blueberry smoothie. He paid and I asked him what his name was, even though at this café we didn't do that thing where you call out the customer's name. He told me it was Brendan.

A minute later, I took the drink to Brendan's table. He was poring over that notebook of his, completely engrossed. I stole a glance at the page and noticed that it was full of numbers.

I stared, remembering the day I met Alex. The day he taught me to crack binary code.

But this was a memory, and memories generated thoughts, and thoughts generated other thoughts. Because I couldn't afford to ruin the empty state my mind had achieved, I shook the memory off, tapped Brendan on the shoulder, and handed him his drink, barely acknowledging his smile. Then I headed back behind the counter where, with no more customers to serve, I took up my father's book again and read the next chapter.

> YESOD is the second vessel from the bottom of the Tree. Literally, it means foundation. Just as a building's foundation is its grounding, its union with the earth, Yesod grounds the divine realm of the upper vessels in the physical realm symbolized by Ani. It is what guarantees balance and stability, prevents a structure from collapsing.

So far, so good, I thought. Foundation, balance, stability — this doesn't sound too difficult. But then, a bit further down, I read something that left me feeling cold with dread:

> All the vessels are associated with human organs; Yesod is symbolized as the male phallus. Inasmuch as this organ corresponds to the male reproductive ability, it is the foundation of generations to come. Yesod's primary association, then, is with male sexuality.

I shuddered at the thought of what I'd have to do next.

EVEN THOUGH IT seemed obvious what I needed to do, I didn't make my move right away. I had to be patient and wait for the perfect opportunity. The trick would be to make him think it was all his idea.

Two weeks later, Hannah called to say she was sick and Tyler would need someone to help him close up. The only catch was that Lily, Hannah's niece, was supposed to spend the afternoon at the café that day. Would that be a problem? No, of course not. Lily could be a difficult kid, but her mother would come by to pick her up no later than five — could I watch her until then? Of course I could. Hannah thanked me profusely, coughed, and hung up.

Perfect.

When I got to the café, Lily didn't seem to be in one of her difficult moods. While I served coffee, she sat down at a table, set up her sketchpad and watercolour kit, ignored me. Every so often the paintbrush would fall from her pudgy fist, and she would stare off into space, kicking the leg of the table or picking her nose. Then she would get a second wind and begin a new painting. Hours passed. Customers came and went. Clearly Lily had zero interest in talking to me, and this suited us both perfectly. But then, just a few minutes before five o'clock rolled around, she put down her brush, waved me over, and told me to look.

I looked. In her hands was a painting of a house and three stick figures — father, mother, and little girl. I smiled. The mother and the little girl had been drawn to scale, but the father loomed impossibly large; he measured as high as the house.

"That one's my dad."

"Oh."

"He left."

"Oh?"

"But he's coming back."

"Oh. That's nice."

"He's coming back," she repeated, and her voice reached for but failed to hit the note of perfect faith. As if aware of her own failure, she let her voice fall into a colder, meaner register. "Where's your dad?"

"My dad? He left, too."

"Is he coming back?"

I said nothing.

"Hello?"

I said nothing.

"I *said*, is he coming back?"

The word NO ballooned in my head, but right at that moment the door opened and Lily's mother walked in. She marched toward her daughter and ordered her to pack away her things. Lily picked up her brush and started to paint flowers by the house. Her mom counted down from three, her voice growing harsher with each number. Three. Two. One! Only then did Lily surrender her brush, leaving her mom to stuff her watercolour kit into her backpack and yank her by the wrist toward the door.

As much as I hated watching the kid be dragged out like that, I was glad she was gone. The café was empty now. It was five o'clock — closing time — and there was no one left but Tyler and me. The sun was sinking and I urged it to sink faster; darkness would make it easier for me to do what I was about to do.

As we wiped down the tables, Tyler grinned at me and I grinned back, then lowered my gaze to telegraph shyness — a look I'd perfected over the past two weeks. When he asked if I smoked, I lied and said yes. Did I want to join him for one last smoke behind the café before heading home? Sure, why not. He turned off the lights, then placed his fingers on the small of my back, as if I couldn't figure out how to make it out the door and needed to be guided.

We emerged into the gold autumn light of the alley. Leaning against a brick wall, he reached into the back pocket of his jeans and pulled out a pack of smokes. He put one between his lips, then held another out toward me. But, instead of taking it, I opened my mouth slightly. He raised his eyebrows before slipping the cigarette between my lips. I leaned toward him. He searched my eyes. Then he lit my cigarette and his, took a deep drag, exhaled.

I glanced around. The sunlight — there was still too much of it. It glinted off everything: the nearby garbage bags, the shards of broken beer bottles, the black asphalt. Tyler was talking now, saying something about his brother, something about how good he used to be at sports. Immediately, I tuned him out. This wouldn't do, this image of Tyler as an actual person, a person who had a brother. Instead,

I focused my attention on his stubbled chin, where the dying light was making the tiny reddish hairs gleam.

Tyler dropped his cigarette onto the ground and stubbed it out with a toe. I did the same. I pretended to shiver, nestling closer to him. Laughing, he took off the jacket he had on over a T-shirt and draped it around my shoulders. I put my palm on his neck and he grinned. And then, with the confidence of a prince collecting his birthright, he leaned in to kiss me.

I pushed him off with a single outstretched hand. He opened his mouth in protest, but my hand was already moving down his chest. I grabbed his belt buckle and yanked it toward me. His body froze, eyes filled with disbelief. I sank toward the ground.

I saw myself unbuckling his belt and I died. I saw his pants swirling around his ankles and I died. I saw my knees jammed against the pavement and his cock in my mouth and I died. But I repeated the word *Yesod* in my head. I was ready to *Yesod Yesod Yesod* all night if I had to. He vaulted above me, I arched under him, sweat pooled in the salty cradle of my neck. I was so close but still not close enough. And he, he was getting too close, I begged him in my head, not yet, not yet, not yet. Not until I've done what I came here to do. He didn't listen; he came, and still I hadn't found it. If his body contained the secrets, it was not divulging them, but I was determined and my tongue wrapped around his cock, slipped over his kneecap, darted along his inner arm, dipped blindly into the concave shadow of his elbow, pushed into the space between each knuckle, all the while with an ear trained on the skin the way a safe-cracker presses his cheek to metal as he listens for the sounds of the twisting dial. *Click-click* I'm searching for the combination *click-click* I know it's here somewhere *click-click* I keep expecting it to surrender to my touch, but the safe remains uncracked, the body keeps its secrets.

THE RADIO CLOCK read 3:02 a.m. I needed a shower, so I peeled off my clothes and turned on the tap, even though I knew it would wake Jenny. The water hit my body and pierced the skin, each drop pulling up flesh with the force of a thousand fishhooks. I wanted to stay there forever, washing the stench of this day off me: the blowjob, and then all the bars I'd gone to, all the drinks I'd poured down my throat in an effort to drown out the taste of Tyler, which was the taste of my own stupidity. What the hell was wrong with me? Had I actually believed I could attain a mystical key via the power of a back-alley blowjob? My reading of Yesod had been laughably simplistic, and so, standing in the shower now, I laughed.

When I finally stepped out, wrapping myself in a towel in front of the mirror, Jenny came up behind me. I turned.

"Hi."

I laughed.

"Samara."

More laughter.

"Are you drunk?"

I couldn't help it; I laughed even harder.

"Come to bed."

Her tone was so uncharacteristically sharp that I stopped laughing immediately. But not because I was unhappy; on the contrary, this made me extremely happy. I was an orphan and finally she was treating me with the bossiness that orphans secretly crave.

I followed her meekly to bed. She leaned down, brought the covers up to my chin, then stopped. She sniffed the air above my head. Suddenly, I became intensely aware that I had forgotten to wash my hair. Could she smell the betrayal on me? She settled herself in the chair by the window and ordered me to close my eyes. I knew I wouldn't be able to sleep — I was still too buzzed — but I obeyed for the sheer pleasure of it. If she knew that I had cheated, she said nothing to indicate it.

But when I woke, I saw her suitcase standing open in the middle of the apartment. Clothes spilled out of it, as though she'd decided to leave but had lost the nerve before she could finish packing. I hated her for her weakness. The apartment was empty, she'd gone out, and I hated her for that, too. "Leave then! Leave!" I wanted to scream at her, because I knew she never would; that was the reason I loved and hated her so much.

I dragged myself out of bed, my feet landing on a black square tile. It gave me a weirdly constricted feeling. In this apartment, options were limited. You could only move across the chessboard in specific, pre-ordained ways. This was sometimes awkward: if you wanted to get from the bed to the fridge, you had to do it in a series of L-shaped moves, even though the shortest distance between the two points was a straight line. Some objects were beyond reach entirely. Could you touch the easel, for example? You could not. You could see it, it was right there by the window, but it stood on a white square and you could only travel on black. What about that person beside you, could you reach out and graze her shoulder? You could not.

Some time later, Jenny came home. Her eyes were red, her arms were full of groceries, and I knew she had told Kyle everything. She put the bags on the kitchen table and pulled items from their dark interiors. She placed each item in the fridge slowly, carefully, with a painstaking precision.

Every chess player knows that in an end game pawns suddenly become very important. Winning the game often involves advancing a pawn to the centre of the board. To do this, it sometimes becomes necessary to sacrifice the queen.


ONE DAY IN NOVEMBER, Hannah and I worked the same shift at Two Moons. It was late afternoon, and the place was calm, just a handful of customers reading or talking in the crisp autumn light. As I rinsed and she stacked teacups, Hannah kept up a steady stream of chatter about this song and that boy, this versus that type of yoga, the healing properties of various crystals. I thought for the hundredth time how grateful I was for the sound of her voice. It spilled on and on like thread off a tumbling spool.

Brendan came up to order a drink and Hannah started to prepare it. He had his notebook in hand and I asked if I could see what he was working on. When he showed me a giant grid filled with digits, I recognized it as one of those magic squares, where each row and column adds up to the exact same number. Impressed, I said, "You must be really good at math."

"Actually, I'm pretty much the worst in my class."

"Seriously? But you're always messing around with numbers."

"Numbers don't like me, but I like them."

"What do you mean?"

"Have you ever heard of synesthesia?"

I nodded. "Why, do you have it?"

"Yeah. For me, numbers have colours."

"Really?"

"I know, it's weird, right? When I look at a number, all of a sudden I can see a colour — or, well, I can feel it. Like one thing triggers the other thing in my head, and then it just seems so obvious that six is blue, or that three is green, you know? It's kind of hard to explain."

"No, actually, I think I know what you mean."

Hannah had finished making his drink. I turned to give it to him —

And then the door opened, and a woman walked in. A green dress swirled about her knees. Her dark hair fell a few inches below her shoulders. In her arms was a stack of books. As she placed them on a table, she blew the bangs out of her eyes with an upward puff of air. Then she walked toward the counter. Toward me.

The teacup slipped from my hand and fell to the floor, shattering.

"What the — ?" Hannah said, but before she could even turn around I was racing to the bathroom, locking myself in a stall, a flood of hot tears gushing up my throat.

I lowered the lid of the toilet and sat. Fists clenched, heart racing.

My breath came in sharp, staccato rhythms that ripped the oxygen from my lungs instead of filling them with air.

It was her. She was wearing a different dress now — not the black one she'd worn at the funeral, or the black one she'd worn at the hospital — but I recognized her. I'd have recognized her anywhere, even though we'd never been introduced, even though I'd only ever heard her name spoken in muffled tones, late at night, through closed doors. Valérie, for the most part. On occasion, Val. And, once or twice, Valkyrie.

I remembered the rumours I'd heard floating around the girls' bathrooms at McGill ("Did you hear about David Meyer's latest love interest?" "*Another* student?" "Yes! Another one!"), rumours of the kind I'd been hearing since my first year of undergrad. It hadn't exactly come as a shock — I'd been all of twelve years old when I figured out why Dad "worked late" so many Friday nights — but the campus gossip had rankled. As had the smell of her perfume in his shirts (which, no, Lev, I couldn't bring myself to want), as had her insistence on stalking us the day of his funeral, when she had shown up first at the burial site, then at the *shiva* house.

And now she was *here*, and I had no idea what to do. She might know things I didn't know about my father's climb up the Tree. Clues that could lead me to the second vessel — the vessel I was failing, so pathetically, to find. But at that thought I squared my shoulders, clenched my jaw. Why should I go running to her for help? My dad's lover, the keeper of his secret life, a life he obviously valued more than his family because he spent so much more time with her than he ever did with us?

When I finally unbolted the door and re-entered the café, she was gone.

The room was peaceful. Behind the counter, the floor was clear; Hannah had swept up my mess. She had gone back to stacking cups, placing them in the precarious pyramid that I would never even dream of attempting but that she pulled off beautifully, effortlessly.

The cups sat atop one another high up on their shelf, their angles straight and stable. I smiled at the sight. And then, just like that, I saw it. Not the cups, but the sheaves of light pouring off them, funneling and streaming into the sky. A perfect foundation, a model of balance — and in my fingers, vibrating with that familiar golden hum, the key to Yesod.

AS JENNY AND I rode the bus to Mile End for Lev's birthday, she stared stonily out the window, her hands folded over a cake box, while I pondered the key.

After the way it had appeared to me freely, it seemed even more absurd that I'd ever tried to wrest it from Tyler. The idea that these keys could be *wrested* at all was a mistake I'd picked up from my dad — I saw that now. You couldn't force the universe's hand. It didn't work that way. But if you waited in utter emptiness, the signs would come to you...

The bus pulled in to the stop beside Katz's house. When we got out, I stared at the tin can tree on his lawn. A bitter laugh escaped me. Jenny threw me a weird look, but I couldn't help it: it had put me in mind of the mystical garden where, according to the old folktale, four entered and only one escaped unscathed. How arrogant my dad had been! To think he could succeed where men so much greater than him had failed, *and by skipping most of the steps!* Such hubris — it was almost tragically funny.

But now we were walking up the path to the house; now Jenny was ringing the bell. The door swung open and she greeted Lev with a loud and bubbly *happy birthday!* He tried to take the cake box from her but she swatted his hand away, laughing. As she hugged him, I thought how well the two of them had always gotten along. The fact that he was hugging her at all was proof of this: his orthodoxy barred him from touching any woman outside his immediate family, but he'd always made an exception for Jenny, who'd grown up alongside him. Who was like a sister to him. Who was — as I knew he knew, even before I'd got up the guts to tell him — dating his sister.

I followed them into the kitchen — where, unexpectedly, Alex sprang up from his seat to greet us.

"Hey, Samara, good to —" he said, and then he saw I hadn't come alone. "Oh, hi, Jenny."

We sat down to eat. Lev passed around the wine and the bread, but didn't recite any blessings. I stole a curious glance at him — had he just forgotten? — but he wasn't making eye contact. I moved food around my plate while Jenny did her best to keep the mood light. She skillfully avoided, in her chatty way, any topic Lev and I might potentially find depressing, such as the ozone layer and melting ice caps and urban sprawl and the fact that we were both now orphans. The morbid irony of celebrating somebody's birth weeks after the person who gave him life has just died — she skated around that, too.

When it came time for dessert, she left the kitchen for a minute and returned with a Black Forest cake in hand and a huge grin on her face. Lev laughed. She'd put two lit candles on top, the ones shaped like numbers that you see at little kids' birthday parties. She placed it on the table in front of him, a pair of glowing 2s reflected in his eyes.

"Make a wish!" Jenny said.

Lev closed his eyes and blew.

Jenny plucked the candles from the droopy frosting and handed a knife to Lev, who cut four slices. She handed one of these to me.

"I'm not hungry," I said.

Jenny studied my dinner plate, still full of food. "Samara," she said quietly, "you've barely eaten anything."

"I'm not hungry," I said again.

"Okay, but. You still have to eat. Your body needs food."

I shrugged. "People are more than just bodies."

"Well yeah, sure, okay, but I mean —"

"Hasn't there ever been a moment in your life when you felt really separate, really far away from your own body?"

"That's really not the point though, is it, because you —"

"I have," Alex said suddenly, and we all swivelled to look at him. A slow smile spread across his face. "It was on my ninth birthday. My mom got me a telescope as a gift, and that night was a clear night, so she helped me set it up on the balcony. She was too tired and cold to stand there searching for stars, but she let me try it out by myself. I pressed my eye to the lens and moved the telescope in these really tiny, really patient increments across the sky — and then, all of a sudden, I was right smack dab in the middle of the Pleiades! They're just seven stars, you know, but they filled my whole field of vision and — I think I forgot to breathe! My feet, it was like they weren't even touching the balcony anymore. I was just up in the sky, surrounded by stars on all sides, totally unaware of the physical —"

"Exactly!" I cried. "It's exactly like that. You get to this place, it's beyond the body and you just — it's just the best feeling — you don't even want to come down anymore because it's so clear up there and everything down on Earth looks so totally unimportant, so pathetic, really, and —"

I faltered. Alex and Jenny and Lev, all of them were staring at me strangely. All of them afraid. Then I realized that I was standing up, though I didn't remember having left my chair, and my voice was piercing, though I didn't remember having raised it. "Anyway," I said. "I'm just not very hungry tonight. But you guys have cake — I'll get these dishes into the dishwasher."

I took the plates and scurried off to the sink.

"Let me help you with that." Alex appeared at my elbow, lifting a dish from my soapy hands and loading it into the dishwasher. He whispered, "Are you okay?"

I looked from him to the dishwasher and back again — and thought I'd never felt better in my life. I'd been so sure there was nobody I could talk to, nobody at all who could possibly understand. I'd been wrong. I'd forgotten about Alex.

**BACK HOME**, around midnight, I got an email from Lev.

> **From:** levmeyer32@gmail.com
> **To:** samsarameyer@gmail.com
> **Subject:** Something I forgot to tell you tonight

At yeshiva we started learning about the Resurrection of the Dead that's supposed to happen when the Messiah comes, which my teacher says could be any day now. Which made me think, hey, maybe I shouldn't give all Dad's clothes away! Because what will he wear when he gets resurrected? But then we got to the part in the Talmud where it says the dead will be resurrected wearing their clothes. So I asked, what do you mean, the clothes they died in? The rabbi said yes. A picture popped into my head then of Dad wearing his jogging clothes, that sweaty T-shirt and grey gym shorts for all eternity, and I burst out laughing. Everyone looked at me like I was crazy. My classmates all take this so literally, you have no idea. As if Dad is just going to magically reappear out of the blue one day, like a zombie? It's weird. Although, on the other hand, I guess maybe it's not any weirder than him just disappearing out of the blue one day. Right?

P.S. Normally I'd talk to Mr. Glassman about this kind of thing but Mrs. Glassman just had another stroke and now the nurse says she's in something called a "persistent vegetative state," which is another thing I forgot to tell you tonight.

P.P.S. Something you forgot to tell me tonight is "happy birthday."

I hit Reply. Then I hit Discard Draft. On the radio clock, one minute, then two, then three ticked by. I reached under the bed and retrieved the letter I'd supposedly sent to Lev weeks ago at Jenny's urging. Really, all I'd managed to do since then was fold the Tree of Life sketch into a paper crane. *Dear —*, it said. I grabbed a pen and completed the salutation.

> *Dear Alex,*
>
> *Remember that day we sat in front of the dishwasher and you taught me to listen for the patterns in the chaos, like SETI scientists do? Remember how I had you feel my pulse and you couldn't believe it because I'd gotten my heartbeat to mimic the pattern in the dishwasher noise, all its whirs and clicks, its os and 1s? I never told you how I did it — never had the words to thank you — but now —*
>
> *I know you weren't at my bat mitzvah but if you had been you would've heard it in my voice. How I let my heart fall into sync with the rhythms of the Hebrew words, and then with the rhythms of the hearts of all the people in the audience, and then once I did that — once I was in — all the noise fell away and I was able to speak to all of them (well, all except one) so that they'd really hear me. It was terrifying, tying my heartbeat to theirs, feeling all of that emotion pour through me. But I did it anyway, and do you want to know how?*
>
> *There's a trick, a very simple trick that I learned that day in front of the dishwasher but later made myself forget. Here it is: stop. Just stop. Stop thinking that you're going to crack the code. Stop trying. You're not going to crack anything. The code is going to crack you.*
>
> *That's something you taught me, even if you didn't realize it. Which is why I owe you my thanks. Because you made it possible for me to do this. To climb the Tree of Life.*

*I'm two vessels up now. I see signs and symbols everywhere.*
*Leaves swirling in the streets, vapours moving over a bowl*
*of soup, cloud formations solidifying and dispersing —*
*everything is full, overfull, ready to explode with meaning*
*at the slightest pinprick. I've combed through my father's*
*book, read the sections on the upcoming vessels. Hod-Netzach.*
*Tiferet. Gevurah-Chesed. I've got them all memorized.*
*I'm ready, now all I have to do is wait.*

**SUDDENLY, IT BEGINS.**

I am behind the counter at Two Moons. The door opens and there she is. Val. Valérie. She sits down at a table, glances nervously at me. I'm about to retreat to the bathroom, but then I remember how well I'm doing on my own now and I think: *I don't need you; I don't need to run from you.* I pick up a mug and a fresh pot of coffee and march straight toward her.

"Coffee?" I ask, my voice pleasant and light.

She looks up at me, startled. "Oh, yes, sure — thank you."

I set the mug down in front of her and begin to pour. I can feel the heat of her gaze on my face. Then, in a low whisper, she asks me, "How are you doing?"

I flash my brightest smile. "Fine, thank you, how are you?"

She doesn't answer. Instead, her eyes search mine for a clue. I watch the question flicker across her face: *does she know who I am? Does she recognize me?*

"Can I get you anything else?" I ask.

"No. Thank you." She studies me for a long moment, then leans in confidentially. "I don't know if you know this, but I'm — I was — I was there at your dad's —"

"Sorry," I cut her off. "I think you have me confused with someone else."

199

It's as if I've slapped her in the face. She shrinks back into her chair. I hold her in the centre of my sightlines, daring her to challenge me. After a second she wilts, drops her gaze. I smile broadly and walk away.

From behind the counter, I watch as Val gulps down her coffee and tries to keep her cool. Her hands are fidgeting around the mug, her lipsticked mouth trembling. The depth of her emotion surprises me, suggests something more than a casual student-professor fling — something like love? A minute later, she drops some cash onto the table and rushes out the door.

I strut back toward her table and slide the coins into my palm. Then I reach for her coffee cup and on the rim I see them. Val's lipstick imprints. They leap out at me, Hod-Netzach, Splendour-Eternity, the complementary vessels that correspond to the two lips. Hod: transitory splendour — Netzach: enduring eternity — Hod-Netzach: the exact combination embodied by Val. Val who loved a man whose life was transitory, but whose impact on her was clearly so enduring, was clearly something she still all too keenly felt —

The key falls into my hand.

Dazed, I turn around. Brendan's left a scrap of paper on the table by the window. I glide over and pick it up. The magic square is huge, a grid of 15 by 15 at least, his biggest one yet — but how can he be manipulating such large numbers in his head? I add up the first row: 37. And the second row: 37. I try the third row and come up with 35. He must have made a mistake there. But then I try the fourth row and it's 81, and all of a sudden it clicks into place; the numbers shift and I see them the way he sees them, in colour. I feel the beautiful calm blue of six, the warm pulsating orange of four, the vibrant zing of three, and now I see what he's been doing — it's an image — blackbird swooping across cloudy sky — a pixilated reality composed entirely of numbers. The colours start to howl in my ears, filling my skull with their wild glow. From cornea to cochlea I'm bursting with it, my insides awash with light. And as quickly as it started, it subsides. The light drains from my ears. The cranial ache fades and I am left with nothing but beauty. Beauty — Tiferet — the crossroads at the very centre of the Tree, where conflicting forces of the divine flow collide, energies smashing into each other and synthesizing as one — one greater harmony, one more delicious key in my hand.

I can hear angry voices now. Lily's mother is here and she is counting down from three. Three. She stuffs the sketchpad into her daughter's bag. Two. Lily's fist clamps stubbornly around her paint-brush. One. The mother slams the watercolour kit shut, takes Lily's wrist, yanks her from her seat. With her free hand, Lily just manages to grab the paint kit, her pudgy fingertips struggling to maintain their grip. She gets dragged outside and the door bangs shut. In the echo I hear something calling me. Something that has fallen. I push open the door and step into the street.

And there it is. On the rain-bleached sidewalk, shining in late afternoon light. A plastic watercolour kit, cracked open upon impact, dropped by two hands — two — two hands that correspond to Gevurah-Chesed, Severity-Kindness, the principle of disciplinary restraint and of the boundless, indiscriminate love that's supposed to counter-balance it. Two pats of paint — Gevurah's red and Chesed's white — have popped out of their lining and landed on the ground. Crushed to pieces by a hurried heel, the colours dissolve into a puddle and form two separate streams. The streams crisscross but the colours do not fade. Two distinct rivers, red and white, race each other through the street, around the block, up that dark alley and down this one — and I chase after them because what else can I do? I follow them homeward and as I race I make a bet with myself. If red gets there first, I will be cruel to her. If white wins, I will be kind. I run until I am out of breath, my heart clenching and unclenching, the keys jangling in my brain, and then I am home. And white has won. I will be kind, I will kiss her on the mouth and speak, I will tell her everything.

But when I open the door, the apartment is quiet and empty, like a graveyard. The seven thousand tubes of paint are gone. The canvases leaning against the walls are gone. The clothes are gone, the suitcase is gone, and she is gone for good. Birds twist in the air above my head. The world dilates, then contracts to the size of a point. I stare down at the chessboard of a floor, all the squares are white, every move seems equally impossible and unnecessary. I drop down to the ground. Checkmate.

SHE DIDN'T TAKE EVERYTHING. I realized this after an hour or two or three in the dark. For example, the easel. It stood in front of the window, submerged in shadows. She had left a single canvas there, its face turned toward the sky, as if she'd hoped birds or pilots might see it and take notice.

When I first learned to read and write, I would make signs and put them up in my bedroom window, facing out. The first one said HELLO. The second one said ANYONE THERE? The third one said IF YOU CAN READ THIS MY NAME IS SAMARA MY ADDRESS IS 5479 HUTCHISON MY PHONE NUMBER IS 514-482-9986 PLEASE CALL.

This last sign stayed up in the window for years. And for years nobody noticed it, because nobody in that neighbourhood ever looked up. The hipsters all had their heads bent over cell phones. The Hasids shunted to and from synagogue with their gaze glued to the ground, the better to avoid temptation-inducing sights: a woman's little finger, a dress hung up on the clothesline to dry.

There was only one exception: Alex.

It had been ten years now. Ten years since that day when, pointing his telescope out at people's houses, he had first seen the sign in my bedroom window. Ten years since he figured out that he could call the house and, without saying a single word, relay his messages to me with perfect clarity and zero chance of being overheard. Ten years since we'd started communicating in binary code, entire conversations conveyed through the receiver in a pattern of rests and taps, 0s and 1s…

**IN THE HUSH OF TWILIGHT** I was painting Jenny's body. Covering every inch of her skin with paint. She lay on the bed, quiet and yielding. Naked. My brush skipped lightly across the contours of her face. Lips, lashes, nostrils, ears. Her blonde hair took a long time, but I coated each strand with care. A canister of house paint sat beside me on the sheet. Taupe, said the label, and my brush dipped again and again. Collarbone, neck, navel. Thirty-three vertebrae, they made the brush skip up and down, and then the small of the back. Hips, thighs, the place between the thighs. The soles of the feet. As I was painting the last of her fingernails, covering up the final traces of sparkly blue polish, I suddenly remembered that if you coat a person's body entirely with house paint, they will die. Panicking, I looked to her eyes for signs of life, but they were already painted over. I screamed, scratched at her face, dug for the human colour beneath the grey. But all my nails brought up were sooty lashes, flakes of skin turned ash.

**I BOLTED UPRIGHT**, gasping for air in the morning light.

The back of her canvas was staring at me. If I turned it around, it would reveal everything she had been thinking and feeling for the past few months. Would it be an expression of hope and happiness in the face of intolerable despair? It would not. Would it be a visual valentine? It would not. I was afraid to look, so instead I lay perfectly still, the golden undersides of birds twirling above my head.

She would go to Kyle's house, I realized with a pang. Jenny would go to Kyle's and move in with her, because she would die before moving back in with her parents, and all her other friends had graduated and moved away, and where else could she turn? Nowhere.

The thought felt too painful to bear.

But when I got out of bed, I found, to my surprise, that it was bearable. Just. Even though being without her felt like nails digging through my skin, scratching at my face, her absence made it easier for me to do what I needed to do. In fact, the pain of this separation *proved* that I was well on my way. Jenny had been trying to tether me to reality, had been holding me back. Now that she was gone — and I accepted she was gone — there was nothing to keep me from rising up the Tree. Without her for ballast, I was light, weightless, free.

And wasn't that, on some level, why I'd misread Yesod to mean a back-alley blowjob — even though I well understood symbol and metaphor, even though my whole academic training had been about preventing me from committing *exactly this type of misreading* — because deep down I'd wanted to push Jenny away? Because deep down I knew that the Tree was a vertical tightrope along which only a single soul could walk?

Instead of getting ready to go to my morning shift, I got my backpack and pulled it into bed with me. I took out the pages of my father's manuscript and recorded my latest dream in the margins: taupe paint, blue nail polish, asphyxiation. Then I started reading:

> BINAH-CHOCHMAH is the final complementary pair.
> It is in Chochmah — Wisdom — that the blueprints
> upon which the world is designed first come into being.
> In Chochmah, however, these blueprints remain at a stage
> of pure potentiality; only in Binah — Understanding —
> do they take concrete form. For this reason, Chochmah
> is referred to as "the original idea" and "the seed of
> creation." It is symbolized as the supernal father.

From the depths of my backpack, my cell phone rang. I ignored it and frowned down at the manuscript. This passage was even more cryptic than the others. How was I supposed to get my hands on such abstract qualities as Wisdom and Understanding? What exactly was the difference between them, aside from the fact that one was about a potential reality and the other a concrete one? The rest of the chapter was not much help:

Some sages read the word Chochmah as *cheich mah*,
"the palate of selflessness." This reading refers to the
mystic's ability to taste God as a result of having shed
any remnants of the ego, as it is written, "Taste and see
that the Lord is good" (Psalms 34). Chochmah is typically
associated with the sense of sight, but the sages interpret
this verse to mean that there is a spiritual sense of taste
in Chochmah that awakens the sense of sight.

A sense of taste that awakens the sense of sight? Over the next few hours, I puzzled over what this could mean. I walked to the market and wandered the stalls. I brought grapes, then cherries, then strawberries to my mouth, tasting one fruit after the other. Nothing transmitted the spark I'd been expecting. The glossy skins were cold to the touch.

*Dear Alex,*

*God is the space between signals — radio and otherwise. In the silence/static/synapse between a moment of desperation and a moment of revelation, that's where faith resides. And that faith isn't a waiting for God. That faith is God.*

*Do you remember the day of the science fair? I was so sure you and Lev were going to crash and burn. Calling the space station? Who ever heard of such a thing? But you sent your lonely voice out into space. Again you called and again silence and again you called and again silence and again your lonely voice crashing into the silencesilencesilence and I couldn't stand to listen, stuffed my fingers in my ears, couldn't stand to watch, squeezed my eyes shut tight, and still you sent your lonely voice...*

*It hit the note of perfect faith. Van Gogh's high yellow note. I thought: where did he learn faith like that? I thought: God is in this classroom. And then your call was answered...*

*I'm trying to have that same sort of faith now. Sufficient faith*
*to achieve the miracle. But it's hard. I'm more than halfway up,*
*I'm stranded here and it's hard. Sometimes I think maybe you*
*should be the one climbing this Tree. Between the two of us,*
*you were always the more faithful.*

**DECEMBER WAS MAKING ME CRAZY.** The days were colder, shorter. The streets were choked, the buses were choked, and in spite of my resolve to remain empty and waiting, I was choking on my own eagerness. Where was the key to Binah-Chochmah? I read and re-read my father's book, raking it for clues which seemed not to exist so I ran my tongue blindly over random objects I encountered — a paring knife, a park bench — but not a single item responded to my touch. The world was a locket that had decided not to open.

I took refuge in every quirky behaviour I had cultivated over the years as a way of making myself unknowable, a byzantine system of codes that no one could crack without the use of a primer or a magic decoder ring. I went to the library and trailed my finger along the spines. I ran warm water over my hands for hours at a time. I went to the downtown café, the one where they called out your name, and ordered a bowl of soup from the woman who had called out "Miranda!" in such a perfect voice. She asked for a name and I gave it to her. She waited, as if giving me a chance to correct myself, to call myself Miranda. I said nothing. She said nothing. I stood at the counter and waited. It felt bad to be confusing her in this way, and I wouldn't have done it if it weren't strictly necessary, but it was, it really was. It was the whole reason I had come. I needed to hear the sweetest name, the name I'd been whispering to myself in the dark, finally spoken aloud.

"Jenny!"

She placed the bowl of soup in front of me. I resisted the urge to hug her. The bowl was steaming hot and I carried it to my table tenderly, like a newborn. For a long time, I simply sat in my seat and studied the vapours moving over the soup. I was searching for patterns in the chaos, for codes in the clouds, but the air around me was bereft of music. By the time I picked up my spoon, the soup was cold.

What is the moral of this story?

Don't see signs in everything. It makes it impossible to live.


THEN ONE EVENING I found myself walking home by way of the McGill campus. This was a detour, but my feet seemed intent on carrying me there and I was happy enough to follow them. It was only five o'clock and already the sky was pitch dark. Wind thudded through the branches overhead. Slightly out of breath from the uphill walk, I paused to adjust the straps on my backpack, redistributing weight. Then I looked up and saw that I had come to a stop in front of Moyse Hall.

Lights were blazing in the university building. A fresh tumult of voices told me a class had just gotten out. The voices sounded dimly familiar. But it wasn't until I saw their owners pour forth, bursting from the double doors and passing between the stone pillars, that I actually recognized them.

Zimmerman's disciples scattered over the wide stairs, talking and laughing loudly. They were pulling on winter coats, huffing into cupped hands, warming them with their breath. They all looked so happy, so healthy, that I felt their normalcy as a physical blow. The preppy student linked arms with a ponytailed girl and emerged into the chilly air. As they chattered, they looked over their shoulders to Zimmerman, who was trailing one step behind them, wrapping a scarf around his neck while he spoke.

The other students filtered past and dispersed into the night, but these three stood on the steps for a while, fervently continuing the conversation. It wasn't hard to guess what they were talking about. Each of them held the insanely thick Norton anthology of literary theory. Zimmerman sent his fist crashing into his copy, again and again, like a Bible-thumper at the pulpit. His acolytes watched the progress of this fist, sweeping first up, then down, as if it carried their fates in its fingers.

And there it was again, the angry ache gnawing at my gut. Every bit as strong as it had been during that initial lesson on Barthes. Turning away from them, I shrugged off my backpack and quickly — almost savagely — ripped it open. I needed to grab onto something meaningful, something that at least didn't swear off the very idea of meaning. I reached for the pages of my dad's manuscript —

But before I could get hold of them, a gust of wind tore toward me and lifted them away. First one page, then two, then three flew out of the backpack and rode the night air. My heart stopped. My hand shot out. My fingers clawed at empty sky. Carried by wind and gravity, sheaves of paper were cascading in a downward spiral. I chased down the slope after them, readying a flat-open palm to smack the pages to pavement. They were too fast — they were getting away from me — and they were all I had left of him in this world —

I dropped to my knees, threw myself over the fluttering papers, pinned them down.

Somewhere above and behind me, I heard the sounds of jeering voices, the preppy boy's laugh and the incredulous giggle of his girlfriend. I whipped around, clutching the manuscript to my chest — and they recognized me. Their smiles faltered but did not fall from their faces. And Zimmerman — he recognized me, too — I could see it in his eyes. But, to my surprise, there was no laughter in them. Only pity.

For a moment I saw myself as they saw me: dishevelled, stringy-haired, pathetic.

My cheeks burned.

I set my face against them all.

Then, for what seemed like the thousandth time, I brought the manuscript close to my face, breathing in the scent of the pages and trying to absorb their meaning through osmosis. My lips brushed up against the words, tasting them. His words, and all around them in the margins, my words, my dreams, my commentary. My mouth grew bolder — teeth biting into paper — a ragged hole ripped right through the middle of the manuscript. I ate and ate and ate. Letters stumbled into my mouth and I swallowed them. Ink poured down my throat and I drank it. Tears filled the cups of my eyes and dangled from my eyelashes like question marks.

And then I blinked, and it was as if my blindness had been washed away.

Through the film of tears, only my scribbles in the margins were visible. The text in the middle of the page had vanished — the middle of the page itself had vanished — and in its place was a naked light.

The night air filled with wild laughter. Mine.

Of course. A tightrope made for one meant that you couldn't take *anyone* with you — not even the earthly teacher who had inspired your climb in the first place. You got to Binah *by destroying* Chochmah. By moving beyond the pure potentiality, the original idea, the seed of all creation. By killing the supernal father.

I let go of the manuscript pages. They flew up into the sky, leaving my hands empty.

But they were not empty.

Instead of the book, I now had a golden key. I took hold of its head and turned.

> *Dear Alex,*
>
> *God can't enter you if you consider yourself something. God is infinite & so can't be held by you unless you make yourself into nothing.*
>
> *Emptied self of everything now. All somethings & all somethingness. Am ready for Ayin.*
>
> *Haven't eaten (except paper) in don't know how long. Time stopped.*

*Separation of self from body = divestment of the physical.*
*Space stopped too.*

*Don't know where Ayin will show up. Could be around any*
*corner. This street or next. Ayin is crown of Ani* → *Highest*
*linked to lowest* → *Return to the beginning? Snakes, ladders.*
*God biting its own tail:* ∞

*Been walking through the city all night ± forever. Don't*
*recognize this place but the bird will find you. Can't sleep.*
*Can't stop. So close. So close. So*

THE SKY WAS ROYAL BLUE and then black and then electric blue
and then gold. I kept on walking through the streets of the city. No,
not walking. Flying. I was flying six inches above ground at all times.
Everywhere I looked, a thousand tiny outstretched hands waited to
pull me up. There was nothing I touched that did not sing, and there
was nothing I saw that did not contain a clue.

I blinked and morning had come. The sign over the coffee shop
said Two Moons. I peered into the window and it looked familiar.
I had worked here once. How long ago? Nine thousand seconds, a
minute, a lifetime.

Someone — a man — what was his name? — stood behind the
counter, scowling. He had his eyes on the table for four where that
little girl always sat. Lily, her name was Lily. She was gleeful, kicking
the leg of her chair as she raised her paintbrush in the air and applied
it to — her own skin. Already she'd painted one arm blue, the other
muddy purple. Now she was setting to work on her hands. That paint
was going to get everywhere. The scowling man marched up to her
and yelled. I couldn't hear what he was saying, maybe the glass was
too thick, or maybe it was my ears, they didn't seem to be working
normally, but from the way his mouth moved I could tell he was yelling. The little girl whipped around, manic delight in her eyes. She
waved her hands in his face, eager to show him.

Her hands were covered in paint. Green paint.

And now, finally, I remembered: Lev's hands. Lev, when he was a kid like this kid. Lev leaning toward me in the kitchen, palms streaked with green. *Can you keep a secret?* He told me about the tree and I told him about the bat mitzvah. *You have to promise you won't tell Dad.* Whispering voices, late summer light. Two of us against the world. Allies in the face of our father's absence. And now, now he was really absent, and instead of allying with Lev I had —

Forgotten he existed.

The wind went out of me. A jolt behind my navel brought me crashing down to earth. Lily was waving her green hands at the window now but I turned away, I couldn't breathe. My eardrums popped. Sound rushed back in. "Samara!" Tyler — that's who it was — called me from the doorway, but he was too late. I was already halfway down the block.

Back home, I dug through drawers, coat pockets, piles of dirty laundry. A pair of jeans crumpled on the floor of the closet. My phone thudded to the ground. I picked it up. Turned it on. The screen showed a list of missed calls.

| | | |
|---|---|---|
| 29 Nov | 6:19 PM | Jenny |
| 30 Nov | 4:23 PM | Lev |
| 1 Dec | 9:02 AM | Hannah |
| 4 Dec | 9:45 PM | Jenny |
| 4 Dec | 11:58 PM | Jenny |
| 5 Dec | 12:03 AM | Jenny |
| 5 Dec | 8:12 PM | Lev |
| 6 Dec | 2:15 AM | Jenny |
| 7 Dec | 9:29 AM | Hannah |
| 12 Dec | 11:28 PM | Lev |
| 13 Dec | 10:03 PM | Lev |
| 14 Dec | 5:06 PM | Lev |
| 14 Dec | 8:30 PM | Lev |
| 15 Dec | 7:35 PM | Lev |
| 16 Dec | 8:48 PM | Lev |
| 17 Dec | 5:00 PM | Lev |
| 17 Dec | 9:36 PM | Lev |
| 18 Dec | 10:15 PM | Lev |
| 19 Dec | 10:49 PM | Lev |
| 19 Dec | 11:38 PM | Lev |

I sank to the ground. My hand rose to my mouth. In the past week, he had called me eleven times. *Eleven times.* And I hadn't returned a single call.

Tears burned in the corners of my eyes, but I made myself blink them back. I looked up from the screen and saw Jenny's canvas waiting on the easel, still facing skyward. The light was waning, and the canvas was growing dark, like a scar fading in reverse. I couldn't ignore it anymore. I went over to it. I turned it around —

It was blank. An unbearable expanse of white. A perfect portrait of the emptiness I'd forced on her. The muscle of my heart clenched at the sight but I bit down on the insides of my cheeks and forced myself not to cry.

I told myself: you had no choice. You had to do this. You were chosen. But I was trembling. I needed reassurance. I dug through my backpack until I found the one remaining page of the manuscript. The dedication page.

*For my children.*

I froze, then read it again. And again. And again. It did not say: *For my daughter.* It said: *For my children.*

A strangled noise escaped me.

All this time I had been banging my head against hallucinations. Caught on the infixed fangs of an obsession. I had passed my desperation through the air like a butterfly net and it caught strange moments of beauty, their tiny wings studded with secrets. But the secrets flaked off the second you touched them — it was all false, all fake — there were no secrets and there were no keys. None of it was real.

In a horrible flash, it came to me: Zimmerman was right! Barthes was right! I had rebelled against it, but it was true. We wanted to believe that, underneath it all, a meaning, a plan, persisted — but this idea could not, *should* not be trusted. The tears I'd been choking back for months poured down my face now, an unstoppable flood. To believe there was a plan just for me — to make keys out of people and means out of ends — what an idiot I'd been! I looked at the blank canvas and hated myself for what I'd done to Jenny. She was not grey, suddenly I understood this. She was not the beautiful maiden without eyes. My need for a person who fit that description was what had robbed her skin of its colour. But the colour was there, had always been there, though for months I hadn't wanted to see it...

I dropped the dedication page and fell into bed.

The window was open. I could hear raindrops hitting pavement. The air around me filled with the noise of crinkling paper, as overhead the cranes rocked and swayed. Goosebumps rose on my flesh. I thought about getting up to close the window, getting up seemed an impossibly difficult and complicated affair, the window stayed open. I fell asleep.

**THAT NIGHT I DREAMED** the birds were crying. Above my head, their thousand dark eyes gleamed in the moonlight. Silvery threads of water fell on my face. At first I didn't notice, because it was a soft, almost imperceptible mist. Then the mist spread out over my whole body. Drops of condensation collecting on my hair, my eyelashes, my collarbone, my belly, my kneecaps, the soles of my feet. The mist deepened to a heavy downpour that lasted just under an hour; then the birds stopped crying, all except one, which hovered right above my chest. I could feel a drip, drip, drip somewhere in the region of my heart, slow but steady, all night long. In the morning, I was washed clean.

**I GRABBED THE PAPER** crane giving Kyle's address (*in case you get lonely*, Jenny had written, how many weeks ago now?) and raced out of the apartment. But the second I stepped into the street, I knew I didn't need it. I could see exactly which way Jenny had gone. She had left traces of herself everywhere, dripping from the branches, twinkling from the streetlamps, sliding down the gutter. That fire hydrant, it was unnaturally red, and I knew that she had passed it. The tree on the corner of Saint-Laurent and Pine, it was impossibly green, and I knew that she had touched it. Beside a parked car was a puddle full of rainbows — amaranth, cadmium, cerulean, heliotrope, atomic tangerine — and I knew that in that spot she had succumbed to tears, drops falling onto pavement until her eyes were grey as marble. Everywhere she had gone, she had shed colour, stained the world around her. This was the breadcrumb trail she had left me. This was her Hansel and Gretel goodbye.

I followed the trail along nineteen city blocks. The path was not always straight; she had meandered, paced in tight circles, retraced her steps. At these points, I knew, she had been filled with doubt. Then there were swathes of thick, uninterrupted colour; this was where she had felt sure that she was making the right, the only possible, decision. On the corner of Milton and Park, I spotted a speck of vermillion, and so I knew that for one second she had even laughed.

As I traced her colours, I wondered if maybe this was love. The ability to detect the mood of your beloved in anything, a stray cat or a stray molecule, weeks after she has come in contact with it. I wondered how she would react when I showed up on her porch. When I told her how sorry I was, how stupid, how wrong I'd been about absolutely everything. When I dropped to my knees and begged her forgiveness.

I was on a quiet, shady street. The trees on either side of me formed a tunnel of dim light. I peered closely at the doorways, and then I saw it. A fleck of sparkly blue on one of the doorknobs, the exact shade of Jenny's nail polish. I climbed the stairs to the front door and knocked. The door opened. It was Kyle.

"Hi," she said.

She was exactly as I had pictured her, except for the fact that she was totally different. I'd been right about the hair, even about the freckles, but she was nothing, she was not cool. She was — normal. Her cheek was bare of any smudges of colour. Her hair was red, but nowhere near impossibly so. Relief flooded my senses.

"Is Jenny here?"

"You must be Samara."

"Yeah. Yes. Is she?"

"She's here."

"Can you?"

"I'll try. Could you wait here?"

I guessed I probably could. She closed the door softly, apologetically. I turned my back toward it and folded my arms across my chest. Branches rustled overhead. The hallucinatory scent of lemon filled the air. The door clicked open behind me.

I was on the swing. I could feel Jenny standing behind me, waiting for me to do it: *Fall! Fall!* I knew that if I turned around now, there would be no more secrets, no more silences. She would want to know me and I would have to let her. With my back still facing the door, I spoke.

"Jenny?" I said and unfolded my arms.

"Yeah?"

"I'm," I said and raised them in the air.

"Yeah?"

"Sorry," I said —

Or almost said. Just as I turned to face her, a huge wind filled the space between us, stealing my breath, stealing the words from my mouth. It tugged me toward the sky. I dug my heels downward, but the wind was too strong for me. It howled in my ears, drowning out all sound. Jenny was mouthing my name, mouthing questions at me, but my limbs were shaking violently, I couldn't feel my hands or feet. My senses were shutting down, collapsing in on themselves one by one. The last thing I saw, the last thing I expected or wanted to see, was Jenny, on the doorstep, holding her arms out toward me, the final key gleaming in her hands.

MILE END

**W**HEN, IN EARLY DECEMBER, an oddly bird-shaped letter began its slow, spiralling descent over the neighbourhood of Mile End, nobody was there to see it. Winter had driven everyone indoors, leaving the streets deserted. The bird swooped lower and lower in the sky, fluttering, first, above a tree-lined block, then above the ancient oak at the end of that block. It circled the tree, eyeing the tin cans that dotted its branches, before going into a sharp nosedive and settling itself in its newfound nest. There, it folded its wings and waited patiently, as if confident of being picked up soon by the right hands.

Alex, turning the corner on his way to visit his best and possibly only friend in the world, passed beneath the wind-tossed branches — and paused. He could have sworn he'd just heard a girl's voice whispering in his ear. As the bird-letter flapped its wings in the breeze, the noise was picked up and amplified by the elaborate system of tin and twine which, despite its unorthodox appearance, the residents of Mile End had not yet had the heart to tear down. Reaching his mittened hand into a can, Alex pulled out the source of the whispers and peered at its mottled back.

At the sight of Samara's handwriting, his heart leapt into his throat.

The letter, a tight scrawl that spanned the wings as well as the bird's dark interior, was stamped and addressed to him. *Dear Alex*, it began. He froze, then read it again. And again. And again. It did not say: *Dear Lev*. It said: *Dear Alex*.

He devoured the message, his gaze skipping and bobbing on certain words — *dishwasher* — *terrifying* — *a very simple trick* — until finally it landed with a thud on a phrase near the end: *You made it possible for me to do this. To climb the Tree of Life.*

He gaped up at the tree in front of him. The contents of the letter were confusing enough. But the letter itself — how had it gotten there in the first place? Perhaps a gust of wind had lifted the bird out of a mailman's hand and swept it up into one of Katz's tin cans. That didn't seem likely (since when had a postal service ever delivered origami?) — so maybe Samara had placed it there herself? What if, knowing his tendency to look up at the sky instead of down at other people, she had purposely stashed the letter someplace high, someplace only he might find it? Or, even better: what if, against all odds, the girl he'd always loved had finally decided she felt the same way? And what if, buoyed by that love, her letter had actually flown there of its own accord?

The idea was ridiculous — imagine a scrap of paper like that winging its way across the city! — and for that reason all the more appealing. It was the first ridiculous thought Alex had permitted himself in over ten years, and he clung to it now with a keen and unsuspected joy.

He tucked the bird into the breast pocket of his jacket and locked it in with a click of the snap. He wouldn't show it to Lev — not yet. Samara hadn't written or even called her brother in weeks; how would Lev feel if he knew she was reaching out to Alex and not him? He walked the rest of the way to Lev's house, climbed the stairs, and knocked.

As soon as Lev opened the door and mumbled his hello, Alex knew he was right to keep Samara's letter from him. Over the past few weeks Lev had become increasingly pale, his face strangely drawn, his shoulders pulled taut. His eyes, which had always been so clean and fresh and blue, twitched faintly at the corners now. And there was a hardness in them that had never been there before. Samara's disturbing words would only make him more anxious, and that was the last thing he needed now.

Lev raised a hand to scratch at the tiny scar above his brow — an old nervous habit — and Alex remembered with a pang how he himself had inflicted that scar all those long years ago. How he'd pushed his telescope out of the way — hitting Lev in the process — to keep him from seeing Samara's message in the window. *Please call*. For reasons he hadn't fully understood then, he'd wanted to be the only one to see those words. Now, as Lev motioned him inside, he realized that he had been hiding Samara's messages from her brother — his best friend — for over a decade. In his pocket, the bird's wings flapped against his chest, and, guiltily, he opened his mouth to say something — but it was too late. Lev's back was already turning, his slim figure receding into the darkness of the house.

CHAIM GLASSMAN HAD been watching from his bedroom window when the bird first made its presence known. Unable to leave his wife, who lay comatose in the dim paisley-walled room, he had taken to surveying the street through the pair of plastic binoculars that his wife's cousin, Reuben, had sent to him a few months earlier. Reuben, who worked in the plastics industry in New York City, now regularly mailed samples of his cheaply made products, presumably as a way to salve his guilt over his own absence at his cousin's bedside. The other products — children's toys, baby bottles — had all been useless, but Glassman liked the binoculars. They kept him entertained during the long hours of his vigil.

And so it happened that, at the exact moment when Alex discovered the strange avian dispatch, Glassman had his gaze trained on Katz's tin can tree. He watched as Alex unfolded the letter and scanned its contents. Whatever they were, they wrought a remarkable transformation in him. Pinpricks of light danced in the boy's eyes. The unmistakable flush of young love rose high in his cheeks. A moment later, a shade of alarm passed over his face, subduing the flush, and Glassman felt an unusual pang. But in the next moment the boy was folding the letter and putting it in his pocket and the light on his face was so bright that Glassman was forced to turn away.

That was why, when Glassman spotted the boy approaching his house the next day, he frowned. He heard a knock, but closed his eyes and pretended he'd heard nothing. The knocking persisted. He ignored it. But the knocking would not stop. Glassman cursed under his breath. He knew he would have to answer the door but declined to do so right away. He counted out ten heartbeats before going down the stairs. When he finally opened the door, the boy was shivering. The wind smelled capable of snow.

"Yes?"

"Um. Hello."

"Yes, yes, hello. So, what can I do for you?"

"My name's Alex."

"And my name's King Solomon, what do you *want* already, it's freezing out here in case you haven't noticed?"

"Can I come in?"

"To come in, he wants? So come in, who's stopping you? But make it fast. My wife is baking ruggelach and she wants I should help with the dough."

Inside the house, the air was odourless and stale.

"So?" Glassman said.

"Excuse me?"

"What do you want?"

"I want — to study. To learn from you."

"To *learn* from me?"

"Yeah. Yes."

"Tell me, what exactly do you want to learn? Geography? Mathematics? Political Science?"

"Kabbalah."

Glassman's eyes narrowed.

"I want to know about the Tree of Life. About the ten —"

"The Tree of Life, he wants to know! How old?"

"What?"

"How old are you? Fifteen? Sixteen?"

"Twenty-one."

"That is a problem."

"It is?"

"Yes. It is."

"Why?"

Glassman shuffled off into the living room, where his formidable library took up three of the four walls. He pulled a large volume from one of the shelves, flipped to the page he wanted, and thrust the book into Alex's hands. "You see? It says here, a man must be at least forty years of age, and married, before he may be allowed to study the kabbalah." He opened another volume and dropped it onto the book that Alex was already holding. "And here, you see? When Rabbi Johanan wished to teach mystical matters to Rabbi Eliezer, Rabbi Eliezer answered, 'I am not yet old enough.' He was already much older than you." He pulled a third volume off the shelf and thrust it, too, into Alex's arms. "And here it tells the story of a boy who, when he was still young and beardless like you, recognized the meaning of Ezekiel's holy vision. You know what happened to him? I'll tell you what happened to him. He was consumed by fire."

Alex's arms trembled, but his expression remained resolute. It was as if the two of them were gladiators crossing swords. Any sign of weakness and the duel would immediately be lost.

Glassman stared him down. "You are not Jewish."

"No."

"That is another problem."

"Oh?"

"It is not permitted to study such matters with *goyim*." Glassman pulled a fourth volume from the shelves, flipped it open, and added it to Alex's pile. "You see? 'It is not proper to study mysticism unless one's belly is filled with bread and meat, that is, knowledge of what is permitted and what is forbidden, according to the Torah.' That means no *goyim*."

"I see."

"And there is another problem."

"There is?"

"You are only one. You need at least two."

"Two…?"

Glassman threw a fifth volume down onto Alex's unwieldy pile, and quoted: "'Mystical matters must not be explained before one, unless he be wise and understands it by himself.' That means you need more than one person in the room, or you may not discuss it."

"Well, that's okay then, isn't it? You and me, that's two people right there!"

"Two *students*. The teacher doesn't count."

Alex opened his mouth as if to retort — but then his mouth fell shut. The boy had nothing more to say, and he knew it. Glassman smiled a triumphant smile. Defeated, Alex tipped the books onto the couch. He retreated down the hall and out of the house, closing the door behind him. Its click was loud and, Glassman told himself as he watched the boy walk out of his life, immensely satisfying.

LEV RUSHED THROUGH THE STREETS, hands shoved deep into pockets, pace quickened by the biting wind — but not just by that.

Minutes ago, he'd been praying the Friday afternoon service, surrounded by his fellow yeshiva students and their bearded, wizened teachers. He had always loved these prayers, the peace and calm that descended on him as he mouthed the words with eyes closed, lips moving silently. But today he had found himself unable to focus. He opened his eyes and stared at his classmates. Their brows were furrowed in identical expressions of fervour. Their upper bodies lurched back and forth in a way that seemed, suddenly, strangely mechanical. During the cantor's repetition, they murmured in unison like an automated, bloodless chorus. For the first time in his life, Lev had slipped out of the sanctuary before the service even came to an end, emerging into the chilly winter air.

As he rounded the block leading up to his house, he spotted a red-cheeked Mr. Katz sitting out on his front lawn in a puffy coat and boots. The man was wearing two scarves but no hat, and one of his red woollen mittens had fallen to his feet. He looked like he was freezing. Yet, with his bare hand, he began to wave merrily at Lev, his flushed face beaming.

"Lev," he called.

Pretending he hadn't heard, Lev turned away.

"Lev!" Katz called again.

But Lev only quickened his pace. Out of the corner of his eye, he saw his old friend half-rise from his lawn chair, the smile sliding off his face, a look of confusion replacing it.

"*Gut shabbes!*" the man tried, his voice a little weaker this time.

But Lev kept his eyes on the ground, ignoring the guilt churning in his stomach and hurrying down the street. He just couldn't deal with Katz right now. Moments later, he turned his key in the lock and stepped into the house.

A rush of silence greeted him like a slap to the face.

Slowly, he removed his coat and boots, then wandered into the kitchen. Opening the fridge, he took out a loaf of challah bread and a bottle of white wine. He placed them on the table and sat down to wait. But after a minute, he got up again. What was the point of waiting around for Samara and Jenny? Aside from his birthday, they hadn't come over for dinner in weeks. He thought about calling Samara now, but he knew she wouldn't answer. All through the end of November and the beginning of December, he'd been calling and texting and emailing her and getting nothing in response. Clearly, his sister did not want to be reached.

He flicked off the kitchen light and went to his father's study.

The room was already full of shadows, the afternoon light fading fast, but Lev didn't bother to reach for the lamp. He sat in his father's high-backed chair, elbows propped on the glass-topped desk, chin in his hands. With his eyes fixed on the darkening window, he waited.

By the time a pair of headlights cut through the night, the windowpane was speckled with drops of condensation. A veil of mist hung in the air, heralding rain or snow. A silver car pulled up directly across the street and its lights went out. In the driver's seat, a shadowy figure sat motionless, delicate hands on the wheel.

Lev had seen the car before, on the day of the funeral. And then again on the first Friday night Samara had failed to show up for dinner. He'd gone to the window to watch for her, thinking maybe she was just late, but saw the silver car glide up instead. The driver sat there for well over an hour. Lev thought about going over, saying hello, but something like shyness held him back. And it kept holding him back the next Friday, and the next — because, for some reason, the silver car kept showing up.

Taking a deep breath, he left the study, pulled on his coat and boots, and opened the front door. For a second he just stood on the stoop and felt the mist collecting on his skin. Then he sliced through the mist, walked up to the car, tapped on the window.

The driver jumped. She looked at Lev, then at the lit joint pinched between her fingers. After a long minute, she rolled down the window.

"Hello," Lev said as the smell of pot reached his nose.

"Hello," the woman answered.

"I know you," he said. "I mean, I've seen you before. You were at the hospital, when my dad got released? And at the funeral." He waited for her to say something, but she just stared at him as if he were a ghost. That sustained gaze was making him uncomfortable. Aside from the two of them, the street was empty, and he wasn't used to being alone with women. Especially not women as pretty as this.

A confusing thrill tingled at the base of his spine. A second later he heard himself say, "Do you want to come in?"

She studied him a moment longer, ashed the joint, then opened the car door. Smiling uncertainly, Lev led the way back to the house.

In the bright hallway, as he took her coat, he noticed how pale and tense her face was, how her eyes — red, swollen — twitched faintly at the corners. Suddenly, he had the distinct impression that he was looking at his mirror image. The woman was younger than he'd thought; there couldn't have been more than five years between them. "What's your name?" he asked.

"Val. Valérie."

"I'm Lev."

Val smiled then — a strangely knowing smile, Lev thought. He motioned for her to come into the kitchen, and when she did, he followed her gaze to the untouched bottle on the table.

"Can I get you a drink?" he said to be polite.

"Why not," she shrugged. "*Un tout petit peu.*"

He poured them each a little wine. They sat down and sipped it in awkward silence.

"So," Lev said. "How well did you know my dad?"

"What?" Val spluttered. A bit of white wine dotted her black dress, and she wiped at it with the back of her hand.

"I mean, were you one of his students or something?"

"Yes. His student. He was a great teacher. And he was my thesis advisor, too, so — so that's why — so I saw him a lot," she finished, taking a gulp of wine.

"Oh."

A moment passed. Then Val said, "Your sister, she's not here?"

Lev's eyes widened.

"He said—your father said—he told us he had a son and a daughter," she explained. "In class. He was always talking about the two of you."

"Oh." Lev looked down at his hands. "She's not here right now. She — I haven't seen her in a long time."

"Me neither," Val said, and immediately her cheeks began to crimson. Her head dipped down for another gulp of wine.

"What do you mean?" he asked. "What do you mean, 'me neither'?"

"I mean ... I just mean ... you know, after the funeral. I didn't see your sister after that." Val stood abruptly. "I'm sorry," she murmured. "I — thank you — but I really have to go now," she said, rushing out.

Before Lev could even make it to his feet, she was halfway down the hall.

From the front door he watched her headlights illuminate the falling snow, then recede into the darkness.


**THAT EVENING BROUGHT** the first real storm of the season. After weeks of terrorizing the city with empty threats, winter finally pulled out the heavy artillery. All night long, the winds howled, the sky creaked and groaned. Glassman listened to the frost-laden boughs scraping the bedroom windowpane.

His wife, hooked up to a feeding tube, breathing independently but shallowly, lay very still with her eyes closed. The home health nurse who usually stopped by to check on her vitals, change her catheter, and turn her to prevent bed sores would not be coming this evening as planned. Peering through his binoculars, Glassman found he couldn't really complain. The streets were icy and deserted; sub-zero temperatures and knee-high snow had chased everyone inside, at least until the snowplows could do their work. In the meantime, everything — roofs, lampposts, Katz's tin can tree — was bedecked with icicles. And still the snow kept falling.

Minutes passed. Then hours.

The wind hurled itself at the walls, threatening to rip the roof right off the house. The power lines went down. Thrown into darkness, Glassman fumbled around for matches and a candle, and, having lit it, watched its tiny blue flame cast shadows on the bedroom's sloping walls. Then he sat at the ancient rolltop desk, opened its drawer, and rummaged around until he found the book.

Samara's copy of *King Lear* was a dog-eared paperback scarred by weeks of jockeying for backpack space with a seventh grader's pencil case, calculator, bagged lunch, and other juvenilia — yet Glassman handled it like a sacred text. He opened it to one of his favourite passages. He had never fully understood its meaning, and was still perplexed by the use of the word "germens" — which, being one himself, he had always known, or believed himself to have known, was spelled "Germans." But the rhythm of the verses — that was fantastic, that he loved.

> Blow, winds, and crack your cheeks! Rage! Blow!
> You cataracts and hurricanoes, spout
> Till you have drench'd our steeples, drown'd the cocks!
> You sulphurous and thought-executing fires,
> Vaunt-couriers to oak-cleaving thunderbolts,
> Singe my white head! And thou, all-shaking thunder,
> Smite flat the thick rotundity o' the world!
> Crack nature's moulds, all germens spill at once,
> That make ingrateful man!

Glassman read on, smiling, until the candle sputtered and went out.

Cast into shadows, he was forced to put aside the text — but not the storm. No, for the hundredth time his memory dragged him back to that terrible day — to that other storm — late last summer, when he had gone out into the streets, railing against the world. It was the day he'd found out that his wife's illness was not going to go away, that her atrial fibrillation was resisting treatment, that she could suffer another stroke at any moment and that, if that happened, he might well be forced to live in this world without her. His wits began to turn. Half blind with despair, he'd rushed out bareheaded, with nothing but a thin black trench coat to shield him from the clouds rolling in overhead. Soon rain pelted his skin, wind whipped at his white hair, but it was all so much nothing. He was being stripped of everything that had made him who he was. Was man no more than this? He would out-storm the storm!

It was in this frame of mind, thoroughly shaken and shaking his fist at the heavens, that he had turned the corner onto Hutchison and seen what he had seen: a man, collapsed in a heap on the ground, clutching at his heart and gasping for breath. Glassman raised a hand to shield his eyes from the rain, squinted through the downpour, and recognized — his neighbour. David Meyer's body, like a giant spider overturned on its back, was all abuzz in a fit of spasms, arms and legs twitching grotesquely. Glassman suppressed a shiver of disgust and, seeing no one else around, moved to help. But by the time he reached the body, the spasms had already passed over it and left something else in their place, something wondrously different from the arachnid creature he'd just seen flailing so desperately on the cold, hard pavement.

In death, his neighbour's features had been transformed. They now bore the sort of beauty they'd never borne in life. Forehead relaxed and smooth as marble. Lips tilted upward in the vague suggestion of a smile. A calm so deep and pure and perfect that Glassman felt a surge of envy.

And then a shout, and harried footsteps, and bodies pressing in on all sides — strangers bursting in with their cries of "Oh God!" and "Call an ambulance!" — and then the rush of noise, the roaring of sirens...

In all this hubbub, Glassman managed to slip away unnoticed. Nobody wondered who the strange old man hovering over the corpse had been. Nobody observed, in his changing expression, the shift from shock to envy to ironclad resolve. And nobody suspected he had just decided that, should his wife fall prey to the dreaded lethal stroke, he too was determined to die.

But determined he was. That was why he could not allow Alex entrance into his world. A youthful pull back into life? That was the last thing he needed. He was careening toward death, full-throttle, and nothing could stop him.

Nothing — except two problems.

First: how would he do it? He needed to depart at the same time as his wife — he hadn't followed her across decades and continents only to be parted at the last moment by something as trivial as death — and he needed to do it in a proper way. A way that fit in with the narrative of their life together. With the terrible story they'd signed onto years ago, at dawn, by a fountain, in a place far away.

The second problem was this: How would he make sure that, before he actually died, he would succeed in rectifying that old mistake — that dreadful blunder that had gone unrecognized for decades but that now, in the crushing silence of his wife's last days, had returned to torture him, demanding to be seen for what it was? Until he found a way to make that right, he would not be able to depart. Because, however desperately he might yearn for death, he was not yet worthy of it.

THE NEXT MORNING, Alex picked and pushed his way through the slush-lined street, nervous but determined. He held Samara's letter in his hands like a talisman. Compulsively, he folded and unfolded the paper crane as he walked, and the air filled with the noise of flapping wings. The temperature had risen slightly, a soft rain was falling, and he was wearing a yellow raincoat that stood out sharply against the grey. As he reached the Glassmans' stoop and knocked on the door, he suddenly felt self-conscious. For one wild second he considered running home and changing into a suit. He wanted to make a strong impression. But it was too late.

Scowling, Glassman yanked the door open and shaded his eyes against the sudden light of the outdoors. "You again!"

"Sorry to bother you, Mr. Glassman. I was wondering..."

"What?"

"Well, I was hoping…"

"What, what? Speak already! Don't you know it is rude to keep an old man waiting?"

But the angrier Glassman looked, the more tongue-tied Alex got. He blinked at the old man with woeful, desperate eyes. Eventually, Glassman threw up his hands and grunted, "So come in already, if you won't speak!" before turning his back and walking into the living room.

Alex followed, closing the door behind him and breathing a sigh of relief. But as soon as he entered the living room, Glassman seemed not only angry but afraid. Eyes bulging, he raised a trembling finger and pointed.

"What is this? What are you wearing?"

"Um, a raincoat?"

"Where did you get this?"

"At… the mall?"

"Take it off!"

"What?"

"Take it off! Take it off immediately!" Glassman shouted, covering his eyes and turning his back on Alex.

Alex's heart sank. He should have worn the suit! He stripped off the offensive coat, folded it up into a ball, and half-hid it beneath a couch cushion. "All — all done, Mr. Glassman. Sorry about that," he said.

Glassman turned. He seemed to have calmed down a bit, but he still looked like he'd just seen a ghost. Then he barked: "So? What does the young kabbalist have to say today? Have you grown a long white beard overnight, like Elazar ben Azaryah? No? No, I see you have not. Then I'm afraid I cannot help you!"

Alex stammered, "Actually, that's what I've come to talk to you about. The whole age restriction thing."

"What about it?"

"Well, for one thing, I think it's all a bunch of — of — well. I don't think it's true at all."

"I see. And what *authority* do you have for saying such things?"

"Well, it's not my authority actually, it's Abraham Azulai's? The famous 17th-century kabbalist? Do you —"

"I have heard the name once or twice, yes."

"Well, so, he thought the ban on mystical study should be lifted. Like, entirely. He wrote that…" Alex closed his eyes to summon up the quote he had committed to memory. "That from the year 1540 on, the basic levels of kabbalah must be taught publicly to everyone, young and old — that's a direct quote, young and old, that's exactly what he says — because only through kabbalah will we eliminate war, destruction, and man's inhumanity to his fellow man."

Glassman's eyebrows had risen so high on his forehead that they were in danger of disappearing into his white hair. "Where did you find this information?"

"The internet," Alex shrugged. "Also, that whole thing about needing to be Jewish?"

"Yes, now, now that — that is a big problem."

"Not really. I mean, didn't the great Vilna Gaon say, 'There was never any ban or enactment restricting the study of the wisdom of kabbalah; anyone who says there is has never studied kabbalah, and speaks as an ignoramus'? And, I mean, that was the Vilna Gaon! So, like, how do you top that, right?"

"Very good," Glassman conceded, the glimmer of a smile flitting across his face. "But you are forgetting one thing. Mystical matters cannot be taught —"

"I know, I know, unless there are at least two students present. That comes up in the second chapter of Tractate Hagigah. But then, just a bit later, we're told that the chapter headings of such matters can be taught. The teacher reads the headings of the chapters, and then the student's allowed to read to the end of the chapter. Rabbi Hiyya did it that way."

"Yes, but Rabbi Zera says that even the chapter headings can only be communicated to an honoured and established sage. A person who is the head of a school."

"I'm top of my class in McGill's physics department."

"Very nice, but I do not think that is what Rabbi Zera had in mind."

"Well, there's always your wife."

Glassman's face drained of enjoyment. "My wife?"

"Sure. I mean, she's just upstairs, isn't she?"

"So?"

"So she could be the second student in the room! And, now, before you start — just listen — before you start listing all the reasons why women aren't allowed to —"

"My wife is — not well."

Alex blinked.

"She is not ever really awake anymore."

"I'm sorry to hear that."

"So she would probably not make a very good student. That is what I am telling you. Not at this minute. But, when she was young, you know she —" He broke off. Silence fell between them. Almost immediately, the old man pressed the heels of his hands into his ears, as if being subjected to a frequency that was the sonic equivalent of murder. It was to put an end to this private torture, perhaps, that he suddenly looked down and, doing so, noticed the letter in Alex's hands.

Between its well-worn creases, beneath its scribbled words, a drawing of the Tree of Life was visible.

"What is this?" Glassman asked, his voice deathly serious. "Who is this from?"

Alex felt himself blushing. "Samara."

"She is . . . climbing the Tree of Life?"

He nodded.

"This is why you wanted to study with me?"

He nodded again, the blush creeping up his neck.

"You want to help her?"

He nodded a third time, the tips of his ears burning.

"How?"

"I don't know exactly," Alex confessed. "But I have this feeling that, once she's gotten high enough, something bad might happen. Because, I mean, it's dangerous what she's trying to do — isn't it? I remember this story Lev told me once, about these four rabbis who got so obsessed with kabbalah that it drove them insane. What if Samara —" He took a breath, trying to edge the fear out of his voice. "I just think that if I understand exactly what she's trying to do, and exactly how it works, I might be able to help her once she's ready to come down again."

Glassman brushed his hand across his eyes. "All right."

"All right, what?"

"I will teach you."

Alex gaped. "But, what about that whole thing about needing two students in the room? Just a second ago you were —"

"Well, the sages do not say anything about the second student being awake!" Glassman interrupted. "Am I right? Awake, asleep, it doesn't matter, yes?" he asked Alex, as though Alex knew best what the sages had to say.

Incredulous, but not wanting to push his luck, Alex said, "Yes."

And Glassman, as if glimpsing in him the solution to some all-consuming problem, looked back at him — and smiled.

The next day their lessons began.


IF LEV HAD SEEN Katz's face in the window, he would have made a detour, turning around on the sidewalk and taking the long way home to avoid running into his old friend again. But, seeing only an empty front lawn, Lev dared to pass right by — and immediately regretted it.

"Lev!" Katz called as he dashed out of his house, wrapping a scarf around his neck and toddling up the walkway at the same time.

Lev marched on, head down.

Quickening his pace, Katz seized Lev's arm and wheeled him around. "Hello!" he said joyfully, his shining face — so slow to anger, quick to forgive — rousing in Lev a confusing mixture of ire and scorn and sadness. Such innocence! Such simple faith!

Katz was watching him intently, as if he could tell that a violent upheaval was taking place within him. "Where are you going in such a hurry?" he asked. "Should you not be praying with the others right now?"

Lev looked up at the man whose faith had so enchanted him as a boy. He could feel a strange grin twisting his face, even as Katz's face filled with dismay.

"So," the man said, his voice sorrowful. "So quickly you lose your faith in the Kadosh Baruch Hu?"

Lev shrugged and, still without answering, turned to walk away.

But again Katz laid a hand on his arm. "You must be patient! Be patient and have some *emunah*, and the Kadosh Baruch Hu will make a miracle, wait and see!" he cried, but Lev didn't want to hear it anymore, couldn't hear it anymore, and with one jagged motion he threw the man's hand off his arm, sending him stumbling backward.

Katz teetered for a second, arms windmilling in the air, before regaining his balance.

Lev walked away, fast, faster, his vision blurry, his heart sick, the strange grin still twisting his face.


WHEN HE GOT HOME, Lev didn't even bother to take off his coat but stood, not moving a muscle, in front of the two framed photographs on the credenza. Thinking, remembering.

His mother: young, married, her beautiful dark hair tucked under a scarf. Her modest dress covering up every inch of skin. Her shining face — like Katz's face — lit up with belief.

His father: bearded, seated at his desk, the deep crease between his eyebrows a sure sign that he was annoyed at having been interrupted.

Open books lay in front of him — books he was obviously anxious to return to. Already he seemed sure that somewhere in these scholarly tomes, the antidote to all his ills awaited him.

Lev ran a finger over the photo of his dad and found it coated in a thick layer of dust. He hadn't picked it up in years. But he'd picked up his mom's photo a thousand times. Faced with these two models — complete faith or complete lack thereof — he had chosen hers. And had always believed in the rightness of that choice — until now.

Katz's voice echoed in his head. *So quickly you lose your faith in the Kadosh Baruch Hu?* He felt a surge of guilt, but also a surge of anger. He knew he'd been cruel to Katz and regretted the way he'd treated him — and yet he couldn't help it. He couldn't stomach the man's simple faith anymore, just like he could no longer stomach his mom's. And it wasn't even for the reasons Katz suspected.

Losing his dad a few months ago had been bad enough. But did he have to lose his sister, too? They had vanished one after the other with no explanation, and no matter how many times Lev turned it over in his head he couldn't come up with a story to help make these losses livable. Now he was forced to consider the possibility that there was simply no meaning underlying any of it. They were gone. Just gone.

And God, God was still there — Lev wasn't so reactionary as to stop believing in God — but clearly, he thought, clearly this was a God without a plan.

GLASSMAN WAS SITTING very still in his darkening bedroom. The sloping walls and his wife's breathing made him feel that he was trapped inside a giant muscle. A lung, perhaps, or a heart. Slumped over the desk, he held his head in his hands.

Then, rousing himself, he opened the drawer and pulled out *King Lear*. Though this was the book he had grown to treasure above all others, it also inspired in him a fair amount of guilt. Samara had forgotten it in his classroom after one of her bat mitzvah lessons. He'd made a mental note to return it to her. But then he picked it up and started reading it. And, once he started, he found he couldn't stop. Later, after she had abandoned him, he kept the book as a memento of his favourite student. A few months ago he had finally made an effort to return it to her, but her resentful father had slammed the door in his face. And really, who could blame him? When Glassman first agreed to those after-school lessons, he hadn't known Samara was contravening her father's wishes. But the more information little Lev let slip about the man's views on religion, the more he began to suspect it. And yet. He hadn't stopped.

Now, gripping the worn copy of *Lear* in his pockmarked hand, he was grateful for that slammed door. More and more these days, Glassman found himself appealing to the pleasure of carefully measured, beautifully proportioned words to stave off the spectre of the old mistake that encroached on his mind when everyone else in the world was asleep.

If only, if only he could understand what the old lunatic was raving about! Because these Shakespearean words, beautiful as they were, were horribly confusing. Their meaning was grey and dim, like a dream that slipped away at the first signs of daylight. Glassman hated that night after night he kept brushing up against the limits of his own abilities. He wanted to *understand*. But he had no method, no teacher or friend who could help him push those limits further out.

Which was why it was so exciting when Alex showed up one Tuesday afternoon bearing a volume that looked distinctly different from the science textbooks he usually toted around. *King Lear.*

Throughout that day's lesson, Glassman struggled to concentrate. He and the boy were seated side by side at the rolltop desk in the second-floor bedroom, where his wife also lay, inert in bed, helping to fulfill the Talmud's two-student requirement. They had finished their study of Ani and begun their study of Yesod, with Glassman reading aloud and translating from the Hebrew while Alex asked questions and occasionally challenged his interpretation of this or that passage. Glassman worked to keep his eyes from straying off the page at hand onto the volume that Alex had placed on the floor at his feet.

But the boy, too, seemed distracted. Was he embarrassed to be studying Yesod, a divine vessel associated with the male phallus, with a strange Jewish man old enough to be his grandfather? Glassman decided to hurry through this part of the Tree. What did it really matter, after all, if the boy's knowledge of Yesod was a little more superficial than his knowledge of the other nine vessels? Besides, it seemed clear what Samara — possibly the first woman ever to attempt this dangerous climb — would have to do to attain the key that would fit this particular lock. And he assumed Alex wasn't especially keen on picturing that.

"Why don't we stop there for today," Glassman said.

Alex nodded and started to pack up his things.

But before he could finish, Glassman said, "I see you have a new book?"

"Oh, this? I picked it up at The Word on my way home. Um, do you know The Word? It's a used bookstore on Milton."

Glassman took the book and, with strenuous casualness, asked, "What is it about?"

"*Lear?* Oh, well, it's the story of this king and his three daughters. Two of the daughters are real pieces of work, and they totally betray the king, who eventually goes, you know, kind of mad. But the third daughter, her name's Cordelia? She's sort of okay, I guess."

"Yes? And what happens to her?"

"Oh, she dies."

"And the evil sisters?"

"They die, too."

"And the king?"

"He dies, too."

"I see."

"That's Shakespeare."

"That's life."

Alex's eyes veered toward Glassman's wife — pale, motionless, shrouded in blankets.

Glassman flipped, as if by chance, to the scene where Lear goes raving into the storm. He poked Alex's shoulder to get his attention, then jabbed his finger at a line in the text. "What does this mean?"

"What does what mean?"

"This. The old man, who is he talking to?"

"Well, he's talking to — the storm, I guess."

"The storm."

"Yes."

"He is crazy?"

"Yes."

"Here he says, 'Singe my white head!' What does he mean, 'singe'?"

"Singe is like, you know, burn."

"Burn? He wants the storm should burn his head? Why?"

"Well, he's kind of... nuts. Plus he's all upset about his daughters' betrayal, you know?"

Glassman grunted his acknowledgment and pointed at another line. "And this? 'Crack nature's moulds, all germens spill at once, that make ingrateful man!' Why is he talking about Germans all of a sudden?"

"He's — he's not actually talking about Germans. He's talking about, um." Alex's cheeks glowed red. "He's talking about the seeds from which human beings grow."

Glassman frowned, then nodded. This explanation reminded him of another perplexing passage, and he flipped to it now with a speed that smacked of familiarity. Alex regarded him curiously. But Glassman was too excited to turn back now.

"Look at this, here. What does this mean?" he asked, pushing the book into Alex's hand.

Hear, nature, hear; dear goddess, hear!
Suspend thy purpose, if thou didst intend
To make this creature fruitful!
Into her womb convey sterility!
Dry up in her the organs of increase;
And from her derogate body never spring
A babe to honour her! If she must teem,
Create her child of spleen;... that she may feel
How sharper than a serpent's tooth it is
To have a thankless child!

Alex cleared his throat. "He's asking the gods to make his daughter, you know, sterile."

Glassman stared.

"Childless."

"Why would he do such a thing?"

"Well, because he hates her. Why else would you inflict childlessness on someone?"

Glassman winced. He closed the book and turned away. He adjusted the pillows beneath his wife's head. He took her hand.

Alex cleared his throat again. "It's getting late."

"Yes," Glassman said absently. "Late."

"I'll see you on Thursday?"

"Yes. Thursday."

"Goodbye," Alex said, leaving the bedroom and shutting the door quietly behind him.


"WHAT'S THAT BRIGHT STAR over there?" Lev asked.

Alex looked up from his telescope and followed Lev's finger to a patch of sky. They were standing on Alex's balcony, where they sometimes spent time stargazing on clear winter nights like this one. He grinned. "That's not a star, actually. That's a planet."

"Oh. Which one?"

"Venus."

Lev was quiet. He seemed to be in a brooding mood that night. Earlier, over dinner with Alex and his mom, Lev had been uncharacteristically terse. He nodded now, blowing into his hands to keep them warm.

To make conversation, Alex said, "Know why they called it Venus?"

"Why?"

"Because, a long time ago, they looked up at it and thought that it was so beautiful and bright and wonderful-looking — kind of like a goddess. And up until pretty recently, scientists thought that Venus had conditions similar to Earth's. They thought it could be our sister planet."

Lev's shoulders stiffened at the word "sister."

Alex could have kicked himself. "Sister" — what a stupid thing to say! Being an only child, he knew he couldn't fully understand Lev's connection to his sibling, but he still had a pretty shrewd idea how miserable Lev must be feeling in her absence. Alex was feeling pretty miserable himself. And to think, if he and Lev had actually succeeded in bringing their parents together all those years ago, that's what Samara would be to him right now — "sister"! He had never confessed this to Lev, but he'd been glad when it became clear they'd failed in their matchmaking efforts. He would have loved to have become Lev's brother. But the more time he spent around Samara, the more he realized that, when it came to her, a sibling relationship was not exactly what he had in mind.

Anxious to cover up the awkward moment, Alex rushed on. "Of course, later scientists discovered that Venus is pretty much a hellhole. The surface is over 462 degrees, and it's bone dry, and the atmosphere is full of poisonous gasses and sulfuric acid rain. So, not really that goddess-like after all," he laughed.

Lev echoed his laugh, quietly, and then the two of them stared up at the sky in silence.

It was no wonder people once mistook the stars and planets for gods and goddesses, Alex thought. It wasn't just that they were bright and beautiful. It was that, looking up at them in the literal sense, you almost couldn't help but look up to them in the figurative sense, too. That was what he had done all his life — what he still did. He kept his hopes pinned on the stars because a message from them would be the most beautiful and incontrovertible, the most elegant and meaningful thing of all.

And if he was honest, wasn't that why Samara's strange letter had so appealed to him? It wasn't just that it was from her. It was that the message had fallen on him from up above — just like, come to think of it, every message she'd ever transmitted to him: the sign taped to her bedroom window, the wordless conversations passing through telephone wires overhead. Above was where meaning lay, if it lay anywhere; above was the source of the truest answers we could ever hope to find. Samara understood this. And whether she herself had climbed up Katz's tree to stash the letter in a tin can, or whether it had flown up there of its own accord — it didn't matter. What mattered was that she understood. It was because she had always understood, right from day one, that he'd fallen in love with her in the first place.


**WHILE ALEX WAS LOOKING** out at the night sky, Glassman was looking out at Katz's tree. The tin cans caught the starlight and reflected it back into his eyes at crazy angles, and this irritated him. The whole tree irritated him. Ragged lines, slings of sloppy string — a chaotic contraption designed to catch, what, a miracle? It offended his Misnagedish sensibilities, that German part of him that viewed reason and logic as the ultimate tools for interpreting Judaism and life in general.

This taste for reason was what had led him to excel in math class as a boy — and, later, to take comfort in his wife's habit of working out logical proofs under her breath. When she talked to herself, she spoke in the language of truths and falsities, validities and invalid-ities, theorems and propositions and QEDs. For decades, he had found this — more than their quiet walks together, more than their three-times-daily meals together, more even than their sporadic love-making — endlessly soothing.

Then came the day of his wife's last stroke. Just before she col-lapsed in the kitchen, he heard her murmur to herself: *If p then q . . . and not p entails q or not q . . . we derive p if and only if . . .* This was no different from her usual murmurs, and so he did not look up from his afternoon tea. But then she began to grow agitated, shaking her head violently, saying: *No, no, you cannot derive this, this would be invalid, I would dispute this . . .* And then she was sinking to the floor.

He rushed over to her, crouched down on the tiles, and stared with horror at her stuttering mouth, her fluttering eyelids. For a split second she took the extravagant step of looking him straight in the eye. She repeated, "I would dispute this!" Then she fell into a coma.

That phrase had haunted him ever since. As it echoed in his mind, he heard in it a valiant, almost heroic correctional gesture. A final attempt to prove the invalidity of an argument he had been making for decades without even knowing it . . .

Now, sitting beside her unconscious body, Glassman had to grind his teeth to keep from crying out in pain. Desperate for a distraction, he looked out the window again. Katz's tree stared back at him. But this time, instead of catching on the tin cans, his attention snagged on those low-hanging branches. He remembered a spring day many years ago when he'd watched Samara pass beneath them.

She had been eight, maybe nine years old. A beautiful, curious little girl. The morning sun haloed her hair as she left her house and set out down the block for school, alone. As she passed beneath the branches of Katz's tree, she paused. After a long winter the branches were finally coming alive, little green buds opening stickily. She pulled a branch toward her. She touched the tips of a brand-new bud. She brought it right up to her lips and — after turning her head quickly this way and that to make sure no one was watching — closed her eyes and kissed it. Then she released the branch — it went flying backward — and, just as she was opening her eyes again, it swung forward and slapped her in the face.

She jumped back, startled.

For years afterward Glassman saw her body veering (perhaps unconsciously) away from that tree any time she walked down the street, as though not just her brain but her muscles had formed a grudge against it. Forever trying to expand his vocabulary, he'd wondered if this was what was meant by "muscle memory."

And then, immediately after her bat mitzvah, as though she'd reached out and been slapped in the face by an invisible branch, she ran away from the very religious tradition that she had weeks earlier begged him to teach her. When he chased after her, she only shook her head, and veered (perhaps unconsciously) away from him. She never tried to get near religion again.

But now, inexplicably, she *was* trying. And what a thing she was trying! The Tree of Life. Something extraordinary must have happened. She must have seen some sort of a sign — or thought she'd seen one. But as he well knew, signs could be misleading, and attempting to do what she was doing on that basis was a terrible mistake. A mistake not unlike the one he'd made so long ago, the one his wife had tried so hard to dispute with her last conscious words. And so he thought that if only he could help Samara, then maybe his problem would be solved, maybe he'd be worthy of rest...


LEV HAD BARELY taken two steps out of his house when he heard a voice calling to him from up above. Craning his neck in the morning light, he saw Glassman leaning out of his bedroom window and waving. "Lev!" he called. "Come up here, *boychick!* I want to talk to you."

Lev sighed. He hadn't seen the old man in weeks, and yet he wasn't entirely surprised to hear himself being summoned this way now. This was something Glassman had been doing for years — calling him into the house to pose a question, or tell a story, or ask after his formerly shining pupil, Samara. Lev was running late for school, but out of respect for his old teacher, he climbed the front steps, walked into the house, and made his way up to the second floor.

"*Boychick!* So good it is to see you," Glassman said. But Lev, standing in the doorframe, couldn't help noticing that the old man wasn't even facing him; he was sitting on the bed, facing his unconscious wife. Half-turning toward him, Glassman said, "Sit, sit!" and waved him into the chair by the desk.

"How are you, Mr. Glassman?"

"Fine, fine."

"How's Mrs. Glassman?"

"She will also be fine, with the help of the Kadosh Baruch Hu."

Lev said nothing. Mrs. Glassman was comatose. Her basic bodily needs required a nurse who seemed to be forever clomping up and down the street to the Glassman house. She would obviously not be fine, with or without God's help. But he didn't have time to dwell on it.

"So," the old man said matter-of-factly. "You will mind if I tell the story in Hebrew?"

"Um, what story?"

"Yankel's story! The story my wife's brother wrote — the one I promised to tell you!"

Lev's mind cast around wildly. Finally, he remembered that the old man had indeed promised to tell him such a story. He had promised it *ten years ago*. Now he was acting as if no time at all had elapsed, as if nothing could be more natural than for him to tell this story today.

"Well?" Glassman sounded impatient. "If I tell it in Hebrew, you will mind?"

"No," Lev said. He did understand Hebrew — not perfectly, but well enough to get the gist of a story. It was Glassman who'd taught him, after all, all those long years ago. "But I —"

"Good," Glassman cut in. "Because, you know, Yankeleh, he told the story in Hebrew, and this is how I remember it. These are the words I know by heart."

Lev said nothing, and Glassman rocked gently back and forth, speaking in a soft, singsong voice.

"In the beginning was the word," he said. "Only one word, that's all there was. You know what the word was. Close your eyes and it will come to you. It will be the first word that comes to mind."

Lev, leaning back in his chair, closed his eyes obediently. He cleared his mind and waited for the first word to make its presence known. But even before a single letter could pop into his head, the old man continued chanting.

"In the beginning was the word and the word was with the king," Glassman said. "The king loved the word and so, to protect it, he planted it in the centre of the royal garden and placed a flaming sword at its gate.

"The king watered the word every day. With time, it grew into a beautiful tree. It grew so tall that it could be seen from anywhere in the kingdom. Rumours began to spread. It was said that the tree bore 613 fruit. Each fruit contained 613 seeds. Each seed contained a single word. What exactly a word was, nobody knew. Nobody in the kingdom had ever sung or spoken. This was a kingdom of silence.

"The tree was a delight to the eyes.

"The royal subjects longed to get close to it. Their fingers itched to pluck its fruit. Their mouths craved the taste of its words. But nobody ventured to make a move.

"Until one night, a daring man snuck into the garden all alone. Nobody knows how he did it, how he got past the flaming sword, though if you close your eyes now it will come to you. It will be the first thing that comes to mind."

Once more, Lev squeezed his eyes shut and waited for the daring man's method to spring to mind, but again Glassman's voice moved on without giving him time to think. As if, even though Glassman had seemed desperate for him to come and listen to this story, the old man wasn't really speaking to him at all.

"The daring man stood in the centre of the garden. He plucked a fruit from the lowest branch of the tree. It was like no other fruit he had ever seen before. Dark, dark red, and soft as velvet. He cracked it open and its insides glittered with hundreds of seeds. He picked one out and placed it on his tongue. His eyes popped open.

"The pleasure was so intense that he dropped the fruit. He raced out of the garden with the single seed still in his mouth, guarding it carefully under his tongue as he ran.

"When he got home, he woke up his wife, who was fast asleep in their bed. The fruit had stained his hands and lips and teeth, and she gasped at his appearance, then gasped again when he opened his mouth and out tumbled — a word. *Taste!* he told her, offering his mouth to hers. Because that was the word he had been guarding. That was the first word anyone in the kingdom ever spoke.

"With fear in her eyes, the woman kissed her husband. He transferred the seed delicately from his mouth to hers. It rolled around on her tongue. Her eyes popped open.

"The couple stared at each other as if for the first time. They were naked, suddenly they understood this. That night, they tasted each other as they had never done before."

Lev, blushing furiously, opened his eyes and inspected the old man's profile. But Glassman gave no sign of embarrassment. He was rocking quickly now, his voice speeding up to keep pace with his body.

"Over the next few days, the couple went crazy for the word. *Taste, taste, taste,* they told one another. They discovered that the word could mean many things. It could be said curiously, flatly, bossily, snobbily, seductively. They practiced saying it as a noun, as a verb, and finally as a command. *Taste, taste, taste!* And seven days later, they yielded to its bold demand.

"The couple snuck into the garden under cover of night. They told themselves what they were doing was for the good of the kingdom.

They were not selfish people. They planned to share the gift of language with all the royal subjects. Awed by the beauty of the tree, they could only bring themselves to pluck a single fruit off its branches. But this fruit, with its hundreds of glistening seeds, was more than enough. Never before had they felt so rich.

"The couple went from door to door, waking up all the royal subjects. The neighbours gasped at their appearances, then gasped again when they opened their mouths and out tumbled — words. *Table!* the daring man said, pointing at the coffee table in his neighbour's living room. *Glass!* the woman said, pointing at the glass of water that sat upon the table. *Cold!* they said together, shivering in the chilly night air.

"But they did not shiver for long. Soon all the neighbours were inviting them in. The seeds were transferred from mouth to mouth to mouth, until all the royal subjects in the kingdom had tasted the words. Their eyelids fluttered. Their breath quickened with pleasure. Words! How they loved the words! How they lent sharpness to age-old experience! Had there ever been anything more delicious?

"The royal subjects were happier than they had ever been. They became greedy, craving ever more words, believing that the more words they had, the better they would be able to communicate with the people around them.

"They snuck into the garden under cover of night, robbing the tree of all its precious fruit and sinking their teeth into the velvet rinds. Words dribbled down their chins, dripped from their fingers. They carried the stolen goods home with them and passed the seeds from mouth to mouth to mouth.

"There spread throughout the kingdom thousands of new words. A word for every object and every experience under the sun. The crisp, supernatural light of autumn. The itchiness that overcomes the upper lip just before taking a sip of whisky. Homesickness caused by an uncertainty of where home really is.

"The words were so precise they could distinguish between even the subtlest shades of meaning. There was a word that meant *sadness of broken bicycles abandoned in the snow.* Another meant *sadness of never having learned to swim.* Still another meant *sadness of knowing the boy you like will never like you back.*

"But there were no general words, not for sadness or anything else. And because of this, the royal subjects could no longer speak to each other vaguely. Yet without vagueness, they realized, human relationships could not be sustained. A wife could no longer simply shrug her shoulders when her husband asked why she hadn't smiled in days. She could no longer say: *I'm not sure exactly, it's just this sort of funny feeling I have.* She had to say: *It's because you're going bald,* or, *The truth is I never really loved you.*

"But the royal subjects soon discovered that, although words could be used to reveal the human heart, they could also be used to conceal it. By heaping one word on top of another, by creating endless layers of noise, they could disguise, for example, the real reasons for their sadness.

"And so the royal subjects began to waste words. They used more words than they needed in order to make their points. They used words to utter things that were not even close to true. Sometimes, they used words as a way of concealing what they really thought and felt and knew to be true, but were too shy to say.

"Talk became cheap.

"The veins and arteries of the royal subjects became clogged with an excess of vowels and consonants, which blocked their hearts until they could no longer speak the truth beating inside them. Sick, pale, bloated with language, an entire generation wasted away and died."

Glassman paused infinitesimally for breath and into that pause leapt an image of Lev's father, his heart clogging with thousands of words, which, in their trapped state, began to murmur against him. Was that what had killed him in the end?

"With tears of sorrow in his eyes, the king descended into the houses of his dead subjects and examined their bodies. So that such a tragedy would never again befall the land, he issued a decree. Every new child born into the kingdom would be given a finite number of words — ten times one hundred thousand — to be stored in the chambers of the person's heart. Four chambers for the four seasons of a person's lifetime: childhood, adolescence, adulthood, and old age. The instant the person had used up all their words, they would die. This way, the king believed, people would be able to enjoy the pleasure of words without being tempted to waste them.

"The first generation of royal subjects seldom wasted words. But there arose a new generation who did not know the king. They and the generations that followed forgot about the decree. They began to waste words again. Within the space of a few centuries, the average life expectancy in the kingdom dropped from one thousand years to one hundred.

"This is still the way the kingdom works today. We are each given at birth a finite number of words, stored in the four chambers of our hearts. If we use them well, we may live to a ripe old age.

"The foolish among us speak often and die young.

"The wise among us speak seldom and die old.

"The wisest among us never speak a single word. They guard their words as carefully as if they were precious stones. They know that there is nothing better for the body than silence. The wisest of the royal subjects live forever."

Glassman's voice stopped. But his body kept rocking back and forth, back and forth. Lev's palms were clammy, his heart hammering in his chest. He had the sense that the old man was trying to communicate something, yet he had no idea what.

He waited a few minutes for Glassman to speak, but the old man seemed to have exhausted himself. Lev stood up carefully in the tiny room. "Thanks, Mr. Glassman," he said. "I'll come and see you again soon." Then he made his way out into the sunlit street, alone.

A COUPLE OF WEEKS after discovering the first avian dispatch, Alex pulled a second from its nest and, unfolding it, scanned its contents. At first he smiled, but as he kept reading, his smile faded. Clutching the bird tightly, he hurried over to his teacher's house. And for the next three hours, they threw themselves into the study of Tiferet.

With the light fading from the bedroom window, Glassman, looking a little sheepish, asked if they could go over the next section of *King Lear*. He opened his book to the soliloquy in Act 2.

"Here," he said, running his finger down the page. "'Man's life's as cheap as beast's!' — well, of course, we all know that. 'A poor old man, as full of grief as age, wretched in both!' That too is easy to see. But here. 'I will do such things — what they are, yet I know not, but they shall be the terrors of the earth. You think I'll weep? No, I'll not weep. I have full cause of weeping. But this heart shall break into a hundred thousand flaws, or ere I'll weep. O fool, I shall go mad!'" The old man stopped, shoulders heaving.

"Mr. Glassman, do you want to take a break?"

But Glassman wasn't listening. Instead, he jabbed at a line in the text. "What does he mean here? 'This heart shall break into a hundred thousand flaws.' What are flaws? A flaw is a mistake, no?"

Alex grinned. "Well, no. I mean yes. But not in this context. Here, it means that his heart will break into a hundred thousand pieces."

Glassman stared at him.

"Mr. Glassman?"

"What did you say?"

"His heart —"

"Yes?"

"Will break —"

"Yes, yes?"

"Into a hundred thousand pieces?"

"Yes!" For the second time that winter, Glassman was searching Alex's face as if it might contain the solution to some terribly important, terribly oppressive problem. Then he leaned in confidentially. "But how?"

"How what?"

"His heart, how will he get it to break into a hundred thousand pieces?"

Alex lifted his palms to the ceiling, smiling apologetically. "It's just a figure of speech, you know?" Then he saw how Glassman was hanging on his every word, staring at him with hunger in his eyes, with a kind of noble anger — and, somewhere in the very back of Alex's mind, an alarm bell went off. "I mean, he's not planning... he's not actually planning to do... anything that would cause that to happen. You know?"

Glassman leaned back, averting his eyes. "Yes," he said. "I know."

AFTER ALEX HAD GONE, Glassman watched through the window as snowflakes twirled down from the sky. Lear had it exactly right. The answer to Glassman's first problem — the problem of how to die — lay in those hundred thousand flaws. The trick was to get the heart to burst open, to release its contents... But how to make that happen?

There was a place halfway between consciousness and unconsciousness where Glassman did his best thinking. He tried to slip into it now, letting his eyes shift in and out of focus so that first the foreground — little white snowflakes — jumped into view, only to be replaced a moment later by the background — the Meyers' house across the way — before the foreground leapt up again. It was like looking at one of those optical illusions his students had shown him years ago: first you saw two faces, then a vase, then two faces again. No matter how hard you tried, you couldn't see both images at the same time. That was the power of the illusion, that rule that could not be broken.

Glassman frowned. Usually this exercise helped to clear his mind.

Tonight it was just giving him a headache. He massaged his temples. He closed his eyes. A few minutes later, he began to slip into a doze...

And that was when the rule — just for a moment — bent.

Imprinted on the undersides of his eyelids, Glassman saw both images, the house and the snowflakes, superimposed — and, trapped in that juxtaposition, caught in that dance between background and foreground — the solution to his problem.

It had been there all winter long.

It had been staring him right in the face.

He laughed — and his eyes popped open.

Last summer: David Meyer, framed by his kitchen window, was talking to Lev and holding a pill bottle; now he was taking the cap off with one hand; now he was sending into his other hand a blizzard of little white pills — pills that looked, through the binoculars in Glassman's grip, just like snowflakes. A flurry of words flew out the open window.

*Besides, Dr. Singh gave me this. Digitalis, it's called.*

*What does it do?*

*These little white helpers? Lub-dub, lub-dub, lub-dub.*

*What?*

*They help the ticker tick faster.*

*What?*

*The heart. They make it contract. Make it pump harder.*

*Harder? But is that, you know, safe?*

*Doctor's orders...*

Glassman sat bolt upright in his chair. Here it was! Here was the solution to his problem!

Well, not so much *here* as *there*. Over there, in David Meyer's house. That complicated things — but he needed those pills. It seemed to him an admittedly unfortunate but ultimately forgivable fact that, in order to get them, he would have to steal.

IT WOULD HAVE TO BE in the evening, Glassman decided. Not the weekend — people's schedules were too unpredictable — and not on a Tuesday or a Thursday, when Alex came for his afternoon lessons on the Tree of Life and didn't leave until late. It would have to be one of the other weeknights, in between Lev's departure for evening prayers and his return from synagogue. Just under half an hour: enough time to sneak into the house, locate the pills, and sneak back out again. But how would Glassman get into the house to begin with? That was the trouble, and he spent days turning it over in his mind.

And then, just as he was about to despair, an opportunity presented itself.

Unfortunately, it was a Thursday. Alex was seated at Glassman's rolltop desk. The two of them were knee-deep in the study of Chesed and the five o'clock sky was already dark.

Glassman was distracted. Ever since he'd seen Lev leave for evening prayers, he'd been glancing outside every ten seconds. Was he imagining things, or had Lev really left the window to the study ajar? His hands kept flapping on the desktop; finally, he sat on his fingers as if to prevent them from flying away. Alex asked a question and Glassman answered it, barely. When Alex challenged him, he leapt from his seat and began to pace back and forth.

"Are you okay?" Alex said.

"What?"

"Are you feeling okay? You look, I don't know, tired or something. Maybe I —"

"Yes, yes, tired. Not at all well. We could continue with this next time?"

"Sure," Alex said, gathering up his things. "I'll see you on Tuesday."

Glassman ushered him to the door, then crumpled his features into an expression of weakness. "Yes. Yes. Goodbye."

As soon as Alex left the room, Glassman sprang into action. He pulled on a sweater and went back to the window to check — yes,

Alex was headed home, the coast was clear, the Meyer house was dark — before hurrying down the stairs and out the back door.

Only a few feet of snowy ground separated the Glassmans' house from the Meyers'. He could see it clearly now. The window to the study was open.

It was only open a crack, barely one inch, and there was such a small difference between one and zero. But Glassman, who had long experience in such matters, knew that that small difference was enough. After all, had not the Kadosh Baruch Hu said, "Open for me a door as big as a needle's eye, and I will open for you a door through which camels may enter"? And that crack of empty space between the window and the sill was much wider than the eye of a needle.

With surprising agility for a man of his age, Glassman pried the window open and climbed through it.

Glancing around the dark library, waiting for his eyes to adjust, he allowed himself exactly three seconds of emotional discomfort over the fact that he had just broken into his dead neighbour's house, with the intention of stealing his dead neighbour's pills, before his dead neighbour's son — a boy who was the closest thing Glassman had ever had to a child — came home again. Then he got over it.

Glassman moved to turn on a lamp, tripped on something at the foot of the desk, and fell forward onto the glass-topped surface, knocking something over in the process.

He cried out in pain. Grasping the edge of the desk to steady himself, he cursed under his breath while he waited for the throbbing in his foot to subside. After a moment, he turned on the lamp and looked down for what had tripped him. A small stack of books. He shook his head. What in the world were books doing on the floor? Mindful of covering up his tracks, he bent down to straighten the stack his foot had dislodged, and noticed a small cylinder rolling into the shadows a few inches from his fingertips. Wincing, he reached for it, picked it up, and peered at it in the dim half-light. He gasped — and then laughed.

In his hand was a pill bottle, full of white capsules.

Digitalis.

He could hardly believe his luck. Already his heart was racing madly, as if to signify its eagerness to burst into a hundred thousand flaws right there on the spot. But the time for that had not yet come. And so, to calm his nerves, he put the pill bottle down on the desk and took a look around the room.

And now he gasped for a second time. David Meyer's library was a mess. All over the floor, volumes were piled into high, haphazard towers. Paperbacks overflowed the windowsills, their covers dusty and discoloured, their pages moisture-curled. On the shelves, academic tomes had been mixed in with volumes of poetry, plays, even picture books. How could anyone work in such an illogical, unreasonable place? Why would anyone want to?

He stared at the library. The library stared back, a locked door that refused to open, a chaos that would not be ordered. Neither a vase nor two faces — just randomness.

Then, all of a sudden, he heard something that made his heart twist with fear. A front door opening and closing, boots clattering to the ground. He made a mad dash toward the window, swung one leg over the sill — and groaned. The pills! He had forgotten the pills! Twisting back, he saw that they were sitting right where he had left them, bathed in warm lamplight. He lunged toward them —

The door to the study clicked open.

Lev stood in the doorway, one coat sleeve off, a prayer book gripped in the other hand, his mouth hanging open.

Had the boy stared at him then with eyes devoid of words, with eyes that steered clear of even the vaguest intuition of language, Glassman might have remained paralyzed, poised on that windowsill, forever. But Lev stared with a single question in his eyes — why? — which, instead of eliciting a response, had the effect of releasing its victim. With a last despairing look at the pill bottle, Glassman sprang free of his trap and, swinging himself off the window ledge, disappeared into the night.

DISAPPEARED INTO THE NIGHT— but why? Lev, sitting at his father's glass-topped desk, rolled the pill bottle between thumb and forefinger. Glassman had been trying to get at this, he was sure of it. But what could he possibly want with a bunch of old pills? And besides, if Glassman needed something, why didn't he just ask?

Then a dark possibility occurred to him: what if the old man wanted the pills for some unspeakable purpose — say, to put his wife out of her misery?

A flicker of light came on in Glassman's house. He had obviously gone home. And so, even though a confrontation was the last thing Lev needed, he stood up, intending to go over and engage in just that.

But even as he stood, a silver car pulled up across the street. She'd come back!

He ran out onto the porch, waving at Val. A second later she emerged, waving back but without raising her palm up into the air the way people normally do. Instead, her hand made a sort of horizontal movement at waist level, awkward even from a distance. Then she walked slowly — hesitantly, Lev thought — up the pathway.

"Come in!" he said, gesturing her into the house, surprised at how happy he was just to see her.

Smiling faintly, she obeyed. But once he had closed the door, the smile slid off her face.

"What's wrong?" he asked. "You look —"

"I lied."

"What?"

"Before. When I was here. I lied to you."

Lev didn't know what to say, so he said nothing.

"You asked me if I'd seen your sister since the funeral," she explained. "I said no."

"You..."

"I did see her, yes." Val's cheeks were flushed — from cold, nerves, or wine, Lev couldn't tell. "She was working at this café, not far from where I live, and I walked in one day and I saw her. I went up to talk to her, but she..."

"She what?"

"She saw me coming, and she ran into the back."

Lev's head was spinning. "But — then — how do you know she even recognized you? Maybe she just —"

"I know," Val murmured. "I just thought, you know, I just thought I should tell you. It didn't feel right... lying to you," she added.

But even now that she'd told him the truth, she didn't look relieved.

"Wait a second," he said. "You said she was working at a café? Which one? Do you remember the name of it? Because maybe I could go and find —"

"She doesn't work there anymore."

"How do you know?"

"Because I went back. I went back a few times, looking for her. In the end I even asked the girl who worked there, but she said your sister stopped coming to work a while ago."

Lev stared at her for a long minute. "Oh," he sighed, and turned his back to her, blinking into the darkness of the house.

"I'm sorry," she whispered.

He took a deep breath. "It's not your fault." When he'd swallowed the lump in his throat, he turned back to face her. She was looking down the hall in the direction of the study, where a strip of lamplight shone out from the door.

"That's my dad's study," Lev explained. "Would you like to see it?"

Val shrugged, but her eyes lit up, giving her away.

When they entered the room, her jaw dropped and Lev smiled apologetically. "It's really chaotic, I know. He was never very good at keeping things organized."

Val didn't answer. Instead, she wandered around the room, taking in bookcase after bookcase. Then she stopped, tilted her head sideways, stepped backward, stared at the books, stepped forward again, stared at the books, and stopped again, her face beaming.

Lev came up beside her. "What is it?"

"It's just — wow," she said. "It's amazing, isn't it?"

"Um. What is?"

"The books. The way they're arranged."

"But — they're not arranged. It's just a big mess in here. I mean they're not organized alphabetically, or thematically, or —"

Val laughed. "Don't you see it? They're arranged *geographically*."

She grabbed his arm and pulled him after her (there was that tingling at the base of his spine again), pointing toward first this shelf, then that.

"See? Here, for example. *King Lear*. That's in England, right? But then, if you look one shelf up — north — yes, yes, here, you see, here's *Macbeth*, the Scottish play. And then — go southeast — and now here's *Les Misérables, Les Trois Mousquetaires* — *voilà,* all French, you see? Go east again, and here you have Nietzsche, Schopenhauer — Germany!"

And suddenly Lev did see. The whole study was a shining replica of the world, mapping the contours of countries and oceans and islands with books so precisely that, glancing around the room, he had the dizzy feeling that he was compassing the globe.

"But... why would someone do this?" he asked weakly.

"Because!" Val laughed. "Your father, you know, he always wanted to travel the world, to see it all! But then your sister was born, and you, and then when your mother — well, you know, when it became just the three of you — he realized that he couldn't do a major trip like that. But — no, don't look like that — it's okay! Believe me, he didn't even mind. You see? He found his own way to travel. As he did in so many things." Her voice vibrated with admiration.

She seemed to be waiting for Lev to say something, but he was silent. He had been coming into this room for twenty years, and in all that time he had seen nothing in these books but chaos. Now a stranger swooped in and — in one second flat — she managed to see straight through to the secret order hidden within them.

She turned from the books to face him, cheeks flushed, eyes bright, and a sudden insight flashed inside him. Her tone when she talked of his father. More than admiration. So. Not really a stranger after all.

THE NEXT MORNING, Glassman paced the bedroom while the nurse pressed a stethoscope to his wife's chest and listened to her heart for a considerably long time. An unreasonably long time.

The minute he'd come home the night before, he'd taken his Chayaleh's hand and noticed that her breathing was troubled. He'd dropped down onto the bed in a spasm of guilt. He should never have left her side. Throughout their years together he had understood very well the concept of *therefore shall a man leave his father and his mother, and shall cleave unto his wife*, et cetera, et cetera, and in the past three months he had not left her alone in the house once — until last night. Her face was deathly pale. And her breathing, yes, there was definitely something abnormal about that.

The nurse straightened up and fixed him with a look so full of compassion it rendered her next words unnecessary. She was afraid it did not look good. His wife's heartbeat was very weak. She was slipping away.

Glassman said nothing.

The nurse patted him on the shoulder and he flinched. She told him to call if there was any change, any change at all, he should not hesitate. He should really not be alone at a time like this — but here Glassman flinched again and clicked his tongue impatiently. He understood very well the concept of *it is not good that the man should be alone, I will make him a helper suitable for him*, et cetera, et cetera. Oh yes, this he understood. Not that understanding it had ever changed anything for the better.

Goodbye, the nurse said, and left.

The room filled with silence.

Glassman sat on the bed. He took his wife's hand and laced fingers with her. The light from the window spread all around them and seemed, for a while, to be opening and closing like a Chinese fan. It was a golden light, young, energetic, full of promise. He watched it inch its way along the carpet, glide over the bedspread, and, having gained the tip of his wife's nose, slink away again as if wary of making vows it did not intend to keep.

The silence in the room was growing louder. It was a presence between them, seeking their attention, a selfish eyed thing that clutched at their chests and scrabbled at the backs of their hands. It cried, like the child they never had.

Glassman glanced around the room, desperate for something to do. He tried to read, but couldn't focus. He pressed the heels of his hands into his ears, but this did not help either. He longed for rest, mental and physical rest, but he was not yet worthy. The terrible mistake oppressed him. It was a sign of his tenacity and willpower that, even though his wife was lying right there before him — a captive audience, a perfect sounding board — he did not break the silence in the room. He did not break the rules.

It was only when he glanced out the window and saw Lev walking out into the late afternoon light that, unable to withstand another moment, he called out, "*Boychick!* Lev, come up here! There is something I want you to hear."


LEV TOOK THE STAIRS UP TO THE bedroom two at a time, feeling worried about Mrs. Glassman and the possible use of his father's pills, and guilty that he'd let himself be so easily distracted by Val.

When he entered, he found Glassman sitting once again at his wife's side, his back to the door. This time, instead of waving Lev into the chair beside the desk, he waved him onto the other side of the bed, where, at his urging, Lev perched uncomfortably.

"Mr. Glassman, I —"

"Listen," Glassman instructed him hoarsely. "I want you to listen to her heart."

Lev blinked. The old man waved him closer to the ancient woman, his manner insistent, almost gruff. And so, leaning over the immobile body, Lev pressed his ear close to her chest.

He heard... nothing.

No, not nothing.

A tinny, rattling emptiness. An absence so profound, it was almost a presence.

And suddenly he was eleven years old. Again he was wading through the peculiar weight, the muffled heaviness, of the air in the Glassman house. Again he was wondering how come Mr. and Mrs. Glassman's conversations could never be heard filtering out through their open windows, despite how close-set the Glassman and Meyer houses were. And now, sitting beside the old man and his wife, he realized that not a single word had ever passed between them in his presence. Mrs. Glassman had never addressed Mr. Glassman directly, only Lev. She had lured him to her kitchen — the smell of freshly baked ruggelach was a powerful, ubiquitous draw — with a kind of intensity he had thought was friendliness but now saw was desperation.

And Mr. Glassman, too — hadn't he always called Lev in when there was something he wanted to communicate to his wife? Hadn't he always communicated those things to her *through* Lev? Wasn't that what he was doing right now?

"Lev," Glassman croaked. "You understand now, yes? You remember the story? You see why I have to have your father's pills? They will push the words from my heart. She has already emptied hers... and there is not much time..." His head fell into his hands. "All those years she knew, she knew to spend her words freely, to talk to herself and you and everyone else as much as possible, but I guarded mine and now she will leave and I will have to stay... but I cannot, I cannot..."

A clammy nervousness overtook Lev's body. *That* was why the old man had stared at the pill bottle with such desire in his eyes. The pills were for *him*, not for her. He needed to catch up to her, to get all his words out in time, to die together with his wife.

Lev knew what the Torah had to say about such things. He knew, too, what the rabbis in his yeshiva would have to say. And yet, he asked himself as he gently squeezed Glassman's shoulder and left him in the shadowy room, what kind of *mensch*, what kind of God-fearing boy, would it make him if he denied a man the right to cleave unto his wife, even in death?

STANDING UNDER A gunmetal sky, leaning against the cold bark of Katz's tin can tree, Alex opened Samara's third letter and his chest seized up with pure, unadulterated fear. Of all her strange dispatches, this one was the strangest. And the shortest. The use of mathematical notation, the & and = and ∞ and ± that normally would have delighted him, only heightened his panic now. The words in between were fragmented, scattered, nonsensical — she was eating nothing "except paper"?! — and one word was glaringly absent: "I."

He and Glassman had just finished studying Binah-Chochmah, so he knew that the higher up you got on the Tree, the greater the dangers that awaited you. Samara was moving toward Ayin, the vessel of ego-annihilation, a stage at which communication with others became difficult if not impossible. The idea of Samara detached from him, dangling in some lofty realm where he wouldn't be able to reach or save her, terrified Alex. He stood under the tree for a long time, furling and unfurling the bird's white wings.

"Alex!"

He stuffed the letter into his pocket just as Katz came bounding up the path.

"Hello, Mr. Katz," he said in his best approximation at nonchalance. "How are you?"

"Thank God, thank God," Katz replied, smiling as he struggled to catch his breath. "Your friend Lev — have you seen him recently?"

"No," Alex admitted with a twinge of guilt. He'd been so preoccupied with Samara's letters and Glassman's lessons that he hadn't been a very good friend lately. "Why do you ask?"

"He is acting..." Katz paused, looking up at the clouds as if expecting them to supply the words he wanted. "Not himself."

"What do you mean?"

"He seems... disturbed. Something is bothering him."

"How do you know? Did he say something? Do something?"

Katz shrugged uncomfortably. "Go to him," was all he added. "Or call. You should call."

But the bird in Alex's pocket flapped its wings. He needed to show Samara's letter to Glassman right now.

As he turned away, Katz grabbed him by the shoulder and forced him back around, issuing an urgent whisper. *"Please call."*

Alex froze. For a second he stared into those wild, crazy eyes. The bird fluttered its wings again. Shaken, he stammered, "I will," and hurried down the street.

When Glassman opened the door, he took one look at Alex and didn't even mention that Friday wasn't their usual day for lessons. "What is it?" he asked, once they'd climbed the stairs to the bedroom.

Alex pulled the bird from his pocket and waited while Glassman squinted at it in the dim light. After a minute, the old man put the letter on the desk and sat down heavily. He placed a hand over his eyes, which scared Alex even more. "Is she in danger?" he asked, his voice small and tight.

Glassman squared his shoulders and said vaguely, "It is not always so easy to tell who is in danger and who is safe."

Alex had to work to keep the irritation out of his voice. "I only care if Samara is safe. And we're on Ayin now anyway, right? So, if you're not busy..."

Glassman sighed and opened the book on the desk.

The deeper they delved, the deeper Alex's concern grew. "What's all this about a person becoming akin to nothing? That makes it sound permanent."

"Yes," Glassman said. "It can be."

Alex stared.

"Sometimes," Glassman said, choosing his words carefully, "it is not always easy for the mind to rejoin the body, once the two have been separated. What goes up," he raised his palms to the ceiling, "does not always come down."

"What do you mean? You mean she might never go back to normal?"

"It is hard to predict. If she has grounded herself properly, she may be able to come back down." Glassman sighed. "What you must understand is that the person, at a certain point, is no longer in control. When she decides to climb the Tree, at first, yes, it is by choice. But after a while..."

"After a while, what?"

"The climb — it starts to take on a power of its own. In the person's mind, you see? Because once the person gives herself to this climb, once she sacrifices everything for it, it is no longer just she who is struggling to go up. The Tree itself is *pulling* her up... And it will keep on pulling her and pulling her, even if..."

"Even if what, what?"

"Even if she no longer wants to go."

"But that's — what you're saying is — you're saying she can be forced, psychologically, to keep climbing *against her will?*"

A strangled noise came from the doorway.

With a sick feeling in his stomach, Alex whipped around — and saw Lev.

It was impossible to tell how long he'd been standing there. But it had been long enough. Lev's face was livid, his fists clenched. What was that in his hand? A pill bottle? Why was he carrying pills?

"Hello, Lev," Glassman murmured.

Lev marched to the desk, snatched up the bird, and read the message scrawled across its wings. For a moment, the air around him seemed to crackle with electricity, as if his body were generating a private lightning storm. When he finally spoke, it was with a deathly quiet that was more terrifying than the loudest crack of thunder. "How could you keep this from me?"

"Lev, I —"

"This whole time, she's been writing to you, she's been climbing the Tree of Life and you —" His voice trembled. "You've been hiding her letters from me?"

"I'm sorry! I'm really, really —"

Lev shook his head, one violent motion that cut into Alex like the sharpest gust of wind. "Are you crazy? Do you know how dangerous this is? It's not safe, she's not safe! You should have told me. I could have helped her!"

"I'm sorry! I didn't want to bother you, you were already so worried and unhappy and this would just be one more —"

"Exactly! You knew how unhappy I was, you knew how much I wanted to hear from her! And this whole time, you just watched and — you said nothing!"

"I thought —"

"What? That you could help her more than I could? That you know her better than me? You don't know anything about her! You think she's in love with you? You're so blind! Don't you know — don't you even see —"

Alex felt cold all over. "See what?"

Lev turned on Glassman. "And you!" he said. A look of fury passed over his face, a mixture of betrayal and hurt and anger and confusion that played out over his features and cast them, somehow, in a light of beauty.

Alex was filled with the terrible sensation of having knocked over a piece of glassware that has yet to strike ground. In that split second before it crashes into a thousand pieces, a pristine silence seems to be all that exists in the world. It was because that silence had lodged itself firmly in his throat that, when his best friend threw the pill bottle down on the desk and stormed out of the house a second later, all he could do was blink.

LEV SLAMMED THE DOOR behind him. He paced the hallway, cold fury like a hand at his back, driving him first this way, then that. The framed photographs of his parents blurred in the edges of his vision as he whipped past, and that, too, added to his fury — the sensation of looping ceaselessly between their two gravitational pulls, like some crazed planet that couldn't decide which star to orbit.

Tears climbed up his throat. How could they? His best friend and his oldest teacher. The only two people he'd thought he had left. Though he'd stopped being able to believe in God's plan, he'd never stopped believing in them — their faithfulness, their good intentions toward him. But now.

He struck the tears from his eyes. He refused to be sad. He was done with sadness. Reaching into his pocket, he located the scrap of paper she'd given him. The scrap of paper with her phone number on it. He dialled and she answered on the first ring. Half an hour later, she was standing there in front of him. Val. Valérie.

He greeted her at the door with two empty wineglasses in hand. The wine was waiting for them on the desk in his father's library.

"What's wrong?" she said.

"Nothing," he said, smiling brightly and leading her into the study.

But instead of returning that smile, she inspected him gravely. The tips of her hair were very dark against her red woollen coat, and when she took the coat off and draped it over the chair, they stood on end, static fanning them around her face in a black halo. His pulse quickened at the sight of it.

"You're lying," she said. "Something *is* wrong."

"How do you know?"

"I know."

"But *how* do you know?"

"I know," she said again, a tiny smile twinkling in the corner of her mouth, as though she were enjoying a private joke at his expense.

"Fine," he said, turning his back to her and reaching for the wine bottle on the desk. He filled both their glasses and clinked his to hers — somewhat savagely — before bringing it to his lips and draining it.

She sipped her wine more slowly. He could feel the heat of her gaze on his face. Whatever she saw there must have softened her because after a minute she said, "It's Friday night."

"So?"

"So it's Friday night, and you're a religious Jew, which means you're not supposed to be using the phone. And yet," she said, "you called me."

The cold fury was pressing at his back again; it pushed the next words out of his heart, up his throat, and off his tongue in a voice that was almost a snarl. "Did my dad tell you that?"

"I'm sorry?"

"That I'm religious. Did he tell you that?"

"Yeah. Yeah, he must have mentioned it at some point, I guess. Why?"

A deep V had appeared between her eyebrows. He said, more calmly, "No reason. I was just wondering, you know, what he used to say about me. What he thought of me." Sitting on the edge of the desk, he put down his glass and gave a sad little grin. "I miss him, that's all."

The V vanished from her forehead. She put her glass down next to his and perched beside him on the edge of the desk, where, very briefly, she hesitated. Then she reached out and touched his hand. He laced fingers with her, and found that her palm was warm. Her pulse, beating against his thumb, was racing. "I miss him, too," she whispered.

He looked up.

Their eyes connected.

And in that instant, he could tell she saw something in his gaze that troubled her — but before her brain could process it and tell her body to stop him, he leaned in and kissed her.

Val's mouth was petal-soft, and for one full moment it surrendered to his mouth breathlessly, passionately, almost gratefully. As if these were the lips she loved and missed all these months. Her cardigan was slipping off one shoulder; he brushed it aside and ran his fingers over her skin. He brought his hands to her hips — and felt her body seize up beneath his touch. She froze, her torso ramrod-straight, before pushing him off with both hands.

"You knew," she said.

He stared down at the carpet.

She took his chin and forced it up. "This whole time, you knew about your dad and me, and you didn't say anything! And now —" she gestured at the space between them, "now *this?*"

With a violent downward motion, he shook his head free of her grasp.

In a whisper that was suddenly strangely kind, strangely void of anger and full of pity, she said, "Why? Why would you want to do a thing like this?"

His mouth broke open and an anguished noise escaped him. "Because," he groaned, "I didn't want to believe anymore... I needed to *not* believe... and I just had to do something, something not good, so I could prove to myself that I don't believe. I needed to do something so bad..."

He stopped. How could he explain it to her? How he'd needed to do something so bad he'd be shut out of faith for good, no more looping back and forth. How seducing his father's lover was the worst possible thing he could think of to do. How he'd come to her seeking his own perdition.

A look of astonishment came over her face. "No," she said. "I won't let you. I won't let you do this to yourself. Do you hear me?"

Lev said nothing.

"Do you hear me?" she repeated, louder now.

His throat felt tight.

"Do you hear me?" she said again, and this time she took him by the shoulders and shook.

At her touch something in him released. Tears came to his eyes and he didn't try to stop them. He was nodding, laughing and crying, his shoulders suddenly wonderfully light. He had spent the past few months dangling over the edge of an abyss, psyching himself up to jump — and, just when he'd been about to do it, Val had flung out an arm and caught him. And in catching him, in refusing to let him go through with his self-destructive plan, she had performed an act of kindness that he now understood was the very mirror and mechanism of God's kindness. It was not from on high but from on low, not through miracles but through human hands that the divine plan was carried out.

The people in Glassman's story — the ones who had words to describe every experience under the sun — he envied them. Right now, he couldn't find the words to thank her. But they would come. And when they did, she would be around to hear them. So, instead of speaking, he shot her a smile. This time, she returned it.

SITTING WITH HIS BACK to the window the next day, Glassman watched the late afternoon sunlight brushing his wife's skin with gold. It was unseasonably warm, but he felt cold all over. Earlier that day the nurse had said his wife probably wouldn't make it through the night. Glassman had pressed his ear to her chest and inwardly agreed with the nurse's assessment. The heartbeat was so hollow that he was struck by admiration for his wife's diligence. She had expelled those words, all right. Had disposed of them thoroughly. In her veins and arteries, the blood was running freely now, not a single noun or verb to slow its passage from the heart.

She had expelled the unspoken punctuation of life long since: the exclamation points she'd used up in their lovemaking, nights when they gestured wildly on one another's bodies. The commas she'd baked into curled pastries, never-ending ruggelach whose trips in and out of the oven broke each day into smaller, more digestible clauses. And the ellipses, those she had been expressing all winter long. Because what was this extended sleep if not one last protracted pause before the sentence of life was studded with its final period? After months of waiting, a beautiful and forgiving full stop was finally coming into view, and at the sight of it Glassman breathed a sigh of relief. He was all readiness, all eager anticipation to end this passage and come up, flush left, against the first paragraph of whatever story awaited them in the next new life.

On the nightstand beside the bed the bottle of white pills beckoned.

He picked it up but did not open it. For a few minutes, he allowed himself the pleasure of floating out into a future he knew he would not inhabit. Allowed himself to picture Alex knocking on the door, climbing the stairs, entering the bedroom. Finding his teacher. Retracing his steps only to return minutes later, breath short and eyes wide, with his only friend in the entire world. They would stand in the doorway and survey the scene. And what a scene it would be! On the bed, his dead body splayed out. His exploded chest unburdened. The raw flesh of his heart sluggishly leaking the last of what was spattered all around the room. Words. Sticking to the sheets, hanging from the bedposts, clinging to the grooves of the rolltop desk, plastered to the window. All the words he would never have been able to pump from his heart in time if it hadn't been for those little white helpers, contracting the muscle faster and faster and —

The sound of a car honking outside roused him from this fantasy.

Rising from his wife's side, he went to the window. A taxi had stopped in front of the Meyer house. The car door opened and a girl he vaguely recognized stepped out onto the curb. She had pale blonde hair and deep concern etched across her face. She waited, apparently for someone else to step out of the car.

When nobody did, she reached her hand inside and helped another girl out of the cab. And this girl Glassman recognized instantly, his breath catching in his chest. Joy flared up inside him. But, a second later, it was snuffed out again. Because, looking at her, he knew immediately that something was wrong.

Samara stood stock-still on the sidewalk, her hair blowing out behind her in the breeze. Her gaze dull and hollow. Her mouth a thin, flat line. She was staring straight at her childhood house, and yet her face registered not even the barest recognition.

**LEV HOPPED DOWN** Katz's front steps with a smile. At the curb, he turned around and saw the man waving from the window. He waved back, his heart full of gratitude. He had been nervous about coming over here, afraid of the reaction he might get, but Katz had accepted his apology instantly. The sick fluid of dread running through his body dissolved and made way for relief. A few weak rays of light landed on his face and he savoured them, bending his steps toward home.

But when he rounded the corner, the smile fell from his face.

Jenny was pounding on the door and ringing the bell. His sister stood absolutely still, staring into space. Her gaze passed over him and in it he saw neither love nor remorse, just a terrifying nothingness. He felt the dread seep back into every corner and crevice of his body, spilling out onto the sidewalk in a long, dark shadow.

Jenny turned and saw him. "Lev!" she called, relief flooding her face as she ran down the stone path to meet him. "Thank God you're here, I need your help, I don't know what to do. It's Samara — she showed up on my doorstep, and she fainted, and ever since then she's hardly spoken or eaten or —"

But he was running past Samara, running past Jenny. Climbing the steps to the door, turning his key in the lock, stepping over the threshold. Jenny scrambled up behind him, grabbing his shoulder.

"What are you doing?" she cried. Her eyes were full of fear and her fingernails were digging into his jacket. "You can't just leave us here! You need to help her!"

"I am," he said before pulling away and racing into the darkness of the house. "I'm calling Alex."

**TEN MINUTES LATER** Alex was at the door, rain drizzling down the neck of his yellow raincoat, fists balled up tight in his pockets. Lev opened it before he could knock. "Is she okay?" Alex said.

Lev led the way into the hall, then raised a hand to scratch at the tiny scar above his brow. "I don't know," he murmured, blue eyes blinking fast. "She won't talk. Not to me, not to anyone. She doesn't even really move that much, you know, except when someone kind of pulls her along. Jenny brought her here, and they're in her old room now, so."

"What do you want me to do?" Alex asked, trying to keep the tremor out of his voice.

"Talk to her. Try to get her to talk to you." Lev studied the floor, shifting his feet. "You . . . I mean . . . you're the only one who really knows what's going on with her, right?"

"Yeah, I guess. But, honestly? I don't really know that much."

"But you know what she's trying to do and . . . you probably also know why?"

"It's — I don't know if you know this but — it's something your dad was working on. The Tree of Life, I mean. Before he died, he was writing a book on it, and I think — I think maybe he wasn't just writing about it, you know?"

Lev's gaze shifted over to something on the credenza — an old photo of his dad — and stayed there.

"Lev?"

"Yeah?"

"What is it?"

"Nothing... It's just — I just remembered — last summer, before my dad died, I saw him once in front of the yeshiva. He had his hand raised to his chest, like this, and he looked like he was..."

"Was what?"

Lev ripped his gaze away from the photo. "Praying."

"Praying? *Your* dad?"

Lev smiled faintly.

"Anyway," Alex said, "I think Samara is trying to finish what he started. And I think the reason she sent me those letters was because she needed to — ground herself, sort of. Tie herself to something, or someone, before she got too high up. Sort of like ballast."

Lev blinked. Alex was hoping against hope that he wouldn't ask why Samara would want to tie herself to *him* and not her own brother — and, luckily, he didn't. Instead he led the way to Samara's bedroom.

Samara was sitting cross-legged on the bed with her back against the wall. Jenny was leaning over her and whispering in scared, pleading tones.

Lev cleared his throat. "Alex is here."

"Oh!" Jenny turned around. "Hi. Thank you so much for coming."

Alex nodded, wondering why in the world *she* would thank *him* for coming. Of course he'd come. Where else would he be?

"I think Alex might be able to help," Lev said. "Can we maybe give him a minute alone with Samara?"

"Of course, of course," Jenny said, smiling gratefully at Alex as she passed him on her way out the door.

Alex edged closer to Samara. Her skin was paler than he'd ever seen it. She was thinner, too. Her dark hair, which had always been full and wavy and beautiful, looked stringy now, as if she hadn't showered in days. The sight of her sitting like a statue with those empty, unfocused eyes pained him and he looked away toward the window. The old paper sign was gone from it, but he could still see the gummy residue left behind by the Scotch tape that had held her message in place all those years. *Please call.* And he had, easily deciphering her series of taps and rests, the long strings of binary code through which she conveyed her innermost thoughts. But the silence emanating from her now was different. There were no ones, just zeros. One big zero, to be precise. A zero so large you could crawl through it.

Was that what she was trying to do? Crawl straight through silence, straight through nothingness, to the other side?

Chilled by that thought, he glanced over at her bookshelf, seeking comfort and familiarity. Sure enough, there were all her old books, lined up in a row in the order he knew so well. Five volumes of the Pentateuch interspersed with the five volumes of *Scientific American* he'd given her: her way of telling him without telling him that religious mysticism and scientific study weren't as distinct as he liked to believe. On impulse, he trailed a finger along them. Samara's body suddenly shivered, as if he had run a finger down her spine.

He crouched by the bed. "Samara?"

Silence.

"Can you hear me?"

Silence.

"I know you can hear me."

Silence.

"Listen, I got your letters. I know — I think I know what you're trying to do. But it's enough now, okay? You've gone far enough, don't you think? Lev's getting scared now. And Jenny. And me, too — I'm scared, too. Do you think..." He watched her closely. "Do you think you could come back now? Please?"

For a second, he thought he saw a flicker of recognition in her eyes. His heart leapt, lit up with fire — but in the next second her eyes went blank, and a thick fog of silence blanketed the room.

He panicked. All this time he had assumed that he was the one who would be able to save her. That was why she had sent him the letters, wasn't it? Him and not somebody else? That was the simplest explanation. All things being equal, the simplest explanation tended to be the right one. And yet here he was, helplessly rocking on his heels, babbling on and on, hardly knowing what he said. Trying to drown out the silence. But the silence was winning. It was becoming acrid, corrosive. Sulfuric. It burned his throat and bleached his insides. Maybe he couldn't save her. Maybe no one could. He fled.

When he found Lev and Jenny in the living room, the naked hope in their faces was almost more than he could bear.

"I'm sorry," he said. "I couldn't... she wouldn't talk to me."

Jenny burst into tears, dissolving before his eyes, her shoulders crumpling under the weight of her sorrow.

She wept for a long time, tears rolling freely down her cheeks. And the more she cried, the more the darkness was washed from his eyes, ebbing away in small, cold waves. A strange lump was rising in his throat. He was slowly coming to understand that, even if Samara did return, she would not be returning to him.

He looked at Lev and saw a deep sympathy in his friend's face.

"I'm going to get help," he murmured. "I'll be back soon." When he left the house a moment later, the cold rain that sluiced through his raincoat and bit into the back of his neck came as a beautiful distraction, an exquisite relief.

SOMEONE WAS KNOCKING on Glassman's front door, but it took a few seconds for the sound — desperation on wood — to register in his brain. Even then, he did not rise from his wife's side. Because, just then, he had his hands full: in the left, his wife's palm, and in the right, a pill bottle.

When the knocking stopped, Glassman breathed a sigh of relief. But a second later he heard footsteps clambering up the stairs. Dimly, he remembered that when the nurse had left the house earlier that day, he hadn't bothered to lock the door behind her.

"Mr. Glassman!" Alex's voice ricocheted off the bedroom walls, hitting him between the shoulder blades. "I'm so glad you're still up. I need your help!"

But Glassman, his back to the door, did not respond.

A floorboard creaked as the boy stepped into the room. "Hello?"

Glassman's fingers tightened around the pill bottle, hiding it from view. "Go away," he said. "I am tired."

"But — it's Samara — she's back, and she won't talk to anyone, and…" The boy's voice faltered, close to hysteria. "I don't know what to do. I mean, I explained to Lev what was happening at least, but — now what?"

Glassman didn't answer.

"Because I mean, before, when I was here, you said she might not be able to come down, and you were right. She's — stuck. But there must be something you can do, right? I mean, there must be some method, some way of helping her? Please, just tell me. What should I do?"

Glassman saw a wretched road forking at his feet. He was being forced to choose between the dying and the living. Between his wife and Samara. He loved them both, wanted to travel both paths simultaneously, but with every passing second he could feel the boy's impatience growing, could feel the pressure mounting to choose, choose already! Left, right, left, right, his eyes flicked from side to side. He heard Alex take another step toward him and the pressure broke him and he blurted, "Come back tomorrow."

"Tomorrow?" Alex paused. "If I come back tomorrow, you'll help me?"

He had struck out on a path. Now momentum compelled him down it.

"Come back tomorrow," Glassman repeated.

The boy hesitated. "Okay. I'll come back first thing in the morning, I guess." He hesitated again. "Are you okay?"

"Thank God," Glassman said. "Thank God."

"Okay. Well. See you tomorrow, then, Mr. Glassman. Good night."

The boy left.

Glassman listened to his receding footsteps. As he heard the front door click shut downstairs, his shoulders relaxed. In a way, he was glad Alex had come. At least now he could be sure he and his wife would be found quickly, before they had a chance to decay.

On the bed, their dead bodies splayed out. Just that. Nothing more.

Because, of course, he knew. That story about the human heart and its ration of words? It was just a story. Just a *meshugganeh* story. But it was the story he'd signed onto, because that was what he'd thought she wanted, that was what he'd thought she needed — a story that would justify a life of silence. For sixty-three years he had lived by that story. Sixty-three years and no "I love you," no "I hate you," sixty-three years without — without even "hello"! What he would not have paid for this one little word, this one little nothing of a word. Hello! And still he did not break the contract. Not even inside his own head! He thought: she wants silence? I will give her silence! He thought: she wants to believe in a *meshugganeh* story? So I, too, will believe. And he had gone on believing for so many years that to abandon the narrative now, at this stage, was inconceivable.

And Samara? He had done his part. He had taught Alex the basics of the Tree of Life. The boy didn't think he'd be able to help her, but surely, in time, he would. He was a bright kid. And if Samara had chosen to write to him, she must have had her reasons. She must have known that Alex would eventually be the one to help her.

As for Glassman, he'd already started down this path. To reverse course now would require great energy. And he didn't have any energy left at all.

He tilted the bottle and the pills spilled out onto his palm.

In the darkness of the bedroom, they shone out like stars.

Because he wanted to see their brighter counterparts one last time, he went over to the window, but the sky was grey and full of mist. Even that he would not be granted. Even that.

So.

He raised his palm, opened his mouth, tilted his head backward and —

The pills rolled off his palm and clattered to the floor, skittering in all directions. He blinked. There in the branches of Katz's tin can tree, a sign no amount of mist could obscure. A bright yellow raincoat.

For one beautiful second, he believed — with all his heart and all his soul and all his might — that the girl in the yellow raincoat was his wife. Not the woman wasting away behind him, but his wife as a girl, the girl she'd been on the day they reunited after the war. In the moments right before the terrible mistake. But it wasn't his wife. It was Samara.

What was she doing there? In Alex's raincoat. And alone. Through the window of the Meyer house he saw that Alex, Lev, and the blonde-haired girl had all fallen asleep in the same room, their tired child limbs splayed out across two couches and a chair. The girl they were all there to keep an eye on had apparently snuck past them.

Samara was halfway up the tree. She was reaching for a branch that did not look strong enough to support her weight. Glassman's body flooded with pity. Not for the girl. For itself. Its tired limbs, its creaking bones. Its envelope of loose skin, stamped with secrets and age spots and numbers, a worn letter someone had forgotten to send. To be sent at last was all he wanted now. But in that instant, he knew he would not be able to leave the world that night. He would not get to depart at the same time as his wife. Because, although it was too late to save his wife, to pry her out of the shell of silence she was stuck in, it was not too late to save Samara.


GLASSMAN CALLED HER NAME from his doorway, but his voice was snatched by the wind. Bareheaded, a light drizzle pricking the skin of his face and hands, he wrapped his arms around himself and ventured deeper into the night. *Blow, winds, and crack your cheeks! Rage! Blow!*

Trudging down the street, wiping mist from his eyes, he made out Katz's old oak tree shining in the distance. Its tin cans jangled crazily. He sliced toward it until the figure in the yellow raincoat stood out in sharp relief.

He tried again: "Samara!"

Nothing but wind and water rushed back at him.

He came nearer still, shielding his eyes. The girl was perched in the middle branches of the tree, upper body hunched over, hair plastered to her forehead, hands blue with cold. She was deliberately forcing her body to suffer. Ayin. Divestment of the physical. Ego-annihilation.

What could he do, what could he possibly say in the face of such resolve?

In that moment, the mistake that had haunted him for months returned to him in full force. And, though it cost him everything to finally give it voice, he knew it was the only way.

"Samara," he began. "It is very cold. Are you not cold up there, all by yourself? You are not warm enough — a thin raincoat like that! Just such a raincoat my Chayaleh wore, long, long ago. Soon after the war. So young she was, so like you. Such a mind. Such a spirit. If you will permit me, I will tell you the story."

The girl said nothing, so he went on.

"It was a night like this one. Cold. Very cold. The air that night was ice and also fire, air so cold it burned. She said I should meet her in the park, you see? Or, well, her cousin Reuben says she says I should meet her in the park. Lower... East... Side, he says, slowly, slowly, into the telephone. As if I am a simpleton. But it doesn't matter, it's not important, the important thing is she is alive and I am going to see her, tonight, tonight!

"So, good, I go to the park. I sit by the fountain. I wait. And, let me tell you, the wind is freezing! The skin on my hands, freezing! My face and my hair and my eyeballs and my *tuches*, freezing, freezing! But, let me also tell you, I do not even think of the cold. Do not even

281

remember I have a body. All I can think of is her. Will she cry? Will I hold her? Will she give me this small gift — her crying, me holding her, not the other way around? Will we talk all night long until our tongues fall out? So much to say to each other! About every brother and sister and mother and father and cousin and friend, so many questions to answer. For example: left or right? For example: dead or alive? For example: how? And I think it will take us a very long time, the rest of our lives maybe, to answer all of these questions.

"It is cold. The stars are going down. Almost a whole night I am waiting for her in this park. I think: she is testing me. I think: this silence is a test. But I like tests, I am good at tests. So easy she thinks it is to push me away? Ha! I will show her.

"A whole night I have waited, and now it is dawn. The first streak of light appears in the sky and I think, for the first time, maybe she is not coming. Then I turn around — and look, there, look! There she is! A thin shape in the grey half-light. I open my mouth to call to her — and then I see it. And my mouth falls shut.

"She is wearing a yellow raincoat.

"A yellow raincoat.

"Yellow."

Glassman paused, waiting to see if the girl would give him some kind of response. She gave nothing — not even a twitch. He inched closer.

"This yellow raincoat is a problem. This yellow raincoat is a mathematical puzzle. She stands still so I can examine it. She does not move. And she does not speak.

"This much I understand right away: the problem is not with the raincoatness of the raincoat. The problem is with the yellowness of the yellow. Because this yellow, this bright shining happy beautiful yellow — ah, what a colour! It is hard to believe such a colour could exist in the same world as. In the same world where. Not hard. Impossible.

"Once I understand this, the next steps of the proof fall into my head, one after the other after the other.

"The colour is a statement.

"The statement is: life is pretty.

"To wear the colour means: I believe the statement is true.

"But if this is so, then there is a problem. The problem is: life is not pretty. I know this. She knows this. How do I know that she knows this? Because all the answers are already in her eyes. Left. Dead. Birkenau.

"The yellow raincoat is a contradiction. She is asking me to embrace a contradiction.

"I open my mouth —

"Again my mouth falls shut.

"Suddenly I remember a story I read in the newspaper. About the thousands of Jewish musicians who were sent to die in the camps. In some places, like Auschwitz, there were multiple orchestras, each with dozens of musicians. The Nazis, may their names be erased, forced them to play while their fellow prisoners marched to the gas chambers and the ovens. But this was not all. In one of the camps, there was a very famous composer. The Nazis ordered this man to compose a score. This man considered his options. What could he do? Refuse? Cry? Scream *NO* at the top of his lungs? His life was anyways going to end by their hands. A score they wanted from him now? So. Very nice. He would compose a score. But ah, what a score this man composed!

"The score called for one hundred musicians. It called for one hundred instruments. And it ordered that the one hundred musicians should play the one hundred instruments *closed*. The lid of the piano *closed*. The violins inside their cases, *closed*. And so, in front of the whole camp, in front of the burning eyes of the Nazis, the entire orchestra played their instruments, but silently, silently. This silence was their protest, their last great *NO*.

"And now, now I am looking at Chayaleh in this yellow raincoat, and I am thinking to myself: this raincoat is the same idea. This raincoat is a great big *NO* to life. Because, you know, life has rules. Rules such as, a thing can be true or not true, but it cannot both be true and not true at the same time. Life can be pretty or not pretty, but it cannot both be pretty and not pretty at the same time. She knows this. She has a better *kop* for mathematics than even me, and I know she knows this. And so I know that what she is saying to me, when she comes to me wearing this contradiction, is: *NO* to all the rules. *NO* to life.

"I open my mouth —

"Again my mouth falls shut. What can I say? What can she say? I realize that if I accept her strange world of yellow raincoats, nothing at all can be said. To say *sky* would be a lie. To say *tree* would be a lie. The yellow raincoat is revealing a world where nothing can be spoken."

Glassman looked up; the light drizzle was not so light anymore; it was beginning to deepen to a heavy downpour. Samara lifted her face to let the needles of rain pierce her skin. He plunged on, his voice rising.

"Still, in mathematics one must be empirical. I decide I will put the theorem to the test. I will open my mouth and speak the simplest statements, the truest statements I know.

"I try: my name is Chaim Glassman. (The words will not come out.)

"I try: I love you. (The words will not come out.)

"I try: hello. (The word will not come out.)

"Now I hear the sound of my own heart beating. It is the yellow raincoat that reveals this sound to me. The yellow raincoat tells me that, for its sake, I must forget what I know. I know, for example, that the heart does not contain a finite number of words. That silence is not better than speech. The yellow raincoat tells me to forget this. To make a life of silence possible between my Chayaleh and me, to give it a reason and a history and a meaning that will make it easier for us to bear, I must begin to believe new things.

"The yellow raincoat is a contradiction, and it is also a contract. The terms are clear: *what we cannot speak of, we must pass over in silence.* Therefore, life must be passed over in silence.

"The sky is full of light now. In this light, her raincoat is brighter than anything I have ever seen. In this light, she is revealed. She opens her arms and I embrace her.

"The next steps happen so easily, so quickly, they are like dance steps learned in advance.

"She bends down and holds my ankle and kisses it. I bend down and hold her ankle and kiss it. She gives me a kiss, a small kiss, right in the corner of my mouth. I give her a kiss, a small kiss, right in the corner of her mouth. She presses a finger to my lips. I press a finger to hers. *Sha*, she tells me without words. Quiet, be quiet, listen.

"I listen. The silence is closing all around us. On the air there is a smell like paper burning. We stand with our fingers on each other's lips and wait. Somewhere, she knows, her brother is watching. He will see her this way and understand."

Glassman paused. Rain was slashing down like knives, wind tearing at the branches. And the girl, the girl was still sitting statuesque in the tin can tree, clinging to her cold patch of sky. Her behaviour bore all the hallmarks of Ayin, and yet the set of her muscles, the tiny ropes of misery moving beneath her face, made plain that she didn't want this — not anymore. Still, she did not, perhaps could not, move.

A bolt of lightning exploded in the sky.

Thunder shook the air and the cans howled their pain. A phrase flashed across his brain: *You sulphurous and thought-executing fires, vaunt-couriers to oak-cleaving thunderbolts, singe my white head!*

His eyes darted from the shivering girl in the branches to the flickering tin cans, and a tremor of fear ran through him. He needed to get her down from there fast, fast, before it was too late — and yet, he knew, she had to come down of her own volition or else this — these words, this sacrifice — would all be useless.

"Samara!" he called up, neck craning, voice straining. "Do you see? Do you see what I am telling you? I thought — I thought I understood the sign — but what if I was wrong? What if," he cried, "the yellow raincoat was not a great big *NO* to life? What if what she was trying to say to me was *YES?* What if she saw, all those years ago, something it took me decades to understand: that the world is not pretty, but human beings need to try to make it so. Not by escaping into some higher world, not by seeking some invisible sign up in the sky — but by seeking it here, here on the earth, here in the people around you —"

Thunder buried his voice again, and again he raised it.

"But that was not how I chose to read the sign. A wiser man might have read it that way, but I — I was not wise. I wanted what was comfortable, and this — this silence — this was comfortable. Because even though it was not an easy way to live, there were rules, there was a clear path to follow. You are making the same mistake, Samara!"

Had she just turned her head slightly toward him?

"You think, because you are sitting in a tree and it is raining and you have not eaten and you have not slept, that you are uncomfortable? You are following a clear path, and that is comfortable!" Through the downpour, he thought he saw her jaw tighten. "You think, now that you have been dragged up this path, you have no choice but to stay there? You have a choice! You can still fight back! But," he screamed, "not for long! Because, believe me, the longer you stay this way, the more strength you give it and the more you will be stuck. And soon you will wake up like me, you will find you really do have almost no choice left at all." Drawing a painful breath, he boomed, "So fight this, Samara. Fight this now!"

Samara's eyes flicked down to meet his. Another crack of thunder burst directly above her. The tree swayed wildly and the blood drained from her face.

"Come down now, Samara. It is not so far to fall. And I will be here to catch you. It will be like flying, yes? So. Come on now. Fly!"

And in one jagged motion, he thrust out his hand —

She leapt from her branch —

She flew —

A ball of fire hit the tree.

The force of the blow — lightning striking age-old oak — pushed her into his arms and threw him off his feet, so that in the end it was earth that caught them both, holding them together in a wet, tangled heap. They gasped for breath. They gaped upward. A horrible creaking filled their ears. And then they watched as the tree split down the middle, branches splintering on either side, and hundreds of tin cans spilled, clanging, to the ground. The cans groaned as they rolled out over the lawn, onto the sidewalk, and down the street, where they were carried away by a surge of rainwater, their rusty complaint fading into the night.

ALEX WAS NOT AWAKE. But he was not fully asleep either. He could feel the first rays of dawn warming his closed eyelids. He was conscious, too, of the vague ache in his back, the crick in his neck. He'd been sleeping at a right angle all night, and his limbs were very much aware of that fact. The muscles at the edges of his eyes — they, too, were slowly becoming aware of something. Of someone.

There was a presence hovering above him. Blocking the light filtering in from the window and casting a shadow on his frame. His mind took stock of that shadow's dimensions. Its height. Its slimness. Its silence. Even before he opened his eyes, he knew who it was.

Samara stood in a beam of light. Her hair was soaking, her clothes dripping. Her face was pale. But her lips curved upward in a wan smile. She brought a finger to them. For a second he thought she was telling him not to speak, because they had always communicated best in code. But she tilted her head slightly to where Lev and Jenny were still asleep on their respective couches, and he realized she didn't want to wake them. He gave a miniscule nod.

A ray of pain shot up his neck. Here he was, doing it again. Looking up at her, looking up *to* her, searching for a sign. He'd been doing this all his life — craning his neck skyward, assuming meaning would rain down on him from the stars. But if Samara's letters had taught him anything, it was that messages from the stars were apt to be misinterpreted.

With this realization, something in the air shifted, swayed. The old architecture of their relationship was crumbling, making way for a new order to be established in its place. And so, before the whole structure collapsed around their ears, he took a moment to savour it.

The silence between them was cold and bright and elegant. It had a glassy, abstract beauty, like the beauty of pure math. It sparkled in the morning light and he admired it. And then he stood up, and the glass splintered, sliding down.

The two of them stood eye to eye. Samara, whose face he had once invested with divinity, flashed him a shy smile. Not the smile of a false goddess. The smile of a new friend.

And so, in a whisper, he greeted her. "Hello."

The word landed on his eardrum with the softness of a feather. Its weight was modest, but it was there, with a mass and a density and a volume all its own. Gone were the elegance and abstractness of silence. That "hello" was perhaps less pure. But he found, to his surprise, it was more beautiful.


THE FIRST STREAKS of dawn slanted into the house as Glassman climbed the stairs to the second floor. He shivered as he went, his clothes wet, his skin cold. He was exhausted but also strangely exhilarated. Reaching the landing, he peered into the bedroom and saw, through the window opposite, a sky glazed with pink and purple, orange and gold. He looked over at his wife in bed. Her skin was grey.

He opened his mouth —

His mouth fell shut.

He stood in the doorframe for a long time.

By the time he made his way over to her side, her face was bathed in light. He extended a finger and traced her last expression — the

corners of her lips, their upward tilt — his heart swelling with gratitude for this impossible gift: a final smile, a closing parenthesis.

He sat down beside her.

He pressed his ear to her chest.

He heard nothing.

No, not nothing. A metallic lub-dub, lub-dub seemed to fly up
through his wife's heart and out her chest and into the air, falling upon
his ears with shocking clarity. His eyes widened. His breath caught.
He lifted his head to look into her face and realized that the sound he
was hearing was not a lub-dub but a thud-thud, a rhythmic thwack-
ing coming from outside his bedroom, outside his house.

He left his place at his wife's side. From the window he saw Katz
standing on his front lawn with an axe in his hands and a smile on his
face. He was crouched over the remains of his weather-beaten tree —
and cutting away at it while singing a cheerful tune.

Another sound fell on Glassman's ears. A happy, indiscernible
babble. Laughter and the clinking of bottles. The glug of glasses being
filled. He leaned out the window and saw two girls and two boys celebrating on the lawn.

"L'Chaim!"

At the sound of it, he almost laughed. L'Chaim: to life! But also:
to Chaim!

He turned back to his wife, who was still smiling, and knew in
that moment that wherever she was, she was not angry at him. He had
not been able to depart at the same time as her, and that was just as it
should be. His time had not yet come. His wife knew and she was glad.

And yet.

He could not let her leave like this.

There was still so much he needed to say to her.

"L'Chaim!" the voices sang again.

He cleared his throat. He extended a finger and traced his own
mouth. He parted his lips, experimentally. He tried to move his
tongue — to push it forward to the teeth, pull it backward to the

throat, roll it sideways, even — but, in her presence, the muscle was heavy and dry. A wad of sandpaper. A bloodless mass.

He opened his mouth —

Again his mouth fell shut.

In that moment, he broke down and cried. He cried because of what his muscles remembered. He cried because, by constantly choosing silence over sound, he had accustomed his tongue to a life of stillness. But the tongue, like anything else, was a creature of habit. When you finally needed to express something truly significant, you would find it frozen, atrophied, paralyzed in the position it knew so well — the position you had trained it to assume.

"L'Chaim!" sang a voice for the third time.

Samara's voice, he realized.

And then he thought: a muscle can always be retrained.

He opened his mouth —

*Acknowledgements*

**THANK YOU** to my editor, Barbara Scott, who understood this book and brilliantly nudged it toward its ideal version; to Kelsey Attard, who impeccably oversaw every step of the process; to Deborah Willis, for first sensing potential in this manuscript; and to everyone at Freehand Books.

To my savvy agent, Samantha Haywood, who believed in this book from the start and worked tirelessly to find it the perfect home.

To everyone at the University of British Columbia MFA program: Steven Galloway, who was generous with time and advice; Keith Maillard, whose enthusiasm for the book increased my faith in it; Kim Fu, Andrea Bennett, Indrapramit Das, Taylor Brown-Evans, Chelsea Rooney, Krissy Darch, Emily Davidson, Anna Maxymiw, Michelle Turner, Jordan Hall, Bill Radford, Ben Rawluk, Meredith Hambrock, Melissa Sawatsky, Kevin Spenst, Emily Urness, Margret Bollerup, Lauren Forconi, Erika Thorkelson, Michelle Deines, Cara Woodruff, Emily Walker, Kari Lund-Teigen, Cara Cole, and Jill Margo, all of whom offered feedback and encouragement. Special thanks to Michelle Kaeser, whose sustained advice shaped the structure and substance of this book.

To Amanda Perry, my intellectual *chevruta,* who read thousands of manuscript pages and brainstormed countless ideas. She demanded her own paragraph and she deserves it.

To Rhoda Sollazzo, for keeping me company and offering insight at a tricky juncture. To Vahid Bazargan, for inspiration. To Emily Myles, for helping me pin down Lev's voice. To Ali Kaufman, for listening and advising. To Julie Sugar, for attending to the details. To Anne Cohen, for fine-tuning the French and more. To Annie Greene, for reading the book in its zygote stage and flagging her favorite parts. To Rebecca Lenetsky, for giving me the gift of an author photo.

To Crystal Sikma, whose keen editorial eye, poetic insight, moral support, and generosity kept making this book possible, day after day, year after year.

I am grateful for the support of the Social Sciences and Humanities Research Council of Canada. My research was guided by the writings of Jewish mysticism scholars Daniel Matt, Aryeh Kaplan, and Sanford Drob. The Vladimir Nabokov letter quoted in this book is from the June 13, 2011, issue of *The New Yorker.* The phrase "What we cannot speak of, we must pass over in silence" is from Ludwig Wittgenstein's *Tractatus.*

Most of all, thank you to my family — my father, Michael Samuel; my grandmother, Rachel Meyers; my sister, Simcha Samuel; and my brother-in-law, Erick Provost — who have always supported me as a writer. You are my greatest cheerleaders. I love you.

¶ This book was typeset in Lexicon by Bram de Does at The Enschedé Font Foundry, with Tungsten by Hoefler & Co. as the accompanying sans serif.

**SIGAL SAMUEL** is an award-winning fiction writer, journalist, essayist, and playwright. Currently a writer and editor for *The Jewish Daily Forward*, she has also published work in *The Daily Beast*, *The Rumpus*, *BuzzFeed*, and *The Walrus*. Her six plays have been produced from Vancouver to New York. Originally from Montreal, Sigal now lives and writes in Brooklyn. *The Mystics of Mile End* is her first novel.